Praise for *New York Times* bestselling author Linda Lael Miller

"Linda Lael Miller creates vibrant characters I defy you to forget."

—Debbie Macomber,
#1 *New York Times* bestselling author

"Miller is one of the finest American writers in the genre."

—*RT Book Reviews*

"[Linda Lael] Miller tugs at the heartstrings as few authors can."

—*Publishers Weekly*

Praise for *USA TODAY* bestselling author Michelle Major

"A dynamic start to a series with a refreshingly original premise."

—*Kirkus Reviews* on *The Magnolia Sisters*

"A sweet start to a promising series, perfect for fans of Debbie Macomber."

—*Publishers Weekly* on
The Magnolia Sisters (starred review)

"*The Magnolia Sisters* is sheer delight, filled with humor, warmth and heart.... I loved everything about it."
—*New York Times* bestselling author RaeAnne Thayne

A RANCHER'S HONOR

#1 *NEW YORK TIMES* BESTSELLING AUTHOR

Linda Lael Miller

Previously published as *Sierra's Homecoming* and
Her Soldier of Fortune

Special thanks and acknowledgment to
Michelle Major for her contribution to the
Fortunes of Texas: The Rulebreakers continuity.

Recycling programs
for this product may
not exist in your area.

ISBN-13: 978-1-335-40986-7

A Rancher's Honor
First published as Sierra's Homecoming in 2006.
This edition published in 2021.
Copyright © 2006 by Linda Lael Miller

Her Soldier of Fortune
First published in 2017.
This edition published in 2021.
Copyright © 2017 by Harlequin Books S.A.

This edition published by arrangement with Harlequin Books S.A.

For questions and comments about the quality of this book,
please contact us at CustomerService@Harlequin.com.

Harlequin Enterprises ULC
22 Adelaide St. West, 40th Floor
Toronto, Ontario M5H 4E3, Canada
www.Harlequin.com

Printed in U.S.A.

CONTENTS

SIERRA'S HOMECOMING   7
Linda Lael Miller

HER SOLDIER OF FORTUNE   273
Michelle Major

The daughter of a town marshal, **Linda Lael Miller** is a *New York Times* bestselling author of more than one hundred historical and contemporary novels. Linda's books have hit #1 on the *New York Times* bestseller list seven times. Raised in Northport, Washington, she now lives in Spokane, Washington.

Books by Linda Lael Miller

HQN Books

Painted Pony Creek

Country Strong

The Carsons of Mustang Creek

A Snow Country Christmas
Forever a Hero
Always a Cowboy
Once a Rancher

The Brides of Bliss County

Christmas in Mustang Creek
The Marriage Season
The Marriage Charm
The Marriage Pact

The Parable series

Big Sky Secrets
Big Sky Wedding
Big Sky Summer
Big Sky River
Big Sky Mountain
Big Sky Country

Visit the Author Profile page
at Harlequin.com for more titles.

SIERRA'S HOMECOMING

Linda Lael Miller

To Little Angels Everywhere

Chapter 1

"Stay in the car," Sierra McKettrick told her seven-year-old son, Liam.

He fixed her with an owlish gaze, peering through the lenses of his horn-rimmed glasses. "I want to see the graves, too," he told her, and put a mittened hand to the passenger-side door handle to make his point.

"Another time," she answered firmly. Part of her knew it was irrational to think a visit to the cemetery could provoke an asthma attack, but when it came to Liam's health, she was taking no chances.

A brief stare-down ensued, and Sierra prevailed, but barely.

"It's not fair," Liam said, yet he sounded resigned. He didn't normally give up so easily, but they'd just driven almost nonstop all the way from Florida to northern Arizona, and he was tired.

"Welcome to the real world," Sierra replied. She set the emergency brake, left the engine running with the heat on High, and got out of the ancient station wagon she'd bought on credit years before.

Standing ankle-deep in a patch of ragged snow, she took in her surroundings. Ordinary people were buried in churchyards and public cemeteries when they died, she reflected, feeling peevish. The McKettricks were a law unto themselves, living *or* dead. They weren't content with a mere plot, like other families. Oh, no. They had to have a place all their own, with a view.

And what a view it was.

Shoving her hands into the pockets of her cloth coat, which was nearly as decrepit as her car, Sierra turned to survey the Triple M Ranch, sprawling in every direction, well beyond the range of her vision. Red mesas and buttes, draped in a fine lacing of snow. Copses of majestic white oaks, growing at intervals along a wide and shining stream. Expanses of pastureland, and even the occasional cactus, a stranger to the high country, a misplaced wayfarer, there by mistake.

Like her.

A flash of resentment rose suddenly within Sierra, and a moment or two passed before she recognized the emotion for what it was: not her own opinion, but that of her late father, Hank Breslin.

When it came to the McKettricks, Sierra *had* no opinions that she could honestly claim, because she didn't know these people, except by reputation.

She'd taken their name for one reason and one reason only—because that was part of the deal. Liam needed health care, and she couldn't provide it. Eve McKettrick—Sierra's biological mother—had set up a medical trust fund for her grandson, but there were strings attached.

With the McKettricks, she heard her father say, as surely as if he were standing there beside her, *there are always strings attached.*

"Be quiet," Sierra said, out loud. She was grateful for Eve's help, and if she had to take the McKettrick name and live on the Triple M Ranch for a year to meet the conditions, so be it. It wasn't as if she had anyplace better to go.

Resolutely she approached the cemetery entrance, walked under the ornate metal archway forming the word "McKettrick" in graceful cursive.

A life-size bronze statue of a man on horseback, broad-shouldered and imposing, with a bandanna at his throat and a six-gun riding on his hip, took center stage.

Angus McKettrick, the patriarch. The founder of the Triple M, and the dynasty. Sierra knew little about him, but as she looked up into that hard, determined face, shaped by the rigors of life in the nineteenth century, she felt a kinship.

Ruthless old bastard, said the voice of Hank Breslin. *That's where McKettricks get their arrogance. From him.*

"Be quiet," Sierra repeated, thrusting her hands deeper into her coat pockets. She stood in silence for a long moment, listening to the rattle-throated hum of the station wagon's engine, the lonely cry of a nearby bird, the thrum of blood in her ears. A piney scent spiced the air.

Sierra turned, saw the marble angels marking the graves of Angus McKettrick's wives—Georgia, mother of Rafe, Kade and Jeb. Concepcion, mother of Kate.

Look for Holt and Lorelei, Eve had told her, the last time they'd spoken over the telephone. *That's our part of the family.*

Sierra caught sight of other bronze statues, smaller than

Angus's but no less impressive in their detail. They were
works of art, museum pieces, and if they hadn't been sol-
idly anchored in cement, they probably would have been
stolen. It said something about the McKettrick legend, she
supposed, that there had been no vandalism in this lonely,
wind-blown place.

Jeb McKettrick, the youngest of the brothers, was rep-
resented by a cowboy with his six-gun drawn; his wife,
Chloe, by a slender woman in pioneer dress, shading her
eyes with one hand and smiling. Their children, grandchildren, great-and a few great-great-grandchildren surrounded
them, their costly headstones laid out in neat rows, like the
streets of a western town.

Next was Kade McKettrick, easy in his skin, wearing a
six-shooter, like his brother, but with an open book in his
hand. His wife, Mandy, wore trousers, a loose-fitting shirt,
boots and a hat, and held a shotgun. Like Chloe, she was
smiling. Judging by the number of other graves around
theirs, these two had also been prolific parents.

The statue of Rafe McKettrick revealed a big, powerfully
built man with a stubborn set to his jaw. His bride, Emmeline, stood close against his side; their arms were linked and
she rested her head against the outside of his upper arm.

Sierra smiled. Again, their progeny was plentiful.

The last statue brought up an unexpected surge of emotion in Sierra. Here, then, was Holt, half brother to Rafe,
Kade and Jeb, and to Kate. In his long trail coat, he looked
both handsome and tough. A pair of very detailed ammu-
nition belts criss-crossed his chest, and the badge pinned
to his wide lapel read Texas Ranger.

Sierra stared into those bronze eyes and, once again, felt
something stir deep inside her. I came from this man, she
thought. We've got the same DNA.

Liam gave a jarring blast of the car horn, impatient to get to the ranch house that would be their home for the next twelve months.

Sierra waved in acknowledgment but moved on to the statue of Lorelei. She was mounted on a mule, long, lace-trimmed skirts spilling on either side of her impossibly small waist, face shadowed, not by a sunbonnet but by a man's hat. Her spirited gaze rested lovingly on her husband, Holt.

Liam laid on the horn.

Fearing he might decide to take the wheel and drive to the ranch house on his own, Sierra turned reluctantly from the markers and followed a path littered with pine needles and the dead leaves of the six towering white oaks that shared the space, heading back to the car.

Back to her son.

"Are all the McKettricks *dead?*" Liam asked, when Sierra settled into the driver's seat and fastened the belt.

"No," Sierra answered, waiting for some stray part of herself to finish meandering among those graves, making the acquaintance of ancestors, and catch up. "*We're* McKettricks, and we're not dead. Neither is your grandmother, or Meg." She knew there were cousins, too, descended from Rafe, Kade and Jeb, but it was too big a subject to explain to a seven-year-old boy. Besides, she was still trying to square them all away in her own mind.

"I thought my name was Liam *Breslin,*" the little boy said practically.

It should have been Liam Douglas, Sierra thought, remembering her first and only lover. As always, when Liam's father, Adam, came to mind, she felt a pang, a complicated mixture of passion, sorrow and helpless fury. She and Adam had never been married, so she'd given Liam her maiden name.

"We're McKettricks now," Sierra said with a sigh. "You'll understand when you're older."

She backed the car out carefully, keenly aware of the steep descent on all sides, and made the wide turn that would take them back on to the network of dirt roads bisecting the Triple M.

"I can understand *now*," Liam asserted, having duly pondered the matter in his solemn way. "After all, I'm *gifted*."

"You may be gifted," Sierra replied, concentrating on her driving, "but you're still seven."

"Do I get to be a cowboy and ride bucking broncs and stuff like that?"

Sierra suppressed a shudder. "No," she said.

"That bites," Liam answered, folding his arms and settling deeper into the heavy nylon coat she'd bought him on the road, when they'd reached the first of the cold-weather states. "What's the good of living on a ranch if you can't be a cowboy?"

Chapter 2

The elderly station wagon banged into the yard, bald tires crunching half-thawed gravel, and came to an obstreperous stop. Travis Reid paused behind the horse trailer hitched to Jesse McKettrick's mud-splattered black truck, pushed his hat to the back of his head with one leather-gloved finger and grinned, waiting for something to fall off the rig. Nothing did, which just went to prove that the age of miracles was not past.

Jesse appeared at the back of the trailer, leading old Baldy by his halter rope. "Who's that?" he asked, squinting in the wintry late afternoon sunshine.

Travis spared him no more than a glance. "A long-lost relative of yours, unless I miss my guess," he said easily.

The station wagon belched some smoke and died. Travis figured it for a permanent condition. He looked on with interest as a good-looking woman climbed out from behind the wheel, looked the old car over, and gave the driver's-side door a good kick with her right foot.

She was a McKettrick, all right. Of the female persuasion, too.

Jesse left Baldy standing to jump down from the bed of the trailer and lower the ramp to the ground. "Meg's half sister?" he asked. "The one who grew up in Mexico with her crazy, drunken father?"

"Reckon so," Travis said. He and Meg communicated regularly, most often by email, and she'd filled him in on Sierra as far as she could. Nobody in the family knew her very well, including her mother, Eve, so the information was sparse. She had a seven-year-old son—now getting out of the car—and she'd been serving cocktails in Florida for the last few years, and that was about all Travis knew about her. As Meg's caretaker and resident horse trainer, not to mention her friend, Travis had stocked the cupboards and refrigerator, made sure the temperamental furnace was working and none of the plumbing had frozen, and started up Meg's SUV every day, just to make sure it was running.

From the looks of that station wagon, it was a good thing he'd followed the boss-lady's orders.

"You gonna help me with this horse," Jesse asked testily, "or just stand there gawking?"

Travis chuckled. "Right now," he said, "I'm all for gawking."

Sierra McKettrick was tall and slender, with short, gleaming brown hair the color of a good chestnut horse. Her eyes were huge and probably blue, though she was still a stride or two too far away for him to tell.

Jesse swore and stomped back up the ramp, making plenty of noise as he did so. Like most of the McKettricks, Jesse was used to getting his way, and while he was a known womanizer, he'd evidently dismissed Sierra out of hand. After all, she was a blood relative—no sense driving his herd into *that* canyon.

Travis took a step toward the woman and the boy, who was staring at him with his mouth open.

"Is this Meg's house?" Sierra asked.

"Yes," Travis said, putting out his hand, pulling it back to remove his work gloves, and offering it again. "Travis Reid," he told her.

"Sierra Bres—McKettrick," she replied. Her grip was firm. And her eyes were definitely blue. The kind of blue that pierces something in a man's middle. She smiled, but tentatively. Somewhere along the line, she'd learned to be sparing with her smiles. "This is my son, Liam."

"Howdy," Liam said, squaring his small shoulders.

Travis grinned. "Howdy," he replied. Meg had said the boy had health problems, but he looked pretty sound to Travis.

"That sure is an ugly horse," Liam announced, pointing towards the trailer.

Travis turned. Baldy stood spraddle-footed, midway down the ramp, a miserable gray specimen of a critter with pink eyes and liver-colored splotches all over his mangy hide.

"Sure is," Travis agreed, and glowered at Jesse for palming the animal off on him. It was like him to pull off a dramatic last-minute rescue, then leave the functional aspects of the problem to somebody else.

Jesse flashed a grin, and for a moment, Travis felt territorial, wanted to set himself between Sierra and her boy, the pair of them, and one of his oldest friends. He felt off balance, somehow, as though he'd been ambushed. What the hell was *that* all about?

"Is that a buckin' bronc?" Liam asked, venturing a step toward Baldy.

Sierra reached out quickly, caught hold of the fur-trimmed hood on the kid's coat and yanked him back. Cold sunlight glinted off the kid's glasses, making his eyes invisible.

Jesse laughed. "Back in the day," he said, "Baldy was a rodeo horse. Cowboys quivered in their boots when they drew him to ride. Now, as you can see, he's a little past his prime."

"And you would be—?" Sierra asked, with a touch of coolness to her tone. Maybe she was the one woman out of a thousand who could see Jesse McKettrick for what he was—a good-natured case of very bad news.

"Your cousin Jesse."

Sierra sized him up, took in his battered jeans, work shirt, sheepskin coat and very expensive boots. "Descended from…?"

The McKettricks talked like that. Every one of them could trace their lineage back to old Angus, by a variety of paths, and while there would be hell to pay if anybody riled them as a bunch, they mostly kept to their own branch of the family tree.

"Jeb," Jesse said.

Sierra nodded.

Liam's attention remained fixed on the horse. "Can I ride him?"

"Sure," Jesse replied.

"No way," said Sierra, at exactly the same moment.

Travis felt sorry for the kid, and it must have shown in his face, because Sierra's gaze narrowed on him.

"We've had a long trip," she said. "I guess we'll just go inside."

"Make yourselves at home," Travis said, gesturing toward the house. "Don't worry about your bags. Jesse and I'll carry them in for you."

She considered, probably wondering if she'd be obligated in any way if she agreed, then nodded. Catching Liam by the hood of his coat again, she got him turned from the horse and hustled him toward the front door.

"Too bad we're kin," Jesse said, following Sierra with his eyes.

"Too bad," Travis agreed mildly, though privately he didn't believe it was such a bad thing at all.

The house was a long, sprawling structure, with two stories and a wraparound porch. Sierra's most immediate impression was of substance and practicality, rather than elegance, and she felt a subtle interior shift, as if she'd been a long time lost in a strange, winding street, thick with fog, and suddenly found herself standing at her own front door.

"Those guys are *real cowboys*," Liam said, once they were inside.

Sierra nodded distractedly, taking in the pegged wood floors, gleaming with the patina of venerable age, the double doors and steep staircase on the right, the high ceilings, the antique grandfather clock ticking ponderously beside the door. She peeked into a spacious living room, probably called a parlor when the house was new, and admired the enormous natural-rock fireplace, with its raised hearth and wood-nook. Worn but colorful rugs gave some relief to the otherwise uncompromisingly masculine decor of leather couches and chairs and tables of rough-hewn pine, as did the piano set in an alcove of floor-to-ceiling windows.

An odd nostalgia overtook Sierra; she'd never set foot on the Triple M before that day, let alone entered the home of Holt and Lorelei McKettrick, but she might have, if her dad hadn't snatched her the day Eve filed for divorce, and carried her off to San Miguel de Allende to share his expatriate lifestyle. She might have spent summers here, as Meg had, picking blackberries, wading in mountain streams, riding horses. Instead, she'd run barefoot through the streets of San Miguel, with no more memory of her mother than a faint scent of expensive perfume, sometimes encountered among the waves of tourists who frequented the markets, shops and restaurants of her home town.

Liam tugged at the sleeve of her coat. "Mom?"

She snapped out of her reverie, looked down at him, and smiled. "You hungry, bud?"

Liam nodded solemnly, but brightened when the door bumped open and Travis came in, lugging two suitcases.

Travis cleared his throat, as though embarrassed. "Plenty of grub in the kitchen," he said. "Shall I put this stuff upstairs?"

"Yes," Sierra said. "Thanks." At least that way she'd know which rooms were hers and Liam's without having to ask. She might have been concerned, sharing the place with Travis, but Meg had told her he lived in a trailer out by the barn. What Meg hadn't mentioned was that her resident caretaker was in his early thirties, not his sixties, as Sierra had imagined, and too attractive for comfort, with his lean frame, blue-green eyes and dark-blond hair in need of a trim.

She blushed as these thoughts filled her mind, and shuffled Liam quickly toward the kitchen.

It was a large room, with the same plank floors she'd seen in the front of the house and modern appliances, strangely juxtaposed with the black, chrome-trimmed wood cookstove occupying the far-left-hand corner. The table was long and rustic, with benches on either side and a chair at each end.

"Tables like that are a tradition with the McKettricks," a male voice said from just behind her.

Sierra jumped, startled, and turned to see Jesse in the doorway.

"Sorry," he said. He was handsome, Sierra thought. His coloring was similar to Travis's, and so was his build, and yet the two men didn't resemble each other at all.

"No problem," Sierra said.

Liam wrenched open the refrigerator. "Bologna!" he yelled triumphantly.

"Whoopee," Sierra replied, with a dryness that was lost on her son. "If there's bologna, there must be white bread, too."

"Jesse!" Travis's voice, from the direction of the front door. "Get out here and give me a hand!"

Jesse grinned, nodded affably to Sierra and vanished.

Sierra took off her coat, hung it from a peg next to the back door, and gestured for Liam to remove his, too. He complied, then went straight back to the bologna. He found a loaf of bread in a colorful polka-dot bag and started to build a sandwich.

Watching him, Sierra felt a faint brush of sorrow against the back of her heart. Liam was good at doing things on his own; he'd had a lot of practice, with her working the night shift at the club and sleeping days. Old Mrs. Davis from the apartment across the hall had been a conscientious babysitter, but hardly a mother figure.

She put coffee on to brew, once Liam was settled on a bench at the table. He'd chosen the side against the wall, so he could watch her moving about the kitchen.

"Cool place," he observed, between bites, "but it's haunted."

Sierra took a can of soup from a shelf, opened it and dumped the contents into a saucepan, placing it on the modern gas stove before answering. Liam was an imaginative child, often saying surprising things. Rather than responding instantly, Sierra usually tried to let a couple of beats pass before she answered.

"What makes you say that?"

"Don't know," Liam said, chewing. They'd had a drive-through breakfast, but that had been hours ago, and he was obviously starving.

Another jab of guilt struck Sierra, keener than the one before. "Come on," she prodded. "You must have had a reason." Of course he'd had a reason, she thought. They'd just been to a graveyard, so it was natural that death would be on his mind. She should have waited, made the pilgrimage on her own, instead of dragging Liam along.

Liam looked thoughtful. "The air sort of…buzzes," he said. "Can I make another sandwich?"

"Only if you promise to have some of this soup first."

"Deal," Liam said.

An old china cabinet stood against a far wall, near the cookstove, and Sierra approached it, even though she didn't intend to use any of the dishes inside. Priceless antiques, every one.

Her family had eaten off those dishes. Generations of them.

Her gaze caught on a teapot, sturdy looking and, at the same time, exquisite. Spellbound, she opened the glass doors of the cabinet and reached inside to touch the piece, ever so lightly, with just the tips of her fingers.

"Soup's boiling over," Liam said mildly.

Sierra gasped, turned on her heel and rushed back to the modern stove to push the saucepan off the flame.

"Mom," Liam interjected.

"What?"

"Chill out. It's only soup."

The inside door swung open, and Travis stuck his head in. "Stuff's upstairs," he said. "Anything else you need?"

Sierra stared at him for a long moment, as though he'd spoken in an alien language. "Uh, no," she said finally. "Thanks." Pause. "Would you like some lunch?"

"No, thanks," he said. "Gotta see to that damn horse." With that, he ducked out again.

"How come I can't ride the horse?" Liam asked.

Sierra sighed, setting a bowl of soup in front of him. "Because you don't know how."

Liam's sigh echoed her own, and if they'd been talking about anything but the endangerment of life and limb, it would have been funny.

"How am I supposed to *learn* how if you won't let me try? You're being overprotective. You could scar my psyche. I might develop psychological problems."

"There are times," Sierra confessed, sitting down across from him with her own bowl of soup, "when I wish you weren't quite so smart."

Liam waggled his eyebrows at her. "I got it from you."

"Yeah right," Sierra said. Liam had her eyes, her thick, fine hair, and her dogged persistence, but his remarkable IQ came from his father.

Don't think about Adam, she told herself.

Travis Reid sidled into her mind.

Even worse.

Liam consumed his soup, along with a second sandwich, and went off to explore the rest of the house while Sierra lingered thoughtfully over her coffee.

The telephone rang.

Sierra got up to fetch the cordless receiver and pressed Talk with her thumb. "Hello?"

"You're there!" Meg trilled.

Sierra noticed that she'd left the china cabinet doors open and went in that direction, intending to close them. "Yes," she said. Meg had been kind to her, in a long-distance sort of way, but Sierra had only been two when she'd last seen her half sister, and that made them strangers.

"How do you like it? The ranch house, I mean?"

"I haven't seen much of it," Sierra answered. "Liam and I just got here, and then we had lunch...." Her hand went, of its own accord, to the teapot, and she imagined she felt just the faintest charge when she touched it. "Lots of antiques around here," she said, thinking aloud.

"Don't be afraid to use them," Meg replied. "Family tradition."

Sierra withdrew her hand from the teapot, shut the doors. "Family tradition?"

"McKettrick rules," Meg said, with a smile in her voice. "Things are meant to be used, no matter how old they are."

Sierra frowned, uneasy. "But if they get broken—"

"They get broken," Meg finished for her. "Have you met Travis yet?"

"Yes," Sierra said. "And he's not at all what I expected."

Meg laughed. "What did you expect?"

"Some gimpy old guy, I guess," Sierra admitted, warming to the friendliness in her sister's voice. "You said he took care of the place and lived in a trailer by the barn, so I thought—" She broke off, feeling foolish.

"He's cute and he's single," Meg said.

"Even the teapot?" Sierra mused.

"Huh?"

Sierra put a hand to her forehead. Sighed. "Sorry. I guess

I missed a segue there. There's a teapot in the china cabinet in the kitchen—I was just wondering if I could—"

"I know the one," Meg answered, with a soft fondness in her voice. "It was Lorelei's. She got it for a wedding present."

Lorelei. The matriarch of the family. Sierra took a step backward.

"*Use* it," Meg said, as if she'd seen Sierra's reflexive retreat.

Sierra shook her head. "I couldn't. I had no idea it was that old. If I dropped it—"

"Sierra," Meg said, "it's not china. It's cast iron, with an enamel overlay."

"Oh."

"Kind of like the McKettrick women, Mom always says." Meg went on. "Smooth on the outside, tough as iron on the inside."

Mom. Sierra closed her eyes against all the conflicting emotions the word brought up in her, but it didn't help.

"We'll give you time to settle in," Meg said gently, when Sierra was too choked up to speak. "Then Mom and I will probably pop in for a visit. If that's okay with you, of course."

Both Meg and Eve lived in San Antonio, Texas, where they helped run McKettrickCo, a multinational corporation with interests in everything from software to communication satellites, so they wouldn't be "popping in" without a little notice.

Sierra swallowed hard. "It's your house," she said.

"And yours," Meg pointed out, very quietly.

After that, Meg made Sierra promise to call if she needed anything. They said goodbye, and the call ended.

Sierra went back to the china cabinet for the teapot.

Liam clattered down the back stairs. "I *told* you this place was haunted!" he crowed, his small face shining with delight.

The teapot was heavy—definitely cast iron—but Sierra was careful as she set it on the counter, just the same. "What on earth are you talking about?"

"I just saw a kid," Liam announced. "Upstairs, in my room!"

"You're imagining things."

Liam shook his head. "I *saw* him!"

Sierra approached her son, laid her hand to his forehead. "No fever," she mused, worried.

"Mom," Liam protested, pulling back. "I'm not sick—and I'm not delusional, either."

Delusional. How many seven-year-olds used that word? Sierra sighed and cupped Liam's eager face in both hands. "Listen. It's fine to have imaginary friends, but—"

"He's *not* imaginary."

"Okay," Sierra responded, with another sigh. It was possible, she supposed, that a neighbor child had wandered in before they arrived, but that seemed unlikely, given that the only other houses on the ranch were miles away. "Let's investigate."

Together they climbed the back stairs, and Sierra got her first look at the upper story. The corridor was wide, with the same serviceable board floors. The light fixtures, though old-fashioned, were electric, but most of the light came from the large arched window at the far end of the hallway. Six doors stood open, an indication that Liam had visited each room in turn after leaving the kitchen the first time.

He led her into the middle one, on the left side.

No one was there.

Sierra let out her breath, admiring the room. It was

spacious, perfect quarters for a boy. Two bay windows overlooked the barn area, where Baldy, the singularly unattractive horse, stood stalwartly in the middle of the corral, looking as though he intended to break loose at any second and do some serious bucking. Travis was beside Baldy, stroking the animal's neck as he eased the halter off over its head.

A quivery sensation tickled the pit of Sierra's stomach.

"Mom," Liam said. "He was here. He had on short pants and funny shoes and suspenders."

Sierra turned to look at her son, feeling fretful again. Liam stood near the other window, examining an antique telescope, balanced atop a shining brass tripod. "I believe you," she said.

"You don't," Liam argued, jutting out his chin. "You're *humoring* me."

Sierra sat down on the side of the bed positioned between the windows. Like the dressers, it was scarred with age, but made of sturdy wood. The headboard was simply but intricately carved, and a faded quilt provided color. "Maybe I am, a little," she admitted, because there was no fooling Liam. He had an uncanny knack for seeing through anything but the stark truth. "I don't know what to think, that's all."

"Don't you believe in ghosts?"

I don't believe in much of anything, Sierra thought sadly. "I believe in you," she said, patting the mattress beside her. "Come and sit down."

Reluctantly, he sat. Stiffened when she slipped an arm around his shoulders. "If you think I'm going to take a nap," he said, "you're dead wrong."

The word *dead* tiptoed up Sierra's spine to dance lightly

at her nape. "Everything's going to be all right, you know," she said gently.

"I like this room," Liam confided, and the hopeful uncertainty in his manner made Sierra's heart ache. They'd always lived in apartments or cheap motel rooms. Had Liam been secretly yearning to call a house like this one home? To settle down somewhere and live like a normal kid?

"Me, too," Sierra said. "It has friendly vibes."

"Is that supposed to be like a closet?" Liam asked, indicating the huge pine armoire taking up most of one wall.

Sierra nodded. "It's called a wardrobe."

"Maybe it's like the one in that story. Maybe the back of it opens into another world. There could be a lion and a witch in there." From the smile on Liam's face, the concept intrigued rather than troubled him.

She ruffled his hair. "Maybe," she agreed.

His attention shifted back to the telescope. "I wish I could look through that and see Andromeda," he said. "Did you know that the whole galaxy is on a collision course with the Milky Way? All hell's going to break loose when it gets here, too."

Sierra shuddered at the thought. Most parents worried that their kids played too many video games. With Liam, the concern was the Discovery and Science Channels, not to mention programs like *Nova*. He thought about things like Earth losing its magnetic field and had nightmares about creatures swimming in dark oceans under the ice covering one of Jupiter's moons. Or was it Saturn?

"Don't get excited, Mom," he said, with an understanding smile. "It's going to be something like five billion years before it happens."

"Before what happens?" Sierra asked, blinking.

"The *collision*," he said tolerantly.

"Right," Sierra said.

Liam yawned. "Maybe I *will* take a nap." He studied her. "Just don't get the idea it's going to be a regular thing."

She mussed his hair again, kissed the top of his head. "I'm clear on that," she said, standing and reaching for the crocheted afghan lying neatly folded at the foot of the bed.

Liam kicked off his shoes and stretched out on top of the blue chenille bedspread, yawning again. He set his glasses on the night stand with care.

She covered him, resisted the temptation to kiss his forehead, and headed for the door. When she looked back from the threshold, Liam was already asleep.

1919

Hannah McKettrick heard her son's laughter before she rode around the side of the house, toward the barn, a week's worth of mail bulging in the saddlebags draped across the mule's neck. The snow was deep, with a hard crust, and the January wind was brisk.

Her jaw tightened when she saw her boy out in the cold, wearing a thin jacket and no hat. He and Doss, her brother-in-law, were building what appeared to be a snow fort, their breath making white plumes in the frigid air.

Something in Hannah gave a painful wrench at the sight of Doss; his resemblance to Gabe, his brother and her late husband, invariably startled her, even though they lived under the same roof and she should have been used to him by then.

She nudged the mule with the heels of her boots, but Seesaw-Two didn't pick up his pace. He just plodded along.

"What are you doing out here?" Hannah called.

Both Tobias and Doss fell silent, turning to gaze guilt-ily in her direction.

The breath plumes dissipated.

Tobias set his feet and pushed back his narrow shoulders. He was only eight, but since Gabe's coffin had arrived by train one warm day last summer, draped in an American flag and with Doss for an escort, her boy had taken on the mien of a man.

"We're just making a fort, Ma," he said.

Hannah blinked back sudden, stinging tears. A soldier, Gabe had died of influenza in an army infirmary, without ever seeing the battleground. Tobias thought in military terms, and Doss encouraged him, a fact Hannah did not appreciate.

"It's cold out here," she said. "You'll catch your death."

Doss shifted, pushed his battered hat to the back of his head. His face hardened, like the ice on the pond back of the orchard where the fruit trees stood, bare-limbed and stoic, waiting for spring.

"Go inside," Hannah told her son.

Tobias hesitated, then obeyed.

Doss remained, watching her.

The kitchen door slammed eloquently.

"You've got no business putting thoughts like that in his head," Doss said, in a quiet voice. He took old See-saw's reins and held him while she dismounted, careful to keep her woolen skirts from riding up.

"That's a fine bit of hypocrisy, coming from you," Hannah replied. "Tobias had pneumonia last fall. We nearly lost him. He's fragile, and you know it, and as soon as I turn my back, you have him outside, building a snow fort!"

Doss reached for the saddlebags, and so did Hannah.

There was a brief tug-of-war before she let go. "He's a kid," Doss said. "If you had your way, he'd never do anything but look through that telescope and play checkers!"

Hannah felt as warm as if she were standing close to a hot stove, instead of Doss McKettrick. Their breaths melded between them. "I fully intend to have my way," she said. "Tobias is my son, and I will not have you telling me how to raise him!"

Doss slapped the saddlebags over one shoulder and stepped back, his hazel eyes narrowed. "He's my nephew—my brother's boy—and I'll be damned if I'll let you turn him into a sickly little whelp hitched to your apron strings!"

Hannah stiffened. "You've said quite enough," she told him tersely.

He leaned in, so his nose was almost touching hers. "I haven't said the half of it, Mrs. McKettrick."

Hannah sidestepped him, marching for the house, but the snow came almost to her knees and made it hard to storm off in high dudgeon. Her breath trailed over her right shoulder, along with her words. "Supper's in an hour," she said, without turning around. "But maybe you'd rather eat in the bunkhouse."

Doss's chuckle riled her, just as it was no doubt meant to do. "Old Charlie's a sight easier to get along with than you are, but he can't hold a candle to you when it comes to home cooking. Anyhow, he's been gone for a month, in case you haven't noticed."

She felt a flush rise up her neck, even though she was shivering inside Gabe's old woolen work coat. His scent was fading from the fabric, and she wished she knew a way to hold on to it.

"Suit yourself," she retorted.

Tobias shoved a chunk of wood into the cookstove as she entered the house, sending sparks snapping up the gleaming black chimney before he shut the door with a clang.

"We were only building a fort," he grumbled.

Hannah was stilled by the sight of him, just as if somebody had thrown a lasso around her middle and pulled it tight. "I could make biscuits and sausage gravy," she offered quietly.

Tobias ignored the olive branch. "You rode down to the road to meet the mail wagon," he said, without meeting her eyes. "Did I get any letters?" With his hands shoved into the pockets of his trousers and his brownish-blond hair shining in the wintry sunlight flowing in through the windows, he looked the way Gabe must have, at his age.

"One from your grandpa," Hannah said. Methodically, she hung her hat on the usual peg, pulled off her knitted mittens and stuffed them into the pockets of Gabe's coat. She took that off last, always hating to part with it.

"Which grandpa?" Tobias lingered by the stove, warming his hands, still refusing to glance her way.

Hannah's family lived in Missoula, Montana, in a big house on a tree-lined residential street. She missed them sorely, and it hurt a little, knowing Tobias was hoping it was Holt who'd written to him, not her father.

"The McKettrick one," she said.

"Good," Tobias answered.

The back door opened, and Doss came in, still carrying the saddlebags. Usually he stopped outside to kick the snow off his boots so the floors wouldn't get muddy, but today he was in an obstinate mood.

Hannah went to the stove and ladled hot water out of

the reservoir into a basin, so she could wash up before starting supper.

"Catch," Doss said cheerfully.

She looked back, saw the saddlebags, burdened with mail, fly through the air. Tobias caught them ably with a grin.

When was the last time he'd smiled at her that way?

The boy plundered anxiously through the bags, brought out the fat envelope postmarked San Antonio, Texas. Her in-laws, Holt and Lorelei McKettrick, owned a ranch outside that distant city, and though the Triple M was still home to them, they'd been spending a lot of time away since the beginning of the war. Hannah barely knew them, and neither did Tobias, for that matter, but they'd kept up a lively correspondence, the three of them, ever since he'd learned to read, and the letters had been arriving on a weekly basis since Gabe died.

Gabe's folks had come back for the funeral, of course, and in the intervening months Hannah had been secretly afraid. Holt and Lorelei saw their lost son in Tobias, the same as she did, and they'd offered to take him back to Texas with them when they left. She hadn't had to refuse—Tobias had done that for her, but he'd clearly been torn. A part of him had wanted to leave.

Hannah's heart had wedged itself up into her throat and stayed there until Gabe's mother and father were gone. Whenever a letter arrived, she felt anxious again.

She glanced at Doss, now shrugging out of his coat. He'd gone away to the army with Gabe, fallen sick with influenza himself, recovered and stayed on at the ranch after he brought his brother's body home for burial. Though no one had come right out and said so, Hannah knew

Doss had remained on the Triple M, instead of joining the folks in Texas, mainly to look after Tobias.

Maybe the McKettricks thought she'd hightail it home to Montana, once she got over the shock of losing Gabe, and they'd lose track of the boy.

Now Tobias stood poring over the letter, devouring every word with his eyes, getting to the last page and starting all over again at the beginning.

Deliberately Hannah diverted her attention, and that was when she saw the teapot, sitting on the counter. She looked toward the china cabinet, across the room. She hadn't touched the piece, knowing it was special to Lorelei, and she couldn't credit that Doss or Tobias would have taken it from its place, either. They'd been playing in the snow while she was gone to fetch the mail, not throwing a tea party.

"Did one of you get this out?" she asked casually, getting a good grip on the pot before carrying it back to the cabinet. It was made of metal, but the pretty enamel coating could have been chipped, and Hannah wasn't about to take the risk.

Tobias barely glanced her way before shaking his head. He was still intent on the letter from Texas.

Doss looked more closely, his gaze rising curiously from the teapot to Hannah's face. "Nope," he said at last, and busied himself emptying the contents of the coffeepot down the sink before pumping in water for a fresh batch.

Hannah closed the doors of the china cabinet, frowning.

"Odd," she said, very softly.

Chapter 3

Sierra descended the rear staircase into the kitchen, being extra quiet so she wouldn't wake Liam up. He hadn't had an asthma attack in almost a month, but he needed his rest.

Intending to brew herself some tea and spend a few quiet minutes restoring her equilibrium, she chose a mug from one of the cupboards, located a box of orange pekoe, and reached for the heirloom teapot.

It was gone.

She glanced toward the china cabinet and saw Lorelei's teapot sitting behind the glass.

Jesse or Travis must have come inside while she was upstairs, she reasoned, and put it away.

But that seemed unlikely. Men, especially cowboys, didn't usually fuss with teapots, did they? Not that she knew that much about men in general or cowboys in particular.

She'd seen Travis earlier, from Liam's bedroom window, working with the horse, and she was sure he hadn't been back in the house after carrying in the bags.

"Jesse?" she called softly, half-afraid he might jump out at her from somewhere.

No answer.

She moved to the front of the house, peered between the lace curtains in the parlor. Jesse's truck was gone, leaving deep tracks in the patchy mud and snow, rapidly filling with gossamer white flakes.

Bemused, Sierra returned to the kitchen, grabbed her coat and went out the back door, shoving her hands into her pockets and ducking her head against the thickening snowfall and the icy wind that accompanied it. Nothing in her life had prepared her for high-country weather; she'd been raised in Mexico, moved to San Diego after her father died and spent the last several years living in Florida. She supposed it would be a while before she adjusted to the change in climate, but if there was one thing she'd learned to do, on the long journey from then to now, it was adapt.

The doors of the big, weathered-board barn stood open, and Sierra stepped inside, shivering. It was warmer there, but she could still see her breath.

"Mr. Reid?"

"Travis" came the taciturn answer from a nearby stall. "I don't answer to much of anything else."

Sierra crossed the sawdust floor and saw Travis on the other side of the door, grooming poor old Baldy with long, gentle strokes of a brush. He gave her a sidelong glance and grinned slightly.

"Settling in okay?" he asked.

"I guess," she said, leaning on the stall door to watch him work. There was something soothing about the way he attended to that horse, almost as though he were touching her own skin....

Perish the thought.

He straightened. A quiver went through Baldy's body. "Something wrong?" Travis asked.

"No," Sierra said quickly, attempting a smile. "I was just wondering..."

"What?" Travis went back to brushing again, though he was still watching Sierra, and the horse gave a contented little snort of pleasure.

Suddenly the whole subject of the teapot seemed silly. How could she ask if he or Jesse had moved it? And, so what if they had? Jesse was a McKettrick, born and raised, and the things in that house were as much a part of his heritage as hers. Travis was clearly a trusted family friend—if not more.

Sierra found that possibility unaccountably disturbing. Meg had said he was single and free, but she obviously trusted Travis implicitly, which might mean there was a deeper level to their relationship.

"I was just wondering...if you ever drink tea," Sierra hedged lamely.

Travis chuckled. "Not often, unless it's the electric variety," he replied, and though he was smiling, the expression in his eyes was one of puzzlement. He was probably asking himself what kind of nut case Meg and Eve had saddled him with. "Are you inviting me?"

Sierra blushed, even more self-conscious than before. "Well...yes. Yes, I guess so."

"I'd rather have coffee," Travis said, "if that's all right with you."

"I'll put a pot on," Sierra answered, foolishly relieved. She should have walked away, but she seemed fixed to the spot, as though someone had smeared the soles of her shoes with superglue.

Travis finished brushing down the horse, ran a gloved hand along the animal's neck and waited politely for Sierra to move, so he could open the stall door and step out.

"What's really going on here, Ms. McKettrick?" he asked, when they were facing each other in the wide aisle, Baldy's stall door securely latched. Along the aisle, other horses nickered, probably wanting Travis's attention for themselves.

"Sierra," she said. She tried to sound friendly, but it was forced.

"Sierra, then. Somehow I don't think you came out here to ask me to a tea party or a coffee klatch."

She huffed out a breath and pushed her hands deeper into her coat pockets. "Okay," she admitted. "I wanted to know if you or Jesse had been inside the house since you brought the baggage in."

"No," Travis answered readily.

"It would certainly be all right if you had, of course—"

Travis took a light grip on Sierra's elbow and steered her toward the barn doors. He closed and fastened them once they were outside.

"Jesse got in his truck and left, first thing," he said. "I've been with Baldy for the last half an hour. Why?"

Sierra wished she'd never begun this conversation. Never left the warmth of the kitchen for the cold and the questions in Travis's eyes. She'd done both those things, though, and now she would have to explain. "I took a teapot out of the china cabinet," she said, "and set it on the counter. I went up to Liam's room, to help him settle in for a nap, and when I came downstairs—"

A startling grin broke over Travis's features like a flash

of summer sunlight over a crystal-clear pond. "What?" he prompted. He moved to Sierra's other side, shielding her from the bitter wind, increasing his pace, and therefore hers, as they approached the house.

"It was in the cabinet again. I would swear I put it on the counter."

"Weird," Travis said, kicking the snow off his boots at the base of the back steps.

Sierra stepped inside, shivering, took off her coat and hung it up.

Travis followed, closed the door, pulled off his gloves and stuffed them into the pockets of his coat before hanging it beside Sierra's, along with his hat. "Must have been Liam," he said.

"He's asleep," Sierra replied. The coffee she'd made earlier was still hot, so she filled two mugs, casting an uneasy glance toward the china cabinet as she did so. Liam couldn't have gotten downstairs without her seeing him, and even if he had, he wouldn't have been able to reach the high shelf in the china closet without dragging a chair over. She would have heard the scraping sound and, anyway, Liam being Liam, he wouldn't have put the chair back where he found it. There would have been evidence.

Travis accepted the cup Sierra offered with a nod of thanks, took a sip. "You must have put it away yourself, then," he said reasonably. "And then forgotten."

Sierra sat down in the chair closest to the wood-burning cookstove, suddenly yearning for a fire, while Travis made himself comfortable nearby, on the bench facing the wall.

"I know I didn't," she said, biting her lower lip.

Travis concentrated on his coffee for some moments before turning his gaze back to her face. "It's a strange house," he said.

Sierra blinked.

Cool place, Liam had said, right after they arrived, *but it's haunted.*

"What do you mean, 'It's a strange house'?" she asked. She made no attempt to keep the skepticism out of her voice.

"Meg's going to kill me for this," Travis said.

"I beg your pardon?"

"She doesn't want you scared off."

Sierra frowned, waiting.

"It's a good place," Travis said, taking the homey kitchen in with a fond glance. Clearly, he'd spent a lot of time there. "Odd things happen sometimes, though."

Sierra heard Liam's voice again. *I saw a kid, upstairs in my room.*

She shook off the memory. "Impossible," she muttered.

"If you say so," Travis replied affably.

"What *kind* of 'odd things' happen in this house?"

Travis smiled, and Sierra had the sense that she was being handled, skillfully managed, in the same way as the horse. "Once in a while, you'll hear the piano playing by itself. Or you walk into a room, and you get the feeling you passed somebody on the threshold, even though you're alone."

Sierra shivered again, but this time it had nothing to do with the icy January weather. The kitchen was snug and warm, even without the cookstove lit. "I would appreciate it," she said, "if you wouldn't talk that kind of nonsense in front of Liam. He's…impressionable."

Travis raised an eyebrow.

Suddenly, strangely, Sierra wanted to tell him what Liam had said about seeing another little boy in his room, but she couldn't quite bring herself to do it. She wouldn't have Travis Reid—or anybody else, for that matter—thinking

Liam was…different. He got enough of that from other kids, being so smart, and his asthma set him apart, too.

"I must have moved the teapot myself," Sierra said, at last, "and forgotten. Just as you said."

Travis looked unconvinced. "Right," he agreed.

1919

Tobias carried the letter to the table, where Doss sat comfortably in the chair everyone thought of as Holt's. "They bought three hundred head of cattle," the boy told his uncle excitedly, handing over the sheaf of pages. "Drove them all the way from Mexico to San Antonio, too."

Doss smiled. "Is that right?" he mused. His hazel eyes warmed in the light of a kerosene lantern as he read. The place had electricity now, but Hannah tried to save on it where she could. The last bill had come to over a dollar, for a mere two months of service, and she'd been horrified at the expense.

Standing at the stove, she turned back to her work, stood a little straighter, punched down the biscuit dough with sharp jabs of the wooden spoon. Apparently, it hadn't occurred to Tobias that she might like to see that infernal letter. She was a McKettrick, too, after all, if only by marriage.

"I guess Ma and Pa liked that buffalo you carved for them," Doss observed, when he'd finished and set the pages aside. Hannah just happened to see, since she'd had to pass right by that end of the table to fetch a pound of ground sausage from the icebox. "Says here it was the best Christmas present they ever got."

Tobias nodded, beaming with pride. He'd worked all fall on that buffalo, even in his sick bed, whittling it from a chunk of firewood Doss had cut for him special. "I reckon I'll make them a bear for next year," he said. Not a word about carving something for her parents, Hannah noted, even though they'd sent him a bicycle and a toy fire engine back in December. The McKettricks, of course, had arranged for a spotted pony to be brought up from the main ranch house on Christmas morning, all decked out in a brand-new saddle and bridle, and though Tobias had dutifully written his Montana grandparents to thank them for their gifts, he'd never played with the engine. Just set it on a shelf in his room and forgotten all about it. The bicycle wouldn't be much use before spring, that was true, but he'd shown no more interest in it once the pony had arrived.

"Wash your hands for supper, Tobias McKettrick," Hannah said.

"Supper isn't ready," he protested.

"Do as your mother says," Doss told him quietly.

He obeyed immediately, which should have pleased Hannah, but it didn't.

Doss, meanwhile, opened the saddle bags, took out the usual assortment of letters, periodicals and small parcels, which Hannah had already looked through before the mail wagon rounded the bend in the road. She'd been both disappointed and relieved when there was nothing with her name on it. Once, in the last part of October, when the fiery leaves of the oak trees were falling in puddles around their trunks like the folds of a discarded garment, she'd gotten a letter from Gabe. He'd been dead almost four months by then, and her heart had fairly stopped at the sight of his handwriting on that envelope.

For a brief, dizzying moment, she'd thought there'd been a mistake. That Gabe hadn't died of the influenza at all, but some stranger instead. Mix-ups like that happened during and after a war, and she hadn't seen the body, since the coffin was nailed shut.

She'd stood there beside the road, with that letter in her hand, weeping and trembling so hard that a good quarter of an hour must have passed before she broke the seal and took out the thick fold of vellum pages inside. She'd come to her practical senses by then, but seeing the date at the top of the first page still made her bellow aloud to the empty countryside: March 17, 1918.

Gabe had still been well when he wrote that letter. He'd been looking forward to coming home. It was about time they added to their family, he'd said, and got cattle running on their part of the Triple M again.

She'd dropped to her knees, right there on the hard-packed dirt, too stricken to stand. The mule had wandered home, and presently Doss had come looking for her. Found her still clutching that letter to her chest, her throat so raw with sorrow that she couldn't speak.

He'd lifted her into his arms, Doss had, without saying a word. Set her on his horse, swung up behind her and taken her home.

"Hannah?"

She blinked, came back to the kitchen and the biscuit batter, the package of sausage in her hands.

Doss was standing beside her, smelling of snow and pine trees and man. He touched her arm.

"Are you all right?" he asked.

She swallowed, nodded.

It was a lie, of course. Hannah hadn't been all right since the day Gabe went away to war. Like as not, she would never be all right again.

"You sit down," Doss said. "I'll attend to supper."

She sat, because the strength had gone out of her knees, and looked around blankly. "Where's Tobias?"

Doss washed his hands, opened the sausage packet, and dumped the contents into the big cast iron skillet waiting on the stove. "Upstairs," he answered.

Tobias had left the room without her knowing?

"Oh," she said, unnerved. Was she losing her mind? Had her sorrow pushed her not only to absent-minded distraction, but beyond the boundaries of ordinary sanity as well?

She considered the mysterious movement of her mother-in-law's teapot.

Adeptly, Doss rolled out the biscuit dough, cut it into circles with the rim of a glass. Lorelei McKettrick had taught her boys to cook, sew on their own buttons and make up their beds in the morning. You could say that for her, and a lot of other things, too. .

Doss poured Hannah a mug of coffee, brought it to her. Started to rest a hand on her shoulder, then thought better of it and pulled back. "I know it's hard," he said.

Hannah couldn't look at him. Her eyes burned with tears she didn't want him to see, though she reckoned he knew they were there anyhow. "There are days," she said, in a whisper, "when I don't think I can go another step. But I have to, because of Tobias."

Doss crouched next to Hannah's chair, took both her hands in his own and looked up into her face. "There's been a hundred times," he said, "when I wished it was me in that grave up there on the hill, instead of Gabe. I'd give anything to take his place, so he could be here with you and the boy."

A sense of loss cut into Hannah's spirit like the blade of a new ax, swung hard. "You mustn't think things like that," she said, when she caught her breath. She pulled her hands free, laid them on either side of his earnest, handsome face, then quickly withdrew them. "You mustn't, Doss. It isn't right."

Just then Tobias clattered down the back stairs.

Doss flushed and got to his feet.

Hannah turned away, pretended to have an interest in the mail, most of which was for Holt and Lorelei, and would have to be forwarded to San Antonio.

"What's the matter, Ma?" Tobias spoke worriedly into the awkward silence. "Don't you feel good?"

She'd hoped the boy hadn't seen Doss sitting on his haunches beside her chair, but obviously he had.

"I'm fine," she said briskly. "I just had a splinter in my finger, that's all. I got it putting wood in the fire, and Doss took it out for me."

Tobias looked from her to his uncle and back again.

"Is that why you're making supper?" he asked Doss.

Doss hesitated. Like Gabe, he'd been raised to abhor any kind of lie, even an innocent one, designed to soothe a boy who'd lost his father and feared, in the depths of his dreams, losing his mother, too.

"I'm making supper," he said evenly, "because I can."

Hannah closed her eyes, opened them again.

"Set the table, please," Doss told Tobias.

Tobias hurried to the cabinet for plates and silverware.

Hannah met Doss's gaze across the dimly lit room.

A charge seemed to pass between them, like before, when Hannah had come back from getting the mail and found Tobias outside, in the teeth of a high-country winter, building a snow fort.

"It's too damn dark in this house," Doss said. He walked to the middle of the room, reached up, and pulled the beaded metal cord on the overhead light. The bare bulb glowed so brightly it made Hannah blink, but she didn't object.

Something in Doss's face prevented her from it.

Present Day

Travis had long since finished his coffee and left the house by the time Liam got up from his nap and came downstairs, tousle-haired and puffy-eyed from sleep.

"That boy was in my room again," he said. "He was sitting at the desk, writing a letter. Can I watch TV? There's a nice setup in that room next to the front door. A computer, too, with a big, flat-screen monitor."

Sierra knew about the fancy electronics, since she'd explored the house after Travis left. "You can watch TV for an hour," she said. "Hands off the computer, though. It doesn't belong to us."

Liam's shoulders slumped slightly. "I *know* how to use a computer, Mom," he said. "We had them at school."

Between rent, food and medical bills, Sierra had never been able to scrape together the money for a PC of their own. She'd used the one in the office of the bar she worked in, back in Florida. That was how Meg had first contacted her. "We'll get one," she said, "as soon as I find another job."

"My mailbox is probably full," Liam replied, unappeased. "All the kids in the Geek Program were going to write to me."

Sierra, in the midst of putting a package of frozen chicken breasts into the microwave to thaw, felt as though she'd been poked with a sharp stick. "Don't call it the Geek Program, please," she said.

Liam shrugged one shoulder. "Everybody else does."

"Go watch TV."

He went.

A rap sounded at the back door, and Sierra peered through the glass, since it was dark out, to see Travis standing on the back porch.

"Come in," she called, and headed for the sink to wash her hands.

Travis entered, carrying a fragrant bag of take-out food in one hand. The collar of his coat was raised against the cold, his hat brim pulled low over his eyes.

"Fried chicken," he said, lifting the bag as evidence.

Sierra paused, shut off the faucet, dried her hands. The timer on the microwave dinged. "I was about to cook," she said.

Travis grinned. "Good thing I got to you in time," he answered. "If you're anything like your sister, you shouldn't be allowed to get near a stove."

If you're anything like your sister.

The words saddened Sierra, settled bleak and heavy over her heart. She didn't know whether she was like her sister or not; until Meg had emailed her a smiling picture a few weeks ago, she wouldn't have recognized her on the street.

"Did I say something wrong?" Travis asked.

"No," Sierra said quickly. "It was—thoughtful of you to bring the chicken."

Liam must have heard Travis's voice, because he came pounding into the room, all smiles.

"Hey, Travis," he said.

"Hey, cowpoke," Travis replied.

"The computer's making a dinging noise," Liam reported.

Travis smiled, set the bag of chicken on the counter but made no move to take off his hat and coat. "Meg's got it set to do that, so she'll remember to check her email when she's here," he said.

"Mom won't let me log on," Liam told him.

Travis glanced at Sierra, turned to Liam again. "Rules are rules, cowpoke," he said.

"Rules bite," Liam said.

"Ninety-five percent of the time," Travis agreed.

Liam recovered quickly. "Are you going to stay and eat with us?"

Travis shook his head. "I'd like that a lot, but I'm expected somewhere else for supper," he answered.

Liam looked sorely disappointed.

Sierra wondered where that "somewhere else" was, and with whom Travis would be sharing a meal, and was irritated with herself. It was none of her business, and besides, she didn't care what he did or who he did it with anyway. Not the least little bit.

"Maybe another time," Travis said.

Liam sighed and retreated to the study and his allotted hour of television.

"You shouldn't have," Sierra said, indicating their supper with a nod.

"It's your first night here," Travis answered, opening the door to leave. "Seemed like the neighborly thing to do."

"Thank you," Sierra said, but he'd already closed the door between them.

Travis started up his truck, just in case Sierra was listening for the engine, drove it around behind the barn and parked. After stopping to check on Baldy and the three other horses in his care, he shrugged down into the collar of his coat and slogged to his trailer.

The quarters were close, smaller than the closet off his

master bedroom at home in Flagstaff, but he didn't need much space. He had a bed, kitchen facilities, a bathroom and a place for his laptop. It was enough.

More than Brody was ever going to have.

He took off his hat and coat and tossed them on to the built-in, padded bench that passed for a couch. He tried not to think about Brody, and in the daytime, he stayed busy enough to succeed. At night, it was another matter. There just wasn't enough to do after dark, especially out here in the boonies, once he'd nuked a frozen dinner and watched the news.

He thought about Sierra and the boy, in there in the big house, eating the chicken and fixings he'd picked up in the deli at the one and only supermarket in Indian Rock. He'd never intended to join them, since they'd just arrived and were settling in, but he could picture himself sitting down at that long table in the kitchen, just the same.

He rooted through his refrigerator, something he had to crouch to do, and chose between Salisbury steak, Salisbury steak and Salisbury steak.

While the sectioned plastic plate was whirling round and round in the lilliputian microwave that came with the trailer, he made coffee and remembered his last visit from Rance McKettrick. Widowed, Rance lived alone in the house *his* legendary ancestor, Rafe, had built for his wife, Emmeline, and their children, back in the 1880s. He had two daughters, whom he largely ignored.

"This place is just a fancy coffin," Rance had observed, in his blunt way, when he'd stepped into the trailer. "Brody's the one that's dead, Trav, not you."

Travis rubbed his eyes with a thumb and forefinger. Brody was dead, all right. No getting around that. Seventeen, with everything to live for, and he'd blown himself up in the back room of a slum house in Phoenix, making meth.

He looked into the window over the sink, saw his own reflection.

Turned away.

His cell phone rang, and he considered letting voice mail pick up, but couldn't make himself do it. If he'd answered the night Brody called…

He fished the thing out, snapped it open and said, "Reid."

"Whatever happened to 'hello'?" Meg asked.

The bell on the microwave rang, and Travis reached in to retrieve his supper, burned his hand and cursed.

She laughed. "Better and better."

"I'm not in the mood for banter, Meg," he replied, turning on the water with his free hand and then switching to shove his scorched fingers into the flow.

"You never are," she said.

"The horses are fine."

"I know. You would have called me if they weren't."

"Then what do you want?"

"My, my, we *are* testy tonight. I called, you big grouch, to ask about my sister and my nephew. Are they okay? How do they look? Sierra is so private, she's almost standoffish."

"You can say that again."

"Thank you, but in the interest of brevity, I won't."

"Since when do you give a damn about brevity?" Travis inquired, but he was grinning by then.

Once again Meg laughed. Once again Travis wished he'd been able to fall in love with her. They'd tried, the two of them, to get something going, on more than one occasion. Meg wanted a baby, and he wanted not to be alone, so it made sense. The trouble was, it hadn't worked.

There was no chemistry.

There was no passion.

They were never going to be anything more than what they were—the best of friends. He was mostly resigned to that, but in lonely moments, he ached for things to be different.

"Tell me about my sister," Meg insisted.

"She's pretty," Travis said. *Real* pretty, added a voice in his mind. "She's proud, and overprotective as hell of the kid."

"Liam has asthma," Meg said quietly. "According to Sierra, he nearly died of it a couple of times."

Travis forgot his burned fingers, his Salisbury steak and his private sorrow. *"What?"*

Meg let out a long breath. "That's the only reason Sierra's willing to have anything to do with Mom and me. Mom put her on the company health plan and arranged for Liam to see a specialist in Flagstaff on a regular basis. In return, Sierra had to agree to spend a year on the ranch."

Travis stood still, absorbing it all. "Why here?" he asked. "Why not with you and Eve in San Antonio?"

"Mom and I would love that," Meg said, "but Sierra needs…distance. Time to get used to us."

"Time to get used to two McKettrick women. So we're talking, say, the year 2050, give or take a decade?"

"Very funny. Sierra *is* a McKettrick woman, remember? She's up to the challenge."

"She is definitely a McKettrick," Travis agreed ruefully. And very definitely a woman. "How did you find her?"

"Mom tracked her and Hank down when Sierra was little," Meg answered.

Travis dropped on to the edge of his bed, which was unmade. The sheets were getting musty, and every night, the pizza crumbs rubbed his hide raw. One of these days he was going to haul off and change them.

"'Tracked her down'?"

"Yes," Meg said, with a sigh. "I guess I didn't tell you about that part."

"I guess you didn't." Travis had known about the kidnapping, how Sierra's father had taken off with her the day the divorce papers were served, and that the two of them had ended up in Mexico. "Eve knew, and she still didn't lift a finger to get her own daughter back?"

"Mom had her reasons," Meg answered, withdrawing a little.

"Oh, well, then," Travis retorted, "that clears everything up. What *reason* could she possibly have?"

"It's not my place to say, Trav," Meg told him sadly. "Mom and Sierra have to work it all through first, and it might be a while before Sierra's ready to listen."

Travis sighed, shoved a hand through his hair. "You're right," he conceded.

Meg brightened again, but there was a brittleness about her that revealed more than she probably wanted Travis to know, close as they were. "So," she said, "what would you say Mom's chances are? Of reconnecting with Sierra, I mean?"

"The truth?"

"The truth," Meg said, without enthusiasm.

"Zero to zip. Sierra's been pleasant enough to me, but she's as stubborn as any McKettrick that ever drew breath, and that's saying something."

"Gee, thanks."

"You said you wanted the truth."

"How can you be so sure Mom won't be able to get through to her?"

"It's just a hunch," Travis said.

Meg was quiet. Travis was famous for his hunches. Too bad he hadn't paid attention to the one that said his little brother was in big trouble, and that Travis ought to drop everything and look for Brody until he found him.

"Look, maybe I'm wrong," he added.

"What's your real impression of Sierra, Travis?"

He took his time answering. "She's independent to a fault. She's built a wall around herself and the kid, and she's not about to let anybody get too close. She's jumpy, too. If it wasn't for Liam, and the fact that she probably doesn't have two nickels to rub together, she definitely wouldn't be on the Triple M."

"Damn," Meg said. "We knew she was poor, but—"

"Her car gave out in the driveway as soon as she pulled in. I took a peek under the hood, and believe me, the best mechanic on the planet couldn't resurrect that heap."

"She can drive my SUV."

"That might take some convincing on your part. This is not a woman who wants to be obliged. It's probably all she can do not to grab the kid and hop on the next bus to nowhere."

"This is depressing," Meg said.

Travis got up off the bed, peeled back the plastic covering his dinner, and poked warily at the faux meat with the tip of one finger. Talk about depressing.

"Hey," he said. "Look on the bright side. She's here, isn't she? She's on the Triple M. It's a start."

"Take care of her, Travis."

"As if she'd go along with that."

"Do it for me."

"Oh, please."

Meg paused, took aim and scored a bull's-eye. "Then do it for Liam."

Chapter 4

1919

Doss left the house after supper, ostensibly to look in on the livestock one last time before heading upstairs to bed, leaving the dishwashing to Tobias and Hannah. He stood still in the dooryard, raising the collar of his coat against the wicked cold. Stars speckled the dark, wintry sky.

In those moments he missed Gabe with a piercing intensity that might have bent him double, if he wasn't McKettrick proud. That was what his mother called the quality, anyhow. In the privacy of his own mind, Doss named it stubbornness.

Thinking of his ma made his pa come to mind, too. He missed them almost as sorely as he did Gabe. His uncles, Rafe and Kade and Jeb, along with their wives, were all down south, around Phoenix, where the weather was more hospitable to their aging bones. Their sons, to a man, were still in the army, even though the war was over, waiting to be mustered out. Their daughters had all married, every one of them keeping the McKettrick name, and lived in places as far-flung as Boston, New York and San Francisco.

There was hardly a McKettrick left on the place, save himself and Hannah and Tobias. It deepened Doss's loneliness, knowing that. He wished everybody would just come back home, where they belonged, but it would have been easier to herd wild barn cats than that bunch.

Doss looked back toward the house. Saw the lantern glowing at the kitchen window. Smiled.

The moment he'd gone outside, Hannah must have switched off the bulb. She worried about running short of things, he'd noticed, even though she'd come from a prosperous family, and certainly married into one.

His throat tightened. He knew she'd been different before he brought Gabe home in a pine box, but then, they all had. Gabe's going left a hole in the fabric of what it meant to be a McKettrick, and not a tidy one, stitched at the edges. Rather, it was a jagged tear, and judging by the raw newness of his own grief, Doss had little hope of it ever mending.

Time heals, his mother had told him after they'd laid Gabe in the ground up there on the hill, with his Grandpa Angus and those that had passed after him, but she'd had tears in her eyes as she said it. As for his pa, well, he'd stood a long time by the grave. Stood there until Rafe and Kade and Jeb brought him away.

Doss thrust out a sigh, remembering. "Gabe," he said, under his breath, "Hannah says it's wrong of me, but I still wish it had been me instead of you."

He'd have given anything for an answer, but wherever

Gabe was, he was busy doing other things. Maybe they had fishing holes up there in the sky, or cattle to round up and drive to market.

"Take care of Hannah and my boy," Gabe had told him, in that army infirmary, when they both knew there would be no turning the illness around. "Promise me, Doss."

Doss had swallowed hard and made that promise, but it was a hard one to keep. Hannah didn't seem to want taking care of, and every morning when Doss woke up, he was afraid this would be the day she'd decide to go back to her own people, up in Montana, and stay gone for good.

The back door opened, startling Doss out of his musings. He hesitated for a moment, then tramped in the direction of the barn, trying to look like a man bent on a purpose.

Hannah caught up, bundled into a shawl and carrying a lighted lantern in one hand.

"I think I'm going mad," she blurted out.

Doss stopped, looked down at her in puzzled concern. "It's the grief, Hannah," he told her gruffly. "It will pass."

"You don't believe that any more than I do," Hannah challenged, catching up with herself. The snow was deep and getting deeper, and the wind bit straight through to the marrow.

Doss moved to the windward side, to be a buffer for her. "I've got to believe it," he said. "Feeling this bad forever doesn't bear thinking about."

"I put the teapot away," Hannah said, her breath coming in puffs of white. "I know I put it away. But I must have gotten it out again, without knowing or remembering, and that scares me, Doss. That really scares me."

They reached the barn. Doss took the lantern from her and hauled open one of the big doors one-handed. It wasn't easy, since the snow had drifted, even in the short time since he'd left off feeding and watering the horses and the milk cow and that cussed mule Seesaw. The critter was a son of Doss's mother's mule, who'd borne the same name, and he was a son of something else, too.

"Maybe you're a mite forgetful these days," Doss said, once he'd gotten her inside, out of the cold. The familiar smells and sounds of the darkened barn were a solace to him—he came there often, even when he didn't have work to do, which was seldom. On a ranch, there was always work to do—wood to chop, harnesses to mend, animals to look after. "That doesn't mean you're not sane, Hannah."

Don't say it, he pleaded silently. Don't say you might as well take Tobias and head for Montana.

It was a selfish thought, Doss knew. In Montana, Hannah could live a city life again. No riding a mule five miles to fetch the mail. No breaking the ice on the water troughs on winter mornings, so the cattle and horses could drink. No feeding chickens and dressing like a man.

If Hannah left the Triple M, Doss didn't know what he'd do. First and foremost, he'd have to break his promise to Gabe, by default if not directly, but there was more to it than that. A lot more.

"There's something else, too," Hannah confided.

To keep himself busy, Doss went from stall to stall, looking in on sleepy horses, each one confounded and blinking in the light of his lantern. He was giving Hannah space, enough distance to get out whatever it was she wanted to say.

"What?" he asked, when she didn't speak again right away.

"Tobias. He just told me—he told me—"

Doss looked back, saw Hannah standing in the moonlit doorway, rimmed in silver, with one hand pressed to her mouth.

He went back to her. Set the lantern aside and took her by the shoulders. "What did he tell you, Hannah?"

"Doss, he's seeing things."

He tensed on the inside. Would have shoved a hand through his hair in agitation if he hadn't been wearing a hat and his ears weren't bound to freeze if he took it off. "What kind of things?"

"A boy." She took hold of his arm, and her grip was strong for such a small woman. It did curious things to him, feeling her fingers on him, even through the combined thickness of his coat and shirt. "Doss, Tobias says he saw a boy in his room."

Doss looked around. There was nothing but bleak, frozen land for miles around. "That's impossible," he said.

"You've got to talk to him."

"Oh, I'll talk to him, all right." Doss started for the house, so fixed on getting to Tobias that he forgot all about keeping Hannah sheltered from the wind. She had to lift her skirts to keep pace with him.

Present Day

"Tell me about the boy you saw in your room," Sierra said, when they'd eaten their fill of fried chicken, macaroni salad, mashed potatoes with gravy, and corn on the cob.

Liam's gaze was clear as he regarded her from his side of the long table. "He's a ghost," he replied, and waited, visibly expecting the statement to be refuted.

"Maybe an imaginary playmate?" Sierra ventured. Liam was a lonely little boy; their lifestyle had seen to that. After her father had died, drunk himself to death in a back-street cantina in San Miguel, the two of them had wandered like gypsies. San Diego. North Carolina, Georgia, and finally Florida.

"There's nothing imaginary about him," Liam said staunchly. "He wears funny clothes, like those kids on those old-time shows on TV. He's a *ghost,* Mom. Face it."

"Liam—"

"You never believe anything I tell you!"

"I believe *everything* you tell me," Sierra insisted evenly. "But you've got to admit, this is a stretch." Again she thought of the teapot. Again she pushed the recollection aside.

"I never lie, Mom."

She moved to pat his hand, but he pulled back. The set of his jaw was stubborn, and his gaze drilled into her, full of challenge. She tried again. "I know you don't lie, Liam. But you're in a strange new place and you miss your friends and—"

"And you won't even let me see if they sent me emails!" he cried.

Sierra sighed, rested her elbows on the tabletop and rubbed her temples with the fingertips of both hands. "Okay," she relented. "You can log on to the internet. Just be careful, because that computer is expensive, and we can't afford to replace it."

Suddenly Liam's face was alight. "I won't break it," he promised, with exuberance.

Sierra wondered if he'd just scammed her, if the whole boy-in-the-bedroom thing was a trick to get what he wanted.

In the next instant she was ashamed. Liam was direct to a fault. He *believed* he'd seen another child in his empty bedroom. She'd call his new doctor in Flagstaff in the morning, talk to the woman, see what a qualified professional made of the whole thing. She offered a silent prayer that her car would start, too, because the doctor was going to want to see Liam, pronto.

Meanwhile, Liam got to his feet and scrambled out of the room.

Sierra cleared away the supper mess, then followed him, as casually as she could, to the room at the front of the house.

He was already online.

"Just what I thought!" he crowed. "My mailbox is *bulging*."

The TV was still on, a narrator dolefully describing the effects of a second ice age, due any minute. Run for the hills. Sierra shut it off.

"Hey," Liam objected. "I was listening to that."

Sierra approached the computer. "You're only seven," she said. "You shouldn't be worrying about the fate of the planet."

"Somebody's got to," Liam replied, without looking at her. "*Your* generation is doing a lousy job." He was staring, as if mesmerized, into the computer screen. Its bluish-gray light flickered on the lenses of his glasses, making his eyes disappear. "Look! The whole Geek Group wrote to me!"

"I asked you not to—"

"Okay," Liam sighed, without looking at her. "The brilliant children in the gifted program are engaging in communication."

"That's better," Sierra said, sparing a smile.

"You've got a few emails waiting yourself," Liam announced. He was already replying to the cybermissives, his small fingers ranging deftly over the keyboard. He'd skipped the hunt-and-peck method entirely, as had all the other kids in his class. Using a computer came naturally to Liam, almost as if he'd been born knowing how, and she knew this was a common phenomenon, which gave her some comfort.

"I'll read them later," Sierra answered. She didn't have that many friends, so most of her messages were probably sales pitches of the penis-enlargement variety. How had she gotten on that kind of list? It wasn't as if she visited porn sites or ordered battery-operated boyfriends online.

"They get to watch a real rocket launch!" Liam cried, without a trace of envy. *"Wow!"*

"Wow indeed," Sierra said, looking around the room. According to Meg, it had originally been a study. Old books lined the walls on sturdy shelves, and there was a natural rock fireplace, too, with a fire already laid.

Sierra found a match on the mantelpiece, struck it and lit the blaze.

A chime sounded from the computer.

"Aunt Meg just IM'd you," Liam said.

Where had he gotten this "Aunt Meg" thing? He'd never even met the woman in person, let alone established a relationship with her. "'IM'd'?" she asked.

"Instant Messaged," Liam translated. "Guess you'd better check it out. Just make it quick, because I've still got a *pile* of mail to answer."

Smiling again, Sierra took the chair Liam so reluctantly surrendered and read the message from Meg.

Travis tells me your car died. Use my SUV. The keys are in the sugar bowl beside the teapot.

Sierra's pride kicked in. Thanks, she replied, at a fraction of Liam's typing speed, but I probably won't need it. My car is just... She paused. Her car was just what? Old? tired, she finished, inspired.

The SUV won't run when I come back if somebody doesn't charge up the battery. It's been sitting too long, Meg responded quickly. She must have been as fast with a keyboard as Liam.

Is Travis going to report on everything I do? Sierra wrote. She made so many mistakes, she had to retype the message before hitting Send, and that galled her.

Yes, Meg wrote. Because I plan to nag every last detail out of him.

Sierra sighed. It won't be that interesting, she answered, taking her time so she wouldn't have to revise. She was out of practice, and if she hoped to land anything better than a waitressing job in Indian Rock, she'd better polish her computer skills.

Meg sent a smiley face, followed by, Good night, Sis. (I've always wanted to say that.)

Sierra bit her lower lip. Good night, she tapped out, and rose from the chair with a glance at the clock on the mantel above the now-snapping fire.

Why had she lit it? She was exhausted, and now she would either have to throw water on the flames or wait until they died down. The first method, of course, would make a terrible mess, so that was out.

"Hurry up and finish what you're doing," she told Liam, who had plopped in the chair again the moment Sierra got out of it. "Half an hour till bedtime."

"I had a *nap*," Liam reminded her, typing simultaneously.

"Finish," Sierra repeated. With that, she left the study, climbed the stairs and went into Liam's room to get his favorite pajamas from one of the suitcases. She meant to put them in the clothes dryer for a few minutes, warm them up.

Something drew her to the window, though. She looked down, saw that the lights were on in Travis's trailer and his truck was parked nearby. Evidently, he hadn't stayed long in town, or wherever he'd gone.

Why did it please her so much, knowing that?

1919

Hannah stood in the doorway of Tobias's room, watching her boy sleep. He looked so peaceful, lying there, but she knew he had bad dreams sometimes. Just the night before, in the wee small hours, he'd crawled into bed beside her, snuggled as close as his little-boy pride would allow, and whispered earnestly that she oughtn't die anytime soon.

She'd been so choked up, she could barely speak.

Now she wanted to wake him, hold him tight in her arms, protect him from whatever it was in his mind that made him see little boys that weren't there.

He was lonely, that was all. He needed to be around other children. Way out here, he went to a one-room school, when it wasn't closed on account of snow, with only seven other pupils, all of whom were older than he was.

Maybe she should take him home to Montana. He had cousins there. They'd live in town, too, where there were shops and a library and even a moving-picture theater. He could ride his bicycle, come spring, and play baseball with other boys.

Hannah's throat ached. Gabe had wanted his son raised here, on the Triple M. Wanted him to grow up the way he had, rough-and-tumble, riding horses, rounding up stray cattle, part of the land. Of course, Gabe hadn't expected to die young—he'd meant to come home, so he and Hannah could fill that big house with children. Tobias would have had plenty of company then.

A tear slipped down Hannah's cheek, and she swatted it away. Straightened her spine.

Gabe was gone, and there weren't going to be any more children.

She heard Doss climbing the stairs, and wanted to move out of the doorway. He thought she was too fussy, always hovering over Tobias. Always trying to protect him.

How could a man understand what it meant to bear and nurture a child?

Hannah closed her eyes and stayed where she was.

Doss stopped behind her, uncertain. She could feel that, along with the heat and sturdy substance of his body.

"Leave the child to sleep, Hannah," he said quietly.

She nodded, closed Tobias's door gently and turned to face Doss there in the darkened hallway. He carried a book under one arm and an unlit lantern in his other hand.

"It's because he's lonesome," she said.

Doss clearly knew she was referring to Tobias's hallucination. "Kids make up playmates," he told her. "And being lonesome is a part of life. It's a valley a person has to go through, not something to run away from."

No McKettrick ever ran from anything. Doss didn't have to say it, and neither did she. But she wasn't a McKettrick, not by blood. Oh, she still wrote the word, whenever she had to sign something, but she'd stopped owning the name the day they put Gabe in the ground.

She wasn't sure why. He'd been so proud of it, like all the rest of them were.

"Do you ever wish you could live someplace else?" Hannah heard herself say.

"No," Doss said, so quickly and with such gravity that Hannah almost believed he'd been reading her mind. "I belong right here."

"But the others—your uncles and cousins—they didn't stay…."

"Ask any one of them where home is," Doss answered, "and they'll tell you it's the Triple M."

Hannah started to speak, then held her tongue. Nodded. "Good night, Doss," she said.

He inclined his head and went on to his own room, shut himself away.

Hannah stood alone in the dark for a long time.

She'd been so happy on the Triple M when Gabe was alive, and even after he'd gone into the army, because she'd never once doubted that he'd return. Come walking up the path with a duffel bag over one shoulder, whistling. She'd rehearsed that day a thousand times in her mind—pictured herself running to meet him, throwing herself into his arms.

It was never going to happen.

Without him, she might as well have been alone on the barren landscape of the moon.

Her eyes filled.

She walked slowly to the end of the hall, into the room where Gabe had brought her on their wedding night. He'd been conceived and born in the big bed there, just as Tobias had. As so many other babes would have been, if only Gabe had lived.

Hannah didn't undress after she closed the door behind her. She didn't let her hair down and brush it, like usual, or wash her face at the basin on the bureau.

Instead, she sat down in Lorelei's rocking chair and waited. Just waited.

For what, she did not know.

Present Day

After Liam had gone to bed, Sierra went back downstairs to the computer and scanned her email. When she spotted Allie Douglas-Fletcher's return address, she wished she'd waited until morning. She was always stronger in the mornings.

Allie was Adam's twin sister. Liam's aunt. After Adam was murdered, while on assignment in South America, Allie had been inconsolable, and she'd developed an unhealthy fixation for her brother's child.

After taking a deep breath and releasing it slowly, Sierra opened the message. Typically, there was no preamble. Allie got right to the point.

The guest house is ready for you and Liam. You know Adam would want his son to grow up right here in San Diego, Sierra. Tim and I can give Liam everything—a real home, a family, an education, the very best medical care. We're willing to make a place for you, too, obviously. If you won't come home, at least tell us you arrived safely in Arizona.

Sierra sat, wooden, staring at the stark plea on the screen. Although Allie and Adam had been raised in relative poverty, both of them had done well in life. Adam had been a photojournalist for a major magazine; he and Sierra had met when he did a piece on San Miguel.

Allie ran her own fund-raising firm, and her husband was a neurosurgeon. They had everything—except what they wanted most. Children.

You can't have Liam, Sierra cried, in the silence of her heart. *He's mine.*

She flexed her fingers, sighed, and hit Reply. Allie was a good person, just as Adam had been, for all that he'd told Sierra a lie that shook the foundations of the universe. Adam's sister sincerely believed she and the doctor could do a better job of raising Liam than Sierra could, and maybe they were right. They had money. They had social status.

Tears burned in Sierra's eyes.

Liam is well. We're safe on the Triple M, and for the time being, we're staying put.

It was all she could bring herself to say.

She hit Send and logged off the computer.

The fire was still flourishing on the hearth. She got up, crossed the room, pushed the screen aside to jab at the burning wood with a poker. It only made the flames burn more vigorously.

She kicked off her shoes, curled up in the big leather chair and pulled a knitted afghan around her to wait for the fire to die down.

The old clock on the mantel tick-tocked, the sound loud and steady and almost hypnotic.

Sierra yawned. Closed her eyes. Opened them again.

She thought about turning the TV back on, just for the sound of human voices, but dismissed the idea. She was so tired, she was going to need all her energy just to go upstairs and tumble into bed. There was none to spare for fiddling with the television set.

Again, she closed her eyes.

Again, she opened them.

She wondered if the lights were still on in Travis's trailer.

Closed her eyes.

Was dragged down into a heavy, fitful sleep.

She knew right away that she was dreaming, and yet it was so real.

She heard the clock ticking.

She felt the warmth of the fire.

But she was standing in the ranch house kitchen, and it was different, in subtle ways, from the room she knew.

She was different.

Her eyes were shut, and yet she could see clearly.

A bare light bulb dangled overhead, giving off a dim but determined glow.

She looked down at herself, the dream-Sierra, and felt a wrench of surprise.

She was wearing a long woolen skirt. Her hands were smaller—chapped and work worn—someone else's hands.

"I'm dreaming," she insisted to herself, but it didn't help.

She stared around the kitchen. The teapot sat on the counter.

"Now what's that doing there?" asked this other Sierra. "I know I put it away. I know for sure I did."

Sierra struggled to wake up. It was too intense, this dream. She was in some other woman's body, not her own. It was sinewy and strong, this body. She felt the heartbeat, the breath going in and out. Felt the weight of long hair, pinned to the back of her head in a loose chignon.

"Wake up," she said.

But she couldn't.

She stood very still, staring at the teapot.

Emotions stormed within her, a loneliness so wretched and sharp that she thought she'd burst from the inside and shatter. Longing for a man who'd gone away and was never coming home, an unspeakable sorrow. Love for a child, so profound that it might have been mourning.

And something else. A forbidden wanting that had nothing to do with the man who'd left her.

Sierra woke herself then, by force of will, only to find her face wet with another woman's tears.

She must have been asleep for a while, she realized.

The flames on the hearth had become embers. The room was chilly.

She shivered, tugged the afghan tighter around her, and got out of the chair. She went to the window, looked out. Travis's trailer was dark.

"It was just a dream," she told herself out loud.

So why was her heart breaking?

She made her way into the kitchen, navigating the dark hallway as best she could, since she didn't know where the light switches were. When she reached her destination, she walked to the middle of the room, where she'd stood in the dream, and suppressed an urge to reach up for the metal-beaded cord she knew wasn't there.

What she needed, she decided, was a good cup of tea.

She found a switch beside the back door and flipped it.

Reality returned in a comforting spill of light.

She found an electric kettle, filled it at the sink and plugged it in to boil. Earlier she'd been too weary to get out of that chair in the study and turn on the TV. Now she knew it would be pointless to try to sleep.

Might as well do this up right, she thought.

She went to the china cabinet, got the teapot out, set it on the table. Added tea leaves and located a little strainer in one of the drawers. The kettle boiled.

She was sitting quietly, sipping tea and watching fat snowflakes drift past the porch light outside the back door, when Liam came down the back stairway in his pajamas. Blinking, he rubbed his eyes.

"Is it morning?" he asked.

"No," Sierra said gently. "Go back to bed."

"Can I have some tea?"

"No, again," Sierra answered, but she didn't protest when

Liam took a seat on the bench, close to her chair. "But if there's cocoa, I'll make you some."

"There is," Liam said. He looked incredibly young, and so very vulnerable, without his glasses. "I saw it in the pantry. It's the instant kind."

With a smile, Sierra got out of the chair, walked into the pantry and brought out the cocoa, along with a bag of semihard marshmallows. Thanks to Travis's preparations for their arrival, there was milk in the refrigerator and, using the microwave, she had Liam's hot chocolate ready in no time.

"I like it here," he told her. "It's better than any place we've ever lived."

Sierra's heart squeezed. "You really think so? Why?"

Liam took a sip of hot chocolate and acquired a liquid mustache. One small shoulder rose and fell in a characteristic shrug. "It feels like a real home," he said. "Lots of people have lived here. And they were all McKettricks, like us."

Sierra was stung, but she hid it behind another smile. "Wherever we live," she said carefully, "is a real home, because we're together."

Liam's expression was benignly skeptical, even tolerant. "We never had so much room before. We never had a barn with horses in it. And we never had *ghosts*." He whispered the last word, and gave a little shiver of pure joy.

Sierra was looking for a way to approach the ghost subject again when the faint, delicate sound of piano music reached her ears.

Chapter 5

"Do you hear that?" she asked Liam.

His brow furrowed as he shifted on the bench and took another sip of his cocoa. "Hear what?"

The tune continued, flowing softly, forlornly, from the front room.

"Nothing," Sierra lied.

Liam peered at her, perplexed and suspicious.

"Finish your chocolate," she prompted. "It's late."

The music stopped, and she felt relief and a paradoxical sorrow, reminiscent of the all-too-vivid dream she'd had earlier while dozing in the big chair in the study.

"What was it, Mom?" Liam pressed.

"I thought I heard a piano," she admitted, because she knew her son wouldn't let the subject drop until she told him the truth.

Liam smiled, pleased. "This house is so cool," he said. "I told the Geek—the kids—that it's haunted. Aunt Allie, too."

Sierra, in the process of lifting her cup to her mouth, set it down again, shakily. "When did you talk to Allie?" she asked.

"She sent me an email," he replied, "and I answered."

"Great," Sierra said.

"Would my dad really want me to grow up in San Diego?" Liam asked seriously. The idea had, of course, come from Allie. While Sierra wasn't without sympathy for the woman, she felt violated. Allie had no business trying to entice Liam behind her back.

"Your dad would want you to grow up with me," Sierra said firmly, and she knew that was true, for all that Adam had betrayed her.

"Aunt Allie says my cousins would like me," Liam confided.

Liam's "cousins" were actually half sisters, but Sierra wasn't ready to spring that on him, and she hoped Allie wouldn't do it, either. Although Adam had told Sierra he was divorced when they met, and she'd fallen immediately and helplessly in love with him, she'd learned six months later, when she was carrying his child, that he was still living with his wife when he wasn't on the road. It had been Allie, earnest, meddling Allie, who traveled to San Miguel, found Sierra and told her the truth.

Sierra would never forget the family photos Allie showed her that day—snapshots of Adam with his arm around his smiling wife, Dee. The two little girls in matching dresses posed with them, their eyes wide with innocence and trust.

"Forget him, kiddo," Hank had said airily, when Sierra went to him, in tears, with the whole shameful story. "It ain't gonna fly."

She'd written Adam immediately, but her letter came

back, tattered from forwarding, and no one answered at any of the telephone numbers he'd given her.

She'd given birth to Liam eight weeks later, at home, attended by Hank's long-time mistress, Magdalena. Three days after that, Hank brought her an American newspaper, tossed it into her lap without a word.

She'd paged through it slowly, possessed of a quiet, escalating dread, and come across the account of Adam Douglas's death on page four. He'd been shot to death, according to the article, on the outskirts of Caracas, after infiltrating a drug cartel to take pictures for an exposé he'd been writing.

"Mom?" Liam snapped his fingers under Sierra's nose. "Are you hearing the music again?"

Sierra blinked. Shook her head.

"Do you think my cousins would like me?"

She reached out, her hand trembling only slightly, and ruffled his hair. "I think *anybody* would like you," she said. When he was older, she would tell him about Adam's other family, but it was still too soon. She took his empty cup, carried it to the sink. "Now, go upstairs, brush your teeth again and hit the sack."

"Aren't you going to bed?" Liam asked practically.

Sierra sighed. "Yes," she said, resigned. She didn't think she'd sleep, but she knew Liam would wonder if she stayed up all night, prowling around the house. "You go ahead. I'm just going to make sure the front door is locked."

Liam nodded and obeyed without protest.

Sierra considered marking the occasion on the calendar.

She went straight to the front room, and the piano, the moment Liam had gone upstairs. The keyboard cover was down, the bench neatly in place. She switched on a lamp and inspected the smooth, highly polished wood for fingerprints. Nothing.

She touched the cover, and her fingers left distinct smudges.

No one had touched the piano that night, unless they'd been wearing gloves.

Frowning, Sierra checked the lock on the front door. Fastened.

She inspected the windows—all locked—and even the floor. It was snowing hard, and anybody who'd come in out of that storm would have left some trace, no matter how careful they were—a puddle somewhere, a bit of mud.

Again, there was nothing.

Finally she went upstairs, found a nightgown, bathed and got ready for bed. Since Travis had left her bags in the room adjoining Liam's, she opened the connecting door a crack and crawled between sheets worn smooth by time.

She was asleep in an instant.

1919

Hannah closed the cover over the piano keys, stacked the sheet music neatly and got to her feet. She'd played as softly as she could, pouring her sadness and her yearning into the music, and when she returned to the upstairs corridor, she saw light under Doss's door.

She paused, wondering what he'd do if she went in, took off her clothes and crawled into bed beside him.

Not that she would, of course, because she'd loved her husband and it wouldn't be fitting, but there were times when her very soul ached within her, she wanted so badly to be touched and held, and this was one of them.

She swallowed, mortified by her own wanton thoughts.

Doss would send her away angrily.

He'd remind her that she was his brother's widow—if he ever spoke to her again at all.

For all that, she took a single, silent step toward the door.

"Ma?"

Tobias spoke from behind her. She hadn't heard him get out of bed, come to the threshold of his room.

Thanking heaven she was still fully dressed, she turned to face him.

"What is it?" she asked gently. "Did you have another bad dream?"

Tobias shook his head. His gaze slipped past Hannah to Doss's door, then back to her face, solemn and worried. "I wish I had a pa," he said.

Hannah's heart seized. She approached, pulled the boy close, and he allowed it. During the day, he would have balked. "So do I," she replied, bending to kiss the top of his head. "I wish your pa was here. Wish it so much it hurts."

Tobias pulled back, looked up at her. "But Pa's dead," he said. "Maybe you and Doss could get hitched. Then he wouldn't be my uncle anymore, would he? He'd be my pa."

"Tobias," Hannah said very softly, praying Doss hadn't overheard somehow. "That wouldn't be right."

"Why not?" Tobias asked.

She crouched, looked up into her son's face. One day, he'd be handsome and square-jawed, like the rest of the McKettrick men. For now he was still a little boy, his features childishly innocent. "I was your pa's wife. I'll love him for the rest of my days."

"That might be a long time," Tobias said, with a measure of dubiousness, as well as hope. He dropped his voice to a whisper. "I don't want Doss to marry some-body else, Ma," he said. "All the women in Indian Rock are sweet on him, and one of these days he might take a notion to get himself a wife."

"Tobias," Hannah reasoned, "you must put this fool-ishness out of your head. If Doss chooses to take a bride, that's certainly his right. But it won't be me he marries. It's too hard to explain right now, but Doss was your pa's brother. I couldn't—"

"You'd marry some man in Montana, though, wouldn't you?" Tobias demanded, suddenly angry, and this time, he made no effort to keep his voice down. "Some stranger who wears a suit to work!"

"Tobias!"

"I won't go to Montana, do you hear me? I won't leave the Triple M unless Doss goes, too!"

Hannah reddened with embarrassment and anger—Doss had surely heard—and rose to her full height. "To-bias McKettrick," she said sternly, "you go to bed this instant, and don't you ever talk to me like that again!"

Tobias's chin jutted out, in the McKettrick way, and his eyes flashed. "You go anyplace you want to," he told her, turning on one bare heel to flee into his room, "but I'm not going with you!" With that, he slammed the door in her face.

Hannah took a step toward it, even reached for the knob. But in the end she couldn't face her son.

"Hannah."

Doss.

She stiffened but didn't turn. Doss would see too much if she did. Guess too much.

He caught hold of her arm, brought her gently around. She whispered his name, despondent.

He took her hand, led her to the opposite end of the

hall, opened the last door on the right, the one where she kept her sewing machine.

"What are you—?"

Doss stepped over the threshold first, turned, and drew her in behind him. Reached around her to shut the door.

She leaned against the panel. It was hard at her back.

"Doss," she said.

He cupped her face in his hands, bent his head, and kissed her, full on the mouth.

A sweet shock went through her. She knew she ought to break away, knew he wouldn't force himself on her if she uttered the slightest protest, but she couldn't say a word. Her body came alive as he pressed himself against her. His weight was hard and warm and blessedly real.

Doss reached behind her head, pulled the pins from her hair, let it fall around her shoulders, to her waist. He groaned, buried his face in it, burrowed through to take her earlobe between his lips and nibble on it.

Hannah gasped with guilty pleasure. Her knees went weak, and Doss held her upright with the lower part of his body.

She moaned softly.

"We can't," she whispered.

"We'd damn well better," Doss answered, "before we both go crazy."

"What if Tobias…?"

Doss leaned back, opened the buttons on her bodice, put his hands inside, under her camisole, to take the weight of her breasts. Chafed the nipples lightly with the sides of his thumbs.

"He won't hear," he said.

He bent to find a nipple, take it into his mouth. Suckled in the same nibbling, teasing way he'd tasted her earlobe.

Hannah plunged her fingers into his hair, groaned and tilted her head back, already surrendering. Already lost.

She tried to bring Gabe's face to her mind, hoping the image would give her the strength to stop—stop—before it was too late, but it wouldn't come.

Doss made free with her breasts, tonguing them until she was in a frenzy.

She sank against the door, barely able to breathe.

And then he knelt.

Hannah trembled. Even though the room was cold, perspiration broke out all over her body. She made a slight whimpering sound when Doss lifted her skirts, went under them and pulled down her drawers.

She felt him part her private place with his fingers, felt his tongue touch her, like fire. Sobbed his name, under her breath.

He took her full in his mouth, hungrily.

Her hips moved frantically, seeking him, and her knees buckled.

He braced her securely against the door, put her legs over his shoulders, first one, and then the other, and through all that, he drew on her.

She writhed against him, one hand pressed to her mouth so that the guttural cries pounding at the back of her throat wouldn't get out.

He suckled.

She felt a surge of heat, radiating from her center into every part of her, then stiffened in a spasm of release so violent that she was afraid she would splinter into pieces.

"Doss," she pleaded, because she knew it was going to happen again, and again.

And it did.

When it was over, he ducked out from under the hem of

her skirt and held her as she sagged, spent, to her knees. They were facing each other, her breasts bared to him, her body still quivering with an ebbing tide of passion.

"We can stop here," he said quietly.

She shook her head. They'd gone past the place of turning back.

Doss opened his trousers, reached under her skirt and petticoat to take hold of her hips. Lifted her onto him.

She slid along his length, letting him fill her, exalting in the size and heat and slick hardness of him. She gave a loud moan, and he covered her mouth with his, kissed her senseless, even as he raised and lowered her, raised and lowered her. The friction was slow and exquisite. Hannah dug her fingers into his shoulders and rode him shamelessly until satisfaction overtook her again, convulsed her, like some giant fist, and didn't let go until she was limp with exhaustion.

Only when she wept with relief did Doss finish. She felt him erupt inside her, swallowed his groans as he gave himself up to her.

He brushed away her tears with his thumbs, still inside her, and looked deep into her eyes. "It's all right, Hannah," he said gruffly. "Please, don't cry."

He didn't understand.

She wasn't weeping for shame, though that would surely come, but for the most poignant of joys.

"No," she said softly. She plunged her fingers into his hair, kissed him boldly, fervently. "It's not that. I feel..."

He was growing hard within her again.

"Oh," she groaned.

He played with her nipples. And got harder still.

"Doss," she gasped. "Doss—"

Present Day

Sierra awakened with a start, sounding from the depths of a dream so erotic that she'd been on the verge of climax. The light dazzled her, and the muffled silence seemed to fill not only her bedroom, but the world beyond it.

She lay still for a long time, recovering. Listening to her own quick, shallow breathing. Waiting for her heartbeat to slow down.

Liam peeked through the doorway linking her room to his.

"Mom?"

"Come in," Sierra said.

He bounded across the threshold. "It snowed!" he whooped, heading straight for the window. "I mean, it *really* snowed!"

Sierra smiled, sat up in bed and put her feet on the floor.

A jolt of cold went through her.

"It's *freezing* in here!"

Liam turned from the window to grin at her. "Travis says the furnace is out."

"Travis?"

"He's downstairs," Liam said. "He'll get it going."

A dusty-smelling whoosh rose from the nearest heat vent, as if to illustrate the point.

"What's he doing here?" Sierra asked, scrambling through her suitcases for a bathrobe. All she had was a thin nylon thing, and when she saw it, she knew it would be worse than nothing, so she pulled the quilt off the bed and wrapped herself in that instead.

"Don't be a grump," Liam replied. "Travis is doing us a *favor,* Mom. We'd probably be icicles by now if it wasn't for him. Did you know that old stove downstairs *works?* Travis built a fire in it, and he put the coffee on, too. He said to tell you it will be ready in a couple of minutes and we're snowed in."

"Snowed in?"

"Keep up, Mom," Liam chirped. "There was a *blizzard* last night. That's why Travis came to make sure we were all right. I heard him knock, and I let him in."

Sierra joined Liam at the window and drew in her breath.

The whiteness of all that snow practically blinded her, but it was beautiful, too, in an apocalyptic way. She'd never seen anything like it before and, for a long moment, she was spellbound. Then her sensible side kicked in.

"Thank God the power didn't go out," she said, easing a little closer to the vent, which was spewing deliciously warm air.

"It *did*," Liam informed her happily. "Travis got the generator started right away. We don't have lights or anything, but he said the furnace is all that matters."

She frowned. "How could he have made coffee?"

"On the *cookstove,* Mom," Liam said, with a roll of his eyes.

For the first time Sierra noticed that Liam was fully dressed.

He headed for the door. "I'd better go help Travis bring in the wood," he said. "Get some *clothes* on, will you?"

Five minutes later Sierra joined Travis and Liam in the kitchen, which was blessedly warm. Her jeans would do well enough, but she'd had to raid Meg's room for socks and a thick sweatshirt, because her tank tops weren't going to cut it.

"Are we *stranded* here?" she demanded, watching as Travis poured coffee from a blue enamel pot that looked like it came from a stash of camping gear.

He grinned. "Depends on how you look at it," he said. "Liam and I, we see it as an adventure."

"Some adventure," Sierra grumbled, but she took the coffee he offered and gave a grateful nod of thanks.

Travis chuckled. "Don't worry," he said. "You'll adjust."

Sierra hastened over to stand closer to the cookstove. "Does this happen often?"

"Only in winter," Travis quipped.

"Hilarious," she drawled.

Liam laughed uproariously.

"You are *enjoying* this," she accused, tousling her son's hair.

"It's *great!*" Liam cried. "Snow! Wait till the Geeks hear about this!"

"Liam," Sierra said.

He gave Travis a long-suffering look. "She hates it when I say 'geek,'" he explained.

Travis picked up his own mug of coffee, took a sip, his eyes full of laughter. Then he headed toward the door, put the cup on the counter and reclaimed his coat down from the peg.

"You're *leaving?*" Liam asked, horrified.

"Gotta see to the horses," Travis said, putting on his hat.

"Can I go with you?" Liam pleaded, and he sounded so desperately hopeful that Sierra swallowed the "no" that instantly sprang from her vocal cords.

"Your coat isn't warm enough," she said.

"Meg's got an old one around here someplace," Travis said carefully. "Hall closet, I think."

Liam dashed off to get it.

"I'll take care of him, Sierra," Travis told her quietly, when the boy was gone.

"You'd better," Sierra answered.

1919

Hannah knew by the profound silence, even before she opened her eyes, that it had been snowing all night.

Lying alone in the big bed she'd shared with Gabe, she burrowed deeper into the covers and groaned.

She was sore.

She was satisfied.

She was a trollop.

A tramp.

She'd practically thrown herself at Doss the night before. She'd let him do things to her that no one else besides Gabe had ever done.

And now it was morning and she'd come to her senses and she would have to face him.

For all that, she felt strangely light, too.

Almost giddy.

Hannah pulled the covers up over her head and giggled.

Giggled.

She tried to be stern with herself.

This was serious.

Downstairs the stove lids rattled.

Doss was building a fire in the cookstove, the way he did every morning. He would put the coffee on to boil, then go out to the barn to attend to the livestock. When he got back, she'd be making breakfast, and they'd talk about how cold it was, and whether he ought to bring in extra wood from the shed, in case there was more snow on the way.

It would be an ordinary ranch morning.

Except that she'd behaved like a tart the night before.

Hannah tossed back the covers and got up. She wasn't one to avoid facing things, no matter how awkward they were. She and Doss had lost their heads and made love. That was that.

It wouldn't happen again.

They'd just go on, as if nothing had happened.

The water in the pitcher on the bureau was too cold to wash in.

Hannah decided she would heat some for a bath, after the breakfast dishes were done. She'd send Tobias to the study to work at his school lessons, and Doss to the barn.

She dressed hastily, brushed her hair and wound it into the customary chignon at the back of her head. Just before she opened the bedroom door to step out into the new day, the pit of her stomach quivered. She drew a deep breath, squared her shoulders and turned the knob resolutely.

Doss had not left for the barn, as she'd expected. He was still in the kitchen, and when she came down the back stairs and froze on the bottom step, he looked at her, reddened and looked away.

Tobias was by the back door, pulling on his heaviest coat. "Doss and me are fixing to ride down to the bend and look in on the widow Jessup," he told Hannah matter-of-factly, and he sounded like a grown man, fit to make such decisions on his own. "Could be her pump's frozen, and we're not sure she has enough firewood."

Out of the corner of her eye, Hannah saw Doss watching her.

"Go out and see to the cow," Doss told Tobias. "Make sure there's no ice on her trough."

It was an excuse to speak to her alone, Hannah knew, and she was unnerved. She resisted an urge to touch her hair with both hands or smooth her skirts.

Tobias banged out the back door, whistling.

"He's not strong enough to ride to the Jessups' place in this weather," Hannah said. "It's four miles if it's a stone's throw, and you'll have to cross the creek."

"Hannah," Doss said firmly, grimly. "The boy will be fine."

She felt her own color rise then, remembering all they'd done together, on the spare room floor, herself and this man. She swallowed and lifted her chin a notch, so he wouldn't think she was ashamed.

"About last night—" Doss began. He looked distraught.

Hannah waited, blushing furiously now. Wishing the floor would open, so she could fall right through to China and never be seen or heard from again.

Doss shoved a hand through his hair. "I'm sorry," he said.

Hannah hadn't expected anything except shame, but she was stung by it, just the same. "We'll just pretend—" She had to stop, clear her throat, blink a couple of times. "We'll just pretend it didn't happen."

His jaw tightened. "Hannah, it did happen, and pretending won't change that."

She intertwined her fingers, clasped them so tightly that the knuckles ached. Looked down at the floor. "What else can we do, Doss?" she asked, almost in a whisper.

"Suppose there's a child?"

Hannah hadn't once thought of that possibility, though it seemed painfully obvious in the bright, rational light of day. She drew in a sharp breath and put a hand to her throat.

How would they explain such a thing to Tobias? To the McKettricks and the people of Indian Rock?

"I'd have to go to Montana," she said, after a long time. "To my folks."

"Not with my baby growing inside you, you wouldn't," Doss replied, so sharply that Hannah's gaze shot back to his face.

"Doss, the scandal—"

"To hell with the scandal!"

Hannah reached out, pulled back Holt's chair at the table and sank into it. "Maybe I'm not. Surely just once—"

"Maybe you are," Doss insisted.

Hannah's eyes smarted. She'd wanted more children, but not like this. Not out of wedlock, and by her late husband's brother. Folks would call her a hussy, with considerable justification, and they'd make Tobias's life a plain misery, too. They'd point and whisper, and the other kids would tease.

"What are we going to do, then?" she asked.

He crossed the room, sat astraddle the long bench next to the table, so close she could feel the warmth of his body, glowing like the fresh fire blazing inside the cookstove.

His very proximity made her remember things better forgotten.

"There's only one thing we can do, Hannah. We'll get married."

She gaped at him. "Married?"

"It's the only decent thing to do."

The word decent stabbed at Hannah. She was a proud person, and she'd always lived a respectable life. Until the night before. "We don't love each other," she said, her voice small. "And anyway, I might not be—expecting."

"I'm not taking the chance," Doss told her. "As soon as the trail clears a little, we're going into Indian Rock and get married."

"I have some say in this," Hannah pointed out.

Outside, on the back porch, Tobias thumped his boots against the step, to shake off the snow.

"Do you?" Doss asked.

Chapter 6

Present Day

While Travis and Liam were in the barn, Sierra inspected the wood-burning stove. She found a skillet, set it on top, took bacon and eggs from the refrigerator, which was ominously dark and silent, and laid strips of the bacon in the pan. When the meat began to sizzle, she felt a little thrill of accomplishment.

She was actually *cooking* on a stove that dated from the nineteenth century. Briefly, she felt connected with all the McKettrick women who had gone before her.

When the electricity came on, with a startling revving sound, she was almost sorry. Keeping an eye on breakfast, she switched on the small countertop TV to catch the morning news.

The entire northern part of Arizona had been inundated in the blizzard, and thousands were without power. She watched as images of people skiing to work flashed across the screen.

The telephone rang, and she held the portable receiver between her shoulder and ear to answer. "Hello?"

"It's Eve," a gracious voice replied. "Is that you, Sierra?"

Sierra went utterly still. Travis and Liam tramped in from outside, laughing about something. They both fell silent at the sight of her, and neither one moved after Travis pushed the door shut.

"Hello?" Eve prompted. "Sierra, are you there?"

"I'm... I'm here," Sierra said.

Travis took off his coat and hat, crossed the room and elbowed her away from the stove. "Go," he told her, cocking a thumb toward the center of the house. "Liam and I will see to the grub."

She nodded, grateful, and hurried out of the warm kitchen. The dining room was frigid.

"Is this a bad time to talk?" Eve asked. She sounded uncertain, even a little shy.

"No—" Sierra answered hastily, finally gaining the study. She closed the door and sat in the big leather chair she'd occupied the night before, waiting for the fire to go out. Now she could see her breath, and she wished the blaze was still burning. "No, it's fine."

Eve let out a long breath. "I see on the Weather Channel that you've been hit with quite a storm up there," she said.

Sierra nodded, remembered that her mother—this woman she didn't know—couldn't see her. "Yes," she replied. "We have power again, thanks to Travis. He got the generator running right away, so the furnace would work and—"

She swallowed the rush of too-cheerful words. She'd been blathering.

"Poor Travis," Eve said.

"Poor Travis?" Sierra echoed. "Why?"

"Didn't he tell you? Didn't Meg?"

"No," Sierra said. "Nobody told me anything."

There was a long pause, then Eve sighed. "I'm probably speaking out of turn," she said, "but we've all been a little worried about Travis. He's like a member of the family, you know. His younger brother, Brody, died in an explosion a few months ago. It really threw Travis. He walked away from the company and just about everyone he knew. Meg had to talk fast to get him to come and stay on the ranch."

Sierra was very glad she'd brought the phone out of the kitchen. "I didn't know," she said.

"I've already said more than I should have," Eve told her ruefully. "And anyway, I called to see how you and Liam are doing. I know you're not used to cold weather, and when I saw the storm report, I had to call."

"We're okay," Sierra said. Had she known the woman better, she might have confided her worries about Liam— how he claimed he'd seen a ghost in his room. She still planned to call his new doctor, but driving to Flagstaff for an appointment would be out of the question, considering the state of the roads.

"I hear some hesitation in your voice," Eve said. She was treading lightly, Sierra could tell, and she would be a hard person to fool. Eve ran McKettrickCo, and hundreds of people answered to her.

Sierra gave a nervous laugh, more hysteria than amusement. "Liam claims the house is haunted," she admitted.

"Oh, that," Eve answered, and she actually sounded relieved.

"'Oh, that'?" Sierra challenged, sitting up straighter.

"They're harmless," Eve said. "The ghosts, I mean. If that's what they are."

"You know about the ghosts?"

Eve laughed. "Of course I do. I grew up in that house. But I'm not sure *ghosts* is the right word. To me, it always felt more like sharing the place than its being haunted. I got the sense that they—the other people—were as alive as I was. That they'd have been just as surprised, had we ever come face-to-face."

Sierra's mind spun. She squeezed the bridge of her nose between a thumb and forefinger. The piano notes she'd heard the night before tinkled sadly in her memory. "You're not saying you actually *believe*—"

"I'm saying I've had experiences," Eve told her. "I've never seen anyone. Just had a strong sense of someone else being present. And, of course, there was the famous disappearing teapot."

Sierra sank against the back of the chair, both relieved and confounded. Had she told Meg about the teapot? She couldn't recall. Perhaps Travis had mentioned it—called Eve to report that her daughter was a little loony?

"Sierra?" Eve asked.

"I'm still here."

"I would get the teapot out," Eve recounted, "and leave the room to do something else. When I came back, it was in the china cabinet again. The same thing used to happen to my mother, and my grandmother, too. They thought it was Lorelei."

"How could that be?"

"Who knows?" Eve asked, patently unconcerned. "Life is mysterious."

It certainly is, Sierra thought. Little girls get separated from their mothers, and no one even comes looking for them.

"I'd like to come and see you," Eve went on, "as soon

as the weather clears. Would that be all right, Sierra? If I spent a few days at the ranch? So we could talk in person?"

Sierra's heart rose into her throat and swelled there. "It's your house," she said, but she wanted to throw down the phone, snatch Liam, jump into the car and speed away before she had to face this woman.

"I won't come if you're not ready," Eve said gently.

I may never be ready, Sierra thought. "I guess I am," she murmured.

"Good," Eve replied. "Then I'll be there as soon as the jet can land. Barring another snowstorm, that should be tomorrow or the next day."

The jet? "Should we pick you up somewhere?"

"I'll have a car meet me," Eve said. "Do you need anything, Sierra?"

I could have used a mother when I was growing up. And when I had Liam and Dad acted as though nothing had changed—well, you would have come in handy then, too, Mom. "I'm fine," she answered.

"I'll call again before I leave here," Eve promised. Then, after another tentative pause and a brief goodbye, she rang off.

Sierra sat a long time in that chair, still holding the phone, and might not have moved at all if Liam hadn't come to tell her breakfast was on the table.

1919

It was a cold, seemingly endless ride to the Jessup place, and hard going all the way. More than once Doss glanced anxiously at his nephew, bundled to his eyeballs and jostling patiently alongside Doss's mount on the mule, and wished he'd listened to Hannah and left the boy at home.

More than once, he attempted to broach the subject that was uppermost in his mind—he'd been up half the night wrestling with it—but he couldn't seem to get a proper handle on the matter at all.

I mean to marry your ma.

That was the straightforward truth, a simple thing to say.

But Tobias was bound to ask why. Maybe he'd even raise an objection. He'd loved his pa, and he might just put his old uncle Doss right square in his place.

"You ever think about livin' in town?" Tobias asked, catching him by surprise.

Doss took a moment to change directions in his mind. "Sometimes," he answered, when he was sure it was what he really meant. "Especially in the wintertime."

"It's no warmer there than it is here," Tobias reasoned. Whatever he was getting at, it wasn't coming through in his tone or his manner.

"No," Doss agreed. "But there are other folks around. A man could get his mail at the post office every day, instead of waiting a week for it to come by wagon, and take a meal in a restaurant now and again. And I'll admit that library is an enticement, small as it is." He thought fondly of the books lining the study walls back at the ranch house. He'd read all of them, at one time or another, and most several times. He'd borrowed from his uncle Kade's collection, and his ma sent him a regular supply from Texas. Just the same, he couldn't get enough of the damn things.

"Ma's been talking about heading back to Montana," Tobias blurted, but he didn't look at Doss when he spoke.

Just kept his eyes on the close-clipped mane of that old mule. "If she tries to make me go, I'll run away."

Doss swallowed. He knew Hannah thought about moving in with the homefolks, of course, but hearing it said out loud made him feel as if he'd not only been thrown from his horse, but stomped on, too. "Where would you go?" he asked, when he thought he could get the words out easy. He wasn't entirely successful. "If you ran off, I mean?"

Tobias turned in the saddle to look him full in the face. "I'd hide up in the hills somewhere," he said, with the conviction of innocence. "Maybe that canyon where Kade and Mandy faced down those outlaws."

Doss suppressed a smile. He'd grown up on that story himself, and to this day, he wondered how much of it was fact and how much was legend. Mandy was a sharp-shooter, and she'd given Annie Oakley a run for her money, in her time. Kade had been the town marshal, with an office in Indian Rock back then, so maybe it had happened just the way his pa and uncles related it.

"Mighty cold up there," he told the boy mildly. "Just a cave for shelter, and where would you get food?"

Tobias's shoulders slumped a little, under all that wool Hannah had swaddled him in. If the kid took a spill from the mule, he'd probably bounce. "I could hunt," he said. "Pa taught me how to shoot."

"McKettricks," Doss replied, "don't run away."

Tobias scowled at him. "They don't live in Missoula, either."

Doss chuckled, in spite of the heavy feeling that had settled over his heart after he and Hannah had made love and stayed there ever since. Gabe was dead, but it still felt as if he'd betrayed him. "They live in all sorts of places," Doss said. "You know that."

"I won't go, anyhow," Tobias said.

Doss cleared his throat. "Maybe you won't have to."

That got the boy's full attention. His eyes were full of questions.

"I wonder what you'd say if I married your ma."

Tobias looked as though he'd swallowed a lantern with the wick burning. "I'd like that," he said. "I'd like that a lot!"

Too bad Hannah wasn't as keen on the prospect as her son. "I thought you might not care for the idea," Doss confessed. "My being your pa's brother and all."

"Pa would be glad," Tobias said. "I know he would."

Secretly, Doss knew it, too. Gabe had been a practical man, and he'd have wanted all of them to get on with their lives.

Doss's eyes smarted something fierce, all of a sudden, and he had to pull his hat brim down. Look away for a few moments.

Take care of Hannah and my boy, Gabe had said. Promise me, Doss.

"Did Ma say she'd hitch up with you?" Tobias asked, frowning so that his face crinkled comically. "Last night I said she ought to, and she said it wouldn't be right."

Doss stood in the stirrups to stretch his legs. "Things can change," he said cautiously. "Even in a night."

"Do you love my ma?"

It was a hard question to answer, at least aloud. He'd loved Hannah from the day Gabe had brought her home as his bride. Loved her fiercely, hopelessly and honorably, from a proper distance. Gabe had guessed it right away, though. Waited until the two of them were alone in the barn, slapped Doss on the shoulder and said, Don't you be ashamed, little brother. It's easy to love my Hannah.

"Of course I do," Doss said. "She's family."

Tobias made a face. "I don't mean like that."

Doss's belly tightened. The boy was only eight, and he couldn't possibly know what had gone on last night in the spare room.

Could he?

"How do you mean, then?"

"Pa used to kiss Ma all the time. He used to swat her on the bustle, too, when he thought nobody was looking. It always made her laugh, and stand real close to him, with her arms around his neck."

Doss might have gripped the saddle horn with both hands, because of the pain, if he'd been riding alone. It wasn't the reminder of how much Hannah and Gabe had loved each other that seared him, though. It was the loss of his brother, the way of things then, and it all being over for good.

"I'll treat your mother right, Tobias," he said, after more hat-brim pulling and more looking away.

"You sound pretty sure she'll say yes," the boy commented.

"She already has," Doss replied.

Present Day

More snow began to fall at mid-morning and, worried that the power would go off again, and stay off this time, Sierra gathered her and Liam's dirty laundry and threw a load into the washing machine. She'd telephoned Liam's doctor in Flagstaff, from the study, while he and Travis were filling the dishwasher, but she hadn't mentioned the hallucinations. She'd heard the piano music herself, after all, and then Eve had made such experiences seem almost normal.

Sierra didn't know precisely what was happening, and she was still unsettled by Liam's claims of seeing a boy in old-time clothes, but she wasn't ready to bring up the subject with an outsider, whether that outsider had a medical degree or not.

Dr. O'Meara had reviewed Liam's records, since they'd been expressed to her from the clinic in Florida, and she wanted to make sure he had an inhaler on hand. She'd promised to call in a prescription to the pharmacy in Indian Rock, and they'd made an appointment for the following Monday afternoon.

Now Liam was in the study, watching TV, and Travis was outside splitting wood for the stove and the fireplaces. If the power went off again, she'd need firewood for cooking. The generator kept the furnace running, along with a few of the lights, but it burned a lot of gas and there was always the possibility that it would break down or freeze up.

Travis came in with an armload just as she was starting to prepare lunch.

Watching him, Sierra thought about what Eve had said on the phone earlier. Travis's younger brother had died horribly, and very recently. He'd left his job, Travis had, and come to the ranch to live in a trailer and look after horses.

He didn't look like a man carrying a burden, but appearances were deceiving. Nobody knew that better than Sierra did.

"What kind of work did you do, before you came here?" she asked, and then wished she hadn't brought the subject up at all. Travis's face closed instantly, and his eyes went blank.

"Nothing special," he said.

She nodded. "I was a cocktail waitress," she told him, because she felt she ought to offer him something after asking what was evidently an intrusive question.

Standing there, beside the antique cookstove and the wood box, in his leather coat and cowboy hat, Travis looked as though he'd stepped through a time warp, out of an earlier century.

"I know," he said. "Meg told me."

"Of course she did." Sierra poured canned soup into a saucepan, stirred it industriously and blushed.

Travis didn't say anything more for a long time. Then, "I was a lawyer for McKettrickCo," he told her.

Sierra stole a sidelong glance at him. He looked tense, standing there holding his hat in one hand. "Impressive," she said.

"Not so much," he countered. "It's a tradition in my family, being a lawyer, I mean. At least, with everyone but my brother, Brody. He became a meth addict instead, and blew himself to kingdom-come brewing up a batch. Go figure."

Sierra turned to face Travis. Noticed that his jaw was hard and his eyes even harder. He was angry, in pain, or both.

"I'm so sorry," she said.

"Yeah," Travis replied tersely. "Me, too."

He started for the door.

"Stay for lunch?" Sierra asked.

"Another time," he answered, and then he was gone.

1919

It was near sunset when Doss and Tobias rode in from the Jessup place, and by then Hannah was fit to be tied. She'd paced for most of the afternoon, after it started to snow again, fretting over all the things that could go wrong along the way.

The horse or the mule could have gone lame or fallen through the ice crossing the creek.

There could have been an avalanche. Just last year, a whole mountainside of snow had come crashing down on to the roof of a cabin and crushed it to the ground, with a family inside.

Wolves prowled the countryside, too, bold with the desperation of their hunger. They killed cattle and sometimes people.

Doss hadn't even taken his rifle.

When Hannah heard the horses, she ran to the window, wiped the fog from the glass with her apron hem. She watched as they dismounted and led their mounts into the barn.

She'd baked pies that day to keep from going crazy, and the kitchen was redolent with the aroma. She smoothed her skirts, patted her hair and turned away so she wouldn't be caught looking if Doss or Tobias happened to glance toward the house.

Almost an hour passed before they came inside— they'd done the barn chores—and Hannah had the table set, the lamps lighted and the coffee made. She wanted to fuss over Tobias, check his ears and fingers for frostbite and his forehead for fever, but she wouldn't let herself do it.

Doss wasn't deceived by her smiling restraint, she could see that, but Tobias looked downright relieved, as though he'd expected her to pounce the minute he came through the door.

"How did you find Widow Jessup?" she asked.

"She was right where we left her last time," Doss said with a slight grin.

Hannah gave him a look.

"She was fresh out of firewood," Tobias expounded importantly, unwrapping himself, layer by layer, until he stood in just his trousers and shirt, with melted snow pooling around his feet. "It's a good thing we went down there. She'd have froze for sure."

Doss looked tired, but his eyes twinkled. "For sure," he confirmed. "She got Tobias here by the ears and kissed him all over his face, she was so grateful that he'd saved her."

Tobias let out a yelp of mortification and took a swing at Doss, who sidestepped him easily.

"Stop your roughhousing and wash up for supper," Hannah said, but it did her heart good to see it. Gabe used to come in from the barn, toss Tobias over one shoulder and carry him around the kitchen like a sack of grain. The boy had howled with laughter and pummeled Gabe's chest with his small fists in mock resistance. She'd missed the ordinary things like that more than anything except being held in Gabe's arms.

She served chicken and dumplings, in her best Blue Willow dishes, with apple pie for dessert.

Tobias ate with a fresh-air, long-ride appetite and nearly fell asleep in his chair once his stomach was filled.

Doss got up, hoisted him into his arms and carried him, head bobbing, toward the stairs.

Hannah's throat went raw, watching them go.

She poured a second cup of coffee for Doss, had it waiting when he came back a few minutes later.

"Did you put Tobias in his nightshirt and cover him

with the spare quilt?" she asked, when Doss appeared at the bottom of the steps. "He mustn't take a chill—"

"I took off his shoes and threw him in like he was," Doss interrupted. That twinkle was still in his eyes, but there was a certain wariness there, too. "I made sure he was warm, so stop fretting."

Hannah had put the dishes in a basin of hot water to soak, and she lingered at the table, sipping tea brewed in Lorelei's pot.

Doss sat down in his father's chair, cupped his hands around his own mug of steaming coffee. "I spoke to Tobias about our getting married," he said bluntly. "And he's in favor of it."

Heat pounded in Hannah's cheeks, spawned by indignation and something else that she didn't dare think about. "Doss McKettrick," she whispered in reproach, "you shouldn't have done that. I'm his mother and it was my place to—"

"It's done, Hannah," Doss said. "Let it go at that."

Hannah huffed out a breath. "Don't you tell me what's done and ought to be let go," she protested. "I won't take orders from you now or after we're married."

He grinned. "Maybe you won't," he said. "But that doesn't mean I won't give them."

She laughed, surprising herself so much that she slapped a hand over her mouth to stifle the sound. That gesture, in turn, brought back recollections of the night before, when Doss had made love to her, and she'd wanted to cry out with the pleasure of it.

She blushed so hard her face burned, and this time it was Doss who laughed.

"I figure we're in for another blizzard," he said. "Might be spring before we can get to town and stand up in front of a preacher. I hope you're not looking like a watermelon smuggler before then."

Hannah opened her mouth, closed it again.

Doss's eyes danced as he took another sip of his coffee.

"That was an insufferably forward thing to say!" Hannah accused.

"You're a fine one to talk about being forward," Doss observed, and repeated back something she'd said at that very height of her passion.

"That's enough, Mr. McKettrick."

Doss set his cup down, pushed back his chair and stood. "I'm going out to the barn to look in on the stock again. Maybe you ought to come along. Make the job go faster, if you lent a hand."

Hannah squirmed on the bench.

Doss crossed the room, took his coat and hat down from the pegs by the door. "Way out there, a person could holler if they wanted to. Be nobody to hear."

Hannah did some more squirming.

"Fresh hay to lie in, too," Doss went on. "Nice and soft, and if a man were to spread a couple of horse blankets over it—"

Heat surged through Hannah, brought her to an aching simmer. She sputtered something and waved him away.

Doss chuckled, opened the door and went out, whistling merrily under his breath.

Hannah waited. If Doss McKettrick thought he was going to have his way with her—in the barn, of all places—well, he was just...

She got up, went to the stove and banked the fire with a poker.

He was just right, that was what he was.

She chose her biggest shawl, wrapped herself in it, and hurried after him.

Present Day

As soon as Sierra put supper on the table that night, the power went off again. While she scrambled for candles, Liam rushed to the nearest window.

"Travis's trailer's dark," he said. "He'll get *hypothermia* out there."

Sierra sighed. "I'll bet he comes back to see to the furnace, just like he did this morning. We'll ask him to have supper with us."

"I see him!" Liam cried gleefully. "He's coming out of the barn, with a lantern!" He raced for the door, and before Sierra could stop him, he was outside, with no coat on, galloping through the deepening snow and shouting Travis's name.

Sierra pulled on her own coat, grabbed Liam's and hurried after him.

Travis was already herding him toward the house.

"Mom made meat loaf, and she says you can have some," Liam was saying, as he tramped breathlessly along.

Sierra wrapped his coat around him, and would have scolded him, if her gaze hadn't collided unexpectedly with Travis's.

Travis shook his head.

She swallowed all that she'd been about to say and hustled her son into the house.

"I'll start the generator," Travis said.

Sierra nodded hastily and shut the door.

"Liam McKettrick," she burst out, "what were you thinking, going out in that cold without a coat?"

In the candlelight, she saw Liam's lower lip wobble. "Travis said it isn't the cowboy way. He was about to put his coat on me when you came."

"*What* isn't the 'cowboy way'?" she asked, chafing his icy hands between hers and praying he wouldn't have an asthma attack or come down with pneumonia.

"Not wearing a coat," Liam replied, downcast. "A cowboy is always prepared for any kind of weather, and he never rushes off half-cocked, without his gear."

Sierra relaxed a little, stifled a smile. "Travis is right," she said.

Liam brightened. "Do cowboys eat meat loaf?"

"I'm pretty sure they do," Sierra answered.

The furnace came on, and she silently blessed Travis Reid for being there.

He let himself into the kitchen a few minutes later. By then Sierra had set another place at the table and lit several more candles. They all sat down at the same time, and there was something so natural about their gathering that way that Sierra's throat caught.

"I hope you're hungry," she said, feeling awkward.

"I'm starved," Travis replied.

"Cowboys eat meat loaf, right?" Liam inquired.

Travis grinned. "This one does," he said.

"This one does, too," Liam announced.

Sierra laughed, but tears came to her eyes at the same time. She was glad of the relative darkness, hoping no one would notice.

"Once," Liam said, scooping a helping of meat loaf onto his plate, his gaze adoring as he focused on Travis, "I saw this show on the Science Channel. They found a cave man, in a block of ice. He was, like *fourteen thousand* years old! I betcha they could take some of his DNA and clone him if they wanted to." He stopped for a quick breath. "And he was all blue, too. That's what you'll look like, if you sleep in that trailer tonight."

"You're not a kid," Travis teased. "You're a forty-year-old wearing a pygmy suit."

"I'm *really* smart," Liam went on. "So you ought to listen to me."

Travis looked at Sierra, and their eyes caught, with an almost audible click and held.

"The generator's low on gas," Travis said. "So we have two choices. We can get in my truck and hope there are some empty motel rooms at the Lamplight Inn, or we can build up the fire in that cookstove and camp out in the kitchen."

Liam had no trouble at all making the choice. "Camp out!" he whooped, waving his fork in the air. "Camp out!"

"You can't be serious," Sierra said to Travis.

"Oh, I'm serious, all right," he answered.

"Lamplight Inn," Sierra voted.

"Roads are bad," Travis replied. "*Real* bad."

"Once on TV, I saw a thing about these people who froze to death right in their car," Liam put in.

"Be quiet," Sierra told him.

"Happens all the time," Travis said.

Which was how the three of them ended up bundled in sleeping bags, with couch and chair cushions for a makeshift mattress, lying side by side within the warm radius of the wood-burning stove.

Chapter 7

Hannah and Doss returned separately from the barn, by tacit agreement. Hannah, weak-kneed with residual pleasure and reeling with guilt, pumped water into a bucket to pour into the near-empty reservoir on the cookstove, then filled the two biggest kettles she had and set them on the stove to heat. She was adding wood to the fire when she heard Doss come in.

She blushed furiously, unable to meet his gaze, though she could feel it burning into her flesh, right through the clothes he'd sweet-talked her out of just an hour before, laying her down in the soft, surprisingly warm hay in an empty stall, kissing and caressing and nibbling at her until she'd begged him to take her.

Begged him.

She'd carried on something awful while he was at it, too.

"Look at me, Hannah," he said.

She glared at Doss, marched past him into the pantry and dragged out the big wash tub stored there under a high shelf. She set it in front of the stove with an eloquent clang.

"Hannah," Doss repeated.

"Go upstairs," she told him, flustered. "Leave me to my bath."

"You can't wash away what we did," he said.

She whirled on him that time, hands on her hips, fiery with temper. "Get out," she ordered, keeping her voice down in case Tobias was still awake or even listening at the top of the stairs. "I need my privacy."

Doss raised both hands to shoulder height, palms out, but his words were juxtaposed to the gesture. "If we're going to talk about what you need, Hannah, it's not a bath. It's a lot more of what we just did in the barn."

"Tobias might hear you!" Hannah whispered, outraged. If the broom hadn't been on the back porch, she'd have grabbed it up and whacked him silly with it.

"He wouldn't know what we were talking about even if he did," Doss argued mildly, lowering his hands. He approached, plucked a piece of straw from Hannah's hair and tickled her under the chin with it.

She felt as though she'd been electrified, and slapped his hand away.

He laughed, a low, masculine sound, leaned in and nibbled at her lower lip. "Good night, Hannah," he said.

A hot shiver of renewed need went through her. How could that be? He'd satisfied her that night, and the one before. Both times he'd taken her to heights she hadn't even reached with Gabe.

The difference was, she'd been Gabe's wife, in the eyes of God and man, and she'd loved him. She not only wasn't married to Doss, she didn't love him. She just wanted him, that was all, and the realization galled her.

"You've turned me into a hussy," she said.

Doss chuckled, shook his head. "If you say so, Hannah," he answered, "it must be true."

With that, he kissed her forehead, turned and left the kitchen.

She listened to the sound of his boot heels on the stairs, heard his progress along the second-floor hallway, even knew when he opened Tobias's door to look in on the boy before retiring to his own room. Only when she'd heard his door close did Hannah let out her breath.

When the water in the kettles was scalding hot, Hannah poured it into the tub, sneaked upstairs for a towel, a bar of soap and a nightgown. By the time she'd put out all the lanterns in the kitchen and stripped off her clothes, her bathwater had cooled to a temperature that made her sigh when she stepped into it.

She soaked for a few minutes, and then scrubbed with a vengeance.

It turned out that Doss had been right.

She tried but she couldn't wash away the things he'd made her feel.

A tear slipped down her cheek as she dried herself off, then donned her nightgown. She dragged the tub to the back door and on to the step, drained it over one side and dashed back in, covered with gooseflesh from the chill.

"I'm sorry, Gabe," she said, very quietly, huddling by the stove. "I'm sorry."

Present Day

Travis was building up the fire when Sierra opened her eyes the next morning. "Stay in your sleeping bag," he told her. "It's colder than a meat locker in here."

Liam, lying between them throughout the night, was still asleep, but his breathing was a shallow rattle. Sierra sat bolt-upright, watchful, holding her own breath. Not feeling the external chill at all, except as a vague biting sensation.

Liam opened his eyes, blinked. "Mom," he said. "I can't—"

Breathe, Sierra finished the sentence for him, replayed it in her mind.

Mom, I can't breathe.

She bounded out of the sleeping bag, scrambled for her purse, which was lying on the counter and rummaged for Liam's inhaler.

He began to wheeze, and when Sierra turned to rush back to him, she saw a look of panic in his eyes.

"Take it easy, Liam," she said, as she handed him the inhaler.

He grasped it in both hands, all too familiar with the routine, and pressed the tube to his mouth and nose.

Travis watched grimly.

Sierra dropped on to her knees next to her boy, put an arm loosely around his shoulders. *Let it work,* she prayed silently. *Please let it work!*

Liam lowered the inhaler and stared apologetically up into Sierra's eyes. He could barely get enough wind to speak. He was, in essence, choking. "It's—I think it's broken, Mom—"

"I'll warm up the truck," Travis said, and banged out of the house.

Desperate, Sierra took the inhaler, shook it and shoved it back into Liam's hands. It *wasn't* empty—she wouldn't have taken a chance like that—but it must have been clogged or somehow defective. "Try again," she urged, barely avoiding panic herself.

Outside, Travis's truck roared audibly to life. He gunned the motor a couple of times.

Liam struggled to take in the medication, but the inhaler simply wasn't working.

Travis returned, picked Liam up in his arms, sleeping bag and all, and headed for the door again. Sierra, frightened as she was, had to hurry to catch up, snatching her coat from the peg and her purse from the counter on the way out.

The snow had stopped, but there must have been two feet of it on the ground. Travis shifted the truck into four-wheel drive and the tires grabbed for purchase, finally caught.

"Take it easy, buddy," he told Liam, who was on Sierra's lap, the seat belt fastened around both of them. "Take it real easy."

Liam nodded solemnly. He was drawing in shallow gasps of air now, but not enough. *Not enough.* His lips were turning blue.

Sierra held him tight, but not too tight. Rested her chin on top of his head and prayed.

The roads hadn't been plowed—in fact, except for sloping drifts on either side, Sierra wouldn't have known where they were. Still, the truck rolled over them as easily as if they were bare.

What if we'd been alone, Liam and me? Sierra thought frantically. Her old station wagon, a snow-covered hulk in the driveway in front of the house, probably wouldn't have started, and even if it had by some miracle, the chances

were good that they'd have ended up in the ditch somewhere along the way to safety.

"It's going to be okay," she heard Travis say, and she'd
thought he was talking to Liam. When she glanced at him,
though, she knew he'd meant the words for her.

She kept her voice even. "Is there a hospital in Indian
Rock?" She and Liam had passed through the town the
day they arrived, but she didn't remember seeing anything
but houses, a diner or two, a drugstore, several bars and a
gas station. She'd been too busy trying to follow the hand-
drawn map Meg had scanned and sent to her by email—
the McKettricks' private cemetery was marked with an X,
and the ranch house an uneven square with lines for a roof.

"A clinic," Travis said. He looked down at Liam again,
then turned his gaze back to the road. The set of his jaw
was hard, and he pulled his cell phone from the pocket of
his coat and handed it to Sierra.

She dialed 911 and asked to be connected.

When a voice answered, Sierra explained the situation
as calmly as she could, keeping it low-key for Liam's sake.
They'd been through at least a dozen similar episodes during his short life, and it never got easier. Each time, Sierra
was hysterical, though she didn't dare let that show. Liam
was taking his cues from her. If she lost it, he would, too,
and the results could be disastrous.

The clinic receptionist seemed blessedly unruffled.
"We'll be ready when you get here," she said.

Sierra thanked the woman and ended the call, set the
phone on the seat.

By the time they arrived at the town's only medical facil-
ity, Liam was struggling to remain conscious. Travis pulled
up in front, gave the horn a hard blast and was around to

Sierra's side with the door open before she managed to get the seat belt unbuckled.

Two medical assistants, accompanied by a gray-haired doctor, met them with a gurney. Liam was whisked away. Sierra tried to follow, but Travis and one of the nurses stopped her.

Her first instinct was to fight.

"My son needs me!" She'd meant it for a scream, but it came out as more of a whimper.

"We'll need your name and that of the patient," a clerk informed her, advancing with a clipboard. "And of course there's the matter of insurance—"

Travis glared the woman into retreat. "Her *name*," he said, "is McKettrick."

"Oh," the clerk said, and ducked behind her desk.

Sierra needed something, anything, to do, or she was going to rip apart every room in that place until she found Liam, gathered him into her arms. "My purse," she said. "I must have left it in the truck—"

"I'll get it," Travis said, but first he steered her toward a chair in the waiting area and sat her down.

Tears of frustration and stark terror filled her eyes. What was happening to Liam? Was he breathing? Were they forcing the hated tube down into his bronchial passage even at that moment?

Travis cupped her face between his hands, for just a moment, and his palms felt cold and rough from ranch work.

The sensation triggered something in Sierra, but she was too distraught to know what it was.

"I'll be right back," he promised.

And he was.

Sierra snatched her bag from his hands, scrabbled through it to find her wallet. Found the insurance card

Eve had sent by express the same day Sierra agreed to take the McKettrick name and spend a year on the Triple M, with Liam. She might have kissed that card, if Travis hadn't been watching.

The clerk nodded a little nervously when Sierra walked up to the desk and asked for the papers she needed to fill out.

Patient's Name. Well, that was easy enough. She scrawled Liam Bres—crossed out the last part, and wrote McKettrick instead.

Address? She had to consult Travis on that one. Everybody in Indian Rock knew where the Triple M was, she was sure, but the people in the insurance company's claims office might not.

Occupation? Child.

Damn it, Liam was a little boy, hardly more than a baby. Things like this shouldn't happen to him.

Sierra printed her own name, as guarantor. She bit her lip when asked about her job. Unemployed? She couldn't write that.

Travis, watching, took the clipboard and pen from her and inserted, Damn good mother.

The tears came again.

Travis got up, with the forms and the clipboard and the insurance card, inscribed with the magical name and carried them over to the waiting clerk.

He was halfway back to Sierra when the doctor reappeared.

"Hello, Travis," he said, but his gaze was on Sierra's face, and she couldn't read it, for all the practice she'd had.

"I'm Sierra McKettrick," she said. The name still felt like a garment that didn't quite fit, but if it would help Liam in any way, she would use it every chance she got. "My son—"

"He'll be fine," the doctor said kindly. His eyes were a faded blue, his features craggy and weathered. "Just the same, I think we ought to send him up to Flagstaff to the hospital, at least overnight. For observation, you understand. And because they've got a reliable power source up there."

"Is he awake?" Sierra asked anxiously.

"Partially sedated," replied the doctor, exchanging glances with Travis. "We had to perform an intubation."

Sierra knew how Liam hated tubes, and how frightened he probably was, sedated or not. "I have to see him," she said, prepared for an argument.

"Of course" was the immediate and very gentle answer.

Sierra felt Travis's hand close around hers. She clung, instead of pulling away, as she would have done with any other virtual stranger.

A few minutes later they were standing on either side of Liam's bed in one of the treatment rooms. His eyes widened with recognition when he saw Sierra, and he pointed, with one small finger, to the mouthpiece of his oxygen tube.

She nodded, blinking hard and trying to smile. Took his hand.

"You have to spend the night in the hospital in Flagstaff," she told him, "but don't be scared, okay? Because I'm going with you."

Liam relaxed visibly. Turned his eyes to Travis. Sierra's heart twisted at the hope she saw in her little boy's face.

"Me, too," Travis said hoarsely.

Liam nodded and drifted off to sleep.

The doctor had ordered an ambulance, and Sierra rode with Liam, while Travis followed in the truck.

There was more paperwork to do in Flagstaff, but Sierra was calmer now. She sat in a chair next to Liam's bed and filled in the lines.

Travis entered with two cups of vending-machine coffee, just as she was finishing.

"Thank you," Sierra said, and she wasn't just talking about the coffee.

"Wranglers like Liam and me," he replied, watching the boy with a kind of fretful affection, "we stick together when the going gets tough."

She accepted the paper cup Travis offered and set the ubiquitous clipboard aside to take a sip. Travis drew up a second chair.

"Does this happen a lot?" he asked, after a long and remarkably easy silence.

Sierra shook her head. "No, thank God. I don't know what we would have done without you, Travis."

"You would have coped," he said. "Like you've been doing for a long time, if my guess is any good. Where's Liam's dad, Sierra?"

She swallowed hard, glanced at the boy to make sure he was sleeping. "He died a few days before Liam was born," she answered.

"You've been alone all this time?"

"No," Sierra said, stiffening a little on the inside, where it didn't show. Or, at least, she *hoped* it didn't. "I had Liam."

"You know that isn't what I meant," Travis said.

Sierra looked away, made herself look back. "I didn't want to—complicate things. By getting involved with someone, I mean. Liam and I have been just fine on our own."

Travis merely nodded, and drank more of his coffee.

"Don't you have to go back to the ranch and feed the horses or something?" Sierra asked.

"Eventually," Travis answered with a sigh. He glanced around the room again and gave the slightest shudder.

Sierra remembered his younger brother. The wounds must be raw. "I guess you probably hate hospitals," she said. "Because of—" the name came back to her in Eve's telephone voice "—Brody."

Travis shook his head. His eyes were bleak. "If he'd gotten this far—to a hospital, I mean—it would have meant there was hope."

Sierra moved to touch Travis's hand, but just before she made contact, his cell phone rang. He pulled it from the pocket of his western shirt. "Travis Reid."

He listened. Raised his eyebrows. "Hello, Eve. I wouldn't have thought even *your* pilot could land in this kind of weather."

Sierra tensed.

Eve said something, and Travis responded. "I'll let Sierra explain," he said, and held out the phone to her.

Sierra swallowed, took it. "Hello, Eve," she said.

"Where are you?" her mother asked. "I'm at the ranch. It looks as if you've been sleeping in the kitchen—"

"We're in Flagstaff, in a hospital," Sierra told her. Only then did she realize that she and Travis were both wearing the clothes they'd slept in. That she hadn't combed her hair or even brushed her teeth.

All of a sudden she felt incredibly grubby.

Eve drew in an audible breath. "Oh, my *God*—Liam?"

"He had a pretty bad asthma attack," Sierra confirmed. "He's on a breathing machine, and he has to stay until tomorrow, but he's okay, Eve."

"I'll be up there as soon as I can. Which hospital?"

"Hold on," Sierra said. "There's really no need for you

to come all this way, especially when the roads are so bad. I'm pretty sure we'll be home tomorrow—"

"Pretty sure?" Eve challenged.

"Well, he'll need his medication adjusted, and the inflammation in his bronchial tubes will have to go down."

"This sounds serious, Sierra. I think I should come. I could be there—"

"Please," Sierra interrupted. "Don't."

A thoughtful silence followed. "All right, then," Eve said finally, with a good grace Sierra truly appreciated. "I'll just settle in here and wait. The furnace is running and the lights are on. Tell Travis not to rush back—I can certainly feed the horses."

Sierra could only nod, so Travis took the phone back.

Evidently, a barrage of orders followed from Eve's end.

Travis grinned throughout. "Yes, ma'am," he said. "I will."

He ended the call.

"You will what?" Sierra inquired.

"Take care of you and Liam," Travis answered.

1919

That morning the world looked as though it had been carved from a huge block of pure white ice. Hannah marveled at the beauty of it, staring through the kitchen window, even as she longed with bittersweet poignancy for spring. For things to stir under the snowbound earth, to put out roots and break through the surface, green and growing.

"Ma?"

She turned, troubled by something she heard in Tobias's voice. He stood at the base of the stairs, still wearing his nightshirt and barefoot.

"I don't feel good," he said.

Hannah set aside her coffee with exaggerated care, even took time to wipe her hands on her apron before she approached him. Touched his forehead with the back of her hand.

"You're burning up," she whispered, stricken.

Doss, who had been rereading last week's newspaper at the table, his barn work done, slowly scraped back his chair.

"Shall I fetch the doc?" he asked.

Hannah turned, looked at him over one shoulder, and nodded. If you hadn't insisted on taking him with you to the widow Jessup's place, she thought—

But she would go no further.

This was not the time to place blame.

"You get back into bed," she told Tobias, briskly efficient and purely terrified. The bout of pneumonia that had nearly killed him during the fall had started like this. "I'll make you a mustard plaster to draw out the congestion, and your uncle Doss will go to town for Dr. Willaby. You'll be right as rain in no time at all."

Tobias looked doubtful. His face was flushed, and his nightshirt was soaked with perspiration, even though the kitchen was a little on the chilly side. The boy seemed dazed, almost as though he were walking in his sleep, and Hannah wondered if he'd taken in a word she'd said.

"I'll be back as soon as I can," Doss promised, already pulling on his coat and reaching for his hat. "There's whisky left from Christmas. It's in the pantry, behind that cracker tin," he added, pausing before opening the door. "Make him a hot drink with some honey. Pa used to brew up that concoction for us when we took sick, and it always helped."

Doss and Gabe, along with their adopted older brother, John Henry, had never suffered a serious illness in their lives, if you didn't count John Henry's deafness. What did they know about tending the sick?

Hannah nodded again, her mouth tight. She'd lost three sisters in childhood, two to diphtheria and one to scarlet fever; only she and her younger brother, David, had survived.

She was used to nursing the afflicted.

Doss hesitated a few moments on the threshold, as though there was something he wanted to say but couldn't put into words, then went out.

"You change into a dry nightshirt," Hannah told Tobias. His sheets were probably sweat-soaked, too, so she added, "And get into our bed."

Our bed.

Meaning Gabe's and hers.

And soon, after they were married, Doss would be sleeping in that bed, in Gabe's place.

She could not, would not, consider the implications of that.

Not now. Maybe not ever.

She was like the ranch woman she'd once read about in a Montana newspaper, making her way from the house to the barn and back in a blinding blizzard, with only a frozen rope to hold on to. If she let go, she'd be lost.

She had to attend to Tobias. That was her rope, and she'd follow it, hand over hand, thought over thought.

Hannah retrieved an old flannel shirt from the rag bag and cut two matching pieces, approximately twelve inches square. These would serve to protect Tobias's skin from the heat of the poultice, but like as not, he would still have blisters. She kept a mixture on hand for just such occasions, in a big jar with a wire seal. She dumped a big dollop of the stuff on to one of the bits of flannel, spread it like butter, and put the second cloth on top, her nose twitching at the pungent odors of mustard seed, pounded to a pulp, and camphor.

When she got upstairs, she found Tobias huddled in the middle of her bed, and his eyes grew big with recollection when he saw what she was carrying in her hands.

"No," he protested, but weakly. "No mustard plaster." He'd begun to shiver, and his teeth were chattering.

"Don't fuss, Tobias," Hannah said. "Your grandfather swears by them."

Tobias groaned. "My Montana grandfather," he replied. "My grandpa Holt wouldn't let anybody put one of those things on him!"

"Is that a fact?" Hannah asked mildly. "Well, next time you write to the almighty Holt McKettrick, you ask. I'll bet he'll say he wouldn't be without one when he's under the weather."

Tobias made a rude sound, blowing through his lips, but he rolled on to his back and allowed Hannah to open the top buttons of his nightshirt and put the poultice in place.

"Grandpa Holt," he said, bearing the affliction stalwartly, "would probably make me a whisky drink, just like he did for Pa and Uncle Doss."

Hannah sighed. Privately she thought there was a good deal of the roughneck in the McKettrick men, and while she wouldn't call any of them a drunk, they used liquor as a remedy for just about every ill, from snakebite to the grippe. They'd swabbed it on old Seesaw's gashes, when he tangled with a sow bear, and rubbed it into the gums of teething babies.

"What you're going to have, Tobias McKettrick, is oatmeal."

He made a face. "This burns," he complained, pointing to the mustard plaster.

Hannah bent and kissed his forehead. He didn't pull away, like he'd taken to doing of late, and she found that both reassuring and worrisome.

She glanced at the window, saw a scallop of icicles dangling from the eave. It might be many hours—even tomorrow—before Doss got back from Indian Rock with Dr. Willaby. The wait would be agony, but there was nothing to do but endure.

When Tobias closed his eyes and slept, Hannah left the room, descended the stairs and went into the pantry again. She moved the cracker tin aside, looked up at the bottle of whisky hidden behind it, gave a disdainful sniff, and took a canned chicken off the shelf instead. It was a treasure, that chicken—she'd been saving it for some celebration, so she wouldn't have to kill one of her laying hens—but it would make a fine, nourishing soup.

After gathering onions, rice and some of her spices—which she cherished as much as preserved meat, given how costly they were—Hannah commenced to make soup.

She was surprised when, only an hour after he'd ridden out, Doss returned with another man she recognized as one of the ranch hands down at Rafe's place. She frowned, watching from the window as Doss dismounted and left the newcomer to lead both horses inside.

That was odd. Doss hadn't been to Indian Rock yet; he

couldn't have covered the distance in such a short time. Why would he ask someone to put up his horse?

Puzzled, impatient and a little angry, Hannah was waiting at the door when Doss came in.

"Bundle the boy up warm," he said, without any preamble at all. "Willie's going to stay here and look after the horses and the place. Once I've hitched the draft horses to the sleigh, we'll go overland to Indian Rock."

Hannah stared at him, confounded. "You're suggesting that we take Tobias all the way to Indian Rock?"

"I'm not 'suggesting' anything, Hannah," Doss interposed. "I met Seth Baker down by the main house, when I was about to cross the stream, and he hailed me, wanted to know where I was headed. I told him I was off to fetch Doc Willaby, because Tobias was feeling poorly. Seth said Willaby was down with the gout, but his nephew happened to be there, and he's a doctor, too. He's looking after the doc's practice, in town, so he wouldn't be inclined to come all the way out here."

Hannah's throat clenched, and she put a hand to it. "A ride like that could be the end of Tobias," she said.

Doss shook his head. "We can't just sit here," he countered, grim-jawed. "Get the boy ready or I'll do it myself."

"May I remind you that Tobias is my son?"

"He's a McKettrick," Doss replied flatly, as though that were the end of it—and for him, it probably was.

Chapter 8

Present Day

Travis waited until Sierra had drifted off into a fitful sleep in her chair next to Liam's hospital bed. Then he got a blanket from a nurse, covered Sierra with it and left.

A few minutes later, he was behind the wheel of his truck.

The roads were sheer ice, and the sky looked gray, burdened with fresh snow. After consulting the GPS panel on his dashboard, he found the nearest Wal-Mart, parked as close to the store as he could and went inside.

Shopping was something Travis endured, and this was no exception. He took a cart and wheeled it around, choosing the things Sierra and Liam would need if this hitch in Flagstaff turned out to be longer than expected. He'd spent the night at his own place, a few miles from the hospital, showered and changed there.

When he got back from his expedition—a January Santa Claus burdened down with bulging blue plastic bags—he made his way to Liam's room.

Sierra was awake, blinking and befuddled, and so was Liam. A huge teddy bear, holding a helium balloon in one paw, sat on the bedside table. The writing on the balloon said Get Well Soon in big red letters.

"Eve?" Travis asked, indicating the bear with a nod of his head.

Sierra took in the bags he was carrying. "Eve," she confirmed. "What have you got there?"

Travis grinned, though he felt tired all of a sudden, as though ten cups of coffee wouldn't keep him awake. Maybe it was the warmth of the hospital, after being out in the cold.

"A little something for everybody," he said.

Liam was sitting up, and the breathing tube had been removed. His words came out as a sore-throated croak, but he smiled just the same, and Travis felt a pinch deep inside. The kid was so small and so brave. "Even me?"

"Especially you," Travis said. He handed the boy one of the bags, watched as he pulled out a portable DVD player, still in its box, and the episodes of *Nova* he'd picked up to go with it.

"Wow," Liam said, his voice so raw that it made Travis's throat ache in sympathy. "I've always wanted one of these."

Sierra looked worried. "It's way too expensive," she said. "We can't accept it."

Liam hugged the box close against his little chest, obstinately possessive. Everything about him said, I'm not giving this up.

Travis ignored Sierra's statement and tossed her another of the bags, this one fat and light. "Take a shower," he told her. "You look like somebody who just went through a harrowing medical emergency."

She opened her mouth, closed it again. Peeked inside the bag. He'd bought her yoga pants and a hoodie, guessing at the sizes, along with toothpaste, a brush, soap and a comb.

She swallowed visibly. "Thanks."

He nodded.

While Sierra was in Liam's bathroom, showering, Travis helped the boy get the DVD player out of the box, plugged in and running.

"Mom might not let me keep it," Liam said sadly.

"I'm betting she will," Travis assured him.

Liam was engrossed in an episode about killer bees when Sierra came out of the bathroom, looking scrubbed and cautiously hopeful in her dark-blue sweats. Her hair was still wet from washing, and the comb had left distinct ridges, which Travis found peculiarly poignant.

Complex emotions fell into line after that one, striking him with the impact of a runaway boxcar, but he didn't dare explore any of them right away. He'd need to be alone to do that, in his truck or with a horse. For now, he was too close to Sierra to think straight.

She glanced at Liam, softened noticeably as she saw how much he was enjoying Travis's gift. His small hands clasped the machine on either side, as though he feared someone would wrench it away.

Something similar to Travis's thoughts must have gone through her mind, because he saw a change in her face. It was a sort of resignation, and it made him want to take her in his arms—though he wasn't about to do that.

"I could use something to eat," he said.

"Me, too," Sierra admitted. She tapped Liam on the shoulder, and he barely looked away from the screen, where bees were swarming. Music from the speakers portended certain disaster. "You'll be all right here alone for a while, if Travis and I go down to the cafeteria?"

The boy nodded distractedly, refocused his eyes on the bees.

Sierra smiled with a tiny, forlorn twitch of her lips.

They were well away from Liam's room, and waiting for an elevator, when she finally spoke.

"I'm grateful for what you did for Liam and me," she said, "but you shouldn't have given him something that cost so much."

"I won't miss the money, Sierra," Travis responded. "He's been through a lot, and he needed something else to think about besides breathing tubes, medical tests and shots."

She gave a brief, almost clipped nod.

That McKettrick pride, Travis thought. It was something to behold.

The elevator came, and the doors opened with a cheerful chiming sound. They stepped inside, and Travis pushed the button for the lower level. Hospital cafeterias always seemed to be in the bowels of the building, like the morgues.

Downstairs, they went through the grub line with trays, and chose the least offensive-looking items from the stock array of greasy green beans, mock meat loaf, brown gravy and the like.

Sierra chose a corner table, and they sat down, facing each other. She looked like a freshly showered angel from some celestial soccer team in the athletic clothes he'd provided, and Travis wondered if she had any idea how beautiful she was.

"I'm surprised Eve hasn't shown up," he said, to get the conversation started.

Sierra's cheeks pinkened a little, and she avoided his gaze. Poked at the faux meat loaf with a water-spotted fork.

"I don't know what I'm going to say to her," she said. "Beyond 'thank you,' I mean."

"How about, 'hello'?" Travis joked.

Sierra didn't look amused. Just nervous, like a rat cornered by a barn cat.

He reached across the table, closed his hand briefly over hers. "Look, Sierra, this doesn't have to be hard. Eve will probably do most of the talking, at least in the beginning, and she'll feed you your lines."

She smiled again. Another tentative flicker, there and gone.

They ate in silence for a while.

"It's not as if I hate her," Sierra said, out of the blue. "Eve, I mean."

Travis waited, knowing they were on uneven ground. Sierra was as skittish as a spring fawn, and he didn't want to speak at the wrong time and send her bolting for the emotional underbrush.

"I don't know her," Sierra went on. "My own mother. I saw her picture on the McKettrickCo website, but she told me it didn't look a thing like her."

Still, Travis waited.

"What's she like?" Sierra asked, almost plaintively. "Really?"

"Eve is a beautiful woman," Travis said. *Like you,* he added silently. "She's smart, and when it comes to negotiating a business deal, she's as tough as they come. She's remarkable, Sierra. Give her a chance."

Sierra's lower lip wobbled, ever so slightly. Her blue, blue eyes were limpid with feelings Travis could only guess at.

He wanted to dive into them, like a swimmer, and explore the vast inner landscape he sensed within her.

"You know what happened, don't you?" she asked, very softly. "Back when my mother and father were divorced."

"Some of it," Travis said, cautious, like a man touching a tender bruise.

"Dad took me to Mexico when I was two," she said, "right after someone from Eve's lawyer's office served the papers."

Travis nodded. "Meg told me that much."

"As little as I was, I remembered what she smelled like, what it felt like when she held me, the sound of her voice." A spasm of pain flinched in Sierra's eyes. "No matter how I tried, I could never recall her face. Dad made sure there weren't any pictures, and—"

He ached for her. The soupy mashed potatoes went pulpy in his mouth, and they went down like so much barbed wire when he swallowed. "What kind of man would—"

He caught himself.

None of your business, Trav.

To his surprise she smiled again, and warmth rose in her eyes. "Dad was never a model father, more like a buddy. But he took good care of me. I grew up with the kind of freedom most kids never know—running the streets of San Miguel in my bare feet. I knew all the vendors in the marketplace, and writers and artists gathered at our *casita* almost every night. Dad's mistress, Magdalena, home-schooled me. I attracted stray dogs wherever I went, and Dad always let me keep them."

"Not a traumatic childhood," Travis observed, still careful.

She shook her head. "Not at all. But I missed my mother desperately, just the same. For a while, I thought she'd come for me. That one day a car would pull up in front of the *casita*, and there she'd be, smiling, with her arms open. Then when there was no sign of her, and no letters came—well, I decided she must be dead. It was only after I got old enough to surf the internet that I found her."

"You didn't call or write?"

"It was a shock, realizing she was alive—that if I could find her, she could have found me. And she didn't. With the resources she must have had—"

Travis felt a sting of anger on Sierra's behalf. Pushed away his tray. "I used to work for Eve," he said. "And I've known her for most of my life. I can't imagine why she wouldn't have gone in with an army, once she knew where you were."

Sierra bit her lower lip again, so hard Travis almost expected it to bleed. Her eyes glistened with tears she was probably too proud to shed, at least for herself. She'd wept plenty for Liam, he suspected, alone and in secret. It paralyzed him when a woman cried, and yet in that moment he'd have rewritten history if he could have. He'd have been there, in the thick of Sierra's sorrows, whatever they were, to put his arms around her, promise that everything would be all right and move heaven and earth to make it so.

But the plain truth was, he hadn't been.

"I'd better get back to Liam," she said.

He nodded.

They carried their trays to the dropping-off place, went upstairs again, entered Liam's room.

He was asleep, with the DVD player still running on his lap.

Travis went to speak to one of the nurses, a woman he knew from college, and when he came back, he found Sierra stretched out beside her son, dead to the world.

He sighed, watching the pair of them.

He'd kept himself apart, even before Brody died, busy with his career. Dated lots of women and steered clear of anything heavy.

Now, without warning, the whole equation had shifted, and there was a good chance he was in big trouble.

1919

The air was so cold it bit through the bearskin throws and Hannah's many layers of wool to her flesh. She could see her breath billowing out in front of her, blue white, like Doss's. Like Tobias's.

Her boy looked feverishly gleeful, nestled between her and Doss, as the sleigh moved over an icy trail, drawn by the big draft horses, Cain and Abel. The animals usually languished in the barn all winter; in the spring, they pulled plows in the hayfields, in the fall, harvest wagons. Summers, they grazed. They seemed spry and vigorous to Hannah, gladly surprised to be working.

Where other horses or even mules might have floundered in the deep, crusted snow, the sons of Adam, as Gabe liked to call them, pranced along as easily as they would over dry ground.

Doss held the reins in his gloved hands, hunkered down into the collar of his sheepskin-lined coat, his earlobes red under the brim of his hat. Once in a while he glanced Hannah's way, but mostly when he spared a look, it was for Tobias.

"You warm enough?" he'd asked.

And each time Tobias would nod. If his blood had been frozen in his veins, he'd have nodded, Hannah knew that, even if Doss didn't. He idolized his uncle, always had.

Would he forget Gabe entirely, once she and Doss were married?

Everything within Hannah rankled at the thought.

Why hadn't she left for Montana before it was too late?

Now she was about to tie herself, for good, to a man she lusted after but would never love.

Of course she could still go home to her folks—she knew they'd welcome her and Tobias—but suppose she was carrying Doss's child? Once her pregnancy became apparent, they'd know she'd behaved shamefully. The whole world would know.

How could she bear that?

No. She would go ahead and marry Doss, and let sharing her bed with him be her private consolation. She'd find a way to endure the rest, like his trying to give her orders all the time and maybe yearning after other women because he'd taken a wife out of honor, not choice.

She'd be his cross to bear, and he would be hers.

There was a perverse kind of justice in that.

They reached the outskirts of Indian Rock in the late afternoon, with the sun about to go down. Doss drove straight to Dr. Willaby's big house on Third Street, secured the horses and reached into the sleigh for Tobias before Hannah got herself unwrapped enough to get out of the sleigh.

Doc Willaby's daughter, Constance, met them at the door. She was a beautiful young woman, and she'd pursued Gabe right up to the day he'd put a gold band on Hannah's finger. Now, from the way she looked at Doss, she was ready to settle for his younger brother.

The thought stirred Hannah to fury, though she'd have buttered, baked and eaten both her shoes before admitting it.

"We have need of a doctor," Doss said to Constance, holding Tobias's bundled form in both arms.

"Come in," Constance said. She had bright-auburn hair and very green eyes, and her shape, though slender, was voluptuous. What, Hannah wondered, did Doss think when he looked at her? "Papa's ill," the other woman went on, "but my cousin is here, and he'll see to the boy."

Hannah put aside whatever it was she'd felt, seeing Constance, for relief. Tobias would be looked after by a real doctor. He'd be all right now, and nothing else mattered but that.

She would darn Doss McKettrick's socks for the rest of her life. She would cook his meals and trim his hair and wash his back. She would take him water and sandwiches in summer, when he was herding cattle or working in the hayfields. She'd bite her tongue, when he galled her, which would surely be often, and let him win at cards on winter nights.

The one thing she would never do was love him—her heart would always belong to Gabe—but no one on earth, save the two of them, was ever going to know the plain, regrettable truth.

"It's a bad cold," the younger doctor said, after carefully examining Tobias in a room set aside for the purpose. He was a very slender man, almost delicate, with dark hair and sideburns. He wore a good suit and carried a gold watch, which he consulted often. He was a city dweller, Hannah reflected, used to schedules. "I'd recommend taking a room at the hotel for a few days, though, because he shouldn't be exposed to this weather."

Doss took out his wallet, like it was his place to pay the doctor bills, and Hannah stepped in front of him.

She was Tobias's mother, and she was still responsible for costs such as these.

"That'll be one dollar," the doctor said, glancing from Hannah's face, which felt pink with conviction and cold, to Doss's.

Hannah shoved the money into his hand.

"Give the boy whisky," the physician added, folding the dollar bill and tucking it into the pocket of his fine tailored coat. "Mixed with honey and lemon juice, if the hotel dining room's got any such thing on hand."

Doss, to his credit, did not give Hannah a triumphant look at this official prescription for a remedy he'd already suggested and she'd disdained, but she elbowed him in the ribs anyway, just as if he had.

They checked into the Arizona Hotel, which, like many of the businesses in Indian Rock, was McKettrick owned. Rafe's mother-in-law, Becky Lewis, had run the place for years, with the help of her daughter, Emmeline. Now it was in the hands of a manager, a Mr. Thomas Crenshaw, hired out of Phoenix.

Doss was greeted like a visiting potentate when he walked in, once again carrying Tobias. A clerk was dispatched to take the sleigh and horses to the livery stable, and they were shown, the three of them, to the best rooms in the place.

The quarters were joined by a door in between, and Hannah would have preferred to be across the hall from Doss instead, but she made no comment. While Mr. Crenshaw hadn't gone quite so far as to put them all in the same room, it was clearly his assumption, and probably that of the rest of Indian Rock, too, that she and Doss were intimate. She could imagine how the reasoning went: Doss and his brother's widow shared a house, after all, way out in the country, and heaven only knew what they were up to, with only the boy around. He'd be easy to fool, being only eight years old.

Hannah went bright red as these thoughts moved through her mind.

Doss dismissed the manager and put Tobias on the nearest bed.

"I'll go downstairs and fetch that whisky concoction," he said, when it was just the three of them.

Tobias had never stayed in a hotel and, sick as he was, he was caught up in the experience. He nestled down in the bearskins, cupped his hands behind his head and gazed smiling up at the ceiling.

"Do as you please," Hannah told Doss, removing her heavy cloak and bonnet and laying them aside.

He sighed. "While we're in town, we'd best get married," he said.

"Yes," Hannah agreed acerbically. "And let's not forget to place an order at the feed-and-grain, buy groceries, pay the light bill and renew our subscription to the newspaper."

Doss gave a ragged chuckle and shook his head. "Guess I'd better dose you up with whisky, too," he replied. "Maybe that way you'll be able to stand the honeymoon."

Hannah's temper flared, but before she could respond, Doss was out the door, closing it smartly behind him.

"I like this place," Tobias said.

"Good," Hannah answered irritably, pulling off her gloves.

"What's a honeymoon," Tobias asked, "and how come you need whisky to stand it?"

Hannah pretended she hadn't heard the question.

She'd packed hastily before leaving the house, things for Tobias and for herself, but nothing for a wedding and certainly nothing for a wedding night. If the valises had been brought upstairs, she'd have something to do, shaking out garments, hanging them in the wardrobes, but as it was, her choices were limited. She could either pace or fuss over Tobias.

She paced, because Tobias would not endure fussing.

Doss returned with their bags, followed by a woman from the kitchen carrying two steaming mugs on a tray. She set the works down on a table, accepted a gratuity from Doss, stole a boldly speculative look at Hannah and bustled out.

"Drink up," Doss said cheerfully, handing one mug to Hannah and carrying the other to Tobias, who sat up eagerly to accept it.

Hannah sniffed the whisky mixture, took a tentative sip and was surprised at how good the stuff tasted. "Where's yours?" she asked, turning to Doss.

"I'm not the one dreading tonight," he answered.

Hannah's hands trembled. She set the mug down, beckoned for Doss to follow, and swept into the adjoining room. "What do you mean, tonight?" she whispered, though of course she knew.

Doss closed the door, examined the bed from a distance and proceeded to walk over to it and press hard on the mattress several times, evidently testing the springs.

Hannah's temper surged again, but she was speechless this time.

"Good to know the bed won't creak," Doss observed.

She found her voice, but it came out as a sputter. "Doss McKettrick—"

He ran his eyes over her, which left a trail of sensation,

just as surely as if he'd stripped her naked and caressed her with his hands. "The preacher will be here in an hour," he said. "He'll marry us downstairs, in the office behind the reception desk. If Tobias is well enough to attend, he can. If not, we'll tell him about it later."

Hannah was appalled. "You made arrangements like that without consulting me first?"

"I thought we'd said all there was to say."

"Maybe I wanted time to get used to the idea. Did you ever think of that?"

"Maybe you'll never get used to the idea," Doss reasoned, sitting now, on the edge of the bed he clearly intended to share with her that very night. He stood, stretched in a way that could only have been called risqué. "I'm going out for a while," he announced.

"Out where?" Hannah asked, and then hated herself for caring.

He stepped in close—too close.

She tried to retreat and found she couldn't move.

Doss hooked a finger under her chin and made her look at him. "To buy a wedding band, among other things," he said. She felt his breath on her lips, and it made them tingle. "I'll send a wire to my folks and one to yours, too, if you want."

Hannah swallowed. Shook her head. "I'll write to Mama and Papa myself, when it's over," she said.

Sad amusement moved in Doss's eyes. "Suit yourself," he said.

And then he left her standing there.

She heard him speak quietly to Tobias, then the opening and closing of a door. After a few moments she returned to the next room.

Tobias had finished his medicinal whisky, and his eyelids were drooping. Hannah tucked the covers in around him and kissed his forehead. Whatever else was happening, he seemed to be out of danger. She clung to that blessing and tried not to dwell on her own fate.

He yawned. "Will Uncle Doss be my pa, once you and him are married?" he asked drowsily.

"No," Hannah said, her voice firm. "He'll still be your uncle." Tobias looked so disheartened that she added, "And your stepfather, of course."

"So he'll be sort of my father?"

"Sort of," Hannah agreed, relenting.

"I guess we won't be going to Montana now," Tobias mumbled, settling into his pillow.

"Maybe in the spring," Hannah said.

"You go," Tobias replied, barely awake now. "I'll stay here with Uncle Pa."

It wounded Hannah that Tobias preferred Doss's company to hers and that of her family, but the boy was ill and she wasn't going to argue with him. "Go to sleep, Tobias," she told him.

As if he'd needed her permission, the little boy lapsed into slumber.

Hannah sat watching him sleep for a long time. Then, seeing snow drift past the windows in the glow of a gas streetlamp, she stood and went to stand with her hands resting on the wide sill, looking out.

It was dark by then, and the general store, the only place in Indian Rock where a wedding band could be found, had probably been closed for an hour. All Doss would have to do was rap on the door, though, and they'd open the place to him. Same as the telegraph office, or any other establishment in town.

After all, he was a McKettrick.

A tear slipped down her cheek.

She was a bride, and she should be happier.

Instead she felt as if she was betraying Gabe's memory. Letting down her folks, too, because they'd hoped she'd come home and eventually marry a local man, though they hadn't actually come out and said that last part. Now, because she'd been foolish enough, needy enough, to lie with Doss, not once but twice, she'd have to stay on the Triple M until she died of old age.

A tear slipped down her cheek, and she wiped it away quickly with the back of one hand.

"You made your bed, Hannah McKettrick," she told her reflection in the cold, night-darkened glass of the window, "and now you'll just have to lie in it."

By the time Doss returned, she'd washed her face, taken her hair down for a vigorous brushing and pinned it back up again. She'd put on a fresh dress, a prim but practical gray wool, and pinched some color into her cheeks.

He had on a brand-new suit of clothes, as fancy as the ones the doctor's nephew wore, and he'd gotten a haircut and a shave, too.

She was strangely touched by these things.

"I'd have bought you a dress for the wedding," he told her, staring at her as though he'd never seen her before, "but I didn't know what would fit, and whether you'd think it proper to wear white."

She smiled, feeling a tender sort of sorrow. "This dress will do just fine," she said.

"You look beautiful," Doss told her.

Hannah blushed. It was nonsense, of course—she probably looked more like a schoolmarm than anything else in her stern gray frock with the black buttons coming up to her throat—but she liked hearing the words. Had almost forgotten how they sounded, with Gabe gone.

Doss took her hand, and there was an uncharacteristic shyness in the gesture that made her wonder if he was as frightened and reluctant as she was.

"You don't have to go through with this, Doss," she said.

He ran his lips lightly over her knuckles before letting her hand go. "It's the right thing to do," he answered.

She swallowed, nodded.

"I guess the preacher must be here."

Doss nodded. "Downstairs, waiting. Shall we wake Tobias?"

Hannah shook her head. "Better to let him sleep."

"I'll fetch a maid to watch over him while we're gone," Doss said.

Now it was Hannah who nodded.

He left her again, and this time she felt it as a tearing-away, sharp and prickly. He came back with a plump, older woman clad in a black uniform and an apron, and then he took Hannah's hand once more and led her out of the room, down the stairs and into the office where she would become Mrs. McKettrick, for the second time.

At least, she thought philosophically, she wouldn't have to get used to a new name.

Chapter 9

Present Day

The weather hadn't improved, Sierra noted, standing at the window of Liam's hospital room the next morning. Orderlies had wheeled in a second bed the night before, and she'd slept in a paper gown. Now she was back in the sweats Travis had bought for her, rested and restored.

Dr. O'Meara had already been in to introduce herself, check on Liam's progress and do a work-up of her own, and she'd signed the release papers, too. Sierra liked and trusted the woman, though she was younger than expected, no more than thirty-five years old, with delicate features, very long brown hair held back by a barrette and a trim figure.

Armed with a prescription, Sierra was ready to take her son and leave.

Ready to face Eve, and all the emotional spade work involved.

Or not.

Just as she turned from the window, Travis entered the room, wearing slacks and a blue pullover sweater that accentuated the color of his eyes. He'd said he owned a house in Flagstaff, and Sierra knew he'd gone there to spend the night.

There was so much she *didn't* know about his life, and this was unsettling, although she didn't have the time or energy to pursue it at the moment.

"Travis!" Liam crowed, as though he hadn't expected to see his friend ever again. "I get to go home today!"

The word *home* caught in Sierra's heart like a fish hook. The ranch house on the Triple M was Eve's home, and it was Meg's, but it didn't belong to her and Liam. They were temporary guests, and it had troubled Sierra all along to think Liam might become attached to the place and be hurt when they left.

Travis approached the bed, grinned and ruffled Liam's hair. "That's great," he said. "According to reports, the power is back on, the pantry is bulging, and your grandmother is waiting to meet you."

Sierra felt a wrench at the reminder. So much for thinking she was prepared to deal with Eve McKettrick.

Liam inspected Travis speculatively. "You don't look like a cowboy today," he declared.

Travis laughed. "Neither do you," he countered.

"Yeah, but I *never* do," Liam said, discouraged.

"We'll have to do something about that one of these days soon."

Sierra bristled. She and Liam were committed to staying on the ranch for a year, that was the bargain. Twelve months. The time would surely pass quickly, and she didn't want her son putting down roots only to be torn from that hallowed McKettrick ground.

"Liam looks fine the way he is," she said.

Travis gave her a long, thoughtful look. "True enough," he said mildly. "My buddy Liam is one handsome cowpoke. In fact, he looks a lot like Jesse did, at his age."

Another connection to the storied McKettrick clan. Uncomfortable, Sierra averted her eyes. She'd already gathered Liam's things, but now she rearranged them busily, just for something to do.

Half an hour later, the three of them were in Travis's truck, headed back to the ranch. Liam, buckled in between Travis and Sierra, promptly fell asleep, but his hands were locked around his DVD player. Mentally Sierra clutched the new inhaler, prescribed by Dr. O'Meara, purchased at the hospital pharmacy and tucked away in her bag, just as anxiously.

She had been silent for most of the ride, gazing out at the winter landscape as it whipped past the passenger window.

Travis said little or nothing, concentrating on navigating the icy roads, but Sierra was fully aware of his presence just the same, and in a way that disturbed her. He'd been a rock since Liam's asthma attack, and she was grateful but she couldn't afford to become dependent on him, emotionally or in any other way, and she didn't want her son to, either.

Trouble was, it might be too late for Liam. He adored Travis Reid, and there was no telling what fantasies he'd cooked up in that high-powered little brain of his. He and Travis riding the range, probably. Wearing baseball mitts and playing catch. Going fishing in some pristine mountain lake.

All the things a boy did with a dad.

"Sierra?"

She didn't dare look at Travis, for fear he might see the vulnerability she was feeling. All her nerves seemed to be on the outside of her skin, and they were doing the jingle-bell rock. "What?"

"I was just wondering what you were thinking."

She couldn't tell him, of course. He'd think she was attracted to him, and she wasn't.

Much.

So she lied. "All about Eve," she said.

He chuckled at the flimsy joke, but Sierra gave him points for recognizing an obscure reference to an old movie. Maybe they had a thing or two in common after all.

"I imagine the lady's on pins and needles herself, right about now. She wants to see you and Liam more than anything, I'd guess, but it won't be easy for her."

"I don't *want* it to be easy for her," Sierra answered.

Travis hesitated only a beat or two. "Maybe she has good reasons for what she did."

Sierra's silence was eloquent.

"Give her a chance, Sierra."

She glanced at him. "I'm doing that," she said. "I drove all the way here from Florida. I agreed to stay on the Triple M for a full year."

"Would you have done it if it weren't for the insurance?"

Damn it. He *was* a lawyer. "Probably not," she admitted.

"You'd do just about anything for Liam."

"Not 'just about,'" Sierra said. "*Anything* covers it."

"What about yourself? What would you do for Sierra?"

"Are we going to talk about me in the third person?"

"Stop hedging. I understand your devotion to Liam. I'd just like to know what you'd be doing right now if you didn't have a child, especially one with medical problems."

Sierra glanced at Liam, making sure he was asleep.

"Don't talk about him as though he were somehow…deficient."

"I'm not. He's a great kid, and he'll grow up to be an exceptional man. And I'm still waiting to hear what your dreams are for yourself."

She gave a desultory little chuckle. "Nothing spectacular. I'd like to survive."

"Not much of a life. Not for you and not for Liam."

Sierra squirmed. "Maybe I've forgotten how to dream," she said.

"And that doesn't concern you?"

"Up until now, it hasn't been a factor."

"That's unfortunate. Liam will pattern his attitudes after yours. Is that what you want for him? Just survival?"

"Are you channeling some disincarnate life coach?" Sierra demanded.

Travis laughed, low and quiet. "Not me," he said.

"You're just playing the cowboy version of Dr. Phil, then?"

"Okay, Sierra," Travis conceded. "I'll back off. For now."

"What are *your* dreams, hotshot?" Sierra retorted, too nettled to let the subject alone. "You have a law degree, but you train horses and shovel out stalls for a living."

This time there was no laughter. Travis's glance was utterly serious, and the pain Sierra saw in it made her ashamed of the way she'd spoken to him.

"I guess I had that coming," he said quietly. "And here's my answer. I'd like to be able to dream again. *That's* my dream."

"I'm sorry," Sierra told him, after a few moments had passed. The man had lost his brother in a very tragic way. He was probably doing the best he could, like almost everybody else. "I didn't mean to be unkind. I was just feeling—"

"Cornered?"

"That's a good word for it."

"You must have been burned pretty badly," Travis observed. "And not just by Eve." He looked down at Liam. "Maybe by this little guy's dad?"

"Maybe," Sierra said.

After that, conversation fell by the wayside again, but Sierra did plenty of thinking.

When they arrived at the ranch, all the lights in the house seemed to be on, even though it was barely noon. A glowing tangle of color loomed in the parlor window, and Sierra squinted, sure she must be seeing things.

Travis followed her gaze and chuckled. "Uh-oh," he said. "Looks as if Christmas sneaked back in while we weren't around."

Liam's eyes popped open at the magic word. "Christmas?"

Sierra smiled, in spite of the knot of worry lying heavily in the pit of her stomach. What was Eve up to?

Travis pulled up close to the back door, and Sierra braced herself as it sprang open. There was Eve McKettrick, standing on the top step, a tall, slender woman, breathtakingly attractive in expensive slacks and a blue silk blouse.

"Is *that* my grandma?" Liam asked. "She looks like a movie star!"

She *did* look like a movie star, a young Maureen O'Hara. And Sierra was suddenly, stunningly aware that she'd seen this woman before, in San Miguel, not once, but several times. She'd been a periodic guest at one of the better B&Bs when Sierra was small, and they'd had ice cream together at a sidewalk café near the *casita*, several times.

For a moment Sierra forgot how to breathe.

The Lady. She'd always called Eve "the Lady," and she'd

secretly believed she was an angel. But it had been years since she'd given the memory conscious house room.

Now it all came flooding back, in a breathtaking rush.

Travis shut off the truck and opened the door to get out. "Sierra?" he prompted, when she didn't move.

"Hello!" Liam yelled, delighted, from his place next to Sierra. "My name is Liam and I'm seven!"

Eve smiled, and her vivid green eyes glistened with emotion. "My name is Eve," she said quietly, "and I'm fifty-three. Come here and give me a hug."

Sierra finally came unstuck, opened the passenger-side door and climbed down, planting her feet in the crusty snow. Liam scrambled past her so quickly that he generated a slight breeze.

Eve leaned down to gather her grandson in her arms. She kissed the top of his head and met Sierra's gaze again as she straightened.

"I'll see to the horses," Travis said.

"Don't go," Sierra blurted, before she could stop herself.

Eve steered Liam into the kitchen, watching with interest as Travis rounded the front end of the truck and stood close to Sierra.

"You'll be all right," he told her.

She bit her lower lip, feeling like a fool. It was still all she could do not to grab one of his hands with both of hers and cling like some crazy codependent girlfriend about to be hustled out of town on the last bus of the day.

So long. It's been real.

For a few long moments she and Travis just stared into each other's eyes. He was determined; she was scared. And something *else* was happening, too, something a lot harder to define.

Finally Travis broke the impasse by turning and striding off toward the barn.

Sierra drew a deep breath and marched toward the open door of the kitchen and the woman who waited on the threshold.

"There's a surprise in the living room," Eve said to Liam, once they were all inside and she'd shut the door against the unrelenting cold.

He raced to investigate.

"You're the Lady," Sierra said, stricken.

"The Lady?" Eve echoed, but Sierra could see by the expression in her mother's eyes that it was mere rhetoric.

"The one I used to see in San Miguel."

"Yes," Eve said. "Sit down, Sierra. I'll make tea, and we'll chat."

"Wow!" Liam yelled, from the living room. "Mom, there *is* a Christmas tree in here, with *major* presents under it!"

"Oh, Lord," Sierra said, and sank on to one of the benches at the table.

"They're *all* for me!" Liam whooped.

Sierra watched her mother take Lorelei's teapot from the cabinet, spoon tea leaves into it, fill and plug in the electric kettle. "Christmas presents?" she asked.

Eve smiled a little guiltily. "I had seven years of grandmothering to make up for," she said. "Cut me a break, will you?"

Sierra would have tallied the numbers differently, but there was no point in saying so. "I thought you were an angel," she confessed. "In San Miguel, I mean."

Eve busied herself with the tea-brewing process, stealing the occasional hungry glance at Sierra. "You've certainly grown up to be a beautiful woman," she said. Finally she stopped her puttering, clasped her hands together and practically gobbled Sierra up with her eyes. "It's…it's so wonderful to see you."

Sierra didn't answer.

Liam pounded in from the living room. "Can I open my presents?"

"If it's all right with your mother," Eve said.

Sierra sighed. "Go ahead. And calm down, please. You just got out of the hospital, remember? Overexcitement and asthma do not mix."

Liam gave a shout of delight and thundered off again, ignoring her admonition completely.

The electric kettle whistled, and Eve poured the contents into the antique teapot, and brought it to the table. She selected two cups and saucers from the priceless collection and carried those over, too. Then, at last, looking as nervous as Sierra felt, Eve sat down in the chair at the end of the table.

"How's Liam?" she asked.

"He's fine," Sierra answered. "But he's just getting over a crisis, as you know, so he's going to bed as soon as he finishes opening his presents." The bear and the balloon were in the back of Travis's truck, under the heavy plastic cover, and she imagined her mother ordering them for a grandson she'd never seen.

"So many things to say," Eve fretted, "and I haven't the first idea where to start."

Suddenly Sierra was tired. And *not* so suddenly she was overwhelmed. "Why didn't you tell me who you were— when we met in San Miguel?"

Eve poured tea, warmed beautifully manicured and bejeweled hands around a translucent china cup. "Nothing like cutting to the chase," she said, with rueful appreciation.

"Nothing like it," Sierra agreed implacably.

"If I'd told you who I was, you would have told Hank, and he might have taken you and disappeared again. It took me almost five years to find you the first time, so I wasn't about to let that happen."

Sierra absorbed her mother's words quietly. She *had* mentioned "the Lady" to her father, at least after the first encounter, but if he'd suspected anything, he'd probably dismissed the accounts as flights of a child's imagination. Besides, elegant tourists were common in San Miguel, and they were generous to local children.

"If I'd been in that situation—if it were Liam who'd been snatched away and I'd found him—I'd have taken him home with me."

Eve's eyes filled with tears, but she blinked them back. "Would you?" she challenged softly. "Even if he seemed happy and healthy, and you knew he didn't remember you? Would you simply kidnap him—tear him away from everyone and everything he knew? Without thought for any of the psychological repercussions?"

Sierra blinked. She *would* have been terrified if Eve had stolen her back from Hank, whisked her out of the country in some clandestine way. And she would have had to do exactly that, because even though Sierra's father seemed benignly disinterested most of the time, word would have gotten back to him quickly, had Eve tried to spirit her away. He would have called out the *federales,* as well as the municipal authorities, many of whom were his friends, and Eve would probably *still* be languishing in a Mexican jail.

And she'd had another daughter to consider, as well as a home and a business.

"I've been grown up for quite some time," Sierra pointed out, after long reflection. "What stopped you from contacting me after Dad died and Liam and I came to the States?"

Eve looked down into her cup.

Liam burst into the room, making both women start.

"Look, Mom!" he cried, clutching an expensive telescope in both arms, already attached to its tripod. "I'll be able to see all the way back to the Big Bang with this thing!"

"You're getting too excited," Sierra reiterated, sparing a glance for Eve before rising from her chair. "You'd better go and lie down for a while."

Liam balked, of course. He was seven, faced with unexpected largesse. "But I haven't even opened half my presents!"

"Later," Sierra said. She got up, put a hand on her son's shoulder and steered him toward the back stairs.

He protested all the way, clutching Eve's telescope in the same way he had Travis's DVD player. The stuff *she'd* given him for Christmas, all bought on sale with her tips from the bar, paled by comparison to this bounty, and even though she was glad for him, she also felt a deep slash of resentment.

"Look at it this way," she said a few minutes later, tucking him into bed in a fresh pair of pajamas, the telescope positioned in front of the window, beside the antique one that had been there when they arrived. "You've still got a lot of loot downstairs. Rest awhile, and you can tear into it again."

"Do you promise?" Liam asked suspiciously. "You won't make my grandma take it all back to the store or something?"

"When have I ever lied to you?"

"When you said there was a Santa Claus."

Sierra sighed. "Okay. Name one other time."

"You said we didn't have any family. We've got Grandma and Aunt Meg."

"I give up," Sierra said, spreading her hands. "I'm a shameless prevaricator."

Liam grinned. "If that boy comes back, I'm going to show him *my* telescope!"

A tiny chill moved down Sierra's spine. "Liam," she insisted, "there *is* no boy."

"That's what *you* think," Liam replied, and he looked damnably smug as he settled back into his pillows. "This is his room. This is his bed, and that's his old telescope."

Sierra took off the boy's shoes, tucked him under the faded quilt and sat with him until he drifted off to sleep.

And even then she didn't move, because she didn't want to go downstairs again and hear more well-rehearsed reasons why her mother had abandoned her when she was smaller than Liam.

1919

Hannah couldn't help comparing her second wedding to her first, at least in the privacy of her mind. She and Gabe had been married in the summer, in the side yard at the main ranch house. Gabe's grandfather, Angus, had been alive then and, as head of the McKettrick clan, he'd issued a decree to that effect. There had been a big cake and a band and long improvised tables burdened with food. There had been guests and gifts and dancing.

After the celebration, Gabe had driven her to town in a surrey, and they'd stayed right here at the Arizona Hotel, caught the next day's train out of Indian Rock. Traveled all the way to San Francisco for a honeymoon. Tobias had been conceived during that magical time, and the box of photographs commemorating the trip was one of Hannah's most treasured possessions.

Now she found herself standing in the cramped and cluttered office behind the reception desk, a widow about to become a bride. Only, this time there was no cake, no honeymoon trip to look forward to, and certainly no music and dancing.

Those things wouldn't have mattered, Hannah was certain, if she'd loved Doss and known he loved her. It wasn't the modesty of the ceremony that troubled her, but the coldly practical reasons behind it.

While the preacher droned the sacred words, with Mr. Crenshaw and one of the maids for witnesses, Hannah stole the occasional sidelong glance at her groom.

Doss looked stalwart, determined and impossibly handsome.

What will become of us? Hannah wondered, in silent and stoic despair. She'd pasted a wobbly smile on her face, because she wouldn't have the preacher gossiping afterward, saying she'd looked like a deer with one foot stuck in a railroad track, and the train about to come clackety-clacking round the bend at full throttle.

Oh, no. If she did what she really wanted to do, which was either run or break down and cry, that self-righteous old coot would spread the news from one end of the state to the other, and what a time folks would have with that.

A weeping bride.

A grimly resigned groom.

The talk wouldn't die down for years.

So Hannah endured.

She repeated her vows, when she was prompted, and kept her chin high, her backbone straight and her eyes bone dry. The ordeal was almost over when suddenly the office door banged open and Doss's uncle Jeb strolled in. He was still handsome, though well into middle age, and he grinned as he took in the not-so-happy couple.

"Thought I'd missed it," he said.

Doss laughed, evidently pleased to set eyes on another blood-McKettrick.

The minister cleared his throat, not entirely approving of the interruption, it would seem.

"I now pronounce you man and wife," he said quickly.

"Kiss your bride," Jeb prompted, watching his nephew closely.

Hannah blushed.

Doss kissed her, and she wondered if he'd have remembered to do it at all, if his uncle hadn't provided a verbal nudge.

"No flowers?" Jeb asked, after Doss had paid the preacher and the man had gone. He looked around the office. "No guests?"

"It was a hasty decision," Doss explained.

Hannah blushed again.

"Oh," Jeb said. He shook Doss's hand, whacked him once on the shoulder and then turned to Hannah, gently kissing her cheek. "Be happy, Hannah," he whispered, close to her ear. "Gabe would want that."

Tears brimmed in Hannah's eyes, and this after she'd held up so well, made such an effort to play the happy bride. Did her true feelings show? Or was Jeb McKettrick just perceptive?

She nodded, unable to speak.

"I thought you were down in Phoenix," Doss said to his uncle. If he'd noticed Hannah's tears, he was keeping the observation to himself.

"I came up here to take care of some business at the Cattleman's Bank," Jeb explained. "Arrived on the afternoon train. It's a long ride out to the ranch, and the meeting ran long, so I decided to spend the night here at the hotel and head back to Phoenix tomorrow. I was sitting in the dining room, taking my supper, when somebody mentioned that the two of you were shut up in here with a preacher." He glanced at Hannah again, and she saw concern flash briefly in his eyes. "I decided to invite myself to the festivities. Of course when I tell Chloe about it, she'll say I ought to learn a few manners. After all this time, my wife still hasn't given up on grinding off my rough edges."

Doss slipped an arm around Hannah's waist. "We're glad you came," he told Jeb. "Aren't we, Hannah?"

She didn't answer right away, and he had the gall to pinch her lightly under her ribs, through the fabric of her sadly practical gray dress.

"Yes," she said.

"Where's Tobias?" Jeb asked. "Chloe'll skin me if I don't bring back a detailed report. That woman likes to know everything about everybody. How much the boy's grown, how he's doing with his lessons, and all that."

"He's down with a cold," Doss said. "That's why we brought him to town. So he could see the doctor."

"And you just decided to get married while you were here?"

Doss colored up.

Hannah was stricken to silence again.

Jeb smiled. "The boy's here in the hotel, then?"

Hannah nodded, still mute.

Jeb's gaze shifted to Doss. "Why don't you go up there and see if he's agreeable to a visit from his old Uncle Jeb?" he said.

Doss hesitated, then nodded and left the room.

"I'm going to ask Doss the same thing I'm about to ask

you," Jeb said, the moment they were alone with the door closed. "What's going on here?"

Hannah swallowed painfully. "Well, it just seemed sensible for us to get married."

"Sensible?"

"Both of us living out there on the ranch, I mean. You know how folks…speculate about things like that."

"I know, all right," Jeb answered. "Chloe and I stirred up plenty of talk in our day. I guess I just figured if there'd been a wedding in the offing, the family would have heard something about it before now."

"Doss wired his folks, and I was going to write to mine—"

"You're both adults and it's your business what you do," Jeb said. "Do you love Doss, Hannah?"

She fell back on something she'd said to Tobias, out at the ranch, when he'd asked a similar question. "He's family," she replied.

"He's also a man. A young one, with his whole life ahead of him. He deserves a wife who's glad to be his wife."

Hannah lifted her chin. "A few minutes ago you told me Gabe would want this. Doss and me married, I mean. And you're probably right. So I did it as much for him as anybody."

"There's only one person you ought to please in a situation like this, Hannah, and that's yourself."

"Tobias needs Doss."

"I don't doubt that's true. Losing Gabe was hard on everybody in this family, but it was worse for you and Tobias. The question on my mind right now is, do you need Doss, Hannah?"

Hannah needed her new husband, all right, but not in a way she was going to discuss with his uncle—or anyone else on the face of the earth, for that matter. "I'll see that he's happy, if that's what you're worried about," she said, and felt her cheeks burn again, fearing she'd revealed exactly what she'd been so determined to keep secret.

"He'll be happy," Jeb said, with such remarkable certainty that Hannah wondered if he knew something she didn't. "Will you?"

"I'll learn to be," she answered.

Jeb placed his hands on her shoulders, squeezed lightly and kissed her forehead. Then, without another word, he went out, leaving Hannah standing there alone, full of confusion and sorrow.

She was waiting in the lobby when Doss came downstairs, some minutes later, looking shy as a schoolboy. Evidently, Jeb had already spoken to him and was with Tobias now.

Doss tried to smile but fell a little short. Now that they were actually married, he apparently didn't know what to say, and neither did Hannah. They were making the best of things, both of them, and it shouldn't have been that way.

"I guess we ought to have some supper," Doss said. "Tobias has already eaten. The maid went down to the kitchen and brought him up a meal while we were—"

Hannah looked down at her feet. "You deserve somebody who loves you," she said softly, miserable with shame.

Doss put a finger under her chin and raised her head, so he could look into her eyes. "I don't know if your mind and heart love me, Hannah McKettrick," he said solemnly, with no trace of arrogance, "but your body does. And maybe it will teach the rest of you to feel the same way."

She took a gentle hold on the lapels of his new suit,

bought just for the wedding. "Gabe would want this," she said. "Our being married, I mean."

Doss swallowed. "I loved my brother," he told her gravely, "but I don't want to talk about him. Not tonight."

Hannah wept inside, even though her eyes were dry. "All right," she agreed.

He led her into the dining room, and they both ordered fried chicken dinners. It was an occasion, to eat a restaurant meal, almost as unusual, in Hannah's life, as getting married. She was starved, after a long and hectic day, and yet the food tasted like sawdust from the first bite.

Jeb appeared, just as they were trying to choke down dessert. Chocolate cake, normally Hannah's favorite, with powdered sugar icing.

"Tobias," Jeb announced, "is spending the night in the room next to mine. I've already made arrangements for the maid to stay with him."

Hannah laid down her fork, relieved not to have to pretend to eat any longer. It was almost as hard as pretending to be happy, and she didn't think she could manage both.

"I guess that's all right," she allowed.

Doss looked down at his plate. He hadn't eaten much more than Hannah had, though, like her, he'd made a good show of it. Making illicit love on the ranch was one thing, she realized, and being married was quite another. Was he as nervous about the night to come as she was?

Jeb congratulated them both and left.

Their plates were cleared away.

Doss paid the bill.

And then there was nothing to do but go upstairs and get on with their wedding night.

Chapter 10

Tobias's bed was empty, and his things had been removed. Hannah glanced nervously at Doss, now her husband, and put a hand to her throat.

He sighed and loosened his string tie, then unbuttoned his collar. If there had been whisky in that hotel room, Hannah was sure he would have poured himself a double and downed it in a gulp. She felt moved to touch his arm, soothe him somehow, but the urge died aborning. Instead she stood rigid upon the soles of her practical high-button shoes, and wished she'd put her foot down while there was still time, called the whole idea of getting married for the damn fool notion that it was, stopped the wedding and let the gossips say what they would.

She was miserable.

Doss was miserable.

What in the world had possessed them?

"We could get an annulment," she said shakily.

Doss's gaze sliced to her, sharp enough to leave the thick air quivering in its wake. "Oh, I'd say we were past that," he retorted coldly. "Wouldn't you?"

Hannah's cheeks burned as smartly as if they'd been chapped by the bitter wind even then rattling at the windows and seeping in as a draft. "I only meant that we haven't...well...consummated the marriage, and—"

He narrowed his eyes. "I remember it a little differently," he said.

Damn him, Hannah thought fiercely. He'd been so all-fired set on going through with the ceremony—it had been his idea to exchange vows, not hers—and now he was acting as though he'd been wooed, enticed, trapped.

"I will thank you to remember this, Doss McKettrick— I didn't seduce you. You seduced me!"

He hooked a finger in his tie and jerked at it. Took an angry step toward her and glared down into her face. "You could have said no at any time, Hannah," he reminded her, making a deliberate effort to keep his voice down. "My recollection is that you didn't. In fact, you—"

"Stop," Hannah blurted. "If you're any kind of gentleman, you won't throw that in my face! I was—we were both—lonely, Doss. We lost our heads, that's all. We could find the preacher, tell him it was a mistake, ask him to tear up the license—"

"You might as well stand in the middle of Main Street, ring a cowbell to draw a crowd, and tell the whole damn town what we did as do that!" Doss seethed. "And what's going to happen in six months or so, when your belly is out to here with my baby?"

Hannah's back teeth clamped together so hard that she had to will them apart. "What makes you so sure there is a baby?" she demanded. "Gabe and I wanted more children after Tobias, but nothing happened."

Doss opened his mouth, closed it again forcefully. Whatever he'd been about to say, he'd clearly thought better of it. All of a sudden Hannah wanted to reach down his throat and haul the words out of him like a bucket from a deep well, even though she knew she'd be just as furious to hear them spoken as she was right then, left to wonder.

For what seemed to Hannah like a very long time, the two of them just stood there, practically nose to nose, glowering at each other.

Hannah broke first, shattered against that McKettrick stubbornness the way a storm-tossed ship might shatter on a rocky shore. With a cry of sheer frustration, she turned on one heel, strode into the next room and slammed the door hard behind her.

There was no key to turn the lock, and nothing to brace under the knob to keep Doss from coming after her. So Hannah paced, arms folded, until some of her fury was spent.

Her gaze fell on her nightgown, spread by some thoughtful soul—probably the maid who had looked after Tobias while she and Doss were downstairs ruining their lives—across the foot of the bed.

Resignation settled over Hannah, heavy and cold as a wagonload of wet burlap sacks.

I might as well get this over with, she thought, trying to ignore the unbecoming shiver of excitement she felt at the prospect of being alone with Doss, bared to him, surrendering and, at the same time, conquering.

Resolutely she took off her clothes, donned the nightgown and unpinned her hair.

And waited.

Where was Doss?

She sat down on the edge of the mattress, twiddling her thumbs.

He didn't arrive.

She got up and paced.

Still no Doss.

She was damned if she'd open the door and invite him in after the way he'd acted, but the waiting was almost unbearable.

Finally Hannah sneaked across the room, bent and peered through the keyhole. Her view was limited, and while she couldn't actually see Doss, that didn't mean he wasn't there. If he'd left, she would have heard him— wouldn't she?

She paced again, briskly this time, muttering under her breath.

The room was growing cold, and not just because there was no fire to light. She marched over to the radiator, under the window, and cranked on the handle until she heard a comforting hiss. Something caught her eye, through the night-darkened glass, as she straightened, and she wiped a peephole in the steam with the sleeve of her nightgown. Squinted.

Was that Doss, standing in the spill of light flowing over the swinging doors of the Blue Garter Saloon down at the corner? His shape and stance were certainly familiar, but the clothes were wrong—or were they? Doss had worn a suit to the wedding, and this man was dressed for the open range.

Hannah stared harder, and barely noticed when the tip of her nose touched the icy glass. Then the man struck a match against the saloon wall, and lit a cheroot, and she saw his face clearly in the flare of orange light.

It was Doss, and he was looking in her direction, too. He'd seen her, watching him from the hotel room window like some woebegone heroine in a melodrama.

No. It couldn't be him.

They had a lot to settle, it was true, but this was their wedding night.

Hannah clenched her fists and turned from the window for a few moments, struggling to regain her composure as well as her dignity. By now everyone in Indian Rock knew about the hurry-up wedding, knew they ought to be honeymooning, she and Doss, even if they hadn't gotten any further than the Arizona Hotel. If Doss passed the evening in the Blue Garter Saloon, tonight of all nights—

She whirled, fumbling to pull up the sash, meaning to call out to him, though God only knew what she'd say. But before she could open the window, he turned his back on her and went right through those saloon doors. Hannah watched helplessly as they swung on their hinges and closed behind him.

Present Day

Sierra stood with her hands on her hips, studying the January Christmas tree. The lights shimmered and the colors blurred as she took in the mountain of gifts still to be unwrapped, the wads of bright paper, the expensive loot Liam had already opened.

Sweaters. A leather coat, reminiscent of Travis's. Cowboy boots and a hat. A set of toy pistols. Why, there was more stuff there than she'd been able to give Liam in all seven years of his life, let alone for one Christmas.

Eve had done it all, of course. The decorating, anyway. She might have brought the presents with her from Texas, after sending some office minion out to ransack the high-end stores.

Did it mean she genuinely cared, Sierra wondered, or was she merely trying to buy some form of absolution?

Sierra sensed Eve's presence almost immediately, but it was a few moments before she could look her in the eye.

"The pistols might have been an error in judgment," Eve conceded quietly, poised in the doorway as though unsure whether to bolt or stay and face the music. "I should have asked."

"The whole thing is an error in judgment," Sierra responded, her insides stretched so taut that they seemed to hum. "It's too much." She turned, at last, and faced her mother. "You had no right."

"Liam is my grandson," Eve pointed out, and the very rationality of her words snapped hard around Sierra's heart, like some giant rubber band, yanked to its limits and then let go.

"You had no right!" Sierra repeated, in a furious undertone.

To her credit, Eve didn't flinch. "What are you so afraid of, Sierra? That he'll like me?"

Sierra swayed a little, suddenly light-headed. "Don't you understand? I can't give Liam things like this. I don't want him getting used to this way of life—it will be too hard on him later, when we have to leave it all behind."

"*What* way of life?" Eve persisted. Her attitude wasn't confrontational, but it was obvious that she intended to stand her ground. It was all so easy for her, with her money and her power. She could make grand gestures, but Sierra would be the one picking up the pieces when she and Liam made a hard—and inevitable—landing in the real world.

"The *McKettrick* way of life!" Sierra burst out. "This big house, the land, the money—"

"Sierra, you *are* a McKettrick, and so is Liam."

Sierra closed her eyes for a moment, struggling to regain her composure. "I agreed to come here for one reason and one reason only," she finally said, with hard-won moderation, "because my son needs medical attention, and I can't afford to provide it. But the agreement was for one year—*one year*, Eve—and we won't be here a single day after that condition is met!"

"And after that one year is up, you think I'm just going to forget that I have a second daughter and a grandson? Whether you're still too blasted stubborn to accept my help or not?"

"I don't *need* your help, Eve!"

"Don't you?"

Sierra shook her head, more in an effort to clear her mind than to deny Eve's meaning, found a chair and sank slowly into it. "I appreciate what you're doing," she said, after a few slow, deep breaths. "I really do. But if you expect anything beyond what we agreed to, there's a problem."

Eve moved to the fireplace, took a long match from the mantel and lit the newspaper and kindling already stacked in the grate. She waited until the flames caught, crackling merrily, then added more wood from the basket next to the hearth. "What did Hank tell you about me, Sierra?" she asked quietly, turning back to study Sierra's face. "Did he tell you I was dead? Or did he say I didn't want you?"

"He didn't have to say you didn't want me. That was perfectly obvious."

"Was it?" Eve dusted off a place on the raised hearth and

sat down, folding her hands loosely in her lap. "I want to know what he told you, Sierra. After all these years, after all he took from me, I think I have the right to ask."

"He never said you didn't want me. He said you didn't want *him*."

"Well, that was certainly true enough."

Sierra swallowed. "I guess I was five or six before I noticed that other little girls had mothers, not just fathers. I started asking a lot of questions, and I guess he got tired of it. He said there'd been an accident, that you'd been badly hurt and you'd probably have to go to heaven."

Eve lowered her head then, wiped furtively at her cheek with the back of one hand. "Who would have thought Hank Breslin would say *two* true things out of three in the same lifetime?"

Sierra slid to the edge of her chair, eager and tense at the same time.

Don't get sucked in, she heard Hank say, as clearly as if he'd been standing in the room, taking part in the conversation.

"There *was* an accident?" Sierra asked on a breath, mentally shushing her father. Just asking the question meant a part of her hadn't believed Hank, but this, like so many other things, would have to be considered later, when she was alone. And calm.

Eve nodded.

"What kind of accident?"

Eve visibly collected herself, sitting up a little straighter. Her eyes seemed focused on a past Sierra hadn't been a part of. "I was having lunch at an outdoor café in San Antonio— with my lawyer, as it happens. We'd found you after two years of searching, or at least the investigators we'd hired had, and I'd seen you with my own eyes, in San Miguel.

Spoken to you. I wanted to contact Hank, work out some kind of arrangement—"

A peculiar, buzzing sensation dimmed Sierra's hearing.

"Your father had to be handled very carefully. I knew that. It would have been like Hank to take you deeper into Mexico—even into South America—if he'd gotten spooked, and he'd have been a lot more careful to disappear for good the second time."

Sierra waited, willing her head to clear, listening with everything in her. "The accident?" she prompted, very softly.

"A car jumped the curb, crashed through the stucco wall between the tables and the street. We were sitting just on the other side. My lawyer—his name was Jim Furman and he had a wife and five children—was killed instantly. I was in traction for weeks, and it took me another year and a half just to walk again."

The incident sounded like something from a soap opera, and yet Sierra knew it was true. Her stomach churned as horrific images, complete with a soundtrack of crashes and screams, flashed through her mind.

"By the time I recovered," Eve went on, after a few long moments of silence, "I knew it was too late, that I'd have to wait until you were older, when you could make choices for yourself. You were happy and healthy and very bright. You were still so young. I couldn't just waltz into your life and say, 'Hello, I'm your mother.' I was still afraid of what Hank might do, and I was struggling to rebuild my life after the accident. Meg was spending most of her time with nannies as it was, and I had to turn the company over to the board of directors because I couldn't seem to focus my mind on anything. With all that going on, how could I take you away from the only home you knew, only to turn around and leave you in the care of strangers?"

Sierra sat quietly, drawing careful, measured breaths, taking it all in. "Okay," she said, finally. "I can buy all that. But there's still a pretty big gap between then and six weeks ago, when you finally contacted me."

Eve was silent.

So I was right, Sierra thought bitterly. There's more.

"I was ashamed," Eve said.

"Ashamed?"

Silence.

"Eve?"

"After the accident," Eve went on, her voice pitched so low that Sierra had to lean forward to hear, "I took a lot of pain pills. They became less and less effective, while the pain seemed to get worse, so I started washing them down with alcohol."

Sierra's mouth dropped open. "Meg never mentioned—"

"Of course she wouldn't," Eve said. "It was my place to tell you and, besides, you don't just email something like that to somebody. What was she supposed to say? 'Oh, by the way, Mother is a pill-freak and a drunk'?"

"My God," Sierra whispered.

"I was intermittently clean and sober," Eve went on. "But I always fell off the wagon eventually. If Rance hadn't stepped in after I took control of the company again, God bless him, I probably would have run McKettrickCo into the ground."

"Rance?"

"Your cousin."

Sierra struggled to hit a lighter note, because they both needed that. "Which branch of the family tree was *he* hatched in?"

Eve smiled weakly, but with a kind of gratitude that pinched Sierra's heart in one of the tenderest places. "Rance is descended from Rafe and Emmeline," she answered. "Rafe was old Angus's son."

"It took you all this time to get your life back together?" Sierra asked tentatively, after yet another lengthy silence had run its course.

"No," Eve said. Color stained her cheeks. "No, I've been on the straight-and-narrow for ten years or so. I said it before, Sierra—I was ashamed. So much time had gone by, and I didn't know what to say. Where to start. It became a vicious cycle. The longer I put it off, the harder it was to take the risk."

"But you finally tracked me down again. What changed?"

"I didn't have to track you down. I always knew where you were." Eve sighed, and her shoulders stooped a little. "I found out about Liam's asthma, and I couldn't wait any longer." She paused, straightened her back again. "Fair is fair, Sierra. I've answered the hard questions, though I realize there will be more. Now, it's your turn. Why did you spend your life moving from place to place, serving cocktails, instead of putting down roots somewhere and making something of your life?"

Sierra considered her past and felt something sink within her. She'd taken a few night courses, here and there. She'd used her fluent Spanish with customers and volunteered, when she could, at some of Liam's schools. But she'd never had roots or any direction except "away."

"There's nothing wrong with serving cocktails," she said, trying not to sound defensive and not quite succeeding.

"Of course there isn't," Eve readily agreed. "But why didn't you go to college?"

Sierra smiled ruefully. "There are only twenty-four hours in a day, Eve. I had a child to support."

Eve nodded reflectively. And waited.

Sierra waited, too.

"That doesn't explain all the moving from place to place," Eve said at last.

"I wish I had a ready answer," Sierra said, after considerable searching. "I guess I just always had this low-grade anxiety, like I was trying to outrun something."

Eve took that in silently.

"Why did you divorce my father?" Sierra asked. She hadn't seen the question coming, but she knew it had been fermenting in the back of her mind for a long time. Whenever it arose, she pushed it down, told herself it didn't matter, but this was a time for truth, however painful it might be.

"Hank," Eve replied carefully, "was one of those men who believe they're entitled to call the shots, by virtue of possessing a penis. He quit his job a month after we were married—he sold condominiums—planning to become a golf pro at the country club. He never actually got around to applying, of course, and it would have been quite a trick to get hired anyway, since there wasn't an opening and he didn't know a nine-iron from a putter."

Sierra moistened her lips, uncomfortable.

"He was an emotional lightweight," Eve went on, quietly relentless. "But you knew that, didn't you, Sierra?"

She *had* known, but admitting it aloud was beyond her. She did manage a stiff nod, though.

"How did he earn a living?" Eve asked. "Even in Mexico, there's rent to pay, and food costs money."

Sierra blushed. Hank had tended bar at the corner cantina on occasion, and played a lot of backroom poker. The house they'd lived in belonged to Magdalena. "He just seemed to…coast," she said.

"But you had clothes, shoes. Medical care. Birthday cakes. Toys at Christmas?"

Sierra nodded. Her childhood had been marked by two things—a vague, pervasive loneliness, and a bohemian kind of freedom. At last, realization struck. "*You* were sending him money somehow."

"I was sending *you* money, through Hank's sister, from the day he took you away. Nell, your aunt, was pretty clever. She always cashed the check, then wired it to Hank, through various places—sometimes a bank, sometimes the courtesy desk in a supermarket, sometimes a convenience store. Eventually my investigators picked up the trail, but it wasn't so easy in those days."

Sierra flashed on a series of memories—her dad walking away from one of the many *cambio* outlets in San Miguel, where tourists cashed traveler's checks and exchanged their own currency for *pesos*. She'd been very small, but she'd seen him folding a wad of bills and tucking it into his pocket, and she'd wondered. Now she felt a stab of shame on his behalf, recalling his small, secret smile.

Eve was right. Hank Breslin had felt *entitled* to that money, and while he'd always made sure Sierra had the necessities, he'd never been overly generous. In fact, it had been Magdalena not Hank, who had provided extras. Sweet, plump, spice-scented Magdalena of the patient smile and manner.

Sierra's emotions must have been clearly visible in her face. Eve rose, came over to her and laid a hand on her shoulder. Then, without another word, she turned and left the room.

Sierra had loved her father, for all his shortcomings,

and seeing him in this light destroyed a lot of fantasies. Even worse, she knew that Adam, Liam's father, had been a younger version of Hank. Oh, he'd had a career. But she'd been an amusement to him and nothing more. He'd been willing to sell her out, sell out his own wife and daughters, for a good time. Like Hank, he'd felt entitled to whatever pleasures happened to be available, and to hell with all the people who got hurt in the process.

For a moment she hated Adam, hated Hank, hated all men.

She'd been attracted to Travis Reid.

Now she took an internal step back, and an enormous *no!* boiled up from her depths, spewing like a geyser and then freezing solid at its height.

Chapter 11

Doss returned to the room well after midnight, smelling of cigar smoke and whisky. Hannah lay absolutely still, playing possum, watching through her lashes as he shed his hat and coat and kicked off his boots. Maybe he knew she was awake, and maybe he was fooled. She wasn't about to give herself away by speaking to him and, besides, she didn't trust herself not to tear into him like a shrew. Once the first word tumbled out of her mouth, others would follow, like a raging horde with swords and cudgels.

On the other hand, if he had the pure audacity to think, for one blessed moment, that he was going to enjoy his husbandly privileges, she'd come up out of that bed like a tigress, claws bared and slashing.

She breathed slowly, deeply and regularly, making her body soft.

Doss moved to the bureau, filled the china wash basin from the pitcher provided, and washed. She waited, in delicious dread, for him to undress, since he obviously intended to sleep in that room, in that bed, with her.

To her surprise, relief and complete annoyance, he remained fully clothed, sat down on the edge of the bed, and stretched out on top of the covers.

"I know you're not asleep," he said.

Hannah bit down hard on her lower lip. Though her eyes were shut tight, tears squeezed beneath her lids. Gabe would never have done such a thing to her, never have gone out on their wedding night to smoke and drink whisky and carouse with bad companions. Never have subjected her to such a public humiliation.

A sob shook her body. "I hate you, Doss McKettrick," she said.

He sighed, sounding resigned. If he'd apologized, if he'd put his arm around her and held her close, she would have felt better, in spite of it all, but he didn't. He kept to his own side of the bed, a weight atop the blankets, within touching distance and yet as remote from Hannah as Indian Rock was from the Eastern Seaboard.

"We'll have to make the best of things," he told her.

She rolled on to her side, with her back to him. "No, we won't," she whispered snappishly, "because as soon as Tobias is well enough, he and I are getting on the train and leaving for good."

"If it's a comfort to you," Doss replied, "then you just go ahead and think that. The truth of the matter is, you're my wife now, and as long as there's a chance you're carrying my baby, you're not going anywhere."

"I hate you," Hannah repeated.

"So you said," Doss answered, with a long-suffering sigh.

"I'll leave if I want to."

"I'll bring you back. And believe me, Hannah, I can keep up the game as long as you can."

"Then you mean to keep me prisoner." Hannah spoke into the darkness, and it seemed like a shadow, cast by her very soul, that gloom, rather than mere night, with the moon following its ancient course and the stars in their right places. It was, in that moment, as if the sun would never rise again.

"I won't lock you in the cellar, if that's what you mean," Doss told her. "I won't mistreat you or force my attentions on you, and I'll be civil as long as you are. But until I know whether you're pregnant or not, you're staying right here."

Hannah huddled deeper into the covers, feeling small, and wiped away a tear with the edge of the sheet. "I hope I'm not," she whispered. "I hope I'm not carrying your baby."

Even as she said the words, though, she knew they were the frayed and tattered weavings of a lie. She longed for another child, a girl this time, yearned to feel a life growing and stirring under her heart. She just didn't want Doss McKettrick to be the father, that was all.

She cried quietly, lying there next to Doss. Cried till her pillow was wet. She'd have bet money she wouldn't sleep a wink, but at some point she succumbed.

The next thing she knew, it was morning.

Doss's side of the bed was empty, and fat, lazy flakes of snow drifted past the window. The room was cold, but she could hear voices in the next room and the clattering of silverware against dishes. The aroma of bacon teased her nose; her stomach clenched with hunger, and then she was nauseous.

"No," she said, in a whisper, sitting bolt-upright.

Yes, her body replied. She'd had the same reaction within ten days of Tobias's conception.

Tobias appeared in the doorway, with Doss standing just behind him.

"You want some breakfast, Ma?" the boy asked. He looked slightly feverish, but stronger, too, and he was wearing a new suit of clothes—black woolen trousers, a blue-and-white-plaid flannel shirt, even suspenders.

The whole picture turned hazy, and the mention of food, let alone the smell, sent bile scalding into the back of Hannah's throat. Avoiding Doss's gaze, she gulped and shook her head.

Doss laid a hand on Tobias's shoulder and gently steered him back into the other room. He pulled the door closed, too, and the instant he did, Hannah rolled out of bed, pulled the chamber-pot out from underneath, distractedly grateful that it was clean, and threw up until she collapsed onto the hooked rug, utterly spent.

She heard the door open again, heard Doss say her name, but she couldn't respond. She just lay there, on her side, wretched and empty, as though she'd lost her soul as well as the remains of her wedding supper.

Doss knelt, gathered her in his arms, and put her back into bed, covering her gently. He fetched a basin of tepid water from the other room, along with a washcloth, and cleaned her up. When that was done, he handed her a glass, and she rinsed her mouth, then spat into the basin.

"I'll get the doctor," he said.

She shook her head. "Don't," she answered, and the word came out raspy and raw. "I just need to rest."

Doss drew up a chair, sat beside the bed, keeping a silent vigil. Hannah wished he'd go away, and at the same time she dreaded his leave-taking with the whole echoing hollowness of her being.

A maid came in, replacing the fouled chamber pot, washing out the basin, taking the pitcher away and bringing it back full. Although she cast the occasional worried glance in Hannah's direction, the woman never said a word, and when she was gone, Doss remained.

He plumped the pillows behind Hannah's back and adjusted the radiator to warm the room.

"I thought I'd bundle Tobias up," Doss ventured, at some length, "and take him down to the general store. Get him some things to play with, maybe a book to read."

Hannah was in a strange, dazed state, weak all over. "You see that he doesn't take a chill," she muttered. Common sense said Tobias ought to stay in, out of the weather, and if she'd been herself, she would have insisted on that. As things stood, she didn't have the strength, and anyway she knew the boy was desperate to get out, if only for a little while.

Doss stood, tucked the covers in around her. To look at them, Hannah thought, anybody would have thought they were a normal husband and wife, people who loved each other. "Can I bring you something back?"

"No," she said, and closed her eyes, drifting.

When she opened them again, Doss was back, with the chilly scent of fresh air surrounding him. She could hear Tobias in the next room, chatting with somebody.

"Feeling better?" Doss asked. He was holding a parcel in his hands, wrapped in brown paper and tied with string.

"Thirsty," Hannah murmured.

Doss nodded, set the package aside and brought her

another glass of water, this time from the pitcher on the bureau.

She drank it down, waited, and was pathetically pleased when it didn't come right back up.

"You'd best have something to eat, if you can," Doss said.

Hannah nodded. Suddenly she was ravenous.

He left again, was gone so long that she wondered if he meant to hunt down the food, skin it, and cook it over a slow fire. Tobias wandered in, cheeks pink from the cold, eyes bright. "Uncle Jeb wants to buy me a sandwich," he told her. "Downstairs, in the restaurant. Is it all right if I go?"

Hannah smiled. "Sure it is," she said.

Tobias drew a step nearer, moving tentatively, as though approaching something fragile enough to fall over and break at the slightest touch. "Doss says you're not dying," he said.

"He's right," Hannah answered.

"Then what's the matter? You never stay in bed in the daytime."

Hannah extended her hand, and after hesitating Tobias took it. "I'm being lazy," she said, giving his fingers a squeeze.

He clung for a moment, then let go. His eyes were wide and worried. "I heard you being sick," he told her.

A door opened in the distance, and Hannah heard Doss and Jeb exchange quiet words, though she couldn't make them out. "I'll be fine by tomorrow," she promised. "You go and have that sandwich. It isn't every day you get to eat in a real restaurant."

Tobias relaxed visibly. He smiled, planted a kiss on her forehead and fled, nearly colliding with Doss in the doorway. Doss tightened his grip on the tray of food he was carrying. A teapot, with steam wisping from the spout. A bowl of something savory and fragrant.

Hannah's nose twitched, and her formerly rebellious stomach growled an audible welcome.

"Chicken and dumplings," Doss said, with a grin.

He set the tray carefully on Hannah's lap. Poured her a cup of tea and probably would have spoon-fed her, too, if she hadn't taken charge of the situation.

"Thank you," she said, trying to square this attentive man with the one who had left her alone on their wedding night to visit the Blue Garter Saloon.

"You're welcome," he replied. He sat down to watch her eat, and his gaze strayed once or twice to the package on the nightstand, still wrapped and mysterious.

Hannah did not assume it was for her, since she'd clearly refused Doss's earlier offer to bring her something from the mercantile, but she was curious, just the same. The shape was booklike, and before she'd married Gabe, she'd read so much her mother and father used to fret that her eyes might go bad. After she became a wife, she was too busy, and when Gabe went away to war, she found she couldn't concentrate on the printed word. Letters were all she'd been able to manage then.

She ate what she could and sipped her tea, hot and sweet and pale with milk, and Doss took the tray away, set it on the bureau. Jeb and Tobias had long since gone downstairs for their midday meal, and except for the sounds of wagons passing in the street below and the faint hiss of the radiator, the room was silent.

Doss cleared his throat and shifted uncomfortably in his chair. "Hannah, about last night—"

"Stop," Hannah said quickly, and with as much force as

she could manage, given her curiously fragile state. The teacup rattled in its saucer, and Doss leaned forward to take it from her, set it next to the parcel. He looked resigned, and a little impatient.

Hannah leaned back on her pillows, fighting another spate of tears. She would have sworn she'd cried them all out the night before, after Doss came back from the Blue Garter and told her he wouldn't let her go home to Montana, but here they were, burning behind her eyes, threatening to spill over.

"I figure you know what this means, your being sick like this," Doss said presently, and in a tone that said he wouldn't be silenced before he'd finished his piece. "That's the only reason I didn't bring the doctor over here, first thing."

Hannah closed her eyes. Nodded.

"I know you'd rather it was Gabe sitting here," he went on. "That he'd be the one who fathered that child, the one taking you home to the ranch, the one bringing Tobias up to be a man. But the plain fact of the matter is, it'll be me doing those things, Hannah, and you might as well make peace with that."

She didn't speak, because she couldn't. She tried to summon up Gabe's image in her mind, but it wouldn't come to her. All she saw was Doss, coming in after a night at the Blue Garter, taking off his coat and hat and boots, lying down beside her on the bed, keeping a careful distance.

He retrieved the parcel from the nightstand and laid it in her lap. She listened, despondent, as he left the room, closed the door quietly behind him.

She ought to refuse the package, throw it against the wall or into Doss's face when he came back. But some part of her wanted a gift, something frivolous and imprac- tical, chosen purely to bring a smile to her face.

She barely remembered what it was like to smile, with- out thinking about it first, without deciding she ought to, because it was called for or expected.

Her hands trembled as she undid the string, wound it into a little ball to keep, turned back the brown paper, which she would carefully fold and save against some fu- ture need, to find that Doss had indeed given her a book. Her breath caught at the beauty of the green leather cover. The title, embossed in shining gold, seemed to sing be- neath the tips of her fingers.

The Flowers of Western America, Native and Imported: An Illustrated Guide.

Hannah held the thick volume reverently, savoring the anticipation for a few moments before opening it to look at the title page, memorize the author's name, as well as that of the artist who'd done the original woodcuttings and metal etchings for the pictures.

When she couldn't bear to wait another moment, Han- nah turned that page, expecting to read the table of con- tents. Instead, there was a note, written in Doss's strong, clear handwriting.

On the occasion of our marriage, and because I know you long for spring, and your garden. Doss McKettrick January 17, 1919

An emotion Hannah could not recognize swelled in her throat, fairly cutting off her breath. She traced his name with her eyes and then with the tip of her index finger. Doss McKettrick. As if men by that name were common as thorns in a blackberry thicket, and any one of them might be her husband. As if he had to be sure she knew which one would give her a book and which had noticed how fiercely, how desperately she craved that first green stirring in the cold earth and in the bare-limbed branches of trees.

Did he know how she listened for the breaking of the ice on the pond far back in the woods behind the house? How she watched the frigid sky for the first brave birds, carrying back the merry little songs she pined for, in the secret regions of her heart, when the snow was just beginning to seep into the ground?

Hannah closed the book, held it against her chest.

Then she opened it again and carefully turned to the first illustration, a lovely colored woodcut of purple crocuses, blooming above a thin snowfall. She drank them in, surfeited herself on lilacs and climbing roses, sweet williams and peonies.

Doss had given her flowers, in the dead of winter. Just looking at the pictures, she could imagine their distinctive scents, the shape of their petals, the depth upon depth of their various colors—everything from the palest of whites to the fathomless purples and crimsons.

She gobbled them all greedily with her eyes, page after page of them, tumbled flower-drunk into sleep and dreamed of them. Dreamed of spring, of trout quickening in the creeks, of green grass and of fresh, warm breezes teasing her hair and tingling on her skin.

When she wakened, drowsy and confused, the room was lavender with twilight, and a rim of golden light edged the lower part of the door. She heard Doss and Tobias talking in the next room, knew by a series of decisive clicks that they were playing checkers. Tobias gave a shout of triumphant laughter, and the sound seemed so poignant to Hannah that tears thickened in her throat.

She got up, used the chamber pot, washed her hands at the basin. She rummaged for her flannel wrapper, pulled it on and crossed the cold wooden floor to the door.

Opened it.

Tobias and Doss both turned to look at her.

Tobias smiled, delighted.

Doss looked shy, as though they'd just met. He got up suddenly, came to her, took her arm. Escorted her to a chair.

"Don't fuss," she scolded, but it was after the fussing was through.

"I beat Uncle Doss four times!" Tobias crowed.

"Did you?" Hannah asked, deliberately widening her eyes.

Doss went over to the other bed, pulled the quilt off, made Hannah stand, wrapped her up like renderings in a sausage skin and sat her down again.

What am I to make of you, Doss McKettrick? she asked silently.

"I'll go down and order us some supper," Doss said.

"Has your uncle Jeb gone?" Hannah asked Tobias, when they were alone.

Tobias nodded, kneeling on the floor, stacking checker pieces into red and black towers that teetered on the wooden board. "He took the afternoon train back to Phoenix. Said to tell you he hoped you'd be feeling better soon."

"I wish I could have said goodbye," Hannah said, but it wasn't the complete truth. She'd not been eager to face Doss's uncle; he was half again too wise and, besides, he must have known that her new husband had spent much of their wedding night in a saloon, just to avoid her. He'd never have mentioned it, of course, but she'd have seen the knowledge in his eyes.

Would he tell his wife, Chloe, when he got home? Would she, in turn, tell Emmeline and Mandy and the other McKettrick women? Get them all feeling sorry for poor Hannah?

She'd know soon enough. Concerned letters would begin arriving, probably in the next batch of mail, full of wary congratulations and carefully worded questions. The Aunts, as both Gabe and Doss had always referred to them, were not gossips, so she needn't fear scandal from that quarter, but they would have plenty of private discussions among themselves, and they'd give Doss what for when they returned to the Triple M in the spring, settling into their houses on all parts of the ranch, throwing open windows and doors, planting gardens and entertaining a steady stream of children and grandchildren.

Hannah thought she would have welcomed even their curiosity, if it meant the long winter was over.

"Ma?"

Hannah realized she'd let her mind wander and turned her attention to Tobias, who was studying her closely and clearly had something of moment to say. "Yes, sweetheart?"

"Is Uncle Doss my pa, now that you and him are married?"

Hannah blinked. Took in a slow breath and took her time letting it out. "I told you before, Tobias. Doss is still your uncle. Your father will always be—your father."

Tobias's forehead creased as he frowned. "But Pa's dead," he said.

Hannah sighed. "Yes."

"Uncle Doss is alive."

"He certainly is."

"I want a pa. Somebody to take me fishin' and teach me how to shoot."

"Uncles can do those things." Hannah didn't want Tobias within a mile of a gun, but she didn't have the strength to fight that battle just then, so she let it go.

"It isn't the same," Tobias reasoned.

"Tobias, there are some things in this life a person has to accept. Your father is gone. Doss is your uncle, not your pa. You'll just have to make the best of that."

"The best would be if he was my pa instead of my uncle."

"Tobias."

"You said once that Uncle Doss would be my stepfather if you got married. Now, you're his wife. So if you leave off the 'step' part, that makes him my pa."

Hannah rubbed her temples with her fingertips.

Tobias beamed. Eight years old, and he could argue like a senior senator at a campaign picnic.

The door to the corridor opened, and Doss came in, followed by two maids carrying trays laden with food.

"Pa's back," Tobias said.

Hannah's gaze locked with Doss's. Something passed between them, silent and charged.

Hannah looked away first.

Chapter 12

"You need time to absorb all this," Eve told Sierra the next morning at the breakfast table. Eve had made waffles for them all, and everyone had eaten with a hearty appetite. Now Liam was upstairs, dressing for his first visit to Indian Rock Elementary School—Sierra planned to register him but wasn't sure he was ready for a full day of class—and Travis had given the ranch house a wide berth ever since their return from Flagstaff the previous afternoon. "So I'm going to leave," Eve finished, gently decisive.

Sierra, who had spent a largely sleepless night, had mixed feelings about Eve's going away. On the one hand, there were so many things she wanted to know about her mother—things that had nothing to do with their long separation. What kind of books did she read? What places had she visited? Had she loved anyone before or after Hank Breslin? What made her laugh? Did she cry at sad movies, or was she a stone-realist, prone to saying, "It's only a story"?

On the other, Sierra craved solitude, to think and reflect and sort what she had learned into some kind of sensible order. She wanted to huddle up somewhere, with her arms around her knees and decide what she believed and what she didn't.

"Okay," she said.

"There is one thing I want to show you before I go," Eve said, rising from the kitchen table and crossing to the china cabinet to lean down and open one of the drawers. She brought out a large, square object, wrapped in soft blue flannel, and set it before Sierra, who had shoved her plate and coffee cup aside in the meantime and wiped her part of the tabletop clean with a checkered cloth napkin.

Sierra's heart raced a little and, at a nod from Eve, she folded back the flannel covering to reveal an old photo album.

"These are your people, Sierra," Eve said quietly. "Your ancestors. There are journals and other photographs in the attic, and they need cataloging. It would be a great favor to me if you would gather them and make sure they're properly preserved."

"I can do that," Sierra said. Her hand, resting on the album cover, trembled a little, with both anticipation and a certain reluctance to get involved. Biologically she had a connection with the faces and names between the battered leather covers of the book, but in terms of real life, she was just passing through. She couldn't afford to forget that.

Eve laid a hand on her shoulder. "Sorry about the Christmas tree," she said with a slight smile. "I was the one who put it up, and I should be the one to take it down, but the plane will be arriving in an hour, so there isn't time. The corresponding boxes are in the basement, at the bottom of the steps."

Sierra nodded a second time. Liam had finished opening his presents the night before, and the mess had been cleaned up. Putting away the tree, like sorting photos and journals, would be a bittersweet enterprise. She hadn't looked closely at the ornaments, but she supposed they were heirlooms, like so many other things in that house, each one with a meaning she could never fully understand.

So many McKettrick Christmases, and she hadn't been a part of any of them. With Hank the holiday had gone almost unnoticed, although there were always a few gifts. Sierra hadn't felt deprived at the time, because she hadn't known that other people made more of a fuss.

The McKettricks, most likely, made a lot of fuss, not just over Christmas, but other holidays, too. They'd probably kept happy secrets at Yuletide, sung carols around that haunted piano, toasted each other with eggnog poured into cut-glass cups that were older than any of them. . . .

Enough, Sierra told herself sternly. That time is gone. You missed it. Get over wishing you hadn't.

Eve bent to kiss Sierra on top of the head, then went upstairs to the big master bedroom, to pack up her things.

Sierra cleared the table and loaded the dishwasher, but her gaze kept straying to the album. It was as though the people in the photographs, all long dead, were calling to her.

Get to know us.

We are part of you. We are part of Liam.

Sierra shook off the feeling as a nostalgic whim. She was as much a Breslin as a McKettrick, after all. She knew how to be Hank's daughter, but being Eve's was a whole new ball game. It was as though she had an entirely separate and unfamiliar identity, and that person was a stranger to her.

Liam bounded down the back stairs as she was rinsing out the coffee carafe, beaming at the prospect of starting school. He'd been thrilled to learn, through the research he and Sierra had done on Meg's computer, after last night's present-unwrapping frenzy, that there was no "Geek Program" at Indian Rock Elementary.

He wanted to be an "ordinary" kid.

Not sick.

Not gifted.

"Just regular" as he'd put it.

Sierra's heart ached with love and empathy. As a child, home taught by Magdalena, she'd yearned to go to a real school, but Hank had forbidden it.

Now she realized Hank had been hiding her, probably fearful that some visitor, expatriate parent or teacher might catch on to the fact that he'd snatched her, and look into the matter.

For a moment she indulged in a primitive anger so deep that it was visceral, causing her stomach to clench and her jaws to tighten.

"Grandma says we'd better take Meg's car into town today, because ours is a heap, not to mention a veritable eyesore," Liam reported cheerfully. "When are we going to get a new car?"

"When I win the lottery or get a job," Sierra said, deliberately relaxing her shoulders, which had immediately tensed, and taking Liam's new "cowboy" coat, as he'd dubbed it, down from the peg. While she would have objected if she'd known Eve was out buying all those gifts, let alone wrapping them and putting them under a fully decorated Christmas tree, she was glad of this one. It was made of leather and lined with sheepskin, well beyond her budget, and it would definitely keep her little boy warm.

Just then Eve came back, bundled up for winter weather herself, and carrying a small, expensive suitcase in one hand. Her coat was full length and black, elegantly cut and probably cashmere.

"We're in the process of opening a branch office of McKettrickCo in Indian Rock," she announced, evidently unabashed that she'd been eavesdropping. "Keegan is heading it up, but I'm sure there will be a place for you in the organization if you want one. You do speak Spanish, don't you?"

"Keegan," Sierra mused mildly, letting the indirect job offer slide, along with the reference to her language skills, at least for the moment. "Another McKettrick cousin?"

"Descended from Kade and Mandy," Eve confirmed, smiling slightly and nodding toward the album. "It's all in the book."

"How are you getting back to the airstrip—or wherever your jet is landing?" Sierra asked, shrugging into her coat, which looked like something from the bottom of a grungy bin at a thrift store, compared to the ones Eve and Liam were decked out in.

"Travis is taking me in his truck," Eve said, setting her suitcase down by the door, heading to the china cabinet to pluck a set of keys from a sugar bowl, taking Sierra's hand, opening it and placing them on her palm. "Use the SUV. That wreck of yours won't make it out of the driveway, if it starts at all."

Sierra hesitated a moment before closing her fingers around the keys. "Not to mention that it's a veritable eyesore," she said pointedly, but with a little smile.

"You said it," Eve replied brightly. "I didn't."

"Yes, you did," Liam countered. "Upstairs, you told me—"

Outside Travis honked the truck horn.

Eve touched her grandson's neatly groomed hair. "Give your old granny a hug," she said. "I'll be back in a few weeks, and if the weather is good, maybe you'd like to take a ride in the company jet."

Liam let out a whoop.

Sierra didn't get a chance to protest, because Travis rapped lightly, opened the back door and took up Eve's suitcase. He gave Sierra a nod for a greeting and grinned down at Liam.

"Hey, cowpoke," he said. "Lookin' good in that new gear."

Liam preened, showing off the coat. "I wanted to wear the hat, too," he replied, "but Mom said I might lose it at school."

"The world," Travis replied, with a longer glance at Sierra, "is full of hats."

"What's that supposed to mean?" Sierra asked, feeling defensive again.

Travis sighed. A look passed between him and Eve. Then he simply turned, without answering and headed for the truck.

Eve hugged Liam, then Sierra.

Moments later she and Travis were in the truck and barreling away.

Sierra found the door leading into the garage—cleverly hidden in back of the pantry, like the architectural afterthought it surely was—and assessed her sister's shining red SUV. Liam strained to reach the button on the wall, and the garage door grumbled up on its rollers, letting in a shivery chill.

Her station wagon was parked outside, behind the SUV, and Sierra muttered as she started Meg's vehicle, after she and Liam were both buckled in, and maneuvered around the eyesore.

1919

Despite the bitter cold, Hannah sat well away from Doss as they drove home in the sleigh two days after the wedding, Tobias cosseted between them.

She was married.

Each time her thoughts drifted in that direction, she started inwardly, surprised all over again.

She was a wife—but she certainly didn't feel like one.

Doss remained silent for the greater part of the journey, his gloved hands gripping the reins with the ease of long practice. Hannah felt his gaze on her a couple of times, but when she looked in his direction, he was always watching the snow-packed trail ahead.

By the time they reached the ranch, Hannah sorely wished she could simply crawl into bed, pull the covers up over her head and remain there until something changed.

It was an indulgence ranch women were not afforded.

Doss drew the team and sleigh up close to the house, lifted a half-sleeping Tobias from the seat and carried him in. Hannah got down on her own, bringing her valise, the flower book tucked safely inside among her dirty clothes, and followed stalwartly.

The kitchen was frigidly cold.

Doss pulled the string on the lightbulb in the middle of the room as he passed, heading for the stairs with Tobias.

Hannah rose above an inclination to turn it right back off again. She set her valise down and made for the stove. By the time Doss returned, she had a fire going and lamps lighted. She'd fetch some eggs from the spring house, she decided, provided that Willie had gathered them during their absence, and make an omelet for their supper. Perhaps she'd fry up some of the sausage she'd preserved last fall, and make biscuits and gravy, too.

"I'll see to the team," Doss said.

"Where do you suppose Willie's got to?" Hannah asked. She'd seen no sign of the hired man when they were driving in, and she feared for her chickens, along with the livestock in the barn. Like many laborers, Willie was a drifter, and might have taken it into his head to kick off the traces and take to the road anywhere along the line.

"I saw him when we came in," Doss answered, opening the door to go out again. "Out by the bunkhouse, stacking firewood."

Hannah gave a sigh of relief. In the next moment, she wanted to tell Doss to stay inside where it was warm, that she'd have the coffee ready in a few minutes, but it would have been a waste of breath. He was a rancher, born and bred, and that meant he looked after the cattle and horses first and saw to his own comforts later, when the work was done.

"Supper will be on the table in half an hour," she said, as though she were a landlady in a boarding house and he a paying guest, planning the briefest of stays. "Willie's welcome to join us, if he wants."

Doss nodded, raised his coat collar around his ears and went out.

Sometime later, he returned alone. Hannah had already fetched the eggs from the spring house, and they were scrambled, cooked and waiting on a platter in the warming oven above the stove. The kitchen was snug, and the softer light of lanterns glowed, replacing the glare of the overhead bulb.

"Willie's gone on back to the main ranch house," he said. "But he thanks you kindly for the invite to supper."

Hannah wiped her hands on her apron and took plates from the china cabinet to set the table. That was when she noticed the album lying there, as though someone had been perusing it and intended to come back and look some more later.

She stopped in her tracks.

Doss, in the act of shedding his coat and hat, followed her gaze.

"What's the matter, Hannah?" he asked, with a quiet alertness in his voice.

"The album," she said.

"What about it?" Doss asked, passing her to approach the stove. He poured himself a cup of coffee and came to stand beside her.

"Willie wouldn't have gone through our things, would he?"

Doss shook his head. "Not likely it would even have occurred to him to do that," he said. "Judging by how cold it was in here when we got home, he probably didn't set foot in the house once he'd finished off that chicken soup you made before we left."

Hannah wrung her hands, took a step toward the table and then paused. "Do you...do you ever get the feeling we're not alone in this house?" she asked, almost whispering the words.

"No," Doss said, with conviction.

"It was bad enough when the teapot kept moving. Now, the album—"

"Hannah." He touched her arm. "You sound like Tobias, going on about seeing a boy in his room."

"Maybe," Hannah ventured to speculate, almost breathless with the effort of speaking the words aloud, "he's not imagining things. Maybe it wasn't the fever."

Doss cupped Hannah's elbow in one hand and steered her to the table, letting go only to pull back a chair. It was pure fancy, of course, but as Hannah sat down, it seemed to her that the album, fairly new and reverently cared for, was very old. The sensation lasted only a moment or so, but it was so powerful that it left her feeling weak.

"We've all been under a strain, Hannah," Doss reasoned. "One of us must have gotten the album out and forgotten about it."

She looked up into his face. "Did you?" she challenged softly.

He paused, shook his head.

"I know I didn't," she insisted.

"Tobias, then," Doss said.

"No," Hannah replied. "He was too sick."

Doss set his coffee on the table, sat astride the bench, facing her. "There's a simple explanation for this, Hannah. Somebody might have come up from one of the other places, let themselves in."

As close as the McKettricks were, they didn't go into each other's houses when no one was at home. If one of them had wanted to see the album, they'd have said so. Anyway, the aunts and uncles were all in Phoenix, their children grown and gone. The people who looked after their places wouldn't have considered snooping like this, even if they'd been interested, which seemed unlikely.

"The biscuits will burn if you don't take them out of the oven," Hannah said, staring at the album, almost expecting it to move on its own, float through the air like a spirit medium's trumpet at a séance.

Doss got up, crossed the room and rescued the biscuits. The sausage gravy was done, warming at the back of the stove, so he retrieved one of the plates Hannah had gotten out, filled it for her and brought it to the table.

"Tobias will be hungry," she said, thinking aloud. .

"I'll see to him," Doss answered. "Eat."

Hannah moved the album out of the way and pulled the plate toward her, resigned to taking her supper, even though she didn't want it. Doss brought her silverware, then filled another plate for Tobias and took it downstairs.

When he returned, he dished up his own meal and joined Hannah at the table. She was still staring at her scrambled eggs, sausage gravy and biscuits.

"Eat," he repeated.

She took up a fork. "There's someone here," she said. "Someone we can't see. Someone who moves the teapot and now the album, too."

"Let's assume, for a moment, that that's true," Doss ruminated, tucking into his food with an energy Hannah envied. "What do you plan to do about it?"

Hannah swallowed a bite of tasteless food. "I don't know," she answered, but it wasn't the complete truth. An idea was already brewing in her mind.

They finished their supper.

Hannah cleared the table, put the album back in its drawer in the china cabinet, and went upstairs to look in on Tobias while Doss washed the dishes.

Her son was sitting up in bed when she entered his room, his supper half-eaten and set aside on the bedside table. "The boy's not here," he said. "I wonder if he's gone away."

Hannah frowned. "What boy?" she asked, even though she knew.

"The one I see sometimes. With the funny clothes."

Hannah stroked her boy's hair. Sat down on the edge

of his bed. "Does this boy ever speak to you? Does he have a name?"

Tobias shook his head. His eyes were large in his pale face. The trip back from Indian Rock had been hard on him, and Hannah was both worried about her son and determined not to let on.

"We mostly just look at each other. I reckon he's as surprised to see me as I am to see him."

"Next time he shows up, will you tell me?"

Tobias bit his lower lip, then nodded. "You believe me?"

"Of course I do, Tobias."

"Pa said he was imaginary. When we talked about it, I mean."

Hannah sighed. "Tobias, Doss is your uncle, not your pa."

Suddenly, Tobias's eyes glistened with unshed tears. "Why won't you let him be my pa?" he asked. "He's your husband, isn't he? If you can have a husband, why can't I have a pa?"

Had Tobias been older, Hannah thought, she might have explained that Doss wasn't a real husband, that theirs was a marriage of convenience, but he was still far too young to understand.

In point of fact, she didn't entirely understand the situation herself.

"A woman can have more than one husband," she said cautiously. "A boy has only one father. And your father was Gabriel Angus McKettrick. I don't want you to forget that."

"I won't forget," Tobias said. "You can wash my mouth out with soap, if you want to, but I'm still going to call Uncle Doss my pa. I've got enough uncles—Jeb and Kade and Rafe, and John Henry, too. What I need is a pa."

Hannah was too exhausted to argue, and she knew

she wouldn't win anyhow. "So long as you promise me you will never forget who your real father is," she said. "And I would appreciate it if you would include your uncle David—my brother—in that list of relations you just mentioned."

Tobias brightened and put out one small hand for a shake. "It's a deal," he agreed. "I like Uncle David. He can spit a long way."

"Go to sleep," Hannah told him with a smile, reaching to turn down the wick in the lantern next to his bed.

"I didn't wash my face or brush my teeth," he confessed, settling back on to his pillows.

"Just this once we'll pretend you did," she said.

The lamp went out.

She kissed his forehead, found it blessedly cool and tucked the covers in close around him. "Good night, Tobias," she said.

"Good night, Ma," Tobias replied with a yawn.

He was probably asleep before she reached the door.

She'd hoped Doss would have turned in by the time she went downstairs, so she wouldn't have to be alone with him in the intimacy of evening, but he was right there in the kitchen, with the bathtub set out in the middle of the floor and buckets and kettles of water heating on the stove.

"I just came down to say good night," she lied. Actually, she'd been planning to sit up awhile, pondering her plan. It wasn't much, but she was bound and determined to find out something about the strange goings-on in that house.

"You can have this bath if you want," Doss told her. "I can always take one later."

"You have it," Hannah said, even though she would have loved to soak the chill out of her bones in a tub of hot water. She wondered if he was planning to share her bed, but she'd have broken the ice on top of the horse trough and stripped bare for a dunking before asking him outright.

He simply nodded.

"Don't forget to bank the fire," she said.

He grinned. "I never do, Hannah," he reminded her.

She turned, blushing a little, and went back upstairs. Entering her room, the one she'd shared with Gabe, she exchanged her clothes for a nightgown. She took her hair down, brushed it, plaited it into a long braid, trying all the while not to imagine Doss right downstairs, naked as the day he was born, lounging in that tub in front of the stove.

Would he join her later?

He was her legal husband, and he had every right to sleep beside her. She, on the other hand, had every right to turn him away, wedding band or none.

Would she?

She honestly didn't know, and in the end, it didn't matter.

She put out her lamp, threw back the covers on her bed and stretched out, waiting and listening.

Presently she heard Doss climb the stairs, walk along the hallway and pass her room.

His door closed moments later.

Hannah told herself she was relieved, and then cried herself into a fitful sleep.

Present Day

The roads had been plowed, and Sierra was secretly proud of the way she handled the SUV. She'd grown up in Mexico, after all, and spent the last few years in Florida, which precluded driving in snow. This was an accomplishment.

At the elementary school, she got Liam registered and watched as he rushed off to join his class before she could even suggest that he start slowly. His eagerness left her feeling a little bereft.

She shook that off. He had his inhaler. The school nurse had been apprised of his asthma. She had to let go.

She would be living on the Triple M for a year, per her agreement with Eve. Might as well drive around a bit, see what the town was like.

Thirty minutes later she'd seen it all.

The supermarket. The library. The Cattleman's Bank. Two cafés, three bars, a gas station. A dry cleaners, and the ubiquitous McDonald's. The Indian Rock Historical Society. A real estate firm. A few hundred houses, many of them old and, at the edge of town, a spanking-new office complex with the word McKettrickCo inlaid in colored stone over a gleaming set of automatic doors.

I'm sure there will be a place for you in the organization, if you want one, she heard Eve's voice say.

Slowing the car, she studied the place, imagined herself going inside, in her jeans, sweatshirt and ratty coat, her hair combed in a slap-dash method, no mirror required. Face bare of makeup. "Hi, there," she would say to her cousin Keegan, who would no doubt be less than thrilled to see her but manage a polite greeting, anyway. "My name is Sierra and, what do you know? Turns out, I'm a McKettrick, just like you. Go figure. Oh, and by the way, my mother says you're to give me a job. Top-dollar salary and all the fringe benefits, if you don't mind."

She smiled ruefully at the thought. "Of course, all I

know how to do is serve cocktails and speak Spanish," she might add. "No problem, I'm sure."

She pulled up in front of the Cattleman's Bank, patted her purse, which contained a few hundred dollars in traveler's checks, all the money she had in the world, and went in to open a checking account.

"You already have one, Ms. McKettrick," a perky young teller told her, after a few taps on her computer keyboard. The girl's eyes widened as she peered at the screen. "It's pretty substantial, too."

Sierra frowned, momentarily puzzled. "There must be some mistake. I've only been in town a few days, and I haven't—"

And then it struck her. Eve had been up to her tricks again.

The teller turned her pivoting monitor around so Sierra could read the facts for herself. The bottom line made her catch hold of the counter with both hands, lest she faint dead away.

Two million dollars?

"Of course you'll need to sign a signature card," the clerk said, still chipper. "Do you have two forms of personal identification?"

"I need to use your telephone," Sierra managed to say. The floor was still at an odd tilt, and her knuckles hurt where she gripped the edge of the counter.

The teller blinked. "You don't carry a cell phone?" she marveled, in a tone usually reserved for people who think they've been abducted by aliens and subjected to a lot of very painful and explicit medical procedures.

"No," Sierra said, trying not to hyperventilate, "I do not carry a cell phone."

"Over there," the teller said, pointing to a friendly looking nook marked off in brass letters as the Customer Comfort area.

Sierra made her way to the telephone, rummaged through her purse for Eve's cell number and dialed. The operator came on and informed her the call was long distance, and there would be charges.

"Make it collect," Sierra snapped.

One ring. Two. Eve was probably still in flight, aboard the company jet, with her phone shut off. Sierra was about to give up when, after the third ring, her mother chimed, "Eve McKettrick."

"I have a bank account with two million dollars in it!" Sierra whispered into the receiver, bent around it like someone calling a 900 number during a church service.

"Yes, dear," Eve said sweetly. "I know."

"I will not accept—"

"Your trust fund?"

Sierra sucked in her breath. Almost choked on it. "My *trust fund?*"

"Yes," Eve answered. "You also have a share in McKettrickCo, of course."

Sierra swallowed, carefully this time. "I will not take your charity."

"Tell it to your grandfather," Eve responded, unruffled. "Of course, you'll need a clairvoyant to help, because he's been dead for fifteen years."

Sierra held the receiver away from her, stared at it, jammed it to her ear again. "My grandfather left me *two million* dollars?"

"Yes," Eve said. "We kept it safely tucked away in Switzerland, so your father wouldn't get his paws on it."

Sierra closed her eyes.

"Sweetheart?" her mother asked, sounding concerned now. "Are you still there?"

"Yes," Sierra breathed. She could have walked away from all that money. She really could have—if not for Liam. "Why didn't you tell me about this, when you were at the house?"

"Because I knew you weren't ready to hear it, and I didn't want to waste precious time arguing."

Sierra swallowed. "How come you can talk on a cell phone in flight?"

Eve laughed. "Because I patch the number into the phone onboard the plane before takeoff," she answered. "I'm quite the technological whiz. Any more questions?"

"Yes. What am I supposed to do with two million dollars?"

Chapter 13

1919

By the time Hannah came downstairs, Doss had built up the fire, brewed the coffee and left for the barn, like he did every morning. She put on Gabe's old coat—there was nothing of his scent left in it now—and made a trip to the privy, then the chicken house. She was washing her hands in a basin of hot water when Doss came in from doing the chores.

"I guess I'll drive the sleigh down and look in on the widow Jessup again," he said. "This cold snap might outlast her firewood."

"You'll have a good, hot breakfast first," Hannah told him. "While I'm fixing it, why don't you get some preserves from the pantry and pack them up? Mrs. Jessup especially loves those cinnamon pears and pickled crab apples I put up for Christmas."

Doss nodded, a grin crooking one corner of his mouth in a way that made Hannah feel sweetly flustered. "How's Tobias today?"

"He's sleeping in," she said, cracking eggs into a bowl, keeping her gaze averted with some difficulty. "And don't think for a moment you're going to take him with you. It's too cold and he's worn-out from yesterday."

She'd thought Doss was in the pantry, but all of a sudden his hands closed over her shoulders, startling her so that she stiffened.

He turned her around to face him. Looked straight into her eyes.

Her heart beat a little faster.

Was he about to kiss her?

Say something important?

She held her breath, hoping he would. Hoping he wouldn't.

"Before he went back to Phoenix, Uncle Jeb said we ought to help ourselves to some hams from the smokehouse down at Rafe and Emmeline's place," he said. "A side of bacon, too. That means I'll be gone a little longer than usual."

Hannah merely nodded.

They stood, the two of them facing each other for a long moment.

Then Doss let go of Hannah's shoulders, and she turned to whip the eggs and slice bread for toasting. He found a crate and filled it with provisions for the widow Jessup.

After he'd gone, Hannah carried a plate up to Tobias, who seemed content to stay in bed with one of his many picture books.

"I'm getting worried about that boy," Tobias told Hannah solemnly. "He ought to be back by now."

"I'm sure you'll see him again soon," Hannah said moderately. "Remember, you promised to let me know right away when you do."

He nodded, looking glum.

She kissed his forehead and went out, leaving the door open so she'd hear if he called for her. What he needed most right now was rest, and good food to build his strength. When Doss got back with the bacon and hams, she'd make up a special meal.

Downstairs Hannah tidied the kitchen, washed the dishes, dried them and put them away. When that was done, she built up the fire and went to the china cabinet to open the top drawer. The album was there, where it belonged, but a little shiver went up her spine at the sight of it, just the same.

She reached past it, found the small leather-bound remembrance book Lorelei and Holt had sent her for a Christmas present. The cover was a rich shade of blue, the pages edged in shiny gold.

She hadn't written a word in the journal, hadn't even opened it. She hadn't wanted to record her grief, hadn't wanted to make it real by writing it down in dark, formal letters.

Now she had something very different in mind. She carried the remembrance book to the table, and then went to the study for a bottle of ink and a pen. The room was chilly. She rarely went there, because it always brought back memories of Gabe, sitting at the desk, reading or pondering over a ledger.

It was especially empty that day; though, strangely, it was Doss's absence Hannah felt most keenly, not Gabe's. She collected the items she needed and hurried out again.

Back in the kitchen she found a rag to wipe the pen

clean. When she was finished she opened the ink and turned to the first page.

She bit her lower lip, dipped the pen, summoned up all her resolve and began to write.

My name is Hannah McKettrick. Today's date is January 19, 1919...

Present Day

The first thing Sierra noticed when she got back to the house later that morning—with a load of groceries and a head spinning with possibilities now that she was rich—was that Travis wasn't around. The second thing was that the album Eve had brought out to show her was gone.

She'd left it on the kitchen table, and it had vanished.

She paused, holding her breath. Listening. Was there someone in the house?

No, it was empty. She didn't need to search the rooms, open closet doors, peer under beds, to know that.

Her practical side took over. She brought in the rest of the supermarket bags and put everything away. Put on a pot of coffee. Made a tuna salad sandwich and ate it.

Only when she'd rinsed the plate and put it in the dishwasher did she walk over to the china cabinet and open the top drawer, as Eve had done earlier that morning.

The album was back in its place.

Sierra frowned.

Invisible fingers played a riff on her spine, touching every vertebra.

She closed the drawer again.

She would look at the photographs later. Combine that with the job of cataloging the ones stored in the attic.

She brought the Christmas boxes up from the basement, carried them into the living room. Carefully and methodically removed and wrapped each ornament. Some were obviously expensive, others were the handiwork of generations of children.

By the time she'd put them all away and dismantled the silk tree, it was time to drive into town and pick Liam up at school. Backing the SUV out of the garage, she almost ran over Travis, who had the hood up on the station wagon and was standing to one side, fiddling with one of its parts.

He leaped out of her path, grinning.

She slammed on the brakes, buzzed down the window on the passenger side. "You scared me," she said.

Travis laughed, leaning in. "*I* scared *you?*"

"I wasn't expecting you to be standing there."

"I wasn't expecting *you* to come shooting out of the garage at sixty-five miles an hour, either."

Sierra smiled. "Do you always argue about everything?"

"Sure," he said, with an affable shrug of his impressive shoulders. "Gotta stay sharp in case I ever want to practice law again. Where are you headed in such a hurry, anyway?"

"Liam's about to get out of school for the day."

"Right," Travis said, stepping back.

"Do you want to come along?"

Now what made her say *that?* She liked Travis Reid well enough, and certainly appreciated all he'd done to help, but he also made her poignantly uncomfortable.

He must have seen her thoughts playing out in her face. "Maybe another time," he said easily. "Eve told me you were going to take down the Christmas tree. It's a big sucker, so I'll lug it back to the basement if you want."

"That would be good. The coffee's on—help yourself."

Travis grinned. Nodded. Stepped back from the side of the SUV with exaggerated haste.

As she drove away, Sierra wasn't thinking about her two-million-dollar trust fund, the vanishing teapot, the piano that played itself, teleporting photo album or even Liam.

She was thinking about the hired help.

Peering through his new telescope at the night sky, Liam felt that familiar shiver in the air. He knew, even before he turned around to look, that the boy would be there.

And he was. Lying in the bed, staring at Liam.

"What's your name?" the boy asked.

For a moment, Liam couldn't believe his ears. He wasn't scared, but his throat got tight, just the same. He'd planned on telling the boy all about his first day at the new school, and a lot of other things, too, as soon as he showed up, but now the words got stuck and wouldn't come out.

"Mine's Tobias."

"I'm Liam."

"That's an odd name."

Liam straightened his back. "Well, 'Tobias' is pretty weird, too," he countered.

Tobias tossed back the covers and got out of bed. He was wearing a funny flannel nightgown, more suited to a girl than a boy. It reached clear past his knees. "What's that?" he asked, pointing to Liam's telescope.

Liam patiently explained the obvious. "Wanna look? You can see all the way to Saturn with this thing."

Tobias peered through the viewer. "It's bouncing around. And it's *blue!*"

"Yep," Liam agreed. "How come you're wearing a nightie?"

Tobias looked up. His eyes flashed, and his cheeks got red. "This," he said, "is a night*shirt*."

"Whatever," Liam said.

Tobias gave him the eyeball. "Those are mighty peculiar duds," he announced.

"Thanks a lot," Liam said, but he wasn't mad. He figured "duds" must mean clothes. "Are you a ghost?"

"No," Tobias said. "I'm a boy. What are you?"

"A boy," Liam answered.

"What are you doing in my room?"

"This is *my* room. What are *you* doing here?"

Tobias grinned, poked a finger into Liam's chest, as though testing to see if it would go right through. "My ma told me to let her know first thing if I saw you again," he said.

Liam put out his own finger and found Tobias to be as solid as he was.

"Are you going to?" he asked.

"I don't know," Tobias said. He put his eye to the viewer again. "Is that *really* Saturn, or is this one of those moving-picture contraptions?"

1919

Hannah blew on the ink until it dried. Then she wiped the pen clean, sealed the ink bottle and closed the remembrance book.

Now that she'd written in it, she felt a little foolish, but what was done was done. She took the book back to the china cabinet and placed it carefully beneath the top cover of the family album.

She was just mounting the steps to go and check on Tobias when she realized he was talking to someone. She couldn't make out the words, just the conversational tone of his voice. He spoke with an eager lilt she hadn't heard in a long time.

She stood absolutely still, straining to listen.

"Ma!" he yelled suddenly.

She bolted up the stairs, along the hallway, into his room.

She found him lying comfortably in bed, wide awake, his eyes shining with an almost feverish excitement. "I saw the boy," he said. "His name is Liam and he showed me Saturn."

"Liam," Hannah repeated stupidly, because anything else was quite beyond her.

"I said it was a strange name, Liam, I mean, and he said Tobias was a weird thing to be called, too."

Hannah opened her mouth, closed it again. Twisted the hem of her apron in both hands. Her knees felt as though they'd turned to liquid, and even though she'd asked Tobias to let her know straight away if he saw the boy again, she realized she hadn't been prepared to hear it. She wished Doss were there, even though he'd probably be a hindrance, rather than a help.

"Ma?" Tobias sounded worried, and his eyes were great in his face.

She hurried to his bed, sat down on the edge of the mattress, touched a hand to his forehead.

He squirmed away. "I'm not sick," he protested. "I saw Saturn. It's blue, and it really does have rings."

Hannah withdrew her hand, and it came to rest, fluttering, at the base of her throat.

"You don't believe me!" Tobias accused.

"I don't know what to believe," Hannah admitted softly. "But I know you're not lying, Tobias."

"I'm not seeing things, either!"

"I— It's just so strange."

Tobias subsided a little, falling back on to his pillows with a sigh. "He told me lots of stuff, Ma," he said, his voice small and uncertain.

Hannah took his hand, squeezed it. Tried to appear calm. "What 'stuff,' Tobias?" she managed, after a few slow, deep breaths.

"That Saturn has moons, just like the earth does. Only, it's got four, instead of just one. One of them is covered in ice, and it might even have an ocean underneath, full of critters with no eyes."

Hannah swallowed a slight, guttural cry of pure dismay. "What else?"

"People have boxes in their houses, and they can watch all kinds of stories on them. Folks act them out, like players on a stage."

Tears of pure panic burned in Hannah's eyes, but she blinked them back. "You must have been dreaming, Tobias," she said, fairly croaking the words, like a frog in a fable. "You fell asleep, and it only seemed real—"

"No," Tobias said flatly. "I saw Liam. I talked to him. He said it was the twenty-first century, where he lives. I told him he was full of sheep dip—that it was 1919, and I'd get the calendar to prove it. Then he said if I was eight years old in 1919, I was probably dead or in a nursing home someplace in his time." He paused. "What's a nursing home, Ma? And how could I be two places at once? A kid here, and an old man somewhere else?"

Dizzy, Hannah gathered her boy in both arms and held him so tightly that he struggled.

"Let me go, Ma," he said. "You're fair smothering me!"

With a conscious effort, Hannah broke the embrace. Let her arms fall to her sides.

"What's happening to us?" she whispered.

"I need to use the chamber pot," Tobias announced.

Hannah stood slowly, like a sleepwalker. She moved out of that room, closed the door behind her and got as far as the top of the back stairs before her legs gave out and she had to sit down.

She was still there when Doss came in, back from his travels to the smokehouse and the widow Jessup's place. As though he'd sensed her presence, he came to the foot of the steps, still in his coat and hat.

"Hannah? What's the matter? Is Tobias all right?"

"He's...yes."

Doss tossed his hat away, came up the steps, sat down next to Hannah and put an arm around her shoulders. She sagged against his side, even as she despised herself for the weakness. Turned her face into his cold-weather-and-leather-scented shoulder and wept with confusion and relief and a whole tangle of other emotions.

He held her until the worst of it had passed.

She sniffled and sat up straight. Even tried to smile. "How was the widow Jessup?" she asked.

Present Day

That night Sierra invited Travis to supper. Just marched right out to his trailer, knocked on the door and, the moment he opened it, blurted, "We're having spaghetti tonight. It's Liam's favorite. It would mean a lot to him if you came and ate with us."

Travis grinned. Evidently, he'd been changing clothes, because his shirt was half-unbuttoned. "If you're trying to make up for almost running over me backing out of the garage this afternoon, it's okay," he teased. "I'm still pretty fast on my feet."

Sierra was doing her level best not to admire what she could see of his chest, which was muscular. She wondered what it would be like to slide her hands inside that shirt, feel his skin against her palms and her splayed fingers.

Then she looked up into his eyes again, saw the knowing smile there and blushed. "It's more about thanking you for taking the Christmas tree downstairs," she fibbed.

"At your service," he said with a slight drawl.

Was that a double entendre?

Don't be silly, she told herself. Of course it wasn't.

"There's wine, too," she blurted out, and then blushed again. At this rate, Travis would think she'd already had a few nips.

"Everything but music," he quipped.

Afraid to say another word, she turned and hurried back toward the house, and she distinctly heard him chuckle before he closed the trailer door.

Liam was strangely quiet at supper. He usually gobbled spaghetti, but tonight he merely nibbled. He had a perfect opportunity to talk "cowboy" with Travis, or chatter on about his first day of school; instead, he asked to be excused so he could take a bath and get to bed early. At Sierra's nod, he murmured something and fled.

"He must be sick," Sierra fretted, about to go after him.

"Let him go," Travis counseled. "He's all right."

"But—"

"He's *all right,* Sierra." He refilled her wineglass, then his own.

They finished their meal, cleared the table together, loaded the dishwasher. When Sierra would have walked away, Travis caught hold of her arm and gently stopped her. Switched on the countertop radio with his free hand.

Soft, smoky music poured into the room.

The next thing she knew, Sierra was in Travis's arms, close against that chest she'd admired earlier at the door of his trailer, and they were slow dancing.

Why didn't she pull away?

Maybe it was the wine.

"Relax," he said. His breath was warm in her hair.

She giggled, more nervous than amused. What was the matter with her? She was attracted to Travis, had been from the first, and he was clearly attracted to her. They were both adults. Why not enjoy a little slow dancing in a ranch-house kitchen?

Because slow dancing led to other things, especially when it was wine powered. She took a step back and felt the counter flush against her lower back. Travis naturally came with her, since they were holding hands and he had one arm around her waist.

Simple physics.

Then he kissed her.

Physics again—this time, not so simple.

"Yikes," she said, when their mouths parted.

He grinned. "Nobody's ever said that after I kissed them."

She felt the heat and substance of his body pressed against hers, right where it counted. If Liam hadn't been just upstairs, and likely to come back down at any moment, she might have wrapped her legs around Travis's waist and kissed him nuclear-style.

"It's going to happen, isn't it?" she heard herself whisper.

"Yep," Travis answered.

"But not tonight," Sierra said on a sigh.

"Probably not," Travis agreed, grinding his hips a little. His erection burned into her abdomen like a firebrand.

"When, then?"

He chuckled, gave her a slow, nibbling kiss. "Tomorrow morning," he said. "After you drop Liam off at school."

"Isn't that…a little…soon?"

"Not soon enough," Travis answered. He cupped a hand around her breast, and even through the fabric of her shirt and bra, her nipple hardened against the chafing motion of his thumb. "Not nearly soon enough."

After Travis had gone, Sierra felt like an idiot.

She looked in on Liam, who was sound asleep, and then took a cool shower. It didn't help.

She would come to her senses by morning, she told herself, as she stood at her bedroom window, gazing down at the lights burning in Travis's trailer.

She'd get a good night's sleep. That was all she needed.

She slept, as it happened, like the proverbial log, but she woke up thinking about Travis. About the way she'd felt when he kissed her, when he backed her up against the counter…

She made breakfast.

Took Liam to school.

Zoomed straight back to the ranch, even though she'd intended to drive around town for a while, giving herself a chance to cool down.

Instead, she was on autopilot.

But it wasn't as if she gave up easily. She raised every argument she could think of. It was *way* too soon. She didn't know Travis well enough to sleep with him.

She would regret this in the morning.

No, long *before* then.

The truth was, she'd denied herself so much, for so long, that she couldn't stand it anymore.

She didn't even bother to park the SUV in the garage. She shut it down between the house and Travis's trailer, up to the wheel wells in snow, jumped out, and double-timed it to his door.

Knocked.

Maybe he's not home, she thought desperately.

Let him be here.

Let him be in China.

His truck was parked in its usual place, next to the barn. The trailer door creaked open.

He grinned down at her. "Hot damn," he said.

Sierra shoved her hands into her coat pockets. Wished she could dig her toes right into the ground somehow and hold out against the elemental forces that were driving her.

Travis stepped back. "Come in," he said.

So much for the toehold. She was inside in a single bound.

He leaned around her to pull the door shut.

"This is crazy," she said.

He began unbuttoning her coat. Slipped it back off her shoulders. Bent his head to taste her earlobe and brush the length of her neck with his lips.

She groaned.

"Talk some sense into me," she pleaded. "Say this is stupid and we shouldn't do it."

He laughed. "You're kidding, right?"

"It's wrong."

"Think of it as therapy."

She trembled as he tossed her coat aside. "For whom? You or me?"

He opened her blouse, undid the catch at the front of her bra, caught her breasts in his hands when they sprang free.

"Oh, I think we'll both benefit," he said.

Sierra groaned again. He sat her down on the side of his bed, crouched to pull off her snow boots, peel off her socks. Then he stood her up again, and undressed her, garment by garment. Blouse…bra…jeans…and, finally, her lacy underpants.

He suckled at her breasts, somehow managing to shed his own clothes in the process; Sierra was too dazed, and too aroused, to consider the mechanics of it.

He laid her down on the bed, gently. Eased two pillows under her bottom. Knelt between her legs.

"Oh, God," she whimpered. "You're not going to—?"

Travis kissed his way from her mouth to her neck.

"I sure am," he mumbled, before pausing to enjoy one of her breasts, then the other.

He kept moving downward, stroking the tender flesh on the insides of her thighs. He plumped up the pillows, raising her higher.

Sierra moaned.

He parted the nest of moist curls at the junction of her thighs. Breathed on her. Touched her lightly with the tip of his tongue.

She arched her back and gave a low, throaty cry of need.

"I thought so," Travis said, almost idly.

"You—thought—what?" Sierra demanded.

"That you needed this as much as I do." He took her full into his mouth.

She welcomed him with a sob and an upward thrust of her hips.

He slid his hands under her buttocks and lifted her higher still.

She was about to explode, and she fought it. It wasn't

as though she had orgasms every day. She wanted this experience to *last*.

He drove her straight over the edge.

She convulsed with the power of her release—once—twice—three times.

It was over.

But it wasn't.

Before she had time to lament, he was taking her to a new level.

She came again, voluptuously, piercingly, her legs over his shoulders now. And before she could begin the breathless descent, he grasped the undersides of her knees and parted them, tongued her until she climaxed yet again. Only, this time she couldn't make a sound. She could only buckle in helpless waves of pleasure.

And still it wasn't over.

He waited until she'd opened her eyes. Until her breathing had evened out. After all of the frenzy, he waited until she nodded.

He entered her in a long, slow, deep stroke, supporting himself with his hands pressing into the narrow mattress on either side of her shoulders, gazing intently down into her face. Taking in every response.

She began the climb again. Rasped his name. Clutched at his shoulders.

He didn't increase his pace.

She pumped, growing more and more frantic as the delicious friction increased, degree by degree, toward certain meltdown.

The wave crashed over her like a tsunami, and when she stopped flailing and shouting in surrender—and only then—she saw him close his eyes. His neck corded, like a stallion's, as he threw back his head and let himself go.

His powerful body flexed, and flexed again, every muscle taut, and Sierra almost wept as she watched his control give way.

Afterward he lowered himself to lie beside her, wrapping her close in his arms. Kissed her temple, where the hair was moist with perspiration. Stroked her breasts and her belly.

She listened as his breathing slowed.

"You're not going to fall asleep, are you?" she asked.

He laughed. "No," he said. He rolled on to his back, pulling her with him, so that she lay sprawled on top of him. Caressed her back, her shoulders, her buttocks.

She nestled in. Buried her face in his neck. Popped her head up again, suddenly alarmed. "Did you use…?"

"Yes," he said.

She snuggled up again. "That was…great," she confessed, and giggled.

He shifted beneath her. She felt some fumbling.

"We can't possibly do that again," she said.

"Wanna bet?" He eased her upright, set her knees on either side of his hips.

Felt him move inside her, sleek and hard.

A violent tremor went through her, left her shuddering.

He cupped her breasts in his hands, drew her forward far enough to suck her breasts. All the while, he was raising and lowering her along his length. She took him deeper.

And then deeper still.

And then the universe dissolved into shimmering particles and rained down on them both like atoms of fire.

Chapter 14

Sierra slept, snuggled against Travis's side, one arm draped across his chest, one shapely leg flung over his thighs.

Travis pulled the quilt up over them both, so she wouldn't get cold, and considered his situation.

He'd been to bed with a lot of women in his time.

He knew how to give and receive pleasure.

He said goodbye as easily as hello.

But this was different.

Different feeling. Different woman.

He'd been a dead man up until now, and this trailer had been his coffin.

Rance had sure been right about that.

Sierra McKettrick, who had probably expected no more from this encounter than he had—a roll in the hay, some much-needed satisfaction, a break in the monotony—had resurrected him. Probably inadvertently, but the effect was the same.

"Shit," he whispered. He'd *needed* that all-pervasive numbness and the insulation it provided. Needed *not* to feel.

Sierra had awakened everything inside him, and it hurt, to the center of his soul, like frost-bitten flesh thawing too fast.

She stirred against him, uttered a soft, hmmm sound, but didn't awaken.

He held her a little closer and thought about Brody. His little brother. Brody would never make love to a woman like Sierra. He'd never watch the moon rise over a mountain creek, the water purple in the twilight, or choke up at the sight of a ragged band of wild horses racing across a clearing for no other reason than that they had legs to run on. He'd never throw a stick for a faithful old dog to fetch, watch Fourth-of-July fireworks with a kid perched on his shoulders or eat pancakes swimming in syrup in a roadside café while hokey music played on the jukebox.

There were so many things Brody would never do.

Travis's throat went raw, and his eyes stung.

The loss yawned inside him, a black hole, an abyss.

He'd thought losing his brother would be the hardest thing he'd ever had to do, but now he knew it wasn't. Dying inside was easy—it was having the guts to *live* that was hard.

He shifted.

Sierra sighed, raised her head, looked straight into his face.

It was too much to hope, he figured, that she wouldn't notice the tear that had just trickled out of the corner of his eye to streak toward his ear.

If she saw, she had the good grace not to comment, and the depth of his gratitude for that simple blessing was downright pathetic, by his reckoning.

"What time is it?" she asked, looking anxious and womanly. *Real* womanly.

He stretched, groped for his watch on the little shelf above the bed. "Twelve-thirty," he answered gruffly. He wanted to say a whole lot more, but he wasn't sure what it was. He'd have to say it all to himself first, and make sense of it, before he could tell it to anyone else.

Especially Sierra.

Not that he loved her or anything. It was too early for that.

But he sure as hell felt *something,* and he wished he didn't.

"You okay?" she asked, raising herself on to one elbow and studying his face a lot more intently than he would have liked.

"Fine," he lied.

"This doesn't have to change anything," Sierra reasoned, hurrying her words a little—pushing them along, like rambunctious cattle toward a narrow chute. Was she trying to convince him, or herself?

"Right," he said.

She pulled away, sat on the backs of her thighs, the quilt pulled up to her chin. "I'd better—get back to the house."

He nodded.

She nodded.

Neither of them moved.

"What just happened here?" Sierra asked, after a long time had passed, with the two of them just staring at each other.

Whatever had happened, it had been a lot more than the obvious. He was sure of that, if nothing else.

"I'll be damned if I know," Travis said.

"Me, neither," Sierra said. Then she bent and kissed his forehead, before scrambling out of bed.

He sat up, watched as she gathered her scattered clothes and shimmied into them. He wished he smoked, because lighting a cigarette would have given him something to do.

Something to distract him from the rawness of what he felt and his frustration at not being able to wrestle it down and give it a name.

"I guess you must think I do things like this all the time," she said. Maybe he wasn't alone in being confused. The idea stirred a forlorn hope within him. "And I don't. I *don't* sleep with men I barely know, and I don't—"

He smiled. "I believe you, Sierra," he said. He did, too. Anybody who came with the kind of sensual abandon she had, on a regular basis, would be superhuman, dead of exhaustion or both.

Actually, he admired her stamina, and her uncommon passion.

And she was up, moving around, dressing. He wasn't entirely sure he could stand.

She sat on the side of the bed, keeping a careful if subtle distance, to pull on her socks and boots. "Travis?" she said without looking at him. He saw a pink glow along the edge of her cheek, and thought of a summer dawn, rimming a mountain peak.

"What?"

"It was good. What we did was good. Okay?"

He swallowed. Reached out and squeezed her hand briefly before letting it go. "Yeah," he agreed. "It was good."

She left then, and Travis felt her absence like a vacuum.

He cupped his hands behind his head, lay back and began making a list in his mind.

All the things he had to do before he left the Triple M for good.

She'd made a damn fool of herself.

Sierra let herself into the house, closed the door behind her and leaned back against it.

What had she been thinking, throwing herself at Travis that way? She'd been like a woman possessed—and a *stupid* woman, at that.

Sierra McKettrick, the sexual sophisticate.

Right.

Sierra McKettrick, who had been intimate with exactly two men in her life—one of whom had fathered her child, lied to her and left her behind, apparently without a second thought.

What if Travis hadn't been telling the truth when he said he used protection?

What if she was pregnant again?

"Get a grip," she told herself out loud. Travis had clearly had a lot of experience in these matters, unlike her. Furthermore he was a lawyer. He might not have given a damn whether *she* was protected or not, but he surely would have covered his *own* backside, if only to avoid a potential paternity suit.

She stood still, breathing like a woman in the early stages of labor, until she'd regained some semblance of composure. She had to pull herself together. In a couple of hours she'd be picking Liam up at school.

He'd want to tell her all about his class. The other kids. The teachers.

There would be supper to fix and homework to oversee.

She was a *mother,* for God's sake, not some bimbo in a soap opera, sneaking off to have prenoon monkey sex in a trailer with a virtual stranger.

She straightened.

Her own voice echoed in her mind.

It was good. What we did was good. Okay?

And it *had* been good, just not in the noble sense of the word.

Sierra went slowly upstairs, took a long, hot shower,

dressed in fresh jeans and a white cotton blouse. Borrowed one of Meg's cardigans, to complete the "Mom" look.

By the time she was finished, she still had more than an hour until she had to leave for town.

Her gaze strayed to the china cabinet.

She would look at the pictures in the album. Get a frame of reference for all those McKettricks that had gone before. Try to imagine herself as one of them, a link in the biological chain.

She heard Travis's truck start up, resisted an urge to go to the window and watch him drive away. There was too much danger that she would morph into a desperate housewife, smile sweetly and wave.

Not gonna happen.

Keeping her thoughts and actions briskly businesslike, she retrieved the album, carried it to the table, sat down and lifted the cover.

A small blue book was tucked inside, its corners curled with age.

A tremor of something went through Sierra like a wash of ice water, some premonition, some subconscious awareness straining to reach the surface.

She opened the smaller volume.

Focused on the beautifully scripted lines, penned in ink that had long since faded to an antique brown.

My name is Hannah McKettrick.
I know you're here. I can sense it. You've moved the teapot, and the album in which I've placed this remembrance book.
    Please don't harm my boy. His name is Tobias. He's eight years old.
    He is everything to me.

Sierra caught her breath. There was more, but her shock was such that, for the next few moments, the remaining words might as well have been gibberish.

Was this woman, probably long dead, addressing her from another century?

Impossible.

But then, it was impossible for teapots and photograph albums to move by themselves, too. It was impossible for an ordinary piano to play itself, with no one touching the keys.

It was impossible for Liam to see a boy in his room.

Sierra swallowed, lowered her eyes to the journal again. The words had been written so very long ago, and yet they had the immediacy of an email.

How could this be happening?

She sucked in another breath. Read on.

I must be losing my mind. Doss says it's grief, over Gabe's dying. I don't even know why I'm writing this, except in the hope that you'll write something back. It's the only way I can think of to speak to you.

Sierra glanced at the clock. Only a few minutes had passed since she sat down at the table, but it seemed like so much longer.

She got out of her chair, found a pen in the junk drawer next to the sink. This was *crazy*. She was about to deface what might be an important family record. And yet there was something so plaintive in Hannah's plea that she couldn't ignore it.

My name is Sierra McKettrick. I have a son, too, and his name is Liam. He's seven, and he has asthma. He's the center of my life.

You have nothing to fear from me. I'm not a ghost, just an ordinary flesh-and-blood woman. A mother, like you.

The telephone rang, jolting Sierra out of the spell.

Conditioned to unexpected emergencies, because of Liam's illness, she hurried to answer, squinting at the caller ID.

"Indian Rock Elementary School."

The room swayed.

"This is Sierra McKettrick," she said. "Is my son all right?"

The voice on the other end of the line was blessedly calm. "Liam is just a little sick at his stomach, that's all," the woman said. "The school nurse thinks he ought to come home. He'll probably be fine in the morning."

"I'll be right there," Sierra answered, and hung up without saying goodbye.

Liam is safe, she told herself, but she felt panicky, just the same.

She deliberately closed Hannah McKettrick's journal, put it back inside the album. Placed the album inside the drawer.

Then she raced around the kitchen, frantically searching for the car keys, before remembering that she'd left them in the ignition earlier, when she'd come back from town. She'd been so focused on having an illicit tryst with Travis Reid....

She grabbed her coat, dashed out the door, jumped into the SUV.

The roads were icy, and by the time Sierra sped into Indian Rock, huge flakes of snow were tumbling from a grim gray sky. She forced herself to slow down, but when she reached the school parking lot, she almost forgot to shut off the motor in her haste to get inside, find her son.

Liam lay on a cot in the nurse's office, alarmingly pale. Someone had laid a cloth over his forehead, presumably cool, but he was all by himself.

How could these people have left him alone?

"Mom," he said. "My stomach hurts. I think I'm gonna hurl again."

She went to him. He rolled on to his side and vomited onto her shoes.

"I'm sorry!" he wailed.

She stroked his sweat-dampened hair. "It's all right, Liam. Everything is going to be all right."

He threw up again.

Sierra snatched a handful of paper towels from the wall dispenser, wet them down at the sink and washed his face.

"My coat!" he lamented. "I don't want to leave my cowboy coat—"

"Don't worry about your coat," Sierra said, wondering distractedly how she could possibly be the same woman who'd spent half the morning naked in Travis's bed.

The nurse, a tall blond woman with kindly blue eyes, stepped into the room, carrying Liam's coat and backpack. Silently she laid the things aside in a chair and came to assist in the cleanup effort.

Sierra went to get the coat.

"No!" Liam cried out, as she approached him with it. "What if I puke on it?"

"Sweetheart, it's cold outside, and we can always have it cleaned—"

The nurse caught her eye. Shook her head. "Let's just bundle Liam up in a couple of blankets. I'll help you get him to the car. This coat is important to him—*so* important that, sick as he was, he insisted I go and get it for him."

Sierra bit her lip. She and the nurse wrapped Liam in the

blankets, and Sierra lifted him into her arms. He was getting so big. One day soon, she probably wouldn't be able to carry him anymore.

The main doors whooshed open when Sierra reached them.

"Oh, great," Liam moaned. "Everybody's looking. Everybody knows I *ralphed*."

Sierra hadn't noticed the children filling the corridor. The dismissal bell must have rung, but she hadn't heard it.

"It's okay, Liam," she said.

He shook his head. "No, it *isn't!* My *mom* is carrying me out of the school in a bunch of *blankets,* like a *baby!* I'll never live this down!"

Sierra and the nurse exchanged glances.

The nurse smiled and shifted Liam's coat and backpack so she could pat his shoulder. "When you get back to school," she said, "you come to my office and I'll tell you *plenty* of stories about things that have happened in this school over the years. You're not the first person to throw up here, Liam McKettrick, and you won't be the last, either."

Liam lifted his head, apparently heartened. "Really?"

The nurse rolled her eyes expressively. "If you only *knew,*" she said, in a conspiratorial tone, opening the door of the SUV on the passenger side, so Sierra could set Liam on the seat and buckle him in. "I wouldn't name names, of course, but I've seen kids do a lot worse than vomit."

Sierra shut the door, turned to face the nurse.

"Thanks," she said. Liam peered through the window, his face a greenish, bespectacled moon, his hair sticking out in spikes. "You have a unique way of comforting an embarrassed kid, but it seems to be effective."

The nurse smiled, put out her hand. "My name is Susan Yarnia," she said. "If you need anything, you call me, either here at the school or at home. My husband's name is Joe, and we're in the book."

Sierra nodded. Took the coat and backpack and put them into the rig, after ferreting for Liam's inhaler, just in case he needed it on the way home. "Do you think I should take him to the clinic?" she asked in a whisper, after she'd closed the door again.

"That's up to you, of course," Susan said. "There's been a flu bug going around, and my guess is Liam caught it. If I were you, I'd just take him home, put him to bed and make a bit of a fuss over him. See that he drinks a lot of liquids, and if you can get him to swallow a few spoonfuls of chicken soup, so much the better."

Sierra nodded, thanked the woman again and rounded the SUV to get behind the wheel.

"What if I spew in Aunt Meg's car?" Liam asked.

"I'll clean it up," Sierra answered.

"This whole thing is *mortifying*. When I tell Tobias—" *Tobias.*

If Sierra hadn't been pulling out on to a slick road, she probably would have slammed on the brakes.

Please don't harm my boy, Hannah McKettrick had written, eighty-eight years ago, in her journal. *His name is Tobias. He's eight years old.*

"Who is Tobias?" Sierra asked moderately, but her palms were so wet on the steering wheel that she feared her grip wouldn't hold if she had to make a sudden turn.

"The. Boy. In. My. Room," Liam said very carefully, as though English were not even Sierra's *second* language, let alone her first. "I told you I saw him."

"Yeah," Sierra replied, her stomach clenching so hard that she wasn't sure *she* wouldn't be the next one to throw up, "but you didn't mention having a conversation with him."

Liam turned away from her, rested his forehead against the passenger-side window, probably because it was cool. "I thought you'd freak," he said. "Or send me off to some bug farm."

Sierra drove past the clinic where she and Travis had taken Liam the day of his asthma attack. It was all she could do not to pull in and demand that he be put on life support, or air-lifted to Stanford.

It's stomach flu, she insisted to herself, and kept driving by sheer force of will.

"When have I ever threatened to send you *anywhere,* let alone to a 'bug farm'?"

"There's always a first time," Liam reasoned.

"You were sick last night," Sierra realized aloud. "That's why you were so quiet at supper."

"I was quiet at supper because I figured Tobias would be there when I went upstairs."

"Were you scared?"

Liam flung her a scornful look. "No," he said. And then his cheeks puffed out, and he made a strangling sound.

Sierra pulled to the side of the road, got out of the SUV and barely got around to open the door before he decorated her shoes again.

This is your real life, she thought pragmatically.

Not the two million dollars.

Not great sex in a cowboy's bed.

It's a seven-year-old boy, barfing on your shoes.

The reflections were strangely comforting, given the circumstances.

When Liam was through, she wiped off her boots with handfuls of snow, got back into the car and drove to the

nearest gas station, where she bought him a bottle of Gatorade so he could rinse out his mouth, spit gloriously onto
the pavement, and hopefully retain enough electrolytes to
keep from dehydrating.

Twilight was already gathering by the time she pulled
into the garage at the ranch house, having noticed, in spite
of herself, that Travis was back from wherever he'd gone,
and the lights were glowing golden in the windows of his
trailer.

Not that it mattered.

In fact, she wasn't the least bit relieved when he walked
into the garage before she could shut the door or even turn
off the engine.

Liam unsnapped his seat belt and lowered his window. "I
horked all over the schoolhouse," he told Travis gleefully.
"People will probably talk about it for *years.*"

"Excellent," Travis said with admiration. His eyes
danced under the brim of his hat as he looked at Sierra
over Liam's head, then returned his full attention to the
little boy. "Need some help getting inside? One cowpoke
to another?"

"Sure," Liam replied staunchly. "Not that I couldn't
make it on my own or anything."

Travis chuckled. "Maybe you ought to carry *me,* then."
His gaze snagged Sierra's again. "It happens that I'm feeling a little weak in the knees myself."

Sierra's face heated. She switched off the ignition.

Liam giggled, and the sound was restorative. "You're
too big to carry, Travis," he said, with such affection that
Sierra's throat tightened again, and she honestly thought
she'd cry.

Fortunately, Travis wasn't looking at her. He gathered
Liam into his arms, blankets and all, and carried him in-

side. Sierra followed with her son's things, scrambling to get her emotions under control.

"It's *arctic* in here," Liam said.

"You're right," Travis agreed easily. He set Liam in the chair where Sierra had sat writing in the diary of a woman who was probably buried somewhere among all those bronze statues in the family cemetery, and approached the old stove. "Nothing like a good wood fire to warm a place up."

"Drink your Gatorade," Sierra told Liam, because she felt she had to say something, and that was all that came to mind.

"Can we sleep down here again?" Liam asked. "Like we did when the blizzard came and the furnace went out?"

"No," Sierra answered, much too quickly.

Travis gave her a sidelong glance and a grin, then stuffed some crumpled newspaper and kindling into the belly of the wood stove, and lit the fire. Sierra shivered, hugging herself, while he adjusted the damper.

"Is something wrong with the furnace again?" she asked.

"Probably," Travis answered.

She was oddly grateful that he hadn't called her on asking a stupid question. But then, he wouldn't. Not in front of her son. She knew that much about Travis Reid, at least. Along with the fact that he was one hell of a lover.

Don't even think about that, Sierra scolded herself. But it was like deciding not to imagine a pink elephant skating on a pond and wearing a tutu.

"I think we should all sleep right here," Liam persisted.

Travis chuckled, more, Sierra suspected, at her discomfort than at Liam's campaign for another kitchen campout. "If a man's got a bed," Travis said, "he ought to use it."

Sierra's cheeks stung. "Was that necessary?" she whispered furiously, after approaching the wood box to grab up a few chunks of pine. If she was going to live in this house for a year, she'd better learn to work the stove.

"No," Travis whispered back, "but it was fun."

"Will you *stop?*"

Another grin. He seemed to have an infinite supply of those, and all of them were saucy. "Nope."

"What are you guys whispering about?" Liam asked suspiciously. "Are you keeping secrets?"

Travis took the wood from Sierra's hands, stuffed it into the stove. She tried to look away but she couldn't. "No secrets," he said.

Sierra bit her lower lip.

The kitchen began to warm up, but she couldn't be certain it was because of the fire in the cookstove.

Travis left them to go downstairs and attend to the furnace.

"I wish he was my dad," Liam said.

Sierra blinked back more tears. Lifted her chin. "Well, he's not, sweetie," she said gently, and with a slight quaver in her voice. "Best let it go at that, okay?"

Liam looked so sad that Sierra wanted to take him on to her lap and rock him the way she had when he was younger and a lot more amenable to motherly affection. "Okay," he agreed.

She crossed to him, ruffled his hair, which was already mussed. "Think you could eat something?" she asked. "Maybe some chicken noodle soup?"

"Yuck," he answered. "And I *still* think we should sleep in the kitchen, because it's cold and I'm sick and I might catch pneumonia or something up there in my room."

The mention of Liam's room made Sierra think of Hannah again and Tobias. She went to the china cabinet, opened the drawer, raised the cover on the photo album. The journal was still there, and she looked inside.

Hannah's words.

Her words.

Nothing more.

Did she expect an answer? More lines of faded ink, entered beneath her own ballpoint scrawl?

A tingle of anticipation went through her as she closed the journal, then the album, then the drawer, and straightened.

Yes.

Oh, yes.

She *did* expect an answer.

The furnace made that familiar whooshing sound.

Liam muttered something that might have been a swear word.

Sierra pretended not to notice.

Travis came back up the basement stairs, dusting his hands together. Another job well done.

"It's still going to be *really* cold upstairs," Liam asserted.

"You're probably right," Travis agreed.

Sierra gave him an eloquent look.

Travis was undaunted. He just grinned another insufferable, three-alarm grin. "I'll make you a bed on the floor," he said, and though he was looking at Sierra, he was talking to Liam. Hopefully. "Just until it gets warm upstairs."

Liam yelped with delighted triumph, punching the air with one fist. Then, just as quickly, he sobered. "What about you and Mom?"

"I reckon we'll just tough it out," Travis drawled. With that, he went about carrying in a couple of sofa cushions to lay on the floor, not too close to the stove but close enough for warmth.

Sierra fetched a pillow and fresh blankets.

Liam stretched out on the makeshift bed like an Egyptian king traveling by barge. Sighed happily.

"Are you staying for supper, Travis?" he asked.

"Am I invited?" Travis asked, looking at Sierra.

She sighed. "Yes," she said.

Liam let out another yippee.

Sierra made grilled cheese sandwiches and heated canned spaghetti, but by the time she served the feast, Liam was sound asleep.

Travis, seated on the bench, his sleeves still rolled up from washing in the bathroom down the hall, nodded toward him.

"If I were you," he said, "I'd start checking out law schools. That kid is probably going to be on the Supreme Court before he's thirty."

Chapter 15

1919

Hannah's hands trembled slightly as she raised the cover of the family album and reached for the remembrance book tucked inside. She held her breath as she opened it.

Only her own words were there, alone and stark.

She was a practical woman, and she knew she should not have expected anything else. Spirits, if there was such a thing, did not take up pens and write in remembrance books. And yet she was stricken with a profound disappointment, the likes of which she'd never experienced before. She'd suffered plenty in her life, seeing three sisters perish as a girl and, as a woman grown, losing Gabe, knowing none of the brave dreams they'd talked about with such hope and faith would ever come true.

No more stolen kisses.

No more secret laughter.

No more cattle grazing on a thousand hills.

And certainly no more babies, born squalling in their room upstairs.

Hannah told herself, I will not cry, I have cried enough. I have emptied myself of tears.

So why do they keep coming?

"Hannah?"

She started, looked up to see Doss standing at the foot of the stairs. He'd been working in the barn, the last she knew, doing the morning chores. Chopping extra wood because there was another storm coming. It bothered her that she hadn't heard him come in.

"Tobias is worse," he said.

Alarm swelled into Hannah's throat, cutting off her wind.

She started for the stairs, but when she would have passed Doss, he stopped her.

"I'm going to town for the doc," he told her.

"I'll just wrap Tobias up warm and we'll—"

Doss's grip tightened on her shoulders. Only then did she realize he hadn't merely stepped into her path, he was touching her. "No, Hannah," he said. "The boy's too sick for that."

"Suppose the doctor won't come?"

"He'll come," Doss said. "You go to Tobias. Don't let the fire go out, no matter what. I'll be back as soon as I can."

Hannah nodded, bursting to get to her son, but somehow wanting to cling to Doss, too. Tell him not to go, that they'd manage some way but he oughtn't to leave, because something truly terrible might happen if he did.

"Go to him," Doss told her, letting go of her shoulders.

She felt as though he'd been holding her up. Swayed a little to catch her balance. Then, on impulse, she stood on tiptoe and kissed him right on the mouth. "You be careful, Doss McKettrick," she said. "You come back to us, safe and sound."

He looked deeply into her eyes for a moment, as though he could see secrets she kept even from herself, then nodded and made for the door. The last Hannah saw of him, just before she dashed up the rear stairs, he was putting on his coat and hat.

Tobias lay fitful in his bed, his nightshirt soaked with perspiration, like the sheets. His teeth chattered, and his lips were blue, but his flesh burned to the touch.

Hannah could not afford to let panic prevail.

She had mothering to do, and however inadequate and fearful she felt, there was no one but her to do it.

She pushed up her sleeves, added more pins to her hair so it wouldn't tumble down and get in her way, and headed downstairs to heat water.

Heedful of Doss's warning not to let the fire die, she added wood from the generous supply he'd brought in earlier without her noticing. She pumped water into every bucket and kettle she owned, and put them on the stove to heat. Then she dragged the bathtub out of the pantry and set it in the middle of the floor.

The instructions seemed to come from somewhere inside her. She didn't plan what to do, or take the time to debate one intuition against another. It was as if some stronger, smarter, better Hannah had stepped to the fore, and pushed the timid and uncertain one aside.

This Hannah knew what to do. The regular one stood in the background, wringing her hands and counseling hysteria.

Tobias was practically delirious when Hannah roused

him from his bed, an hour later when the tub was full of hot water, and half carried, half led him downstairs.

In the kitchen she stripped him and put him into the bath. Scrubbed him down, all the while talking quietly, confidently, without ever stopping to think up the words she'd say next.

"You'll be fine, Tobias. Come spring, you'll be able to ride your pony through the fields and swim in the pond. We'll get you that dog you've been wanting—you can pick him out yourself—and he can sleep right in your room, too. On the foot of your bed, if you want. You can call your uncle Doss 'Pa' from now on, and there'll be a brand-new baby in this house at harvest time—think of it, Tobias. A little brother or sister. You can choose the name—"

Tobias shuddered, chilled even in water that would be too hot to stand any other time.

Hannah dried him with towels, put him in a clean nightshirt, got him back upstairs again. Settled him into her own bed while she hastened to put fresh sheets and blankets on his.

All that morning, and all that afternoon, she tended her boy, touching a cold cloth to his forehead. Holding his hands. Telling him that his pa had gone to town for the doctor, and he needn't worry because he was going to be just fine.

They were all going to be just fine.

Tobias had occasional moments of lucidity. "Liam's sick, too," he said once. "I want to be with Liam."

Another time, he asked, "Where's Pa? Is Pa all right?"

Hannah had bitten her lower lip and reassured him gently. "Yes, sweetheart, your pa's just fine."

The day wore on, into evening.

And Doss hadn't returned.

Hannah put more wood on the fire, donned Gabe's coat and made her way out to the barn, through ever-deepening snow, to feed the livestock, because there was no one else to do it.

The wind bit through to Hannah's bones as she worked. Made them ache, then go numb.

Where was Doss?

The other Hannah, the fretful one pushed into the background, kept calling out that question, as if from the bottom of a well.

Where…where…where?

It was completely dark by the time she'd finished, and as she left the barn, she heard the faint rumble of thunder. Rare in a snowstorm, like lightning, but Hannah had seen that, too, there in the high country of Arizona, and in Montana, as well. A staggering sense of foreboding descended upon her, and it had nothing to do with Tobias being sick.

Hannah returned to the house, switched on the kitchen bulb before even taking off Gabe's coat, thinking somehow the light might draw Doss back to her and Tobias, through the storm. Even in daylight, and even for a man as tough and as skilled as Doss, navigating the most familiar trails would be difficult in weather like that, if not impossible. In the dark, it was plain treacherous.

"Ma?" Tobias called. "Ma, are you down there?"

It heartened her, the strength she heard in his voice, but her joy was tempered by worry. Doss should have been home by then. Unless—please, God, let it be so—he'd decided to stay in town.

"Yes," she called back, as cheerfully as she could. "I'm here, and I'm about to fix you some supper."

"Come up, Ma. Right now. That boy's here."

In the process of shedding the coat she'd worn to feed the livestock and the chickens and milk the cow, Hannah let the garment drop, forgotten, to the floor. She took the stairs two at a time and burst into Tobias's room.

With no lamp burning, it was stone dark. She made out the outline of Tobias's bed and him lying there.

"He's here, Ma," Tobias said, in a delighted whisper, as though speaking too loudly might cause his invisible friend to disappear. "Liam's here."

Hannah hurried to the bedside.

"I don't see him," she said.

Just then the sky itself seemed to part, with a great, tearing roar so horrendous Hannah put her hands to her ears. The floor trembled beneath her feet, and the windowpanes rattled. Light quivered in the room—she knew it was snow lightning, but it was otherworldly, just the same—and for one single, incredulous moment, she saw not Tobias lying in that bed, but another little boy. And she saw the woman standing on the other side of the bed, too. Staring at her. Looking every bit as surprised as Hannah herself.

Within half a heartbeat, the whole incident was over.

"Did you see them?" Tobias asked desperately, grasping at her hand. Clinging. "Ma, did you see them?"

"Yes," Hannah whispered. She dropped to her knees next to Tobias's bed, unable to stand for another instant. Tobias had said "them." He'd seen the woman, too, then, as well as the boy. "Dear God, yes."

"She was wearing trousers, Ma," Tobias marveled.

Hannah raised herself from the floor to perch tremulously on the side of Tobias's bed. Fumbled for the matches and lit the lamp on the stand.

"Tell me what else you saw, Tobias," she said. Her

hands were shaking so badly that the lamp chimney rattled when she set it back in place.

"She had short hair. Brown, I think. And she saw us, Ma, just as sure as we saw her!"

Hannah nodded numbly.

"What does it mean, Ma?" Tobias asked.

"I wish I knew," Hannah said.

Present Day

Sierra stood still at Liam's bedside, hugging herself and trembling, trying to understand what she'd just seen.

What the hell *had* she just seen?

Lightning.

A woman in an old-fashioned dress, standing on the opposite side of Liam's bed.

Hannah?

"What's wrong, Mom?" Liam asked sleepily. He'd protested a little, when she'd roused him from his slumbers in the kitchen and brought him up here to sleep in his own bed. Then he'd fallen into natural oblivion.

She couldn't catch her breath.

"Mom?" Liam prompted, sounding more awake now.

"We'll...we'll talk about it in the morning."

"Can I sleep with you?"

Sierra swallowed. Travis had gone back to his trailer several hours before. She'd sat downstairs in the study, with a low fire going, catching up on her email, checking in on Liam at regular intervals. Anything, she realized now, but open the family album and come face-to-face with a long line of McKettricks, every one of them a stranger.

The house seemed empty and, at the same time, too crowded for comfort.

"I'll sleep in here with you," she said. "How would that be?"

"Awesome," Liam said.

"Just let me change." Down the hall, she stripped to the skin, put on sweats and made for the bathroom, where she splashed her face with cool water and brushed her teeth.

Such ordinary things.

In the wake of what she'd just experienced, she wondered if anything would ever be "ordinary" again.

Liam was snoring softly when she got back to his room. She slipped into the narrow bed beside him, turned on to her side and stared into the darkness until at last she, too, fell asleep.

1919

While Doc Willaby's nephew was getting his medical gear together, Doss took the opportunity to slip into the church down on the corner. He hadn't set foot inside it since he and Gabe had come back from the army, him sitting ramrod straight on a train seat and Gabe lying in a pine box.

He'd had no truck with God after that.

Now they had some business to discuss.

Doss opened the door, which was always unlocked, lest some wayfarer seek to pray or to find salvation, and took off his hat. He walked down front, to the plain wooden table that served as an altar, and lit one of the beeswax candles with a match from his pocket.

"I'm here to talk about Tobias," he said.

God didn't answer.

Doss shifted uncomfortably on his feet. They were so cold from the long drive into town that he couldn't feel them. Cain and Abel had been fractious on the way, and he'd had all sorts of trouble with them. Once, they'd just stopped and refused to go any farther, and then, crossing the creek, the team had made it over just fine but the sleigh had fallen through. Sunk past the runners in the frigid water.

He'd still be back there, wet to the skin and frozen stiff as laundry left on a clothesline before a blizzard, if three of Rafe's ranch hands hadn't come along to help. They'd given him dry clothes, fetched from a nearby line shack, dosed him with whisky, hitched their lassos to the half-submerged sleigh and hauled it up on to the bank by horsepower.

He'd thanked the men kindly and sent them on their way, and then spent more precious time coaxing Cain and Abel to proceed. They'd been mightily reluctant to do that, and he'd finally had to threaten them with a switch to get them moving.

The whole day had gone like that, though the frustrations were at considerable variance, and by the time he'd pulled up in front of the doc's house, the worthless critters were so worn-out he knew they wouldn't make it back home. He'd sent to the livery stable for another rig and fresh horses.

Doss cleared his throat respectfully. "Hannah can't lose that boy," he went on. "You took Gabe, and if You don't mind my saying so, that was bad enough. I guess what I want to say is, if You've got to claim somebody else, then it ought to be me, not Tobias. He's only eight and he's got a lot of living yet to do. I don't know exactly what kind of outfit You're running up there, but if there are cattle, I'm a fair hand in a roundup. I can ride with the best of them, too. I'll make myself useful— You've got my word on that." He paused, swallowed. His face felt hot, and he knew he was acting like a damn fool, but he was desperate. "I reckon that's my side of the matter, so amen."

He blew out the candle—it wouldn't do for the church to take fire and burn to the ground—and turned to head back down the aisle.

Doc Willaby was standing just inside the door, leaning on his cane, because of that gouty foot of his, and dressed for a long, hard ride out to the Triple M.

"You ought to tell Hannah," the old man said.

"Tell her what?" Doss countered, abashed at being caught pouring out his heart like some repentant sinner at a revival.

"That you love her enough to die in place of her boy."

Doss heard a team and wagon clatter to a stop out front. "Nobody needs to know that besides God," he said, and slammed his hat back on his head. "What are you doing here, anyhow? Besides eavesdropping on a man's private conversation?"

The doc smiled. He was heavy-set, with a face like a full moon, a scruff of beard and keen little eyes that never seemed to miss much of anything. "I'm going out to your place with you. And we'd better be on our way, if that boy's as sick as you say he is."

"What about your nephew?"

"He'd never stand the trip," Doc said. "My bag's out on the step, and I'll thank you to help me up into the wagon so we can get started."

Doss felt a mixture of chagrin and relief. Doc Willaby was old as desert dirt, but he'd been tending McKettricks, and a lot of other folks, for as long as Doss could remember. His own health might be failing, but Doc knew his trade, all right.

"Come on, old man," Doss said. "And don't be fussing

over hard conditions along the way. I've got neither the time nor the inclination to be coddling you."

Doc chuckled, though his eyes were serious. He slapped Doss on the shoulder. "Just like your grandfather," he said. "Tough as a boiled owl, with a heart the size of the whole state of Arizona and two others like it."

Getting the old coot into the box of the hired wagon was like trying to hoist a cow from a tar pit, but Doss managed it. He climbed up, took the reins in one hand and tossed a coin to the livery stable boy, shivering on the sidewalk, with the other. Cain and Abel would be spending the night in warm stalls, maybe longer, with all the hay they required and some grain to boot, and, cussed as they were, Doss was glad for them.

He and the doc were almost to the ranch house when the lightning struck, loud enough to shake snow off the branches of trees, throwing the dark countryside into clear relief.

The horses screamed and shied.

The wagon slid on the icy trail and plunged on to its side.

Doss heard the doc yell, felt himself being thrown sky high.

Just before he hit the ground, it came to him that God had taken him up on the bargain he'd offered back there in Indian Rock at the church. He was about to die, but Tobias would be spared.

Someone was pounding at the back door.

Hannah muttered a hasty word of reassurance to Tobias, who sat up in bed, wide-eyed, at the sound.

"That can't be Pa," he said. "He wouldn't knock. He'd just come inside—"

"Hush," Hannah told him. "You stay right there in that bed."

She hurried down the stairs and was shocked to see old Doc Willaby limping over the threshold. He looked a sight, his clothes wet and disheveled, his hair wild around his head, without his hat to contain it. His skin was gray with exertion, and he seemed nigh on to collapsing.

"There was an accident," he finally sputtered. "Down yonder, at the base of the hill. Doss is hurt."

Hannah steered the old man to a chair at the table. "Are you all right?" she asked breathlessly.

The doctor considered the question briefly, then nodded. "Don't mind about me, Hannah. It's Doss—I couldn't wake him—I had to turn the horses loose so they wouldn't kick each other to death."

She hurried into the pantry, moved the cracker tin aside and took down the bottle of Christmas whisky Doss kept there. She offered it to Doc Willaby, and he gulped down a couple of grateful swigs while she pulled on Gabe's coat and grabbed for a lantern.

"You'd better take this along, too," Doc said, and shoved the whisky bottle at her.

Hannah dropped it into her coat pocket. She didn't like leaving the old man or Tobias alone, but she had to get to Doss.

She raised her collar against the bitter wind and threw herself out the back door. Out in the barn, she tossed a halter on Seesaw and stood on a wheelbarrow to mount him. There was no time for saddles and bridles.

Holding the lamp high in one hand and clutching the halter rope with the other, Hannah rode out. She soon met two of the horses Doc had freed, and followed their trail backward, until the shape of an overturned wagon loomed in the snowy darkness.

"Doss!" she cried out. The name scraped at her throat, and she realized she must have called it over and over again, not just the once.

She found him sprawled facedown in the snow, at some distance from the wagon, and feared he'd smothered, if not broken every bone in his body. Scrambling off Seesaw's back, she plodded to where he lay, utterly still.

She knelt, setting the lantern aside, and turned him over.

"Doss," she whispered.

He didn't move.

Hannah put her cheek down close to his mouth. Felt his breath, his blessed breath, warm against her skin.

Tears of relief sprang to her eyes. She dashed them away quickly, lest they freeze in her lashes.

"Doss!" she repeated.

He opened his eyes.

"What are you doing here?" he asked, sounding befuddled.

"I've come looking for you, you damn fool," she answered.

"You're not dead, are you?"

"Of course I'm not dead," Hannah retorted, weeping freely. "And you're not either, which is God's own wonder, the way you must have been driving that wagon to get yourself into a fix like this. Can you move?"

Doss blinked. Hoisted himself on to his elbows. Felt around for his hat.

"Where's the doc?" His features tightened. "Tobias—"

"Tobias is fine," she said. "And Doc's up at the house, thawing out. It's a miracle he made it that far, with that foot of his."

A grin broke over Doss's face, and Hannah, filled with joy, could have slapped him for it. Didn't he know he'd nearly killed himself? Nearly fixed it so she'd have to bear and raise their baby all alone?

"I reckon Doc was right," Doss said. "I ought to tell you—"

"Tell me what?" Hannah fretted. "It's getting colder out here by the minute, and the wind's picking up, too. Can you get to your feet? Poor old Seesaw's going to have to carry us both home, but I think he can manage it."

"Hannah." Doss clasped both her shoulders in his hands, gave her just the slightest shake. "I love you."

Hannah blinked, stunned. "You're talking crazy, Doss. You're out of your head—"

"I love you," he said. He got to his feet, hauling Hannah with him. Knocked the lantern over in the process so it went out. "It started the day I met you."

She stared up at him.

"I don't know how you feel about me, Hannah. It would be a grand thing if you felt the same way I do, but if you don't, maybe you can learn."

"I don't have to learn," she heard herself say. "I came out into this wretched snowstorm to find you, didn't I? After I suffered the tortures of the damned wondering what was keeping you. Of course I love you!"

He kissed her, an exultant kiss that warmed her to her toes.

"I'm going to be a real husband to you from now on," he told her. He made a stirrup of his hands, and Hannah stepped into them, landed astraddle Seesaw's broad, patient old back.

Doss swung up behind her, reached around to catch

hold of the halter rope. "Let's go home," he said, close to her ear.

Hannah forgot all about the whisky in her coat pocket.

It was stone dark out, but the lights of the house were visible in the distance, even through the flurries of snow.

Anyway, Seesaw knew his way home, and he plodded patiently in that direction.

Present Day

The world was frozen solid when Sierra awakened the next morning, to find herself clinging to the edge of Liam's empty bed. Voices wafted up from downstairs, along with heat from the furnace and probably the wood stove, too.

She scrambled out of bed, finger combed her hair and hurried down the hallway.

Travis said something, and Liam laughed aloud. The sound affected Sierra like an injection of sunshine. Then a third voice chimed in, clearly female.

Sierra quickened her pace, her bare feet thumping on the stairs as she descended them.

Travis and Liam were seated at the table, reading the comic strips in the newspaper. A slender blond woman wearing jeans and a pink thermal shirt with the sleeves pushed up stood by the counter, sipping coffee.

"Meg?" Sierra asked. She'd seen her sister's picture, but nothing had prepared her for the living woman. Her clear skin seemed to glow, and her smile was a force of nature.

"Hello, Sierra," she said. "I hope you don't mind my showing up unannounced, but I just couldn't wait any longer, so here I am."

Travis stood, put a hand on Liam's shoulder. Without a

word, the two of them left the room, probably headed for the study.

"Everything Mom said was true," Meg told Sierra quietly. "You're beautiful, and so is Liam."

Sierra couldn't speak, at least for the moment, even though her mind was full of questions, all of them clamoring to be offered at once.

"Maybe you should sit down," Meg said. "You look as though you might faint dead away."

Sierra pulled back the chair at the head of the table and sank into it. "When...when did you get here?" she asked.

"Last night," Meg answered. She poured a fresh cup of coffee, brought it to Sierra. "I hope I'm not interrupting anything."

"Interrupting anything?"

Meg's enormous blue eyes took on a mischievous glint. She swung a leg over the bench and straddled it, as several generations of McKettricks must have done before her, facing Sierra.

"Something's going on between you and Travis," Meg said. "I can feel it."

Sierra wondered if she could carry off a lie and decided not to try. She and Meg had been apart since they were small children, but they were sisters, and there was a bond. Besides, she didn't want to start off on the wrong foot.

"The question is," she said carefully, "is anything going on between *you* and Travis."

"No," Meg answered, "more's the pity. We tried to fall in love. It just didn't happen."

"I'm not talking about falling in love."

Wasn't she? Travis had rocked her universe, and much as she would have liked to believe it was only physical, she knew it was more. She'd never felt anything like that with Adam, and she *had* been in love with him, however naively. However foolishly.

Meg grinned. "You mean sex? We didn't even get that far. Every time we tried to kiss, we ended up laughing too hard to do anything else."

Sierra marveled at the crazy relief she felt.

"Too bad he's leaving," Meg said. "Now we'll have to find somebody else to look after the horses, and it won't be easy."

The bottom fell out of Sierra's stomach.

"Travis is leaving?"

Meg set her coffee cup down with a thump and reached for Sierra's hand. "Oh, my God. You didn't know?"

"I didn't know," Sierra admitted.

Damned if she'd cry.

Who needed Travis Reid, anyway?

She had Liam. She had a family and a home and a two-million-dollar trust fund.

She'd gotten along without Travis, and his lovemaking, all her life. The man was entirely superfluous.

So why did she want to lay her head down on her arms and wail with sorrow?

Chapter 16

1919

Come morning Hannah made her way through the still, chilly dawn to the barn. Besides their own stock, four livery horses were there, gathered at the back of the barn, helping themselves to the haystack. Remnants of harness hung from their backs.

Hannah smiled, led each one into a stall, saw that they each got a bucket of water and some grain. She was milking old Earleen, the cow, when Doss joined her, stiff and bruised but otherwise none the worse for his trials, as far as Hannah could see.

They'd shared a bed the night before, but they'd both been too exhausted, after the rigors of the day and getting Doc Willaby settled comfortably in the spare room, to make love.

"You ought to go into the house, Hannah," Doss said,

sounding both confounded and stern. "This work is mine to do."

"Fine," she said, still milking. There was a rhythm in the task that settled a person's thoughts. "You can gather the eggs and get some butter from the spring house. I reckon Doc will be in the grip of a powerful hunger when he wakes up. He'll want hotcakes and some of that bacon you brought from the smokehouse."

Doss moved along the middle of the barn, limping a little. Stopping to peer into each stall along the way. Hannah watched his progress out of the corner of her eye, smiling to herself.

"I meant what I said last night, Hannah," he said, when he finally reached her. "I love you. But if you really want to go back to your folks in Montana, I won't interfere. I know it's hard, living out here on this ranch."

Hannah's throat ached with love and hope. "It is hard, Doss McKettrick, and I wouldn't mind spending winters in town. But I'm not going to Montana unless you go, too."

He leaned against one of the beams supporting the barn roof, pondering her with an unreadable expression. "Gabe knew," he said.

She stopped milking. "Gabe knew what?"

"How I felt about you. From the very first time I saw you, I loved you. He guessed right away, without my saying a word. And do you know what he told me?"

"I can't imagine," Hannah said, very softly.

"That I oughtn't to feel bad, because you were easy to love."

Tears stung Hannah's eyes. "He was a good man."

"He was," Doss agreed gruffly, and gave a short nod. "He asked me to look after you and Tobias, before he died. Maybe he figured, even then, that you and I would end up together."

"It wouldn't surprise me," Hannah replied. Dear, dear Gabe. She'd loved him so, but he'd gone on, and he'd want her to carry on and be as happy as she could. Tobias, too.

"What I mean to say is," Doss went on, taking off his hat and turning it round and round in his hands by the brim, "I understand what he meant to you. You can say it, straight out, anytime. I won't be jealous."

Hannah stood up so fast she spooked Earleen, who kicked over the milk bucket, three-quarters of the way full now, steaming in the cold and rich with cream. She put her arms around Doss and didn't try to hide her tears.

"You're as good a man as Gabe ever was, Doss McKettrick," she said, "and I won't let you forget it."

He grinned down at her, wanly, but with that familiar spark in his eyes. "I'll build you a house in town, Hannah," he said. "We'll spend winters there, so you can see folks and Tobias can go to school without riding two miles through the snow. Would you like that?"

"Yes," Hannah said. "But I'd stay on this ranch forever, too, if it meant I could be with you."

Doss bent his head. Kissed her. His hands rested lightly on the sides of her waist, beneath the heavy fabric of Gabe's coat.

"You go inside and see to breakfast, Mrs. McKettrick. I'll finish up out here."

She swallowed, nodded. "I love you, Mr. McKettrick," she said.

His eyes danced mischievously. "Once we get Doc back to town," he replied, "I mean to bed you, good and proper."

Hannah blushed. Batted her lashes. "When is he leaving?"

Present Day

Travis was packing, loading things into his truck. Even whistling as he went about it. Meg got into her car and drove off somewhere.

Sierra waited as long as she could bear to—she didn't know how she was going to explain this to Liam, who was sleeping off his flu bug—didn't know how to explain it herself.

She got out the album, for something to do, and set the remembrance book aside without opening it. Even after seeing Hannah and Tobias the night before, in Liam's room, she just didn't believe in magic anymore.

So she took a seat at the table and lifted the cover of the album.

A cracked and yellowed photograph, done in sepia, filled most of the page. Angus McKettrick, the patriarch of the family, stared calmly up at her. He'd been handsome in his youth; she could see that. Though, in the picture his thick hair was white, his stern, square-jawed face etched with lines of sorrow as well as joy. His eyes were clear, intelligent and full of stubborn humor.

It was almost as though he'd known Sierra would be looking at the photo one day, searching for some part of herself in those craggy features, and crooked up one corner of his mouth in the faintest smile, just for her.

Be strong, he seemed to say. *Be a McKettrick.*

Sierra sat for a long time, silently communing with the image.

I don't know how to "be a McKettrick." What does that mean, anyway?

Angus's answer was in his eyes. Being a McKettrick

meant claiming a piece of ground to stand on and putting your roots down deep into it. Holding on, no matter what came at you. It meant loving with passion and taking the rough spots with the smooth. It meant fighting for what you wanted, letting go when that was the best thing to do.

Sierra absorbed all that and turned to the next page.

A good-looking couple posed in the front yard of the very house where Sierra sat, so many years later. A small boy and a girl in her teens stood proudly on either side of them, and underneath someone had written the names in carefully. Holt McKettrick. Lorelei McKettrick. John Henry McKettrick. Lizzie McKettrick.

They wore the name like a badge, all of them.

After that came more pictures of Holt and Lorelei together and separately. In one, they were each holding the hand of a laughing, golden-haired toddler.

Gabriel Angus McKettrick, stated a fading caption beneath.

On the facing page, Lorelei sat proud and straight in a chair, holding an infant. Young Gabriel, older now, stood with a hand on her thigh, his ankles crossed, with the toe of one old-fashioned shoe touching the floor. Holt flanked them all, one hand resting on Lorelei's shoulder. The baby, according to the inscription, was Doss Jacob McKettrick.

Sierra continued to turn pages, and moved through the lives of Gabe and Doss along with them, or so it seemed, catching a glimpse of them on important dates. Birthdays. School. Mounted on ponies. Fishing in a pond.

Sierra felt as though she were looking not at mere photographs, but through little sepia-stained windows into another time, a time as vivid and real as her own.

She watched Gabe and Doss McKettrick grow into

young men, both of them blond, both of them handsome and sturdy.

At last she came to the wedding picture. Her gaze landed on Hannah, standing proudly beside Gabe. She was wearing a lovely white dress, holding a nosegay.

Hannah.

The woman with whom, in some inexplicable way, she shared this house. The woman she had seen in Liam's bedroom the night before, caring for her own sick child even as Sierra was caring for hers.

Sierra could go no further. Not then.

She closed the album carefully.

"Mom?"

She turned, looked around to see Liam standing at the foot of the stairs, in his flannel pajamas. His hair was rumpled, his glasses were askew, and he looked desperately worried.

"Hey, buddy," she said.

"Travis is putting stuff in his truck," he told her. "Like he's going away or something."

Sierra's heart broke into two pieces. She got up, went to him. "I guess he was just here temporarily, to look after your aunt Meg's horses."

Liam blinked. A tear slipped down his cheek. "He can't go," he said plaintively. "Who'll make the furnace work? Who'll get us to the clinic if I get sick?"

"I can do those things, Liam," Sierra said. She offered a weak smile, and Liam looked skeptical. "Okay, maybe not the furnace. But I know how to get a fire going in the wood stove. And I can handle the rest, too."

Liam's lower lip wobbled. "I thought...maybe—"

Sierra hugged him, hard. She wanted to cry herself, but

not in front of Liam. Not when his heart was breaking, just like hers. One of them had to be strong, and she was elected.

She was an adult.

She was a McKettrick.

Before she could think of anything to say, the back door opened and suddenly Travis was there. He looked at her briefly, but then his gaze went straight to Liam's face.

"If you came to say goodbye," Liam blurted out, "then don't! I don't care if you're leaving—*I don't care!*" With that, he turned and fled up the stairs.

"That went well," Travis said, taking off his hat and hanging it on the peg. He didn't take his coat off, though, which meant he really *was* going away. Sierra had known that—and, at the same time, she *hadn't* known it. Not until she was faced with the reality.

"He's attached to you," she said evenly. "But he'll be all right."

Travis studied her so closely that for a moment she thought he was going to refute her words. "I know this all seems pretty sudden," he began.

Sierra kept her distance, glad she wasn't standing too close to him. "It's your life, Travis. You've done a lot to help us, and we're grateful."

Upstairs, something crashed to the floor.

Sierra closed her eyes.

"I'd better go up and talk to him," Travis said.

"No," Sierra replied. "Leave him alone. Please."

Another crash.

She found Liam's backpack, unzipped it and took out the inhaler. "I've got to get him calmed down," she said quietly. "Thanks for...everything. And goodbye."

"Sierra..."

"Goodbye, Travis."

With that, she turned and went up the stairs.

Liam had destroyed his new telescope and his DVD player. He was standing in the middle of the wreckage, trembling with the helplessness of a child in a world run by adults, his face flushed and wet with tears.

Sierra picked up his shoes, made her way to him. "Put these on, buddy," she said gently, crouching to help. "You'll cut your feet if you don't."

"Is he—" Liam gulped down a sob "—gone?"

"I think so," Sierra said.

"Why?" Liam wailed, putting a hand on her shoulder to keep from falling while he jammed one foot into a shoe, then the other. "Why does he have to go?"

Sierra sighed. "I don't know, honey," she answered.

"Make him stay!"

"I can't, Liam."

"Yes, you can! You just don't want to! You don't *want* me to have a dad!"

"Liam, that is enough." Sierra stood, handed him the inhaler. "Breathe," she ordered.

He obeyed, puffing on the inhaler between intermittent, heartbreaking sobs. "Make him stay," he pleaded.

She squired him to the bed, pulled his shoes off again, tucked him in. "Liam," she said.

Outside, the truck door slammed. The engine started up.

And suddenly Sierra was moving.

She ran down the stairs, through the kitchen, and wrenched open the back door. Coatless, shivering, she dashed across the yard toward Travis's truck.

He was backing out, but when he saw her, he stopped. Rolled down the window.

She jumped on to the running board, her fingers curved around the glass. *"Wait,"* she said, and then she felt stupid because she didn't know what to say after that.

Travis eased the door open, and she was forced to step back down on to the ground. Unbuttoning his coat as he got out, he wrapped it around her. But he didn't say anything at all. He just stood there, staring at her.

She huddled inside his coat. It smelled like him, and she wished she could keep it forever. "I thought it meant something," she finally murmured. "When we made love, I mean. I thought it *meant something*."

He cupped a gloved hand under her chin. "Believe me," he said gruffly, "it did."

"Then why are you leaving?"

"Because there didn't seem to be anything else to do. You were busy with Liam, and you'd made it pretty clear we had nothing to talk about."

"We have *plenty* to talk about, Travis Reid. I'm not some…some rodeo groupie you can just have sex with and forget!"

"You can say that again," Travis agreed, smiling a little. "Do you mind if we go inside to have this conversation? It's colder than a well-digger's ass out here, and I'm not wearing a coat."

Sierra turned on her heel and marched toward the house, and Travis followed.

She tried not to think about all the things that might mean.

Inside she gestured toward the table, took off Travis's coat and started a pot of coffee brewing, so she'd have a chance to think up something to say.

Travis stepped up behind her. Laid his hands on her shoulders.

"Sierra," he said. "Stop fiddling with the coffeemaker and talk to me."

She turned, looked up into his eyes. "It's not like I was expecting marriage or anything," she said, whispering. Liam was probably crouched at the top of the stairs by then, listening. "We're adults. We had…we're adults. But the least you could have done, after all that's gone on, was give us a little notice—"

"When Brody died," Travis said, "I died, too. I walked away from everything—my house, my job, everything. Then I met you, and when—" He paused, with a little smile, and glanced toward the stairs, evidently suspecting that Liam was there, all ears, just as she did. "When we *were adults,* I knew the game was up. I had to get it together. Start living my life again."

Sierra blinked, speechless.

He touched his mouth to hers. It wasn't a kiss, and yet it affected Sierra that way. "It's too soon to say this," he said, "but I'm going to say it anyway. Something happened to me yesterday. Something I don't understand. All I know is, I can't live another day like a dead man walking. I called Eve and asked for my old job back, and I'll be working in Indian Rock, at McKettrickCo, with Keegan. In the meantime I've got to put my house on the market and make arrangements to store my stuff. But it won't be long before I'm at your door, with every intention of winning you over for good."

"What are you saying?"

Liam came shooting down the stairs, wheeling his arms. "Get a clue, Mom! He's in love with you!"

"That's right," Travis said. He gave Liam a look of mock

sternness. "I *was* planning to break it to her gradually, though."

"You're in…?" Sierra sputtered.

"Love," Travis finished for her. "Just tell me this one thing. Do I have a chance with you?"

"Give him a *chance,* Mom!" Liam cried jubilantly. "That's not too much to ask, is it? All the man wants is a chance!"

Sierra laughed, even as tears filled her eyes, blurring her vision. "Liam, hush!" she said.

"What do you say, McKettrick?" Travis asked, taking hold of her shoulders again. "Do I get a chance?"

"Yes," she said. "Oh, yes."

"If you're going to work in town," Liam enthused, tugging at Travis's shirtsleeve by then, "you might as well just move in with us!"

Travis chuckled, released Sierra to lean down and scoop Liam up in one arm. "Whoa," he said. "I'm all for *that* plan, but I think your mother needs a little more time."

"You're not leaving?" Liam asked, so hopefully that Sierra's heartbeat quickened.

"I'm not leaving," Travis confirmed. "I've got some things to do in Flagstaff, then I'll be back."

"Will you live right here, on the ranch?" Liam demanded.

"Not right away, cowpoke," Travis answered. "This whole thing is real important. I don't want to get it wrong. Understand?"

Liam nodded solemnly.

"Good," Travis said. "Now, get on back upstairs, so I can kiss your mother without you ogling us."

"I broke my DVD player," Liam confessed, suddenly

crestfallen. "On purpose, too." He paused, swallowed audibly. "Are you mad?"

"You're the one who'll have to do without a DVD player," Travis said reasonably. "Why would *I* be mad?"

"I'm sorry, Travis," Liam told him.

Travis set the boy back on his feet. "Apology accepted. While we're at it, *I'm* sorry, too. I should have talked to you—your mother, too—before I packed up my stuff. I guess I was just in too much of a hurry to get things rolling."

"I forgive you," Liam said.

Travis ruffled his hair. "Beat it," he replied.

Liam scampered toward the stairs and hopped up them as though he were on a pogo stick.

"Are you sure he's sick?" Travis asked.

Sierra laughed. "Kiss me, cowpoke," she said.

1919

Doc Willaby was with them for three full days, waiting for his bumps and bruises to heal and the weather to clear. He played endless games of checkers with Tobias, next to the kitchen stove, and Hannah and Doss tried hard to pretend they were sensible people. The truth was, they could barely keep their hands off each other.

"How come I have to move to the other end of the hall?" Tobias asked Doss, on the morning of the third endless day.

"You just do," Doss answered.

Early that afternoon, the sleigh came pulling into the yard, drawn by Cain and Abel and driven by Kody Jackson, from the livery stable. Two outriders completed the procession.

"Glory be," Doc said, peering out the window, along with Hannah. "They've come to fetch me back to Indian Rock." He looked down at Hannah and smiled wisely. "Now you and Doss can stop acting like a couple of old married folks and do what comes naturally."

Hannah blushed, but she couldn't help smiling in the process. "It's been good having you here, Doc," she said, and she meant it, too. "You saved Doss's life the other night, coming all that way to fetch me, in the shape you were in. I'll be grateful all my days."

He took her hand. Squeezed it. "He loves you, Hannah."

"I know," she said softly. "And I love him, too."

"That's all that counts, in the long run. Or the short one, for that matter. We each of us get a certain number of days to spend on this earth. Only the good Lord knows how many. Spend them loving that man of yours and that fine boy, and you'll have done the right thing."

Hannah stood on tiptoe. Kissed the doctor on the cheek. "Thank you," she said.

Doss came out of the barn to greet Kody and the other men.

They all went down the hill together to set the other wagon upright, leading the team along behind them. Doss put Cain and Abel away, while Kody drove the rig up alongside the house.

Doc was outside by then, ready to go, with his medical bag clutched in one hand and his cane in the other. He turned and waved at Hannah through the window, and she waved back, watching fondly as Doss and another man helped him up into the wagon box.

When Doss didn't come back in right away, Hannah busied herself making the kitchen presentable. Tobias was upstairs, resting in his new bedroom at the front of the house. Now that he'd adjusted to the change, he liked being able to see so clear across the valley from the ga-bled window, but what had really swayed him was the reminder that Doss and Gabe had shared that room when they were boys.

She swept the floor and put fresh coffee on to brew and even switched on the lightbulb instead of lighting lamps, as wintry afternoon shadows darkened the room.

Still, there was no sign of Doss, so she built up the fire in the stove, opened the drawer of the china cabi-net, lifted the cover of the album and took out her re-membrance book.

In the three busy days since she'd seen the other woman and her boy, up there in Tobias's bedroom, she'd thought often of the journal, and kept a close eye on the teapot, too.

Nothing extraordinary happened, but inside, in a quiet part of herself, Hannah was waiting. She carried the re-membrance book over to the rocking chair drawn up close to the stove and sat down. Perhaps she'd begin mak-ing regular entries in that journal.

She'd write about her and Doss, and make notes as Tobias grew toward manhood. She'd record the dates the peonies bloomed, and tuck a photograph inside, now and then. Doss had promised her they'd build a house in In-dian Rock, and pass the hard high-country winters there. She would capture the dimensions of the new place in these pages, and perhaps even make sketches. One day she'd take up a pen and write that the baby had come, safe and strong and well.

She was so caught up in the prospect of all the years ahead, just waiting to be lived and then set down on paper,

that a few moments passed before she realized that another hand had written beneath her own short paragraphs.

My name is Sierra McKettrick.
    I have a son, too, and his name is Liam. He's seven,
and he has asthma. He's the center of my life.
    You have nothing to fear from me. I'm not a ghost,
just an ordinary flesh-and-blood woman. A mother,
like you.

Hannah stared at the words in disbelief.
Read them again, and then again.
It couldn't be.
But it was.
The woman she'd seen was a McKettrick, too, living
far in the future. She had the proof right here—not that
she meant to show it to just everybody. Some folks would
say she'd written those words herself, of course, but Hannah knew she hadn't.
She touched the clear blue ink in wonder. It looked
different, somehow, from the kind that came in a bottle.
The door opened, and Doss came in. He took off his
coat and hat, hung them up neatly, like he always did.
Hannah held the remembrance book close against her
chest. Should she let Doss see? Would he believe, as she
did, that two different centuries had somehow managed
to touch and blend, right here in this house?
Her heart fluttered in her breast.
"Hannah?" He sounded a little worried.
"Come and look at this, Doss," she said.
He came, crouched beside her chair, read the two en-
tries in the journal, hers and Sierra's.

She watched his face, hopeful and afraid.

Doss raised his eyes to meet hers. "That," he said, "is the strangest thing I've ever run across."

"There's more," Hannah said. "I saw her, Doss. I saw this woman, and her little boy, the night of your accident."

He closed a hand over hers. "If you say so, Hannah," he told her quietly, "then I believe you."

"You do?"

He grinned. "Does that surprise you?"

"A little," she admitted. "When Tobias mentioned seeing the boy, you said it must be his imagination."

Doss handed back the book. "Life is strange," he said. "There's a mystery just about everywhere you look, when you think about it. Babies being born. Grass poking up through hard ground after a long winter. The way it makes me feel inside when you smile at me."

Hannah leaned, kissed his forehead. "Flatterer," she said.

"Is Tobias asleep?" he asked.

She blushed. "Yes."

He pulled her to her feet, set the remembrance book aside on the counter and kissed her.

"I think we've waited long enough, don't you?" he asked.

Hours later, hair askew, bundled in a wrapper, well and thoroughly loved, Hannah sneaked back downstairs. She gathered ink and a pen from the study and lit a lantern in the kitchen.

Then, smiling, she sat down to write.

Present Day

Travis lay sprawled on his stomach in Sierra's bed, sound asleep. She sat up beside him, stroked his bare back once with a gentle pass of her hand. In the three days since he'd moved out of the trailer, he'd been back several times, on one pretext or another. Finally Meg had packed some of her things and some of Liam's, and the two of them had gone to stay in town with friends of hers.

"You two really need some time alone," she'd said, with a wicked grin lighting her eyes.

Sierra smiled down at Travis. So far they'd made good use of that time alone. They'd talked a lot, in between bouts of lovemaking, and they still had plenty to say to each other—maybe enough to last a lifetime.

She switched on the lamp, took Hannah's remembrance book from the bedside table, and opened it. Her eyes widened, and she drew in a breath.

Beneath her own entry, in the same stately, faded writing as before, Hannah had written:

It's nice to know there's another woman in the house, even if I can't see or hear you, most of the time. We must be family, since your name is McKettrick. Maybe you're descended from us, from Doss and me. I told my son, Tobias, that your name is Sierra. He said that was pretty, and he'd like the new baby to be called that, too, if it's a girl...

There was more, but Sierra couldn't read it, because her eyes were blurred with tears of amazement. She bounded out of bed, not caring if she awakened Travis, and hurried downstairs, switching on lights as she went. She had the album out and was flipping through the pages at the middle when he joined her, blinking and shirtless, with his jeans misbuttoned.

"What's going on?" he asked, yawning.

Sierra's heart thumped at the base of her throat.

She forced herself to slow down, turn the pages gently. And then she found what she was looking for—an old, old photograph of two children, smiling for the camera lens. The little boy she'd seen in Liam's room, with Hannah, holding a baby wearing a long, lacy gown.

Beneath the picture, Hannah had written Tobias's name and the baby's.

Sierra Elizabeth McKettrick.

Sierra put a hand to her mouth and gasped.

Travis drew closer. "Sierra—"

"Look at this," Sierra said, stabbing at the image with one finger. "What do you see?"

Travis frowned. "An old picture of two kids."

"Look at the baby's name."

"Sierra. You must have been named for her."

"I think *she* was named for *me*," Sierra said.

"How could *she* be named for *you*?"

"Sit down," Sierra told him. She reached for Hannah's remembrance book, offered it when he was seated. "Read this."

He read. Looked up at her with wide eyes. "You don't really think—"

"That I've been communicating with a woman who lived in this house in 1919, and probably for years after that? Yes, Travis, that is *exactly* what I think!"

"But, *how?*"

"You said it yourself, when I first got here. Strange things happen in this house."

"This is beyond strange. Are you going to tell anybody else about this?"

"Mother and Meg," Sierra said. "Liam, too, when he's a little older."

He reached for her hand, wove his fingers through hers, squeezed. "And me. You told *me*, Sierra."

"Well, *yeah*."

"You must trust me."

She grinned. "You're right," she said. "I must trust you a whole lot, Travis Reid."

"Can we go back to bed now?"

She closed the album and tucked Hannah's remembrance book carefully inside. "Race you!" she cried, and dashed for the stairs.

* * * * *

Michelle Major grew up in Ohio but dreamed of living in the mountains. Soon after graduating with a degree in journalism, she pointed her car west and settled in Colorado. Her life and house are filled with one great husband, two beautiful kids, a few furry pets and several well-behaved reptiles. She's grateful to have found her passion writing stories with happy endings. Michelle loves to hear from her readers at michellemajor.com.

Books by Michelle Major

Harlequin Special Edition

Crimson, Colorado

Anything for His Baby
A Baby and a Betrothal
Always the Best Man
Christmas on Crimson Mountain
Romancing the Wallflower
Sleigh Bells in Crimson
Coming Home to Crimson

HQN

The Magnolia Sisters

A Magnolia Reunion
The Magnolia Sisters
The Road to Magnolia
The Merriest Magnolia

Visit the Author Profile page
at Harlequin.com for more titles.

HER SOLDIER OF FORTUNE

Michelle Major

To the Fortunes of Texas readers—
thanks for making me a part of your reading life
with these books.

Chapter 1

Nathan Fortune heard car wheels crunching up the driveway through the open kitchen window at his family's ranch outside the tiny town of Paseo, Texas. It was almost noon, but he'd just made his second pot of coffee for the day.

Ignoring whoever was stopping by for an unannounced visit, he poured a steaming stream of coffee into a mug, took a big gulp, then promptly spit it into the sink. Grimacing, he grabbed a container of vanilla creamer from the refrigerator and dumped a generous amount into his cup. While it wasn't up to the standards of his brother's wife, at least it was palatable.

He'd never realized he made coffee that tasted like tar until late last spring when Ariana Lamonte arrived on the ranch. Hope sparked inside him that maybe Jayden and Ariana had returned to the ranch from their research trip down to Corpus Christi. They weren't scheduled to be back until next week, but if they were here now he could definitely convince Ariana to make him a cup of coffee in that fancy espresso maker he and the third triplet, Grayson, had gotten for her last Christmas.

During his time as a navy SEAL, he'd come to master over a dozen different types of guns, but that shiny machine remained a mystery to him. Ariana loved coffee, and Nate needed caffeine like he needed air when memories of that final mission in Afghanistan kept him up at night. Sometimes he slept like the dead, and even managed to convince himself that he was getting over that last tragic mission. But then he'd wake in a cold sweat, nightmares prodding at him like an insistent finger, making sure he knew he could never move past the way he'd failed the man who had been his best friend.

The doorbell rang, and he sighed. Definitely not his brother and Ariana. He took another swig of coffee and wiped a sleeve across his mouth, approaching the front door slowly. Most people in Paseo knew Nate well enough to simply call out a greeting and let themselves in. Actually, most people would assume he was out working the land at this time of day. Normally they'd be right, except he'd been up half the night and needed coffee to keep him going—even the kind that tasted like burnt tar.

He opened the front door almost warily, not sure what to expect. Ever since he and his brothers had discovered that the father they thought had died during their mom's pregnancy was not only alive, but was tech mogul Gerald Robinson, and more specifically Jerome Fortune, there was no telling who might show up on Nate's doorstep. Jerome Fortune had faked his own death over thirty years ago, shortly after a fight with Nate's mom, to make a break with his own controlling father, but as Gerald Robinson, he not only had eight legitimate children with his wife, Charlotte, but a host of illegitimate offspring.

Nothing could have prepared Nate for his body's reaction to the woman who stood on his front porch, glancing around like she was more than a little lost. He didn't recognize her, although there was something familiar in the big brown eyes that looked into his. What was wholly unfamiliar was the sharp prick of desire that stabbed him as he took in her delicate features—those molten chocolate eyes, a pert nose and lips that looked almost bee-stung in fullness despite being pressed into a tight line.

Her hair was thick and dark like her eyes, tumbling around her shoulders. She wore a plain white T-shirt over faded jeans, and Nate swallowed as his gaze took in the perfect curve of her breasts and hips. He promptly cursed himself for his line of thought. Here was a stranger at his front door, and he was ogling her like some sort of randy teenager instead of a grown man of thirty-seven.

"Can I help you?" he asked, hoping he sounded more polite than lecherous.

"Hi, Nate," she said softly. "How are you?"

"Um…fine." He took off his Stetson, slapping it against his thigh, and ran a hand through his hair with his other hand. "Do I know you?"

The woman flashed a shy smile. "I'm Bianca Shaw. Eddie's sister. Don't you remember me?"

Nate lifted one hand to grip the doorframe, whether to steady himself or to keep himself from reaching for Bianca, he couldn't say. The beautiful woman in front of him was Eddie's little sister?

"Busy Bee," he murmured, repeating the nickname Eddie'd used for his younger sister.

She gave a short laugh. "I haven't had someone call me

that since…" Her voice trailed off as her hands clenched in tight fists at her side.

"I'm sorry about Eddie," he offered, the words tasting like dust in his mouth. "He died a hero." Nate cleared his throat. "If it helps."

"Thank you," she whispered, and swiped her fingers across her cheek.

The familiar regret and blame churned through his stomach, turning the coffee he'd drunk to acid in his belly. Eddie Shaw had been like a brother to him. They'd met their first day of Basic Underwater Demolition/SEAL training—more routinely known as BUD/S. Although as a triplet, Nate had always been close to his brothers, he'd formed an immediate bond with the stocky, wisecracking soldier that was just as strong.

From the few times he'd been to Eddie's mom's cramped apartment in San Antonio, he remembered Eddie's sister as a gangly teenager who giggled at everything and constantly tried to tag along with the brother who was nine years older than her. Eddie had been infinitely patient with Bianca, and even when they were stationed overseas or on a ship, he'd always taken the time to answer her overly perfumed letters and all the silly questions she asked about life as a navy SEAL.

"You're here in Paseo," he said, stating the obvious because his brain felt about five steps behind the reality of whatever was happening right now.

"I'm here," she echoed and bit down on her bottom lip, her gaze skittering away from his like she was nervous about something. "I hope I'm not bothering you."

Nate had met people from all over the world and all different walks of life during his stint in the US Navy. He'd become something of an expert on reading body language, and from the splotches of color blooming on Bianca's cheeks to the rigid set of her thin shoulders to the tiny breath she blew out as if her lungs couldn't handle Paseo's clean air, Nate would have sworn on everything he had that the woman standing in front of him was in trouble.

Eddie's sister was in trouble. The brother-in-arms whom Nate had failed to save during their last mission wouldn't have let that happen. Neither would Nate. All he had left of Eddie were memories and the guilt that burned his gut. But he could honor Eddie by taking care of Bianca. It was the only thing he had left to offer.

He pushed aside his reaction to her, pretended he didn't feel attraction pulsing through him like a drum beat and tried to see her as the girl she'd once been. Eddie's baby sister. That was all she could ever be to Nate.

"What do you need, Bianca?" he asked, wishing suddenly he was a different kind of man. One who could give her everything she wanted and more.

Bianca's breath whooshed out in a shuddery rush at Nathan Fortune's simple question.

The summer she was five years old, new renters had moved into the tiny apartment next door to the cramped space where Bianca lived with her mom and Eddie. The walls in the run-down complex were paper-thin, and the young couple stayed up late with friends, music thumping so loud it would make the pictures on the wall vibrate. Bianca's mom had quickly become a regular at the all-night parties, and Bianca would often wake in the middle of the night to laughter or voices yelling out or other strange noises she didn't understand at the time.

She'd tiptoe from her tiny bedroom across the hall to where Eddie slept and listen to his regular breathing. When

Bianca complained about the noise, her mom told her to plug her ears with toilet paper, but that never worked. She'd creep closer to the mattress Eddie slept on. Bianca had a real headboard for her twin bed, but Eddie only had a mattress pushed up against one wall.

Her brother always seemed to know when she was coming because by the time her knobby knees hit the threadbare covers, he'd sigh and ask, "What do you need, Bianca?" at the same time he'd lift one corner of the sheet so she could crawl in next to him.

She never had to answer the question out loud because Eddie always knew what she needed without her even saying it. There in the dark, with her big brother next to her, Bianca would fall back asleep. With Eddie at her side, it didn't matter what was happening in the apartment next door. Eddie would keep her safe.

She was a big girl now and had been taking care of herself for enough time to know she didn't need to rely on anyone. Everyone except Eddie had disappointed or abandoned her, so she'd quickly learned to stand on her own two feet. But recently she'd lost her footing as the angry hurricane of her life pummeled her from all sides. Now when she laid awake in the wee hours of the night, the only thing she wished was not to be so alone.

It was as if the universe had heard her silent plea and answered her need with Nathan Fortune. He stood in front of her, strong and sure, exactly the opposite of how Bianca felt. He was muscled and clearly in shape, his shoulders broad beneath the fabric of the chambray shirt he wore. His skin was tanned from the sun, despite the wide brim of his hat, and she could see a faint patchwork of lines fanning out from his light brown eyes when he smiled.

He was a few inches taller than Eddie had been but

not so much that he towered over her. In fact, it looked as though she'd fit perfectly tucked underneath his shoulder. She locked her knees to keep from stepping into him, wrapping her arms around his lean waist and burying her face in his shirtfront.

"Now that you mention it," she said with an awkward little laugh, "I was hoping I might stay with you for a few days." She swallowed and added, "A week or two at the longest." She glanced to either side of the farmhouse's wraparound porch, as though the house itself might offer up an answer.

The ranch was just as Eddie had described it, with huge fields and rolling hills in the distance. The house was a charming, if modest, two-story stone structure with picture windows and faded trim that gave it a settled-in, well-loved look. "If you have room and it's not too much of an inconvenience."

"Are you in trouble?"

His gaze was unreadable as he studied her.

Yes, she was in big trouble because she'd sought out Nate in place of her brother, but her reaction to him was both unexpected and dangerous, as it threatened to overwhelm her at a time when she was already holding on to her composure by a thin thread.

"No," she answered immediately, which she figured they both knew was a lie. "I just need a break from my life—a fresh start. Eddie thought of you as family, so I came to, as well. Even though you're practically a stranger. He talked a lot about coming to visit Paseo between deployments. He really enjoyed his time on the ranch. So I thought—"

She sucked in a breath when Nate reached out and placed his fingertip against her lips. "You can stay here as long as you want, Bianca. Eddie was my family in every way that counts. In some weird way, that makes you my little sister."

Bianca opened her mouth to argue. There were a hundred things she wanted from Nate, but for him to think of her as his little sister darn sure wasn't one of them. But she needed a place to stay more than she cared to admit, so she simply leaned forward and gave him a small hug, the way she'd done with Eddie all the time. It was a test, she told herself, to see if she could ignore the way he made butterflies dance across her stomach. To see if she could pretend she didn't notice his rock-hard abs when her fingers brushed his shirtfront or how good he smelled—like soap and the outdoors.

She managed it pretty well and didn't even let the soft whimper that bubbled up in her throat escape into the charged air between them.

Instead she gave him one last pat on the back and stepped away, surprised to find him staring down at her like she'd just grabbed his butt.

"I'm alone here," he blurted. "At the ranch."

"Okay," she answered with a shrug.

"My brother Grayson is touring with the rodeo and Mom manages his career, so she's with him. Jayden and his wife won't be back until next week." He crossed his arms over his chest. "Whenever Eddie was here, we had a full house."

She nodded. "I think he was jealous that you were a triplet. He always wanted a brother or two. I look forward to meeting your family."

"You might not be comfortable being out here with only me," he suggested. "It's a haul to town and Paseo is a postage stamp compared to San Antonio."

"San Antonio is too crowded these days," she countered, wondering why Nate suddenly looked so uncomfortable. He hadn't shown a moment's hesitation in offering her a place to stay, but now he seemed to be almost warning her away.

"I'm not great company," he continued, glancing over his shoulder into the entry as if he might find a reason for her to venture inside the cozy farmhouse. "I make terrible coffee."

"I can make my own coffee."

"I'm grumpy in the morning. You might not like me when I'm grumpy."

"As long as you don't turn green and bust out of your clothes, I think I'll manage."

"I can be mean as a grizzly coming out of hibernation."

"If you've changed your mind," she said, crossing her arms over her chest to mimic his stance, "just tell me, Nate. Otherwise, you're not going to scare me away. Remember, I grew up with a navy SEAL. Talk all you want about grizzlies, but I know you guys are big teddy bears at heart."

"A teddy bear?" He shook his head, looking as offended as her late granny had when Bianca's mom cursed in the middle of the Christmas church service. "I'm not a teddy bear and neither was your brother. In fact—"

"Want to see my teddy bear?" a voice called from Bianca's car. The back door opened and a pair of scuffed sneakers hit the dust, the heels lighting up as they did. "His name is Roscoe, and he's my best friend."

"EJ," Bianca called as the boy ran forward, swinging a battered stuffed animal above his head. "I told you to wait—"

"You talked too long, Mommy. Roscoe got bored. He wants to see everything." Her beautiful, energetic, precocious four-year-old son climbed the front porch steps, and she automatically held out a hand. As was typical, EJ ignored it.

"Are you Uncle Eddie's friend?" he asked Nate, who had taken a step back, staring at her boy like EJ was a snake in the grass. Or maybe it was shock over EJ's resemblance to Eddie, with his dark hair, olive-colored skin and deep brown eyes that always seemed to be full of mischief. Mischief and EJ were bosom pals. "Are you a cowboy? Are we staying with you? Can I have a glass of water?"

EJ didn't wait for an answer to any of his questions. He ducked away from Bianca when she reached for him and barreled past Nate, disappearing into the house.

Bianca started to follow but Nate filled the doorway, blocking her way. "Is there something—or someone—you forgot to mention?"

She flashed what she hoped was an innocent smile and managed to only cringe a little when there was a crash from inside the house. "That's my son, EJ," she said quickly. "And we'd better go after him unless all the other breakables in your house are nailed down."

Chapter 2

"I'm sorry, Mommy. It was an accident." EJ clutched the raggedy teddy bear tight to his chest. "Roscoe bumped the lamp when I was looking at the game. He didn't mean it."

"You owe Mr. Nate an apology," Bianca scolded gently. "This is his home and we're guests here." She glanced up at Nate from below her impossibly long lashes. "At least I think we're staying for a bit. But after this—"

"Of course you're staying," Nate told her. "Accidents happen, and I never liked that lamp, anyway."

Bianca offered the hint of a grateful smile. She ruffled her son's dark hair. "EJ."

In that way that mothers of boys had, Bianca seemed to be able to communicate an entire sentence simply by speaking her son's name.

"I'm sorry about your ugly lamp," EJ said solemnly. "Roscoe is sorry, too."

"How old are you, EJ?" Nate asked.

The boy held up four dirt-smudged fingers. "Four."

"How about Roscoe?"

That question earned Nate a smile so like Eddie's it made his chest ache.

"Roscoe is two," EJ explained. "So he's still kinda clumsy."

"Is there a broom in the kitchen?" Bianca asked as she bent to pick up the top half of the lamp, which hadn't cracked. "I'll sweep—"

"I can get it," Nate told her, still shocked that Eddie's little sister had shown up on his doorstep all grown up and with a child of her own. "Did you drive all the way from San Antonio today?"

She placed the broken lamp gently on the table next to the sofa. "It's only six hours. We got an early start."

"Did you stop for lunch?"

"Nope," EJ answered before Bianca could. "I had cheese crackers and a banana."

"I'll make you both lunch."

"You don't have to," Bianca protested at the same time EJ offered, "I like peanut butter and honey with the crusts cut off."

"I can make him a sandwich," Bianca offered, her cheeks flaming bright pink. "He's a picky eater."

"I'm not picky." The boy shook his head, still clinging to the bear. "I just eat what I eat."

"You sound like your uncle," Nate said, a ball of emotion lodging in the back of his throat. "Do you know he put hot sauce on everything?"

Bianca chuckled softly. Nate's gaze tracked to her and they shared a smile, clearly both remembering the man they had in common. "I once saw him shake hot sauce on a brownie."

"Yuck." EJ made a face. "I like ketchup."

"Me, too," Nate agreed. "But not on a peanut butter and honey sandwich."

"Do you own horses?" EJ asked.

"Yes."

"Cows?"

"Yep."

"Pigs?"

Nate shook his head. "No pigs, but we have a chicken coop."

"Do you make nuggets out of them?"

"They lay eggs," Nate explained, grinning at the boy. "I'll make you an omelet in the morning."

"I like cereal," the boy told him. "Where's my room? Do I have a place to put my clothes? Can Roscoe have his own pillow?"

"Let's eat lunch and then I'll give you a tour of the house."

"EJ," Bianca said, putting a hand on the boy's thin shoulder. "Can you thank Mr. Nate for letting us stay with him?"

"Thank you," EJ said, then added, "I need to pee."

"Bathroom's right around the corner," Nate said, pointing toward the hall.

As the boy skipped out of the room, Bianca let out an audible breath. "I'm sorry I didn't mention him at the start."

"It's fine."

"I wasn't sure—"

"Bianca." Nate stepped forward and tucked a strand of hair behind her ear. "I'm happy to have both you and EJ here. He reminds me so much of Eddie. I bet your brother loved having a little mini-me running around. I can't believe he never mentioned a nephew."

"EJ's a great kid," she said, not directly addressing his comments. "He has a lot of energy, just like Eddie."

"It should serve him later in life. Eddie had more stamina in his little finger than the rest of our squadron combined."

"I hope it does," she said, almost wistfully. "He's the light of my life. I'd do anything for him."

She blinked several times and turned to look out the family room's picture window to the fields south of the house. Nate had a million questions, but suddenly she seemed so fragile, and he was afraid she might cry if he pushed her for details on how she'd ended up at his house. He couldn't stand to see a woman cry, especially not one who was clearly trying to hold it together.

As he looked at her more closely, he noticed faint circles under her big eyes, like she hadn't had a decent night's sleep in ages. Where was EJ's father? Nate knew if he had a son, he'd be a part of his life.

Was EJ's father dead or had he deserted Bianca? Nate thought about his newly discovered extended family of Fortunes. He and his brothers had grown up simply, unlike Gerald and Charlotte Robinson's children. But they'd had a mother who loved them and the ranching couple who'd taken Deborah in, pregnant and alone, when she'd had nowhere else to turn. Did his mom ever feel as weary and desperate as Bianca looked right now? His heart clenched at the thought.

"Ham or turkey?" he shouted suddenly, then forced a calming breath when Bianca whirled to him, her brown eyes wide.

"Excuse me?"

"Didn't mean to startle you," he told her. "I'm going to make sandwiches. Would you like ham or turkey?"

"You really don't—"

"I'll choose if you don't."

Her delicate brows furrowed as she stared at him. "Turkey," she said finally, and with that one word Nate felt like he'd won some sort of battle. He liked winning.

"Great. Lunch will be ready in ten minutes." He paused on his way to the kitchen. "Unless you need help unloading your bags from the car."

"No," she said, almost too quickly. "We don't have much. Just a weekend bag. We're not staying that long. I don't want to impose. It won't—"

"You can stay as long as you like," he told her. "Eddie was family, Busy Bee. That makes you family, too. If you want to tell me what's going on, I'll listen. If not, I won't intrude. But know that you have a place here."

He saw the sharp rise of her chest as his words seemed to hit their mark. "Thank you," she whispered, and then hurried out of the room.

"It's quiet here."

EJ flipped onto his side to face Bianca on the double bed in Grayson's room later that night.

"We're in the country," she said, gently pushing back the lock of hair that had flopped into his eyes. It was dark in the room, other than the faint glow from the night-light she'd plugged into the wall near the door. She'd told Nate that she and EJ could share a bedroom, but he'd insisted EJ could take Grayson's room and she could use his mom's since they'd be on the rodeo circuit until spring.

Her son loved claiming the space as his own, and Bianca wondered if she might actually get a decent night's sleep without the noise from the freeway across the street from their run-down apartment building in San Antonio. "There are country sounds here."

"Like the horses and cows," EJ said in wonder, inching closer until his leg pressed against hers and she could smell his toothpaste-scented breath. She'd be sad when her boy got old enough that he didn't want to snuggle any longer.

"Don't forget the chickens," she told him.

"The rooster is my favorite."

She dropped a quick kiss on the tip of his nose. "The rooster might even wake up earlier than you, buddy."

"No one wakes up earlier than me, Mommy."

Bianca sighed. "Think of this as vacation. You can sleep late."

He yawned, then smiled. "I don't like to sleep late."

"I know, bud."

"I like it here," he said sleepily.

"Me, too," she whispered, almost afraid to say the words out loud for fear she'd jinx her new bit of luck. She rolled her shoulders against the mattress, amazed at how light she felt. Strange that the weight she'd been carrying for so long it felt a part of her had already started to lift.

She needed to find a way to earn her keep on the ranch, but not having the pressure of a dead-end job and the stress of worrying about childcare for EJ was a gift. She'd been running on all cylinders for so long with no time to catch her breath or figure out a plan for making a better life. Nate Fortune, with his matter-of-fact demeanor and quiet intensity, seemed to have no issue with giving her space. True to his word, he hadn't pushed her for details about her circumstances. Not during the simple but satisfying lunch he'd made or on the brief tour of the house he'd led them on after they ate.

He seemed to be almost more comfortable with EJ than he was with her, patiently answering EJ's litany of questions while barely making eye contact with her.

She had a healthy dose of curiosity where the former navy SEAL was concerned.

Why did he leave the service and return to Paseo in the first place? She knew he'd been with Eddie on the mission that had killed her brother. Could he give her any more information about how and why her brother had died?

She'd practically memorized the reports and brief news stories she'd found online, but nothing in the official paperwork told her what she wanted to know. Did Eddie suffer? Was it quick? How had things gone so wrong for the brother who'd always seemed invincible?

She hadn't asked any of those questions. If she wasn't willing to share the specifics of her life, could she really expect Nate to open up his past for inspection? But he must have read something in her eyes because in the middle of the tour, his shoulders had stiffened and he'd made some excuse about needing to get back to work and all but bolted out of the house.

Other than a distant trail of dust on the horizon, she hadn't seen him again. He hadn't returned to the house at dinnertime, and she'd eventually heated EJ a meal of chicken nuggets and macaroni and cheese. She'd placed the leftover macaroni in a bowl on the counter in case Nate wanted dinner when he came in. It was a meager offering, and she planned to drive into town for groceries the following morning. The least she could do while she was here was to cook Nate a few decent meals.

She'd learned to cook as a teenager so Eddie would have home-cooked meals when he was on leave, and sitting around the small table listening to her brother tell tales of his adventures in the navy were still some of her happiest memories.

EJ made a tiny whimpering sound and shifted away from

her on the bed. She listened to his steady breathing for a few more minutes, then climbed out of the bed and crossed the hall to Deborah's room, which Nate had offered her without reservation. She heard a noise from downstairs, alerting her that Nate had returned to the house. It was past nine and she wondered what he'd been doing to keep him away for so long. The thought that he might have a girlfriend in town both intrigued and frustrated her. She laughed inwardly as she realized EJ came by his curiosity honestly.

The urge to see Nate again was almost overwhelming, but Bianca walked into her room and closed the door, leaning against it as if that would keep her inside. She was lucky Nate had agreed to let her stay so easily, and didn't want him to regret the decision because she couldn't help but make a pest of herself.

His mother's room was simple, with one chest of drawers and a faded quilt covering the bed. Bianca appreciated the framed photos scattered around the room, all featuring the triplets at various ages. Bianca's photos of EJ and his preschool artwork that she'd framed were among her prized possessions, all of them currently stuffed in the trunk of her car.

She dressed for bed, leaving the window cracked slightly so the night breeze cooled the air. She'd mostly kept her apartment windows shut, even in the blistering heat of a Texas summer, both for security reasons and to limit the outside noise. But the ranch was quiet and peaceful, and she took a deep breath as she slipped between the sheets.

Bianca had gotten used to being tired, but that didn't mean sleep came easily to her. She expected to toss and turn as she normally did into the wee hours, but the next thing she knew she was blinking awake as pale gray light began to creep through the curtains that covered the window.

"It's morning, Mommy."

EJ's face was only inches from hers, and she turned her head to glance at the clock on the nightstand.

"It's six o'clock," she said with a groan and then sat up, yawning widely. "I let you stay up a whole hour past your bedtime last night so you'd sleep later this morning."

"Didn't work," EJ reported with a wide grin. "I haven't even heard the rooster yet. I beat him."

"You sure did," she agreed. She'd slept through the night without waking but somehow felt more exhausted than she had in ages. She struggled to sit up against the pillow, letting the sheet and quilt slip down to her waist. "But it's too early, sweetie. I bet Mr. Nate isn't even—"

"Good morning," a deep voice called from the doorway. "I'm impressed that you two keep ranch hours."

Maybe it was her fuzzy brain, but Bianca felt her mouth drop open as she took in Nate Fortune leaning against the doorjamb, sipping from an oversize mug. He looked even more handsome than he had yesterday, wearing a red-checked flannel shirt and faded jeans molded to his lean hips and muscled thighs. Bianca must have been more desperate than she'd even realized because she was jealous of a pair of pants. His hair was damp at the ends and curled over his collar like he was a couple of weeks past needing a haircut.

"I beat the rooster," EJ repeated, grinning widely.

"Nice work," Nate said with an answering smile.

Bianca stifled a yawn. "This is an unholy hour for people to be awake and chipper."

"Mommy's grumpy in the morning," EJ announced helpfully.

She made a face. "It's practically still the middle of the night."

Nate chuckled, the sound reverberating through her. "At least you're not turning green and busting out of your clothes."

At the mention of clothes, Bianca glanced down to the thin tank top she wore for sleeping. The words *You Can't Make Everyone Happy. You're Not Pizza.* were printed across the front, and she'd taken off her bra before she went to bed last night. She looked up again and Nate's gaze slammed into hers. She automatically crossed her arms over her chest, but at the way his brown eyes sparked, it was obvious he'd already noticed her lack of a bra. Goose bumps rose on her skin in response to the intensity of his stare. Maybe Nate's thoughts where she was concerned weren't so brotherly, after all.

Bianca's heart hammered a frantic beat in her chest. She definitely didn't need coffee to wake her up when Nate looked at her like that.

"Come on, Mommy," EJ urged, tugging at the covers. "You should get out of bed."

She pulled him into her lap, keeping the covers tucked around her. She'd put on a pair of short boxers and wasn't quite ready to expose her legs for Nate's inspection. When was the last time she'd shaved them, anyway?

Nate cleared his throat. "Hey, EJ, maybe we can let your mom catch up on sleep this morning while you help me with chores in the barn. What do you think?"

The boy squirmed out of her grasp, his bare feet hitting the carpet with a soft thud. "Can I go, Mommy?"

"Sure," she mumbled, swallowing to wet her throat when the word came out on a croak. "You need to get dressed, brush your teeth and eat breakfast first."

"We'll handle that," Nate told her as EJ ran past him,

heading across the hall. "You go back to sleep. You obviously need it."

Ouch. Bianca raised a hand to her cheek. She could feel her face flooding with color as she let out a half laugh, half sigh. "I guess it's been rougher recently than I realized. Plus the drive from San Antonio took a lot out of me. I'm not normally this much of a mess."

"You're not a mess." Nate took one step toward the bed then stopped, his fingers gripping the mug so tight his knuckles turned white. He stared at her for several long moments, a muscle ticking in his jaw. "You're beautiful, Bianca. But it's obvious you've been taking on too much. If Eddie were alive, he would have never let that happen. You're here now…with me. I only want to help."

Her toes curled as relief and gratitude whirled through her like a tornado. She hated what her life had come to in the past few months but was so happy to have this chance at a literal do-over. She could make things right for herself and EJ because Nate was in her corner.

"Thank you," she whispered. "I'm going to make this up to you someday. I promise."

"You don't have to do anything. I owe Eddie more than you can ever know. Helping you is the least I can do." His voice was tight with tension as he spoke, as if there were more he wanted to say. Then EJ ran back in wearing his favorite dump truck T-shirt, a pair of baggy jeans and his light-up sneakers.

"I'm ready for breakfast," he said, tugging on Nate's free hand. "I got dressed by myself. My sneakers have Velcro so Mommy doesn't have to tie them."

"Clever," Nate murmured, smiling at her son.

"Do you always wear cowboy boots?" EJ asked, pointing to the toe of Nate's leather boot.

"Almost always."

EJ turned his attention to Bianca. "Mommy, can I get a pair of boots?"

She wondered how much youth-sized cowboy boots would run. "We'll see."

"Get some rest," Nate told her, ruffling EJ's hair as he turned for the door, then quickly added, "Not because you look like you need it. Because you deserve it."

She flashed a smile. "Good save, cowboy."

He nodded then led EJ from the room. Bianca readjusted the pillow, then laid back and stared up at the ceiling. She wasn't sure she'd be able to fall asleep again, but within seconds her eyes drifted shut. Maybe just a few minutes more, she told herself. Just a few.

Chapter 3

"Like this, Mr. Nate?"

"Exactly. Hold the nail steady with one hand and the hammer with the other. Careful of your fingers."

Later that morning, Nate stood next to EJ at the workbench on the far side of the barn, watching as the little boy hammered together two boards to be used as a ramp for the chicken coop. It was a mundane chore Nate had been putting off for weeks, but it was the perfect job for an eager four-year-old.

Nate never would have guessed how much he'd enjoy having a kid shadow him all morning as he fed and watered the livestock and then drove out to check the perimeter fences. EJ's enthusiastic stream of questions and excitement over every new task made the time fly by. EJ wanted to be involved in every piece of the action, reminding Nate of himself and his brothers when they were kids.

Earl and Cynthia Thompson, who'd owned the ranch,

had been like grandparents to the triplets. Had his mother been as exhausted as Bianca seemed?

Probably.

He and his brothers were more than a handful.

Earl had been a quiet man with a surly countenance that hid a gentle heart. From the time Nate could remember, the craggy rancher had worked the Fortune boys, teaching them to manage the land and livestock and giving them a purpose when they might have turned wild with a less steady hand guiding them.

Nate wanted to do that for EJ, the way Eddie would have if he'd survived that last mission. As guilt exploded in Nate's chest, he had to force himself not to step away from the boy. What right did he have to insert himself into this child's life and try to offer direction?

When push had come to shove, he hadn't been able to save his best friend. His brothers and mother had done fine for decades on their own while he was traveling the world with the navy. And shortly after he'd come home, all hell had broken loose with the discovery that Gerald Robinson was their father. Not that Nate could blame himself for that bombshell, but he hated that he hadn't been able to protect his mom from revisiting that old heartbreak.

At the end of the day, he couldn't trust himself to offer support to anyone. Bianca and EJ were far too precious to risk.

But they'd sought him out, and Nate had to believe that meant something. He *needed* to mean something to Eddie's sister and her boy. He placed a hand on EJ's arm to steady him and gave a few quiet instructions about how to position the next nail. The pink tip of EJ's tongue poked out from the corner of his mouth, a sure sign the boy was deep in concentration.

"I thought I might find you two out here."

At the sound of his mother's voice, EJ stopped hammering and jumped off the stool Nate had pushed to the front of the workbench.

"Mommy," he shouted, running toward her and launching himself against her legs. "I petted a cow and scooped horse poop and fed the chickens and now I'm fixing part of the coop. That's what you call the chicken's house—a coop. There are fifteen but only one rooster on account of he doesn't like to share his girlfriends."

"Whoa," Bianca said with a laugh, lifting EJ into her arms. "Slow down, buddy. Take a breath. It sounds like you had a busy morning."

"I got boots, too," EJ said, kicking out his feet. "They used to be Mr. Nate's."

Her grin faltered as she looked to Nate. Damn, she was beautiful. She wore a simple white T-shirt and a pair of snug jeans with a tiny rip above one knee. That small strip of skin was the sexiest thing he'd ever seen because it held the promise of so much more.

Nate had never been one for flash and dazzle in his women, so Bianca's natural beauty hit him hard. Her hair was pulled back into a loose bun at the nape of her neck, exposing the graceful line of her throat. More than anything, he wanted to know if her skin was as soft as it looked.

He was so damn close to making a fool of himself and embarrassing them both.

"Or one of my brother's pairs." He shrugged, feeling suddenly self-conscious that he'd dug through the shed out back to track down the bins of clothes and shoes his mom had kept from his childhood. "It's hard to know, but my mom saved anything we didn't wear out and Earl insisted on good boots, even when we were young. We all had the same style."

"Thank you for sharing them with EJ," she said after a moment.

"He needed a decent pair of shoes for the ranch." The words came out more gruffly than he meant them because he didn't want her to think that after one day he was trying to step in as the boy's father or something. "It's not a big deal."

"Mommy, I got so many things to show you." EJ wriggled to the ground and skipped in a circle around Bianca. "You want to see the poop I scooped or the fence I helped Mr. Nate fix?" He waved his hands in a windmill motion as he moved, a bundle of boy energy even after working for hours. Temperatures in January usually hovered in the low fifties, but today the thermostat had climbed nearly ten degrees above normal. Nothing appeared to dim EJ's enthusiasm.

"Right now," Bianca said gently, pulling a cell phone from the back pocket of her jeans, "I need to talk to Mr. Nate. Why don't you check out your favorite YouTube channel for a few minutes?"

Nate frowned as EJ took the phone and hit a button, the blue light from the screen illuminating his small face. "It's not working, Mommy," EJ said almost immediately, handing the phone back to Bianca.

"No service," Bianca muttered. "I guess it's because we're so far out of town. Do you have a Wi-Fi password?" She glanced from the phone to Nate.

"Nope," he said, massaging a hand over the back of his neck.

"Maybe the signal is bad in the barn," she told her son. "If you take it to the house's front porch—"

"You still won't have any luck." Nate stepped forward. "Cell service out here is spotty, and the ranch doesn't have Wi-Fi."

Bianca and EJ stared at him with mutual horror in their dark gazes.

"You can get internet in town at the library," he added quickly. "Normally it's open on Wednesdays."

EJ's mouth dropped open.

"Once a *week*?" Bianca asked, her tone incredulous.

"I haven't been there for a few months. It might have different hours now."

"I want to watch a show," EJ complained.

"We have a satellite dish," Nate said. "My mom likes to watch the Rodeo Live channel when she's not on the road with Grayson."

"Do you have *Elmer the Elephant*?" the boy asked.

"I'm not sure about that," Nate admitted. He'd heard of a puppet named Elmo but never an elephant called Elmer. "What channel is Elmer on?"

"YouTube," Bianca and EJ answered at the same time, then Bianca crouched down at EJ's side.

"It's okay, buddy. We'll figure out something to watch when you need a break. Besides, there's so much to keep you busy on the ranch, you'll hardly have time to miss Elmer."

"I miss him already, Mommy."

Nate watched Bianca's shoulders deflate as she sighed.

"EJ, would you put extra hay in each of the horse stalls while your mom and I talk?"

For all the boy's earlier enthusiasm, EJ looked like he wanted to refuse. Nate understood the sentiment. As much fun as a ranch could be for a boy, there was always the moment when a kid realized work was work. It was a lesson Nate and his brothers had learned early on, and it had served each of them as they grew to be men. He wanted to make sure he instilled the same work ethic in Bianca's son. He knew Eddie would have done the same thing.

"Remember how we talked about chores," he said gently.

EJ scrunched up his face and nodded. "Taking care of the animals is most important."

"Right," Nate agreed.

EJ looked up at Bianca. "I'll be back after I finish my chore, Mommy."

"I'll be here, sweetie."

Nate gave EJ a few more instructions about how much hay to give each horse, then watched as the boy made his way to the first stall.

"I can't believe how well he listens to you," Bianca murmured. "No access to Elmer would have ended in a full-blown temper tantrum with me."

"Sometimes a boy just needs a man in his life."

He was thinking of how much Eddie would have loved being a part of EJ's world but cringed as Bianca sucked in what looked to be a strained breath.

"You probably think it's terrible that I rely on an animated elephant to help me parent my kid. I do limit his screen time, but sometimes—"

Nate shook his head. "No. I'm sorry. That isn't what I meant. I'm not judging you, Bianca. A single mom raised me, and I know how much trouble we gave her. I don't know how she handled the three of us most days. It's clear you do a wonderful job with EJ, but it kills me that Eddie is missing this."

"Me, too," she said softly. "Sometimes I still can't believe he's gone. And EJ reminds me of him in so many ways."

"He's a great kid."

"Thanks. He clearly loves being with you. My feelings of inadequacy aside," she said with a small laugh, "it's good for him to spend time with a man who can be a role model. But I don't want you to feel like he's a burden."

"That would never happen." He couldn't put into words how much he enjoyed the young boy.

"He's also a handful and his energy is nonstop. Sometimes it gets to be too much for people."

"People like his father?" Nate asked, unable to tamp down his curiosity. EJ talked a mile a minute but all he would say about his dad was that he'd liked when EJ was quiet. Nate couldn't imagine EJ not talking a mile a minute other than when he was sleeping.

"My ex-husband isn't involved in our lives anymore. I've gone back to my maiden name, and I'm working to have EJ's legally changed to Shaw." She bit down on her bottom lip. "Brett walked away two years ago and never looked back."

"He's an idiot," Nate offered automatically.

One side of her mouth kicked up. "You sound like Eddie. He never liked Brett, even when we were first dating. He said he wasn't good enough for me."

"Obviously that's true." Nate took a step closer but stopped himself before he reached for her. Bianca didn't belong to him, and he had no claim on her. But one morning with EJ and he already felt a connection to the boy. A connection he also wanted to explore with the beautiful woman in front of him. "Any man who would walk away from you needs to have his—" He paused, feeling the unfamiliar sensation of color rising to his face. His mother had certainly raised him better than to swear in front of a lady, yet the thought of Bianca being hurt by her ex made his blood boil. "He needs a swift kick in the pants."

"Agreed," she said with a bright smile. A smile that made him weak in the knees. He wanted to give her a reason to smile like that every day. "I'm better off without him, but it still makes me sad for EJ. I do my best, but it's hard with only the two of us. There are so many things we've had to sacrifice." She wrapped her arms around her waist and turned to gaze out of the barn, as if she couldn't bear to make eye contact with Nate any longer. "Sometimes I wish I could give him more."

"You're enough," he said, reaching out a hand to brush away the lone tear that tracked down her cheek. "Don't doubt for one second that you're enough."

As he'd imagined, her skin felt like velvet under his callused fingertip. Her eyes drifted shut and she tipped up her face, as if she craved his touch as much as he wanted to give it to her.

He wanted more from this woman—this moment—than he'd dreamed possible. She'd fit perfectly in his arms and he could show her exactly how it felt to be with a man who appreciated what a gift she was. He let his finger trail over her cheek and trace the line of her jaw, edging down to her throat. He leaned in, so close he could smell her shampoo, something fruity and utterly feminine. A loose strand of hair brushed the back of his hand, sending shivers across his skin.

She glanced at him from beneath her lashes, but there was no hesitation in her gaze. Her liquid brown eyes held only invitation, and his entire world narrowed to the thought of kissing Bianca.

"I finished with the hay, Mommy," EJ called from behind him.

Bianca jumped away like she'd been scalded.

"Nice work, buddy," she said, her voice high and tight. "Want to show me that fence you fixed now?"

"Can you come, too, Mr. Nate?" EJ smiled, his face all wide-eyed innocence.

The boy trusted him. Bianca trusted him. Eddie had trusted him.

And Nate didn't deserve any of it.

He had to put the brakes on the careening desire he felt for his best friend's sister. She'd come to him for help. That was all he had to offer.

"Um… I…" He shook his head, trying to clear his muddled brain. "I promised a neighbor I'd help with some damage to his barn." As excuses went, it was totally lame but also true. In this part of rural Texas, neighbors relied on each other. Nate had made the commitment before Bianca and EJ arrived. "I'll see you later."

The boy looked confused at his change in demeanor, but Bianca kept her gaze on the barn's dirt floor. "Thanks for this morning," she said softly, and he noticed her hands were clenched into fists at her sides.

"No problem." He turned and walked out into the bright January sunlight before he changed his mind and found a reason to spend the day with his houseguests. Keeping Bianca at arm's length was the only way he was going to survive her stay.

The only way.

She and EJ drove into town for lunch and found a surprisingly yummy Mexican restaurant open in the back of the building that housed both the grocery store and gas station. They'd shared a plate of chicken enchiladas and she'd eaten way too many of the crispy chips and tangy salsa the owner, Rosa, had brought to the table.

Lunch at a restaurant might be typical for some people, but it was a real treat for Bianca. She'd cashed the check she received from her crummy apartment deposit in San Antonio before leaving town, so she had an extra five hundred dollars to her name before her finances got precariously tight again.

She and EJ had been equally shocked at how tiny Paseo was compared to their neighborhood in San Antonio. There was something oddly comforting about making her way through a town that only stretched a few short blocks. The pace of life was clearly less rigorous in this part of the state, and everyone she met went out of their way to be welcoming, especially when she mentioned she was a family friend of the Fortunes.

Saying the name out loud almost made her giggle since there were a whole mess of very wealthy and well-known Fortunes living in different parts of Texas. Bianca might not be worldly, but even she'd heard of cosmetics mogul Kate Fortune and her famous youth serum. She'd also read headlines about British Fortunes who had ties to the royal family, and wondered how Nate and his small-town brothers felt about sharing such an illustrious last name.

But despite—or possibly because of—their humble beginnings, Nate, Jayden and Grayson were the famous Fortunes in Paseo. Particularly Grayson, of course, who was so famous he was mainly known by his first name. But all during lunch, she heard a litany of stories and compliments about the brothers and their mom.

After buying enough food at the grocery store to make several days' worth of meals, Bianca stopped into the RV that housed the town's public library. She logged on to their Wi-Fi to check her email, surprised to find a note from her former boss, asking if she'd be willing to make another batch of personalized gift boxes for the shop she'd gotten fired from a week ago.

"He's got some nerve," she muttered under her breath and promptly deleted the email.

"Man trouble?" the older woman behind the counter asked.

Bianca glanced to where EJ was positioned in front of one of the computer screens, a pair of retro-looking headphones engulfing his small head. She'd allotted twenty minutes for him to have a screen break and watch two episodes of the *Elmer the Elephant* cartoon he loved so dearly. Reassuring herself he was engrossed in the show, she turned to the woman.

"I was working in an upscale retail boutique before we came to Paseo. The woman who'd owned the store for years sold it six months ago, and the new owner wouldn't allow any flexibility in my schedule to take care of my son."

"Big city folks," the woman said, spitting out each word like venom.

"I guess," Bianca agreed, not bothering to mention that she was, in fact, born and raised in San Antonio. "I had a great babysitter for EJ. A woman who lived around the corner from the store ran a small day care out of her home. EJ loves her, but he got a bad case of the flu right before Christmas, so I had to take time off work. I had vacation hours banked, but the owner said I couldn't use them during the holidays. I offered to come in on the weekends and afternoons when I could hire a sitter to be with him at the apartment, but he wouldn't budge."

The librarian rolled her eyes. "So much for 'lean in.'"

Bianca felt a grin split her face that this woman had heard of the popular movement.

"I stayed home and raised my two kids," the woman

offered. "They're twenty-eight and thirty now. My daughter works as an attorney in some hoity-toity law firm in Houston. She just had her second baby, and I went down there to stay for a couple weeks. She was answering phone calls from one of the senior partners in the hospital. They barely honored her maternity leave, and that's a law. The stress moms are under these days is crazy. It's not right."

Bianca felt a lump of emotion clog her throat at this stranger's sympathy. Her own mom lived in San Antonio, but when Bianca had swallowed her pride and called to ask for help during EJ's illness, Jennifer Shaw had lectured her about how she shouldn't have taken on more than she could handle in the first place. As if Bianca had had a choice about working since Brett deserted them. She certainly hadn't seen one cent of child support from her ex-husband.

"So does the man want to hire you back?" the librarian asked.

"Not exactly," Bianca admitted. "I like to sew and do crafty stuff, so I spent evenings making specialized gift boxes for the store, celebrating birthdays and other occasions. I knew they sold well, but apparently they were more popular than I realized. He sold out and has customers asking for them. He wants to put in an order."

"Congratulations."

Bianca shrugged. "With what he paid me, I barely covered the money I spent on materials, although he sold them for almost triple the cost. I mainly did it to have something to keep me occupied at night after EJ went to bed."

"Seems like you could use a boyfriend for that," the woman said with a cheeky grin.

"Oh." Bianca pressed a hand to her chest as an image of spending a quiet night at home with Nate popped into her head. "I don't really date."

"You're young," the librarian said, pointing a finger at Bianca. "I tell my daughter she needs to schedule regular date nights with her husband."

Bianca swallowed. "I don't have a husband."

"But that blush tells me you've got someone who's caught your eye. No one would blame you if it was one of Deborah Fortune's boys. Those three are far too handsome for their own good." She tapped a finger against her chin. "Although Jayden got married last year to a lovely girl."

"Ariana," Bianca confirmed. "They're traveling while she researches a book." It felt strange to talk about Nate's brother and sister-in-law as if she knew them.

"Well, that's the great thing about triplets." The woman laughed. "We still have two of them up for grabs." She pushed away from the counter and reached up to one of the bookshelves behind her. "I've got something that might come in handy for you."

Bianca was half afraid the woman would pull out a book on spicing up a single mom's sex life, but instead she handed Bianca a thin paperback titled *Starting a Business That Stands Out.*

"I ordered this when Steph Renner decided she was going to start selling her jewelry on Etsy. She's got a steady revenue stream going now, and I'm sure she'd be willing to give you some tips if you want."

"But I don't have anything to sell."

"Sure you do," the woman countered. "If those gift boxes can sell in a boutique, they can sell online. You could create a business and still be at home with your boy."

Bianca sucked in a breath. She'd never thought of her boxes as a viable business, but why not? If it would give her more time with EJ, she'd try anything. For the first time since she'd gotten fired, hope bloomed in her chest. Maybe she really could get her life back on track here in Paseo.

She stood and impulsively wrapped her arms around the older woman's shoulders. "Thank you," she whispered, "for listening and for the idea."

"You remind me of my daughter," the woman said, patting Bianca's cheek. "You're a good girl."

"Mommy, Elmer ended." EJ pulled off his headphones. "Can I watch another?"

"Not today, buddy." Bianca tightened her grip on the book in her hands. "But I'm sure we'll be back to the library to visit..."

She glanced at the woman who said, "My name's Susan."

"I'm Bianca. Nice to meet you." She took EJ's hand. "We'll come back and visit Susan because Mommy's going to start making the gift boxes again. I'll need to order supplies online."

Susan smiled. "I've expanded my hours now that my husband's retired. He and I need a little space to keep our marriage happy. I'm open ten to two Monday through Thursday and from nine to four on Saturdays."

"Well, then, I'm grateful for your happy marriage," Bianca said and led EJ out of the RV.

She drove back from town feeling happier than she had in ages and couldn't wait to share with Nate her plan for a new business venture. Not that she wouldn't still pull her weight around the ranch, but the idea of having an actual career was so exciting after all the speed bumps she'd hit in the past two years.

It was nearly six before Nate's big silver truck pulled down the driveway again. Bianca had started to think she'd really scared him away after that scene in the barn.

Had she imagined the desire in his eyes and the way he

was leaning in as if to kiss her? The only man she'd been with was her ex-husband and he hadn't been interested in her sexually since she'd gotten pregnant. So maybe she was that out of practice in reading the signs of attraction. Or perhaps she was projecting her own lust onto Nate because every time he looked at her it felt like her skin burst into flames and sparks danced across her stomach.

She'd honestly thought motherhood had sucked all the woman out of her. She hadn't felt a yearning like she did for Nate in—well, she'd never felt anything like it.

But if he truly saw her as only Eddie's little sister, where did that leave her? She wasn't exactly going to throw herself at him and risk losing the second chance she had in Paseo. That didn't stop her heart from racing as she heard the truck door slam shut.

Chapter 4

"Mr. Nate is home," EJ shouted, jumping up from where he sat coloring at the kitchen table. He ran down the hall and a moment later reappeared, holding tight to Nate's hand as he peppered the handsome rancher with questions about his day.

"Something smells great in here," Nate said, his smile making Bianca's heart beat even faster.

"It's dinner," she said. "I hope you like stir-fry."

He chuckled. "I like anything I don't have to cook. Do I have time to take care of a couple things in the barn? The day got away from me."

"I can help," EJ told him, tugging on his hand.

"Sure," Bianca said. "When would you like to eat?"

"Twenty minutes?"

"I'll have it ready."

"Mommy's making fried rice," EJ announced. "Even the vegetables taste good."

"I can't wait to try it."

"It's nothing special," Bianca said quickly. "An easy midweek meal."

Nate studied her for a moment, then said in his deep, rumbling voice, "It's special."

He and EJ headed for the barn. Bianca adjusted the stove's temperature to low, set the small farmhouse table with three place settings, then impulsively ran upstairs and dabbed a light coat of gloss on her lips. She pulled her hair out of its ponytail and ran a brush through it as she studied her reflection in the mirror over the bathroom sink.

Was it too much to leave it down? Did she look like she was trying too hard? Of course she was trying too hard. Any woman in her right mind would try to impress a man like Nate. She grabbed a jeweled clip out of her toiletries bag and fastened it at the back of her head, figuring hair half up and half down was a good compromise. She was trying but not *too hard*, if that was an option.

She hurried back downstairs just as Nate and EJ returned to the house. EJ was still talking a mile a minute, but Nate paused in the doorway to the kitchen, his eyes darkening as he took her in. Clearly he appreciated the small effort she'd made. Feeling like a teenage girl again, she gave her hair a gentle toss over one shoulder, gratified when his lips parted and he simply stared at her.

"Hi," she said, her voice a little breathless.

"Hi," he answered, removing his Stetson and setting it on the kitchen counter.

They stared at each other for several seconds until EJ shouted, "I'm hungry, Mommy."

"Wash your hands," she told him, quickly moving to the stove.

"Would you like something to drink with dinner?"

Nate rubbed a hand against the back of his neck. "Not sure there's any wine in the house, but I've got beer."

"A beer would be great. Thank you."

With Nate's big presence in the kitchen, the space felt smaller—more intimate. It felt like a real family dinner, something simple but an activity Bianca had always craved. She loved the normalcy of it.

"This is a real treat," Nate said as he sat down at the table.

"It's the least I can do," she told him and dished out a generous amount of rice and chicken onto his plate.

"EJ told me you went to town today. Paseo must seem like a speck on the map compared to what you're used to in San Antonio."

"It's a nice change," she said, taking a seat across the table from him.

"Really?" He took a long pull on his beer. "Your brother liked to say that Paseo was a half-a-horse town because there wasn't enough room for a full horse."

She smiled. "He made the worst jokes."

"He cracked himself up every time, though." Nate forked up a big bite of chicken. "This is unbelievable," he said after swallowing. "It's like real Chinese food."

"I can't tell if that's actually a compliment," Bianca said with a laugh.

"It's amazing," he clarified. "Best I've ever had."

"Mommy's a good cook," EJ announced. "Even though she couldn't find the targreron." He stumbled over the last word.

"I'd planned to roast the chicken," she explained when Nate threw her a questioning look. "But they didn't have tarragon at the local market and there's none in your spice cabinet. Stir-fry was my backup plan."

"Hold that thought," Nate said, and pushed back from the table. He walked into the hallway, where Bianca could hear him rummaging through a closet.

"Found it," he announced, and returned with a small camo knapsack rolled tight. "I don't know if the spices are still fresh, but we have tarragon."

"That's the care package I sent to Eddie on his final deployment." She frowned. "No, that's the second one I sent. He wrote and told me he lost the first, but I couldn't find the material I'd used for it so I made that knapsack out of a camo vest I bought at a local thrift store. I forgot that I'd included tarragon along with the basic spices. Eddie loved the licorice flavor."

Nate put the sack down on the kitchen table, looking a little sheepish. "Eddie was the envy of all of us with these little tubes of spices." He unrolled the sack to reveal a row of test tubes, each filled and labeled with a different type of spice. Bianca had gotten the idea for it after Eddie'd complained so bitterly about the bland navy food. "Turns out one of the guys from the squadron had taken the first one you sent. He ended up returning it but not before Eddie had asked you for another. He gave the second package to me for my birthday." He ran his fingers over the labels on the front of each tube. "It was my most prized possession when we were deployed."

"Really?"

Nate nodded. "I'm not a picky eater, but it gets old when every meal starts to taste the same week after week. These spices were a reminder of home, and that somebody cared."

Conflicting emotions unfurled in Bianca's chest, happiness at knowing her gift had meant something to her brother tinged with the familiar ache of missing him.

"You should sell those, too, Mommy." EJ looked at her

matter-of-factly. "If Uncle Eddie and Mr. Nate liked them so much, other soldiers would, too."

"That's a heck of an idea, buddy," Bianca murmured, staring at her son in wide-eyed wonder. As they were driving back to the ranch, she'd told EJ about her conversation with Susan the librarian. That was the thing about being a family of two. EJ might be only four, but he was Bianca's constant companion and often her first sounding board. She tried not to burden him with her stresses, but he'd been as excited as she was at the prospect of a business that would allow her to work from home.

"What else are you selling?" Nate looked confused.

"I haven't had a chance to tell you about my visit with Susan at the library," she said.

"I'm done, Mommy," EJ interrupted, shoveling the last bite of food into his mouth. "Can I go out to the pasture and see if the horses are still eating their hay?"

She let out a small laugh. "Mr. Nate and I have barely started eating. How can you be done already?"

"I was chewing while you talked," EJ answered with a shrug. "I chew fast."

"You do everything fast." Bianca used her napkin to wipe a stray piece of rice from EJ's chin. "Are you sure you don't want to sit here and visit with Mr. Nate while he eats?"

"Nope. I want to visit the horses."

She glanced at Nate, who nodded. "Take your plate and glass over to the sink first," she told her son, who scrambled off his seat to obey.

She took another bite as EJ ran from the room.

"He's sure taken to ranch life," Nate said, humor lacing his tone.

"It's okay for him to be out there by himself?" Bianca

asked. "I kept him close to me this afternoon. Horses aren't really my thing."

Nate nodded. "He'll be fine, and I'll check on him when we're finished. This truly is the best food I've had in ages."

"I'm glad you like it. I've got meals planned through the weekend."

"You don't have to cook for me."

"I want to," she told him honestly. "I like sharing a meal, and it's the least I can do to thank you for letting us stay here."

"You don't owe me—"

She held up a hand. "I do, Nate. I want to pull my weight around the ranch. EJ's not the only one who can help."

"I appreciate that. Tell me more about your visit to the library."

"It started because I got an email from the man I used to work for." She grimaced, then added, "The one who fired me."

To her surprise, Nate didn't look shocked at the news. "EJ told me you lost your job because of him."

His words were a sharp stab to her chest. "I didn't realize he understood that." She sighed. "I guess I didn't do as good of a job hiding it as I thought. The bottom line is, EJ was sick and the shop owner didn't like that I took time off work to be with him."

"Of course you took time off. You're his mother."

She smiled at his matter-of-fact tone. "You sound a lot like Susan at the library. I'm starting to think I could get used to small-town life."

"It doesn't take a million people living in a place to understand what really matters."

"Sometimes all it takes is one," she agreed. "Especially for a mother. Anyway, the boutique owner is upset because he's sold out of the birthday and special occasion gift boxes I made to sell in the store. Susan suggested I look into starting my own business, maybe something online like Etsy or supplying them to other shops around the state." She tapped a finger against her cheek. "I might even focus on gifts for military families to send overseas. I could add the little spice packs to the mix. They weren't difficult to put together and if they were so popular—"

"You can't understand unless you've lived on a carrier for months at a time." Nate grinned, as if remembering. "What about those shampoo bars? Or the homemade lip balm? Whenever a package came for Eddie, we all hung around to see what he'd gotten. He'd show off whatever you sent, mainly to make the rest of us jealous."

"Really?" Pride bubbled up inside her at the thought. She'd missed her older brother so much when he was away and had taken to creating products she thought he could use to keep from getting lonely. "I figured Eddie and his navy buddies thought I was just a silly girl with too much time on her hands."

"He did get some major grief when you went through your boy band phase."

"Oh, my gosh." Bianca covered her face with her hands. "I forgot about that. I used to cut out pictures of all the celebrities I was crushing on and send collages to Eddie. I'd spray them with perfume."

"A *lot* of it," Nate said with a chuckle. "It amazed me your letters arrived still scented, like they'd been dipped in a vat of perfume."

"The funniest part was Eddie used to write me back like he knew stuff about the guys in the photos."

"That's because he did," Nate explained. "Whenever we

were in a place with internet access, he'd troll the gossip sites so he'd have something to add to his letters to you."

Bianca's heart pinged in her chest. She could just imagine her bad-to-the-bone brother, who favored pounding heavy metal music, doing research on the latest boy band craze to make her happy.

"I miss him so much," she whispered.

"I know." Nate reached across the table and took her hand. "He'd be proud of the woman you've become, Busy Bee. You're a great mother, and I'm glad Susan gave you the idea of starting your own business. You're smart and creative and I bet you can make a success of anything you set your mind to."

Tears sprang to her eyes as she pushed away from the table, making a show of clearing plates. Gripping the edge of the counter in front of the sink, she blinked and tried to pull herself together. A few kind words and Nate had all but reduced her to a puddle on the floor. But how long had it been since anyone believed in her?

Even in the best of times during their relationship, Brett had brushed off her creativity as nothing more than a waste of time and money. Her mother, too, complained about Bianca's crafting supplies taking up too much space in their small apartment when she'd still lived at home.

She'd had no idea that Eddie had so much invested in the care packages she'd sent him. Her brother loved her and would have done anything for her, but he'd been a consummate career military man—the strong and silent type. He'd always been the one to take care of her. Bianca had never had a reason to believe she could truly make something of herself.

Until now.

"Did I say something wrong?" Nate asked quietly. His warm hand brushed her shoulder.

She sniffed and turned, pasting on a bright smile. "You said all the right things. I'm simply unaccustomed to hearing them."

"I want to change that, Bianca." His gaze dropped to her mouth. He was going to kiss her now. At least in this moment she had no doubt he wanted her as much as she wanted him.

He leaned in and she closed her eyes, anticipation making her breathless.

Suddenly the sound of frenzied barking blasted through the open window followed by her son's high-pitched shouting.

"EJ!" she screamed and hurried after Nate, who was already rushing through the house toward whatever trouble her son had gotten himself into.

"EJ!"

Nate ran toward the fenced pasture behind the barn as fast as he could.

A small figure was sprawled on the ground near the gate. Nate's heart felt like it was going to beat out of his chest with worry that the young boy was hurt.

As he got closer, EJ lifted his head and then sat up, leaning against the fence post.

"EJ, are you okay?" Nate dropped down next to the boy.

EJ swallowed and nodded, but his face crumpled as Bianca joined them.

"Sweetie, what happened?" She knelt and opened her arms. EJ flung himself into them, his thin shoulders shaking as he sobbed loudly. "Are you hurt?" She let the boy cling to her for several minutes, then set him away from her, running gentle hands over his head and torso as if searching for injuries.

"No. The dog saved me."

"What dog?" Nate straightened and scanned the area, but all he could see were the horses gathered around the feeder, munching on the hay he and EJ had put out before dinner. There was no other sign of life near the barn.

"The black-and-tan one," EJ said, wiping his nose on his sleeve. "One of the horses bit the other. They started fighting so I went over the fence to break it up."

"Cinnamon," Nate muttered. "He's a hay hog and will give the other horses trouble if they get too close when he's eating."

Bianca lifted EJ into her arms and hugged him close. "We talked earlier about staying on this side of the fence."

"But Cinnamon was being a bully," the boy argued. "You told me when Bryson was being mean to Harper at preschool that I should use my words to stop a bully."

"That's with another child, not a thousand-pound animal."

Nate could see from the residual fear in Bianca's brown eyes that she was imagining EJ being trampled under one of the horses. The thought of what might have happened made cold sweat break out along Nate's shoulders.

"What happened when you got close?" he asked quietly, almost afraid to hear the answer.

"I yelled at Cinnamon," EJ reported. "Him and Jobuck tried to bite each other, but then he went after Daisy." He pointed to the dapple-gray mare standing serenely near the edge of the trough. "He was hurting her, and she's my favorite."

"Remember we talked about the hierarchy of the herd?" Nate smoothed the dark hair away from EJ's face, his elbow brushing Bianca's arm. "Cinnamon isn't going to hurt Daisy. He's just letting her know who's boss."

"He was mean," EJ insisted. "I had to help her. But then I tripped and fell and they were still fighting. Cinnamon came up on his back legs, and I thought he was going to land on me. But I kept yelling at him to leave Daisy alone. I didn't give up, Mommy."

So much like Eddie, Nate thought. He wanted to pull both of them against him until the panic gripping him subsided. He could taste metal in his mouth and the familiar prickling sensation, like ants marching under his skin.

He was overreacting but couldn't stop it. A vision of Eddie's lifeless body tore through his mind, and he jerked away from EJ and Bianca.

How many times had he and his brothers had close calls while ignoring directions their mom or Earl gave them as kids? Hell, Grayson had first broken a bone falling off a horse when he was younger than EJ. There was no threat of punishment that could keep his horse-crazy brother away from the barn when they were kids.

He tried to focus on breathing and the fact that now that EJ had calmed down, the boy didn't seem to have a scratch on him. In fact, when he looked to Bianca and her son again, they were staring at him like he was the one who'd been in jeopardy.

"Tell us about the dog." Bianca shifted EJ in her arms and raised a questioning brow toward Nate.

He nodded and forced one side of his mouth to curve, trying to convince both her and himself that he had things under control.

"I saw him yesterday, too. He was behind the house when I went out back to play but ran off when Mr. Nate came out."

"He's a stray," Nate muttered. "He used to come around when Jayden's dog, Sugar, was here. I don't know why because Sugar's mostly blind so it's not like she's going to go rambling with another dog."

"Is he friendly?" Bianca asked.

Nate shrugged. "Hard to say. He won't let me get close. I haven't seen him since Sugar left with Jayden and Ariana on their trip."

"I think he needs a home," EJ said quietly.

"Not this one," Nate answered without hesitation. "I like Sugar, but she's Jayden's responsibility. I've got enough on my plate without taking on one more thing." He saw Bianca cringe slightly at his words. Of course he didn't mean her and EJ. They were the best things that had happened to him in years. How could he explain what a difference they'd made in his lonely life in such a short time without sounding like a fool?

"The dog saved me, Mommy. He ran up to Cinnamon and was barking so loud. He stood in front of me until the horses backed away."

Bianca placed a soft kiss on the tip of EJ's nose. "Your own personal guard dog."

"Don't read too much into it," Nate told her. "Chances are the dog reacted to the commotion. I doubt he was purposely trying to protect EJ."

"Which doesn't change the fact that he did," she countered. "This stray dog is a hero. We need to help him."

"That isn't how things work in the country. Unfortunately, there are always animals on the loose without a true home."

"That's sad." EJ dropped his head to Bianca's shoulder. "Everybody needs a home." He yawned. "I hope the dog comes back so I can thank him. Do you think he has a name, Mommy?"

"Probably not if he doesn't belong to someone," Bianca said.

"I'm going to call him Otis."

She hugged him closer. "Otis is a good name for a dog."

"You can't name a dog that doesn't belong to you." Nate's tone came out sharper than he'd meant.

EJ yawned again, clearly too tired to notice. "I'm still going to call him Otis."

"Let's go inside so you can take a bath tonight," Bianca told the boy. She seemed wary of Nate's mood, which he could understand. He wanted to assure her he was fine, but how was that possible? He hadn't been anywhere close to fine since the day he watched his best friend die. "You've had a big day."

"Did you bring bubbles?" EJ asked.

"I sure did."

"I'm going to check the horses," Nate said. "EJ, from now on, I want you stay on the far side of the fence unless your mom or I is with you. Okay?"

The boy scrunched up his nose. "But what if—"

"Even if it looks like they're fighting. The horses will take care of themselves, but what's most important to me is keeping you safe."

Bianca's shoulders relaxed, and he was happy he'd finally said the right thing. He wanted to wipe away the past few minutes, the shock of hearing EJ scream and the terror of knowing the boy might have been badly hurt on Nate's watch.

He wanted to return to those moments in the kitchen when he and Bianca had the world to themselves and all that mattered was pressing his mouth to hers. He wanted her to want him again.

But that was dangerous territory, especially when what he felt for her was already more complicated than physical attraction. She was smart and strong, and he respected how hard she was working to make a better life for herself and EJ. He'd never met a woman quite like Bianca, but to tell her that would give away too much, so he simply nodded and let himself into the pasture. When he looked up again, his hand pressed to Cinnamon's muscled flank, Bianca and EJ were already gone.

Chapter 5

"Mom, it's me. I've been trying to get a hold of you."

"Where are you? Why are you calling from this area code?" Jennifer Shaw let out an exasperated breath. "I've been getting calls from this number all week."

"I just told you that." Bianca paused and counted to ten in her head. It wouldn't do any good to get angry with her mom. "I'm out of town and there isn't decent cell phone service where we're staying. Why haven't you picked up the phone?"

"Because I didn't recognize the number. For all I know you could have been…" Her voice trailed off.

"A creditor?" Bianca guessed. "Are you in financial trouble again?"

"A telemarketer," Jennifer answered. "You know how persistent they can be."

Not as persistent as collection agencies, Bianca thought. She couldn't help the bitterness that lingered over the college education she'd sacrificed to bail her mom out of a rough patch a few years ago. Normally Jennifer kept her gambling habit low-key, but it had gotten out of control, and Bianca had drained her savings account to pay down her mother's debt. "EJ and I left San Antonio. I wanted to tell you myself instead of leaving a message."

"How could you leave?" her mom demanded. "You have no place to go."

Bianca pressed a hand to her stomach. It felt like her mom had just punched her in the gut. "I'm in Paseo."

"Why does that name sound familiar?"

"It's where Nate Fortune lives. You remember Eddie's navy SEAL friend."

"Tall, handsome, cowboy-looking type?" Jennifer whistled softly. "Oh, I remember him all right." She made a growling sound low in her throat then laughed. "Nate Fortune is the kind of man for whom the term *cougar* was named."

"Um…whatever you say, Mom." Bianca rolled her eyes. "I'm just letting you know we're staying with Nate for a bit. I didn't want you to hear that I'd moved and worry."

Her mother sniffed. "You know I've got my own life to deal with, Bianca. I can't get all involved in yours at this late date."

"Or ever," Bianca muttered.

"What was that?"

"Nothing. Never mind."

There was a long, awkward pause before Jennifer asked, "How long will you be there?"

"I'm not sure. I'm working on a plan for a new business. One that will let me work from home so I can be with EJ."

"Why couldn't you do that in San Antonio?"

"I needed a break. After my boss fired me—"

"Your brother got all my work ethic genes."

"Mom, EJ was *sick*. I had to take time off. I asked you to help but—"

"Now you're blaming me? Like I was supposed to jeopardize my career by asking for personal leave?"

Her mother was the receptionist at a used car dealership, and Bianca didn't think her boss would have minded if she'd taken off an extra day or so since he was also her boyfriend. But it was one more thing not worth the trouble of mentioning.

"It's fine," she said instead. "Maybe it was even a blessing. EJ needs me at home more now that he'll be starting kindergarten in the fall. I want to be there for him after school."

"Another thing you've always held against me," her mother said, her voice tight. "The fact that I had to work to support you and your brother."

"I didn't," Bianca argued. "I always had Eddie at home in the afternoon. He took care of me."

"Your brother took care of everything." The sound of Jennifer blowing her nose reverberated through the phone. "I miss him."

"Me, too," Bianca whispered. Grief over Eddie's death was the one thing she and her mother had in common. "It's actually been nice to be with Nate. Somehow he makes me miss Eddie less."

"I can hear it in your voice that you're getting attached the way you do. It's not a good idea, Bianca. Nate Fortune isn't the man for you."

Bianca blinked several times, unsure of how to answer. She couldn't believe her mother had read her so easily just in their short conversation. Her temper pricked at the same time. Of course her mom would assume Bianca didn't deserve someone like Nate.

"He likes me. We're friends, Mom."

"Of course he likes you. I bet you're *real* grateful he's taken you in."

Jennifer said the words like there was something salacious about Bianca's friendship with Nate. "It's not that way," she said through clenched teeth.

"All I'm saying is you don't know the whole story about Nate Fortune. You might think you do but— Shoot, the office phone's ringing. I gotta answer it, Bianca. Don't do anything stupid and tell EJ his mimi said hi."

Before Bianca could answer, Jennifer had ended the call. Bianca replaced the receiver on the old-school phone that hung on the kitchen wall. As usual, the phone call with her mother made the doubts she'd recently held at bay spring to life with renewed energy.

What was she doing in Paseo? Could Nate really be the right man for her? It had all seemed so clear last night when Nate had been about to kiss her. But once again, she wasn't sure of anything except that the enigmatic rancher made her wish for things he might not be willing to give her.

"I can't decide if you work this late every night or if you're just trying to avoid me."

Nate paused as he climbed the porch steps later that evening. It was dark now, the sky a jumble of stars and planets. Growing up near downtown San Antonio, she'd never appreciated the night sky. But here in Paseo, the vast swath of inky blackness dotted with bright lights fascinated her.

She'd come onto the porch after EJ had fallen asleep, wrapping a blanket around her shoulders to ward off the evening chill. She could imagine the summer air in the country must be as sweltering as it felt in the city, but in January the temperature dipped to the midforties each evening, and she was grateful for the coolness.

"A little of both, I suppose," he said, taking off his hat and running a hand through his hair. Bianca had quickly come to realize the gesture meant Nate was uncomfortable, and she wasn't sure how she felt about him doing it so often when she asked him a question.

She was both grateful for his honesty and disappointed at his answer.

"I'm sorry," she said automatically. "This is your home and I don't mean to chase you away. If it's easier—"

"It's because of how much I want to be near you," he interrupted, and her heart thundered in her chest.

What was she supposed to make of that?

"You stay away because you want to be near me?" she asked with a laugh that sounded breathless to her own ears. "Mixed signals much?"

He flashed a self-deprecating smile and leaned a hip against the porch rail. "That pretty much sums it up. You've got me mixed up like a can of soda someone's shaken too hard. I don't even understand it, but I feel like I'm about to explode from wanting you. I'm happy you found me. Hell, until you showed up I would have sworn I liked being on my own. You and EJ came along and changed everything. But you're Eddie's little sister."

"I'm not a baby."

"Trust me, I know that. You said yourself that Eddie told you I'd take care of you. I don't think wanting you was what he had in mind."

She swallowed. "You want me?"

"I can see where EJ gets his penchant for asking a million questions." He sighed. "Of course I want you. Any man in his right mind would want you."

An image of the door slamming behind Brett flashed in her mind.

"Now don't be thinking about your dirtbag ex-husband." Nate pointed a finger at her. "We've already established he's an idiot."

"Staying away because you want me doesn't make sense." She wrapped the blanket tighter around her shoulders.

"It makes all the sense in the world. I'm trying to be a gentleman." Nate threw up his hands. "For once in my dang life, I'm doing the right thing, even though it's just about killing me. You're a beautiful woman, Bianca. But you're also a mother. What kind of role model would I be to EJ if I took advantage of his mom?"

"It's not taking advantage if your feelings are reciprocated."

"If Eddie were here—"

"He's not," she shouted, then pressed her fingers to her mouth. "Eddie isn't here, and EJ's father wants nothing to do with either of us. You're the first decent man my son can remember in his life."

"Which makes it even more important that I treat you with the respect you deserve. I know what it's like to grow up without a father, Bianca. We were lucky to have Earl Thompson, but there was always something missing. My mom never dated that I can remember. We were her only priority, and I always felt sad that she didn't have someone. That Jayden, Grayson and I didn't have someone."

"Eddie told me your dad died when your mom was pregnant."

Nate's eyes narrowed as he looked out into the night. "That's what we always thought."

"It wasn't true?"

He shook his head. "My mom thought the same thing." He paused, as if weighing how much to share with her.

Whatever he had to say was obviously difficult, so Bianca stood and stepped closer, wanting to offer whatever kind of support she could.

"We found out last year that our father has been living in Austin this whole time," he finally said.

She sucked in a shocked breath, and he turned to look at her. "Have you heard of Gerald Robinson?"

Bianca nodded. "The tech mogul who was revealed to be Jerome…" Her voice trailed off as she thought of the laugh she'd had earlier that Nate and his brothers shared the same last name as a famous Texas family. "You don't mean your dad is Jerome Fortune?"

"He and my mom met in New Orleans. They were in love but argued about something and he stormed out. After he left, he faked his own death to get away from his own controlling father. He created an entirely new identity for himself as Gerald Robinson, married a woman named Charlotte and had eight legitimate children." He gave the approximation of a smile but there was no humor in it. "There are also a bunch of illegitimate offspring. Gerald Robinson was a serial cheater."

"Nate," she whispered. "No."

"We found out when Ariana, Jayden's wife, came to Paseo looking for us. She worked for a magazine in Austin and was profiling several of Gerald's children. She'd heard a rumor of his relationship with my mom and that there was a son from their brief time together. She didn't realize at the time that we were triplets."

"How did your mother react?" she asked without thinking. Bianca couldn't imagine the shock Deborah must have felt.

"She hasn't said much. She and Grayson were on the road when we found out. Jayden told her but by the time they returned to the ranch, she was back to business as usual."

"It has to be hard for her."

"Yeah," he agreed, his voice tight. "I know she loved him. She never talked much about our father, but when she did it was clear her feelings for him hadn't dimmed through the years. To learn that he'd been alive all this time must have been a blow."

"Did he know about the three of you?"

Nate shook his head. "According to Mom, he didn't even realize she was pregnant. She tried to find him—Jerome Fortune—when she found out, but he'd already faked his death and created the Gerald Robinson persona by that time. Jayden met him last year at a grand opening party to celebrate some office complex in Austin designed by one of our half brothers."

"Have you talked to him?"

"No." The word was spoken with so much emptiness, she couldn't help but reach out and put a hand on his arm, encircling his wrist with her fingers. She prayed he wouldn't pull away.

"Do you want to?"

He looked past her shoulder, a muscle working in his jaw, and she wondered if he'd even answer. Finally, he shrugged. "He's nothing to me. I had a father figure in Earl Thompson, and I was never alone thanks to Jayden and Grayson. I don't need more siblings, and I sure don't need a father who doesn't want to be a part of my life."

"What makes you think he doesn't?" she couldn't help but ask.

"He left my mom."

"But it changes things if he didn't know she was pregnant."

"Maybe," he admitted after another long moment. "Ariana believes he really loved her at the time. Jayden seems to think he feels bad about not being a part of our lives."

"It definitely sounds like Gerald Robinson made plenty of mistakes, but family is important. Even new family. Trust me, you don't want to be in a position to have regret plague you."

He jerked back, as if she'd struck a nerve.

"You have nothing to regret, Bianca."

She thought about her son not knowing his uncle. Eddie had been deployed when she'd gotten pregnant with EJ. She knew her brother hadn't approved of Brett, so she hadn't talked to him about her shotgun marriage. She'd planned to, of course, but he'd been under so much pressure as his squadron had endured a series of deadly missions. Then her marriage had started to break down, and she'd been too embarrassed to say anything in the emails and letters she sent.

Eddie had been scheduled for redeployment, but he'd been killed a month before he was supposed to come home on leave. Before she'd been able to tell him about EJ, the boy she'd named in his honor.

Regret had become her constant companion, yet how could she admit that to Nate?

"Neither do you," she told him instead.

He didn't answer, but raised his hand to her cheek, the pad of his thumb stroking back and forth. Shivers raced along her spine at the delicate touch. "Thank you for saying that." He smiled, and this time his eyes appeared less shadowed than they had minutes earlier. He looked younger, more like the soldier she remembered from his visits to San Antonio with Eddie.

This is how I can repay him, she thought suddenly. She

could ease his burden. She could help him remember how it felt to be happy. She knew he'd been injured in the mission that had killed her brother, and between that and his responsibilities running the ranch and the shock of discovering his tie to the Fortune family, Nate had been dealt as much of a blow as she had in the recent past.

Maybe what they both needed was some joy in their lives.

She reached up on tiptoe and pressed her mouth to his. Not a demand, but an invitation. He stilled, and she wondered if her own need had made her misjudge the situation. Nate was a sinfully handsome bachelor. If he wanted a woman—any woman, Bianca imagined—he'd only have to crook his finger.

He'd said he wanted her, but did he want her as much as she did him?

Her answer came a moment later when he reached around her back and pulled her tight against him, angling his head to deepen the kiss. He took control in a way that was both tender and thrilling, as if she was a precious gift he wanted to savor.

Running every day until she dropped into bed, Bianca hadn't had time to savor anything in years. She sank into the kiss, letting the desire swirling through her take over until she was total sensation.

She lost herself in the moment, pressing her breasts against the hard planes of his chest and lifting her hands to grip his biceps. His heat enveloped her, and her body came alive. This was everything she'd ever wanted and more than she'd realized was possible.

And this was just a kiss.

She could so easily lose herself to this man.

The thought had her wrenching away, taking several stumbling steps toward the edge of the porch.

"I'm sorry," she said automatically. "Looks like I'm the one taking advantage now."

He barked out a short laugh. "It's not taking advantage if we both want it."

She glanced over her shoulder. His arms were crossed over his chest like he was having trouble stopping himself from reaching for her again.

"I didn't come here expecting this."

"I know."

"We should—" She paused, not sure how to give voice to the things she knew were right when her body was screaming for so much more.

"Take it slow," Nate finished, rubbing a hand across the back of his neck almost sheepishly.

"Slow," she agreed. "I should…um…go in now."

His brown eyes never left hers. "Good night, Bianca."

"Good night, Nate," she whispered, and hurried past him.

Chapter 6

Nate woke the next morning from a deep sleep.

He blinked and turned to glance at the clock on his nightstand.

Five o'clock.

He'd slept for seven hours.

In a row. Without waking.

It was a damn miracle.

A grin split his face as he sat up. He felt better than he had in months, longer even. Since he could remember.

After Bianca had gone into the house last night, he'd stood on the porch, pulling air in and out of his lungs, as he forced himself not to go after her. He pictured her walking up the stairs, the squeak from the loose floorboard echoing in his brain. She'd undress slowly and slip into the thin tank top she'd worn before—the one he could easily imagine peeling off her to reveal the pale skin beneath.

A movement had caught his attention out of the corner of his eye, and he'd turned to see a four-legged figure trotting toward the barn in the pale moonlight. The stray dog EJ had named Otis. The dog seemed almost feral the first time Nate had seen it on the ranch, but the animal always lurked about when Sugar was in residence. He thought about shooing it away but couldn't bring himself to after the dog had saved EJ.

Instead, he'd gone into the house and scooped up a cup of Sugar's kibble into a bowl he placed at the bottom of the front porch steps. The small business had been enough of a distraction that the pounding urge to follow Bianca had subsided. He'd gone to bed then, reciting SEAL navigation training exercises in his head to keep his mind from wandering.

He'd expected to toss and turn as he did most nights. He'd closed his eyes knowing that the next time he opened them would be in the middle of the night, his body drenched in a cold sweat as memories pummeled him from the deep recesses of his mind.

Although the sky outside his window was still dark, he knew the light of morning would be coming soon, heralding a new day. A fresh start.

He hadn't shared his feelings about Gerald Robinson with anyone. He'd barely discussed his father with Jayden and Grayson. He figured they understood where each other stood. Being triplets, they could often communicate without speaking. Even when careers in the US Army and Navy had sent Jayden and Nate to far-flung locations throughout the world, the bond the three of them shared had never wavered. They might not spend hours talking over their feelings, but Nate never doubted their love for each other or the devotion each had toward their mother.

Maybe he'd thought he was fine after discovering his

father hadn't died like his mother believed. He'd always been the fun-loving triplet, leaving the serious stuff for responsible Jayden and intense Grayson. But nearly twenty years in the navy had tempered him, and that last disastrous mission had all but destroyed his ability to see the bright side of anything.

Today he felt a new sense of hope, and he wasn't going to take it for granted. He got dressed, then slipped out of his room and started for the stairs. But as soon as he passed EJ's room, the door opened and the boy popped out.

"Morning," he said in an overloud voice.

Nate lifted a finger to his lips, then pointed to his mother's room across the hall. "I bet your mommy's still asleep," he whispered.

"I'm awake." EJ grinned. "I got dressed and brushed my teeth so I'm ready for morning chores."

"Then let's get going. If we finish quickly enough, we'll have time to make your mom breakfast in bed. I bet she'd like that."

"She likes pancakes," EJ said, following Nate down the stairs.

"I make darn good pancakes," Nate told him.

EJ frowned. "Mommy told me Daddy used to say making food is women's work, and the man's job is watching sports on TV."

Nate resisted the urge to roll his eyes. It didn't surprise him that Brett would have given that advice to his young son. The more he learned about Bianca's ex-husband, the more he disliked the man.

At the bottom of the stairs, he crouched down in front of EJ. "A real man takes care of the women in his life. That's what my brothers and I were taught." Once again, he was grateful for Earl Thompson's presence in his life.

He wondered what values Gerald Robinson had instilled in the children he'd raised. And whether his other illegitimate offspring had been lucky enough to have the kind of happy childhood Nate had experienced. "I know you love your mommy, and you understand how hard she works to make sure you have a good life. Right?"

EJ nodded solemnly.

"Then sometimes you want to do special things for her to thank her for that. Trust me, buddy, most women appreciate a man who is willing to help in the kitchen. It's an important lesson for you to learn."

The boy scratched his nose, looking about as interested in lessons on women as Nate had been as a boy. That hadn't stopped Earl from teaching them, and Nate would be forever grateful. "Okay."

He didn't say anything against EJ's father. That wasn't his place. But he figured if he made sure to share with EJ his own values—the values Eddie Shaw would have taught his nephew—hopefully Nate could balance whatever stupid, Neanderthal ideas Brett had put into his son's mind.

"Can I learn to ride a horse today?" EJ asked as Nate held open the front door for him.

"We'll need to ask your mom about that."

EJ sighed loudly. "She'll say no because she's afraid of horses. She won't want me to get hurt."

"You won't get hurt on my watch," Nate promised, even though the boy nearly had been the other day.

"Look," EJ shouted, then skipped to the bottom of the porch steps. "There's a dog bowl and paw prints in the dirt."

Nate lifted a brow. "I saw the stray hanging around last night as I was going to bed. I left out a scoop of food for him."

"His name's Otis," EJ said patiently.

"We're not naming him," Nate countered. "He doesn't belong to us."

"You fed him." EJ held up the metal bowl.

"It was a onetime thing," Nate explained a little sheepishly. "To thank him for coming to your rescue with Cinnamon."

"Can I feed him this morning?" EJ bounced on his toes. "Since I was the one he rescued, I should thank him."

Nate grinned but couldn't fault EJ's logic. "One scoop. There's a bin of dog food next to the washer in the laundry room."

EJ let out a whoop of delight then ran into the house, returning a few minutes later carrying the bowl piled high with kibble.

Nate chuckled. "That's a heck of a lot more than one scoop."

"I want to thank Otis a whole bunch." EJ set the food at the bottom of the porch. "Where do you think he sleeps?"

Nate started walking toward the barn, EJ at his side. "I'm not sure. But that dog can take care of himself."

"Everybody needs somebody," EJ reminded him. "Even Otis."

"Right now the horses need their morning hay. Let's get them and the chickens fed, then we'll make pancakes before your mom wakes up."

EJ seemed to have no trouble believing that a real man worked in the kitchen and was so excited at the prospect of surprising Bianca that he made quick work of morning chores. Within an hour they were back in the house, washing their hands and then mixing the pancake batter.

Nate had loved weekend mornings as a kid when his mom made huge stacks of pancakes. He and his brothers would polish off a half dozen each after their morning chores. They didn't make nearly as many now, but EJ was thrilled to pull up a chair in front of the stove and use the wide spatula to flip the pancakes. Nate washed and plated the blueberries Bianca had bought at the grocery store then poured a glass of juice. He didn't bother with coffee. Her first morning on the ranch Bianca had confirmed that his coffee was unpalatable. She'd quickly mastered Ariana's fancy coffee maker and had made him promise that he'd let her handle their morning caffeine.

It was such a little thing, but it felt like they were on the same team. Nate found that idea strangely appealing.

They put everything for breakfast on a tray then headed upstairs. Nate knocked softly on the bedroom door, but EJ just pushed it open.

"We made breakfast, Mommy," he shouted.

Bianca was already awake, sitting up against the pillows, her hair pulled back in a messy ponytail and a notebook propped in her lap.

She gave her son a brilliant smile. "This is a special treat. What's the occasion?"

"Mr. Nate said real men cook." EJ took the tray from Nate and carried it to the bed.

Nate sucked in a breath as Bianca's gaze lifted to his. She looked so fresh and happy, and an adorable blush colored her cheeks when he winked.

"Mr. Nate is a smart man," she murmured. She put aside the notebook and took the tray from EJ. "I love pancakes. Thank you both."

She was wearing an oversize, shapeless scoop-neck T-shirt that was about the sexiest thing he'd ever seen. Maybe because she looked relaxed and a little bit rumpled, and he could easily imagine a night spent with his body curled around hers.

He stayed in the doorway, afraid all his willpower would disappear if he stepped any closer. She took a bite of the pancakes, closed her eyes and then smiled as she chewed.

"They're perfect," she said, forking up a bite and holding it out to EJ.

"I flipped 'em," the boy reported.

"You did a good job." She brushed the hair away from his face, and Nate's heart clenched. He couldn't get enough of Bianca and the love she had for her son. She was exactly the type of woman he would have never chosen for himself. He usually went for the party girls, the ones who wanted a good time and expected nothing more.

No expectations meant nobody got hurt.

But Bianca made him crave more, a different life than the one he'd grown accustomed to. He wanted to be the kind of man she deserved, but could he trust he wouldn't fail her the way he had Eddie? Despite having Earl Thompson as a role model, Nate was still Gerald Robinson's son. What if he took after his dad and hurt the people who cared about him the most?

There was no doubt Gerald had broken Deborah's heart, and Bianca had already had one man desert her. She needed someone who could truly commit to her and EJ. As much as Nate wanted to, he wasn't sure if he had it in him to be that guy.

"What are you working on?" he asked when she glanced toward him again. It was a struggle to do anything except stare at her like a googly-eyed teenager, but despite the amazing kiss they'd shared, Bianca wanted to take things slow. She considered him a friend. He needed to act like one to her. He owed it to Eddie.

She bit down on her bottom lip, looking almost embarrassed. "It's nothing."

"I don't believe that for a minute."

"It's the start of a business plan," she said, dropping her gaze to the plate in front of her. "Just an initial inventory list and some ideas for how to market the care packages and gift boxes."

"That's fantastic," he said, and was rewarded by one of her sweet smiles.

"You don't have to say that. It's probably a silly idea in the first place."

"It's a great idea, and good for you for making a plan. You'll be back on your feet in no time, and you won't need me anymore."

Something flashed in her brown eyes that looked like disappointment, but it was gone a second later. She took another quick bite of pancake, then set the tray aside and threw back the covers. "Hopefully we'll be out of your hair sooner than later."

"That's not what I meant." All the warmth he'd felt from her minutes earlier had disappeared. He wanted to kick himself for his careless words. The last thing he wanted was for Bianca and EJ to leave, not when they'd already made such a difference in his life.

How could he explain that without sounding like a wuss? He was supposed to be a big, strong navy SEAL, not a broken man who was no longer sure of his purpose in life.

"Have you already been helping Mr. Nate with chores?" Bianca asked EJ as she stood.

"Yep," her son confirmed. "We fed the horses and the chickens. After breakfast we're going to fix the gate behind the shed. It needs new hinges."

She wore a pair of pajama pants with a pattern of rubber ducks all over. She was medium height but had a delicate bone structure that made her seem younger than twenty-eight. He had to remind himself she was nine years younger than him. And his best friend's little sister.

Nate sighed. As amazing as their kiss had been, he needed to keep Bianca at arm's length. He had no reason to ask her to stay once she'd gotten her life back on track. Despite the setbacks she'd obviously faced, it was also clear she hadn't lost her sense of hope or her willingness to work hard and try new things.

"Can I join you?" She reached behind her head and pulled out the ponytail holder, her dark hair falling over her shoulders and making his mouth go dry.

He should say no. He should walk away, put some sort of distance between them. Instead he found himself nodding. "It's not easy work."

"I'm good with that," she assured him.

"Meet me at the barn in twenty minutes." He moved forward and picked up the tray from the bed. "I'll take this downstairs."

"I can do it," she told him, her fingers brushing his as she reached for the tray.

He ignored the sparks that raced along his skin and gave EJ a pointed look. "A real man also cleans up the dishes."

The boy nodded and picked up the juice cup Bianca had set on her nightstand. "I'm a real man, Mommy."

"My best man," she murmured. She met Nate's gaze again, the tenderness in her brown eyes almost bringing him to his knees. "Thank you," she whispered.

He nodded. "Let's go, little man," he told EJ, and the boy followed him out of the room.

Chapter 7

The following week Bianca drove into Paseo to pick up the boxes of supplies she'd ordered to start on her stock for military care packages and birthday boxes. The post office was also housed in the general store, so she'd had the packages delivered to town because it seemed quicker than trying to find a delivery driver willing to make the trek out to the Fortune ranch.

Rosa, who owned most of the businesses in town, asked her to open several of the packages then immediately placed an order for two gift boxes for her daughters, who both had birthdays in February.

"They'll feel so special." Rosa clasped her hands in front of her ample chest. She was short with generous curves and a bright smile. "I've gotten into the habit of sending gift cards because it's so easy, but I love giving them something personal."

"I appreciate the business," Bianca told her honestly. "I

can't help but wonder if people will see the point of them. Nothing I offer is extravagant—"

"But you make it look so beautiful," Rosa interrupted. "You have an eye for color and design."

Susan from the library had stopped into the post office while Bianca was still there. Both of the older women oohed and aahed over the photos Bianca had saved on her camera of the gift boxes she'd put together for the store in San Antonio.

"Thanks." Bianca couldn't hide her grin. She was excited to start putting together the boxes. She'd used the internet at the library to go online and set up an Etsy page and a website for her business, which she was calling "Just the Two of Us Designs." She already had a half dozen preorders. It was hard to believe that only a short time ago she'd left San Antonio with no idea what she was going to do with her life. Now she was a small business owner and part-time ranch hand.

She glanced at her watch. "Oh, no. It's almost noon. I told Nate and EJ I'd make lunch and I promised that EJ could start horseback riding lessons this afternoon."

Susan laughed. "Just make sure it's Nate teaching him and not Grayson. Otherwise your son will be bronco riding by the time he starts kindergarten."

Bianca felt her eyes widen. "No way. I'm nervous enough to let him be led around the corral."

"Nate will take care of him," Rosa said matter-of-factly.

"I know," Bianca agreed softly. Rosa gave her a calculated look, but before the women could ask any questions about Bianca's relationship with Nate, she picked up her stack of boxes and walked out into the bright Texas sunshine.

It wasn't exactly a surprise that everyone she'd met on

her regular trips to town knew Nate and his family. Paseo was a tiny, close-knit community. Bianca hadn't been in the area long, but already most of the people she encountered greeted her by name. So different from San Antonio, where the barista at the neighborhood coffee shop she'd frequented for almost two years still got her name wrong almost every day.

Brittany. Bethany. Becky. But never Bianca.

Two weeks in Paseo and she was a regular.

She realized people were curious about how she knew Nate and why she and EJ were staying at the ranch while the rest of the family was away. Bianca doggedly continued with the "family friend" line, unwilling to share any more than that when she barely understood her feelings for Nate.

All she knew was she wanted him to kiss her again, but somehow she'd been relegated back to the realm of "Eddie's little sister." Nate was careful to keep his distance, especially at night after EJ had gone to bed. She tried not to let it hurt her feelings, but the longer she spent with Nate, the harder she fell for him.

She'd gotten so desperate for his company, she'd even made herself into a morning person. Waking before sunrise wasn't in her nature, but a person could train themselves to do anything with the right motivation.

Nate Fortune was it for her.

He'd been surprised the first day she'd stumbled down to the kitchen and offered to make breakfast while he and EJ handled the early morning chores. But now it was a routine, and she'd come to enjoy that quiet time in the kitchen with the scent of coffee filling the air.

She enjoyed everything about her time at the ranch, other than Nate's refusal to admit he felt more for her than physical attraction. Sometimes, though, when they were in the barn or driving down the dirt road that led to the far end of the property, she'd catch him staring at her like she was a hot-fudge sundae and he'd been without dessert for months. It had to be only a matter of time until he kissed her. She'd told herself she would wait for him to make the next move, but it was difficult to be patient.

Still, she was happier in Paseo than she'd been in years. It was more than Nate. There was a sense of community she hadn't realized was missing in her life. The rolling hills and wide pastures gave her a feeling of being grounded to the earth and somehow a better understanding of her place in it. She loved watching the open sky above her as she drove. It was a welcome change from the constant traffic of her San Antonio neighborhood.

Here she could sometimes drive the whole way from town to the ranch without passing another car. And when she did, whoever was driving the approaching vehicle would undoubtedly offer her a friendly wave.

But today, when she pulled into the long driveway, there was an unfamiliar truck parked in front of the barn. EJ burst out the front door and came running toward her car before she'd even turned off the ignition.

"Sugar's here, Mommy!" he shouted as she opened the door. "And Jayden and Ariana. And Mr. Nate bought me a pony."

"He didn't," she whispered.

"I didn't buy the pony," Nate called from the front porch as if he'd read her lips. She heard a deep laugh come from the direction of the barn. A man who was the spitting image of Nate, but somehow totally different, walked toward her.

"You must be Bianca," he said, pulling off a faded leather glove. "I'm Jayden."

"Nice to meet you," she said automatically, relieved her

voice didn't falter. She knew Jayden and his wife would be returning to the ranch, but somehow she'd put the thought out of her mind. This place had begun to feel like home, like it belonged to Nate and her and EJ.

But it wasn't hers, and Nate didn't belong to her. She was the outsider here, as she'd been in every other part of her life. What if Ariana resented a woman other than the triplets' mother being at the ranch? What if neither Jayden nor Ariana could deal with EJ's exuberance the way Nate did?

Bianca prided herself on her resilience—on being able to keep a positive attitude no matter what life threw at her. No one other than Eddie had made her feel valued, so she'd learned early on to value herself. But recently, life's disappointments and misfortunes—both big and trivial—had worn her down until it felt like she was made of tissue paper, easily crumpled, torn and tossed aside.

"The pony's name is Twix." EJ tugged on her pant leg. "Mr. Nate says he's the perfect size for me." He looked up at Jayden. "Can I go get Sugar so Mommy can meet her?"

"You bet." Jayden chuckled as EJ took off for the house. "I'm guessing my brother didn't clear the pony with you?"

Bianca pressed her lips together. "No."

"I didn't plan it," Nate said behind her. She turned to find him standing closer than he'd been to her all week. He was giving her an aw-shucks smile she could imagine had gotten him out of all sorts of trouble when he was younger. "I was over at the Caplans' today and they'd gotten Twix when their grandson came to stay for Christmas. The kid won't be back until spring break, so the pony's on loan until then." He lifted his hands, palms out. "I didn't buy EJ a pony."

"Close enough," Jayden said with a smug grin.

"Not helping," a feminine voice called.

They all turned as a woman walked from the barn, looking both completely out of place on this ranch in the middle of nowhere and utterly like she belonged. She had long dark hair that looked Hollywood A-list shiny and wore a printed shirtdress and the cutest pair of red boots Bianca had ever seen.

Bianca smoothed a self-conscious hand over the front of her faded shirt. She didn't own much in the way of clothes. The day before leaving San Antonio, she'd brought everything decent she had to a local resale shop that bought items outright for a pittance of what they were worth. That left her with jeans, yoga pants, a handful of well-worn T-shirts and a couple of floral-patterned blouses she hadn't been willing to part with because they were her favorites.

She felt shabby in comparison to this woman who she assumed was Jayden's wife, Ariana. Why hadn't she at least taken the time to brush out her hair this morning? Instead, she'd pulled it back into a messy bun, her usual nonstylish style. She'd never considered how much she'd stopped caring about her appearance once she became a mom. Maybe that was part of the reason Nate had backed off. He probably preferred women who were beautiful and pulled together. Women like Ariana.

She didn't realize she'd stepped back until she felt the soft pressure of Nate's warm hand against the small of her back.

"You're perfect," he whispered, and she was once again amazed at how easily he was able to read her.

"I'm a mess," she said under her breath.

"Perfect," he repeated and moved his hand to the collar of her shirt. Her neck was exposed because of the bun, and his thumb gently grazed her skin.

Bianca felt a blush heat her cheeks as her stomach dipped and swirled at his touch. She glanced over to see Jayden watching the two of them, his gaze assessing.

She sidestepped Nate and moved forward to greet Ariana. Instead of taking Bianca's outstretched hand, the other woman enveloped her in a tight hug.

"I'm *so* happy to meet you," she said, squeezing Bianca's shoulders. "Nate told us all about you. EJ is adorable. I'm so sorry about your brother."

"Thank you," Bianca said, slightly overwhelmed at Ariana's warmth. "Congratulations on getting married."

"Thanks." Ariana grinned. "I guess we're still officially newlyweds. Our honeymoon was spent traveling around the state for research on my new book, so it kind of feels like we've been married forever."

"You're definitely stuck with me forever," Jayden said, slipping an arm around Ariana's waist and pulling her closer.

"I'm a lucky girl." Ariana tipped up her face and kissed her husband's cheek. She looked at Bianca again. "We're glad your stay coincides with our visit home."

Jayden nodded. "I only met Eddie a couple of times, but he was a good guy. And he had my brother's back for a lot of years, so we'll always be grateful."

"It goes both ways," Bianca answered, glancing over her shoulder. "Nate was the brother Eddie always wanted."

Something shifted in the air as Nate looked past her to Jayden—a silent communication between the brothers Bianca didn't understand. But she knew it had to do with Eddie, and that made her intensely curious.

"Deborah will be sad she didn't get a chance to meet EJ," Ariana said into the uncomfortable silence. "She loves kids."

"Hard to believe," Jayden said with a smile, "after dealing with us for so many years."

"What were you doing in the barn?" Nate asked Ariana, lifting an eyebrow. "You and Jayden making up for the time you spent working on your honeymoon?" His tone was teasing. He was obviously comfortable with his brother's wife. Bianca felt a pang of jealousy. She'd always imagined becoming best friends with the woman her brother married, but Eddie had remained stubbornly single, making excuses about the SEALs not leaving him time for anything else.

Ariana rolled her eyes. "Get your mind out of the gutter, Nathan Fortune. There's a corner in one of the horse stalls where I can sometimes get a few bars of service on my phone."

"What?" Bianca felt her mouth drop open. "You actually have service on the ranch?"

"It comes and goes, but I always try."

"That would be amazing. Can you show me where?"

Jayden groaned. "Why can't we all just be satisfied with the good ol' landline on the kitchen wall?"

"The ranch is perfect," Ariana agreed, "except for that one little thing. It's not like I'm checking Facebook. I need internet for work." She sent a questioning glance toward Bianca. "I'm guessing you need it for your job, too?"

Embarrassment roared through Bianca, making her stomach twist. Ariana was researching a book and was already a talented writer. Bianca had spent almost an hour at the library in town reading the series of articles Ariana had written last year about different members of the Fortune family. Bianca couldn't possibly compare what she was doing to that.

"I don't—"

"She's starting her own business," Nate interrupted. "Personalized gift boxes people order or buy in stores. Plus care packages for soldiers deployed overseas. She used to send stuff to Eddie and we were all jealous. They're going to be popular. Rosa has already ordered a couple for her daughters."

"That's so exciting," Ariana said. "Do you have pictures? Are you selling them online?"

Bianca nodded, darting a glance at Nate. Of course he knew about her gift boxes, but the pride in his voice as he explained her business idea to his brother and Ariana surprised her. She'd sort of assumed he was just being kind in his support of what she was doing, but he really sounded like he believed in her.

It made her tingle all the way down to her toes.

"I set up an Etsy account." She pulled her phone out of her back pocket. "I just went to town to pick up the supplies I ordered, but I have photos of a few of the boxes I made for the gift shop where I worked in San Antonio. I did different colors and themes." She pulled up the photo stream and handed the phone to Ariana. "They're simple, but it's a start."

Ariana swiped a finger across the screen, her face lighting up as she did. "Oh, my gosh. I love them. I'm totally going to set you up with a couple of high-end boutiques from my old neighborhood in Austin. These would be perfect."

"Thanks," Bianca said softly, wondering why she'd been so intimidated by Jayden's wife. Ariana was one of the friendliest people she'd ever met.

"Mommy, this is Sugar." She turned to EJ, who'd returned with an adorable mutt wearing a red bandana at his side. "She's blind," EJ explained, "but she can get from the house to the barn and that's why there are wind chimes all around. They help Sugar know where she's going."

Bianca smiled. "I just thought this family had a thing for wind chimes." She bent to scratch the dog's head. She could tell by the dog's cloudy eyes that she couldn't see, but Sugar sniffed at Bianca's hand, then gave it a gentle lick.

"She likes you," EJ said, his voice breathless. "She likes me, too." He shaded his eyes with one hand and turned in a circle, surveying the property. "I bet Otis will come out now that Sugar's back. He's been eating the food Mr. Nate and I leave out for him every morning."

"You're feeding that stray dog who hangs around?" Jayden asked with a pointed look toward Nate. "The one you said was nothing but a nuisance."

Nate shrugged, rubbing a hand over his jaw.

"I told you owning a dog would do you some good." Jayden nodded. "It can be lonely out here when no one else is around."

"He's not my dog, and I don't get lonely. I like the quiet."

Bianca tried not to flinch. She knew he didn't mean to direct the comment toward her and EJ, but they'd certainly shown up and disturbed Nate's quiet world.

"Well, I'm glad we're all here together now," Ariana said quickly. "We're going to have so much fun." She scrunched up her nose. "Bianca, I hope Nate hasn't been subjecting you to his coffee."

"It's not that bad," Nate protested.

"I'm making coffee every morning," Bianca assured Ariana.

The other woman smiled. "Smart girl."

"Can I take Sugar to the backyard?" EJ asked. "Maybe Otis doesn't realize she's here."

Nate looked like he wanted to say no, but Jayden cleared his throat and gave a small nod to Bianca.

"Since it's okay with Jayden," she told her son. "But don't go any farther than the shed."

Nate let out a long breath and ruffled EJ's dark hair.

"Jayden and I need to look at one of the tractors that hasn't been running right. When we're finished, I'll bring Twix out to the corral for you to ride."

EJ pumped his little fist in the air. "Best day ever," he said and called for Sugar to follow him around the house.

Bianca leveled a look at Nate. "Back to the subject of you getting my son a pony."

"I think that's our cue," Jayden said quickly, grabbing his wife's hand.

"Good luck," Ariana called over her shoulder as the pair hurried to the house.

"Was she wishing luck to you or me?" Nate stepped closer again, and Bianca ignored the effect his nearness had on certain parts of her body.

She narrowed her eyes.

"Me," he said with a grimace. "Definitely me."

She sighed. "Seriously, Nate. A pony?"

"It's on loan," he said, holding up his hands.

"A pony is the stuff of childhood fantasies. Now it's EJ's reality."

"It's not a big deal in Paseo," he countered. "Most families keep at least one horse, and lots of people have ponies when their kids are little."

She couldn't argue that point, but still…

"How am I supposed to compete with a pony when we leave here?"

"It's not a competition," he insisted. "You're a fantastic mom. Besides, there's no reason you have to leave anytime soon."

My heart, she wanted to tell him. Protecting it was a good reason.

"I thought you liked quiet."

He inclined his head. "I do, but I like you and EJ more."

He reached out and ran a finger along her collarbone. "A lot more."

"We don't belong here."

His mouth went hard, but his eyes stayed gentle. "You belong here for as long as you want. I thought you'd be happy with the pony. EJ's determined to learn to ride, and this way he can start on a horse that's more his size."

"I guess you're right."

He grinned. "Darlin', I'm always right. Trust me."

She laughed, but the truth was she did trust Nate. And she cared about him far more than she was willing to admit to either of them.

"What am I going to do with you?"

"I've got so many ideas," he whispered, and she sucked in a breath when he dropped a quick kiss on her lips. "Right now there's a tractor to fix. We'll meet behind the barn in an hour for EJ's first riding lesson if you want to watch."

Bianca blinked, unable to put a sentence together with how blown away she was by his sudden flirtation. "Sure," she whispered and pressed her fingertips to her lips. She had so many ideas of what she wanted to do with him, as well. Each one of them sexier than the last.

His eyes turned dark as if he knew every erotic thought she'd ever had. But he only winked and walked past her toward the barn.

She brushed her hair out of her eyes and turned for the house like she wasn't about to explode from pent-up need. Bianca was used to wanting things she couldn't have. And she wanted Nate more than anything.

Chapter 8

"You're in deep."

Nate kept the smile plastered to his face as he reached behind his back to give Jayden, standing at the edge of the corral, a one-fingered salute.

"You're doing great, EJ," he called. "Loosen up on the reins a little. Remember you're using them to talk to Twix, not scream at him."

The boy nodded, the tip of his tongue poking out from the corner of his mouth. He gave the reins more slack and the docile pony continued his wide circle in the ring.

Bianca stood on the far side of the corral, leaning against the fence and looking tense as she watched her son. Ariana was at her side, a supportive hand resting on Bianca's shoulder.

"Rude hand gestures don't make it any less true," Jayden said.

"She's Eddie's baby sister." Nate took a few steps back until he was standing next to his brother.

Jayden chuckled. "She's not a baby."

"I'm giving her a helping hand."

"That's not all you want to give her." By his amused tone, Jayden was obviously loving a chance to give Nate grief about a woman.

"Don't make me kick your—"

"Mr. Nate, I want him to go faster." EJ looked over at him hopefully.

Nate saw Bianca stiffen and shook his head. "Next lesson. First you get comfortable, then we'll increase the speed."

"I'm happy for you," Jayden said, nudging his shoulder. "You look better than you have since you left the SEALs. Are you sleeping?"

"Like a rock."

"Like you used to."

Nate sighed. When he'd first gotten back to Paseo, he'd tried to hide the nightmares that plagued him. He didn't want anyone in his family to worry, especially since there was nothing they could do to help him. He hadn't thought anything would help him. Until Bianca.

"What have you told her about Eddie?"

"She hasn't asked many questions," Nate admitted, giving EJ a thumbs-up when the boy tugged on the reins to keep the pony from lowering its head to eat grass. "I haven't offered anything. The official report didn't give details, so why should I?"

"Because you believe you're responsible for her brother's death."

Nate's head jerked back like Jayden had punched him.

"Not that I think that," his brother amended. "No one does." He leaned closer. "Except you. Which is what counts."

"What good would it do to tell her?"

"It's a secret between you. That isn't the way to start a relationship. Trust me."

"There's no relationship to speak of. She's a friend."

"She's more than that," Jayden insisted. "You deserve to be happy, Nate. Eddie would want that for you."

"No one can say what Eddie would want because he's not here. That's on me."

"It's not."

Nate shook his head, his cheeks aching from continuing to smile through this ridiculous conversation. "Did you make a stop in Austin on your way home?"

"Yeah. Ariana wanted to visit her family."

"Did you see any of the others?"

He didn't need to spell out which others he was referring to.

"We had lunch with Keaton. He was the first person Ariana profiled last year in her *Becoming a Fortune* blog series for *Weird Life Magazine*, so they're still friends. He's a good guy. Every one of them I've met has been."

"What about Gerald?"

Jayden shook his head.

Before Nate could ask more questions, EJ called for him. He jogged out to the boy and took hold of the reins. "Done for today?"

"Can Mommy come out while I'm on Twix and pet him?" EJ bit down on his lip, a nervous habit he'd inherited from his mother and one that made Nate's heart melt just a bit. "I think she'll like him better then."

"I like him fine," Bianca called from the fence. "I like him with some space between us."

"Please, Mommy?" EJ called.

Nate arched a brow in her direction, then smiled as Ariana gave her a gentle nudge. She climbed through the slats of the fence and slowly made her way toward them.

Her chest rose and fell in shallow breaths as if she was approaching a man-eating tiger rather than a slightly paunchy and docile pony.

"He smells like a real horse," EJ informed her.

"He is a real horse."

"He's a pony," Nate and EJ said at the same time.

Bianca reached out a hand, which Nate noticed was trembling slightly.

"Are you okay?" he whispered, moving to stand directly behind her.

"Peachy keen," she said through clenched teeth.

"You saw them out here. Twix's as gentle as they come," Nate assured her.

"Right." She stroked her hand up the pony's nose, yanking it away when the animal let out a soft whicker.

"He likes you, Mommy," EJ said brightly.

Bianca nodded, although to Nate it looked like she was about to lose her lunch. He glanced up but Jayden and Ariana had started toward the house.

"End of your lesson," he told EJ, tugging on the reins he held. "Let's get Twix back to the barn."

"I can do it," EJ said.

Nate helped the boy off the pony and handed him the reins. "Put him in his stall and start brushing him down."

"Yes, sir," EJ answered and made his way into the barn, the pony happy to follow since the barn meant rest and food.

"I'm such a wimp." Bianca covered her face with her hands when EJ disappeared around the corner. "I don't want my fear to rub off on him."

"What happened with you and a horse?" Nate gently pulled her hands way from her face, lacing his fingers with hers.

"Nothing."

"Your reaction to Twix isn't nothing."

She took a shuddery breath. "I fell off a horse when I was in third grade and got kicked in the back. My mom blamed the accident on me because I kept sliding off the saddle. The horse wasn't tame like your herd. He belonged to one of her boyfriends, and she insisted I learn to ride so she'd have an excuse to be at his house every weekend."

"I'm sorry, Bianca. That must have been terrifying."

She shrugged. "Eddie had just left for boot camp, so it was Mom and me on our own. That was never a good thing. I missed a couple of days of school, but the next Saturday she dragged me back out there. I had a panic attack and puked all over her new boyfriend. It was kind of the end of their relationship."

"I imagine that didn't sit well with her?"

"Not at all. I missed Eddie so much at that moment. I wanted to call and beg him to leave the navy, to come home so I wouldn't be alone with her. It was miserable with the two of us in the apartment. Eddie could always make her laugh or lighten the mood. I couldn't do anything right. I still can't, according to her."

Nate ignored his resolve to keep a safe distance between the two of them and pulled her closer. He wrapped his arms around her waist and she rested her head against his chest with a sigh that made his heart ache. When he'd enlisted, it hadn't seemed like a big deal. Yes, Jayden also left home for a career in the army, but Grayson was still with their mom, and Nate came back to Paseo during every leave to pitch in at the ranch. Between the three boys, they'd always been able to take care of Deborah.

He knew from the little Eddie had talked about his mom that she was the exact opposite of Nate's mother. Based on how Eddie had described Jennifer Shaw, she was an immature, insecure party girl who'd never grown up. There was no doubt Eddie loved his mother, but he'd often seemed relieved to be far away from home. Nate hadn't given much thought to how Eddie's sister would fare being left alone for so much time with a woman who clearly had very few maternal instincts.

It was a wonder Bianca had turned out as sweet and nurturing as she had with Jennifer as a role model.

"You're amazing," he whispered into her hair, loving how the flowery scent of it seemed to envelop him.

She snuggled closer, and Nate realized that if his brother or Ariana was looking out the window in the kitchen, they'd have a perfect view of this embrace. He should care. He should step away from her, but he didn't.

"And you're not alone," he told her. "Not anymore."

She lifted her head. "Maybe you can teach me to ride?" Her voice shook slightly.

"You don't have to do that."

"I want to," she insisted. "I've made a lot of decisions in my life based on fear. That needs to stop. I want to be brave. I figure if I can get back on the proverbial horse, I can do anything, right?"

He could feel her fear like it was a living thing, radiating from her in waves. "You can do anything."

One side of her mouth kicked up. "Even this?" she asked and pressed her mouth to his.

The kiss was over so quickly he didn't even have time to respond. It was a soft promise, and her eyes danced as she pulled away. "The next move is yours."

He wondered how he'd ever thought he'd be able to stay away from her. His need was a palpable force, humming under his skin and making his blood feel like he'd just taken a shot of adrenaline.

He rubbed a hand over the back of his neck. "I've got all kinds of moves," he said, trying to sound romantic or sexy or something.

But he realized how out of practice he was when Bianca laughed. "I just bet you do. I can't wait to see them." She glanced over her shoulder toward the house then back to him. "Are you okay with EJ in the barn? I'd like to get Ariana's opinion on a couple of marketing descriptions I did for the military care packages."

"He's safe with me," Nate told her, then closed his eyes for a moment as images of Eddie's lifeless body pounded into his brain. *Safe.* His most despised four-letter word, since he no longer believed he had the power to keep anyone safe. "I mean—"

"I know he is," she said with a gentle smile. "I'll be out to check on him in a bit."

She walked away before he could answer, and despite Jayden's advice, Nate knew he'd never tell Bianca the details of Eddie's death. He couldn't stand the thought of hurting her and would do anything he could to make sure that didn't happen.

Anything.

"What inspired the idea for your book?" Bianca asked Ariana later that evening as they worked together in the kitchen. Nate and Jayden had taken EJ with them an hour earlier when they left to go check on the irrigation system in one of the fields at the far end of the property.

Ariana had offered to help Bianca make dinner—homemade meatballs and spaghetti. Bianca was shocked to discover how easy and companionable it was to have a friend in the kitchen.

"It was a local couple actually," Ariana answered as

she chopped tomatoes for the salad. "Paloma and Hector Ybarra. I got stuck on Jayden's ranch last June when my car conked out just before a tornado touched down nearby. There was some minor damage to this ranch, but the Ybarras' house was completely destroyed."

"That's terrible," Bianca whispered.

"It was, but the community immediately pitched in to rebuild it. I went to their farm with Jayden and was shocked at how calm both of them seemed. Paloma told me how blessed they were to have each other and their friends even when they had nothing but the land beneath their feet. They had so much wisdom to offer, and their words really meant a lot. It was a time of transition in my life, and although I had a great job, I felt strangely at loose ends. I'd just met Jayden, and he changed everything for me. Does that make any sense?"

Bianca sighed. "More than you know."

"Once I realized things were getting serious with Jayden—or at least that I wanted them to—I quit the magazine. The Fortunes were no longer simply a family I was reporting on. I was in love with one of Gerald Robinson's sons. It no longer felt right making the family my business, and I'd always wanted to write a book." She laughed softly. "When I first met Jayden after my car died, I accused him of being an ax murderer."

"I'm sure that went over well," Bianca said with a smile.

"He likes to joke that I should write a story about an ax murderer, but I like interviewing real people and learning their stories. The Ybarras inspired me, and I knew there must be more stories like theirs around the state, so I decided to write a book about people who embody the spirit of Texas."

Bianca dumped a box of dried spaghetti into the pot of

boiling water on the stove. "It's a great idea. How do you find your subjects?"

"Articles in local papers, news stories, social media."

"Social media?"

Ariana nodded. "I set up a Facebook page and Instagram account for the book. I posted about what I was doing and asked people to message me if they knew anyone who would be a good fit. The response was unbelievable. Then I sorted through the stories, contacted people for initial interviews and went from there. Jayden and I are visiting the dozen people I'm profiling."

"It's nice of him to travel with you."

"I think he was nervous about letting me go alone, but it's wonderful to have him on the road with me. I've got pages of notes and lots of recorded conversations. In fact, I only have three more people to interview and I'll be ready to start compiling everything."

"Are any of them famous like the Fortunes?"

Ariana shook her head. "A few are well-known in their communities, but very few people in Texas are as famous as the Fortunes."

"Nate told me the story of their mother and Gerald Robinson. Or I suppose she knew him as Jerome Fortune."

"He did?" Ariana paused with the knife in midair. "Was it a secret?"

"No, of course not. It's just that Nate doesn't talk about his father much. He's like Deborah in that way. Both of them like to pretend that discovering Gerald is alive hasn't changed anything."

"That's impossible."

"I know, but it's a pretty overwhelming discovery. Having interviewed several of the Fortune kids, I've seen a span of different reactions. I'm glad Nate finally talked to someone. I'm glad he has you."

"I happened to be here," Bianca said with a shrug, unwilling to allow herself to believe Nate confiding in her meant what Ariana wanted it to.

"It's more than that," the other woman insisted. "Nate is charming and funny, but Jayden said something changed in him when he returned from his last mission."

"The mission where my brother died."

"Right," Ariana agreed, her gaze sympathetic. "Obviously that was a tragedy you can't truly recover from, but I think it affected Nate more than even he realized. I've only known him a short time, but there's a big difference in how he seems with you and EJ here. He's lighter somehow."

"He takes on too much."

"Each of the Fortune brothers does." Ariana dropped the tomatoes into the wooden salad bowl Bianca had placed on the counter. "I think it comes from being raised by a single mom. They're protective of Deborah and feel responsible for anyone they care about."

"I wonder if that's how EJ will be when he grows up." Bianca stirred the tomato sauce simmering on the stove then turned to Ariana. "Nate told me he doesn't care about a relationship with Gerald Robinson. Does Jayden feel the same way?"

"Not exactly. I think Jayden is wary but curious. He's met some of the Fortunes as well as Gerald. And I'm not sure Grayson has actually processed his feelings on having a father. He's been busy with the rodeo circuit and his sponsorship responsibilities. I doubt Deborah's fully dealt with it, either. She spends so much time with Grayson that it's easy for her to lose herself in his life. She does that with all the boys. They've always been her whole world."

"Did you have a normal family growing up?" Bianca couldn't help but ask.

"I did. What about you?"

Bianca shook her head, the familiar disappointment and regret burning a hole in her stomach. "I never knew my dad. According to Mom, he took off after Eddie was born but came back when he was around seven. He wanted another shot and to finally be a family. I guess life was pretty good until I came along. The baby thing just wasn't our dad's cup of tea so he left again—permanently. Mom blamed me, although Eddie never did. He always told me he didn't remember much about those two years with our dad, but now I think he might have been lying. Eddie was a great big brother. I'm so lucky I had him because our mom didn't have much use for me."

"That can't be true," Ariana said, sounding stunned. "You're obviously a great mother. Where did you learn that if not—"

"Maybe it's natural instinct," Bianca said with a tired laugh. "Or maybe I'm trying to make up for what I never had. Either way, I can appreciate how Nate must feel. It breaks my heart because my jerk of an ex-husband walked away two years ago and hasn't contacted EJ since. I don't care that he was done with me, but a boy needs a father."

"You're doing a great job on your own."

Bianca shook her head. "I appreciate you saying that, but you have to understand what I'm talking about after profiling even a few of the Fortune kids." She leveled a look at Ariana. "How many of them have daddy issues?"

Ariana grimaced before quickly schooling her features. "Point taken, but they're also a group of accomplished, smart, talented and generally fun-to-be-around people. They may have some issues to work through, but show me one person who doesn't. I had a great family, but that doesn't make me perfect." She opened the refrigerator and pulled out a bottle of white wine. "Besides," she said, grabbing a corkscrew from a drawer, "perfect is boring."

Bianca smiled and took down two wineglasses from the cabinet next to the stove. "One thing you can say about the Paseo Fortunes is they are *not* boring."

Ariana filled each of the glasses and handed one to Bianca. "To not perfect."

They clinked glasses. "And not boring," Bianca added and took a long sip.

Nate walked out of an empty horse stall, staring at his cell phone's home screen, and almost plowed into Jayden.

"Ariana and Bianca called us in to dinner," his brother told him. "I sent EJ in to wash his hands and—" Jayden's eyes narrowed. "What's wrong? You look like you've seen a ghost."

"Not a ghost," Nate clarified. "But I did just get off the phone with Ben Fortune Robinson in Austin."

Jayden raised a brow.

"Why is it that I can have no service at the house but somehow I get three bars in the back of that stall?"

"Ariana would tell you it's luck."

"Bad luck," Nate muttered.

"Was Ben giving you trouble?"

Nate shook his head. "On the contrary, he was ten kinds of friendly."

"All of Gerald's kids I've met have been. The Robinson brood—Ben, Wes, Kieran, Graham, Rachel, Zoe, Sophie and Olivia—had just as much of a shock as the rest of us."

"I can't believe you can rattle off their names."

"We now have a lot of family around Texas," Jayden said with a shrug. "But I think there are actually more."

"We know there's more," Nate countered. "Keaton for one." He began to tick names off on his fingers. "Then Chloe and—"

"I'm not talking about the kids from Gerald's affairs. Ariana uncovered information while she was doing research last year. It seems Gerald got his wandering eye honestly. His father, Julius, had secrets of his own. And quite possibly Fortune offspring that even Charlotte Robinson isn't aware of. I was thinking—"

"Stop thinking." Nate held up a hand. "Stop talking. Whatever you and Ariana believe you know, I don't want to hear about it. Gerald Robinson was a sperm donor as far as I'm concerned. Leave me out of any sort of search for more Fortunes."

"You know Ben was the one who first reached out to his—I guess our—father's illegitimate kids. He believed everyone had a right to know their roots."

"Yeah. He told me as much during our conversation." Nate blew out a breath. "He also invited me to the Mendoza Winery in Austin for some big Valentine's Day bash. According to Ben, it would be a perfect occasion for me to meet some of the other Fortunes."

"And the Mendozas," Jayden added. "The two families are pretty intertwined at this point. There's a lot of history there, and now Rachel and Olivia—"

"Two of Gerald's legitimate daughters, right?"

Jayden nodded. "They're both married to Mendozas."

"Sounds complicated." Nate gave Jayden a pointed look. "I don't do complicated anymore."

Jayden tipped back his head and laughed. "Right. I'm going to ignore the fact that you've got it bad for your best friend's little sister, who happens to be a single mom and also happens to be living under the same roof as you. Hate to break it to you, bro, but that's kind of the definition of complicated."

"It's not the same thing."

"Right," Jayden repeated with a smirk.

"I'm heading to dinner. This conversation is going nowhere." Nate didn't wait for an answer but started walking toward the barn door.

"So are you going to do it?" Jayden asked, catching up to him in a few strides.

Bianca's beautiful face filled Nate's mind but he shook off the image. "Do what?"

"Make an appearance at the Mendoza Winery party?"

Nathan shrugged. "It's a busy time around here."

"It's always busy at the ranch," Jayden countered. "Make time, Nate. I think it would be good for you."

"I'll take that under consideration," Nate answered, unwilling to admit how curious he was becoming about his extended Fortune family.

Chapter 9

Jayden and Ariana stayed for two more days. The house was crowded in the best way possible with all of them together. When Eddie had joined the navy, Bianca had dreamed of a big family with lots of brothers and sisters instead of the cramped apartment where she could feel the weight of her mother's silence like a boulder balanced on her shoulders. Being on the ranch with the Fortunes was a dream come true.

During the day, she organized her inventory, taking photographs and cataloging everything for her website and Etsy shop. She also spent time with EJ, working with him on letter recognition and writing his name. He'd been in a prekindergarten program at his daycare, and she didn't want him to be behind when they returned to San Antonio.

Although the thought of going back held no appeal.

They couldn't stay in Paseo forever, even though watching the love between Jayden and Ariana made her long for her own happily-ever-after. She and Nate had little time alone with his brother in residence, and she supposed that was a good thing.

Or at least an excuse as to why he hadn't tried to touch her again. She knew he wanted her. Sometimes when no one was looking, she'd meet his gaze and the intensity in his eyes made her feel like she might spontaneously combust.

But he'd stayed up with his brother both nights, although it was clear Jayden would have rather gone out to the tiny guest cottage situated to the west of the house he was sharing with his wife. Bianca didn't understand why Nate insisted on the late-night bonding sessions, and she didn't like not knowing.

Now she stood at the front porch rail, a cool breeze whipping between the house and the barn, as Jayden loaded duffel bags into the cargo bed of his truck, then opened the back door so Sugar could hop in.

EJ was next to Nate a few feet from the car, and she watched her son wipe his eyes on the back of his shirtsleeve. He'd miss that sweet dog. The stray he'd named Otis had indeed been more visible with Sugar at the ranch. The dog still wouldn't let anyone near enough to touch him, but if they let Sugar out on her own, Otis would soon enough be hanging out at her side.

Sugar seemed to take the stray dog's devotion as her due. She was like a queen with one of her loyal subjects. EJ remained determined to tame Otis and had convinced Ariana to help him bake dog treats to lure the animal closer.

Bianca worried about his attachment to a dog whose history they didn't know, but both Jayden and Nate assured her that if Sugar was comfortable with Otis, he must have a decent temperament.

Ariana waved from the passenger-side window. They'd

said their official goodbyes after lunch, and Bianca was only a little embarrassed that she didn't walk all the way to the car to see them off. She was afraid she might lose it in a far more embarrassing way than EJ. In such a short time, Ariana had come to feel like a true friend, and she appreciated the calming effect Jayden had on Nate, who seemed more relaxed at his brother's side.

Jayden said something to Nate and held up a finger toward Ariana, then jogged toward the house and up the porch steps.

"Forget something?" Bianca asked lightly, relieved her voice didn't crack.

"Take care of him," Jayden said quietly, coming to stand in front of her. "He pretends to be stronger than he is."

"I know," she said with a slight nod. "But Nate can take care of himself. He doesn't need me."

"Yes." Jayden crouched down so they were at eye level. "He does."

She blew out a breath, unsure how to answer. What she wanted most in life at the moment was to be needed by Nate Fortune.

"Losing Eddie was a blow to both of you," he continued, "but it isn't the only thing that holds you together. You make him remember what it's like to feel happy. That's special, Bianca."

"I think he's pretty special," she whispered with a shaky smile.

Jayden frowned slightly. "He also doesn't believe he deserves that happiness."

"What do you mean?"

"It's his story to tell, but I'm asking you not to give up on him. Me, Nate and Grayson aren't the sharpest knives in the drawer when it comes to women."

"You were pretty smart choosing Ariana."

His gaze softened. "I almost messed it up, but I loved her too much to let her go."

"It was so nice to meet you both."

"You, too." He reached forward and gave her a friendly hug. For as much as the two brothers—and she guessed Grayson, as well—looked alike, her body didn't react at all to Jayden. It was as if she'd been specifically calibrated to respond to Nate. All she had to do was feel his gaze on her and she'd start to tremble. "I'm guessing we'll be seeing more of you."

She lifted one shoulder. "I'm not sure how long we'll be staying. I don't want to take advantage of Nate's hospitality."

Jayden laughed at that. "No one takes advantage of Nate. Stay as long as you like. You're good for him. EJ is good for him."

"Are you going to talk all afternoon?" Nate called, impatience clear in his tone.

"He's jealous," Jayden said with an eye roll, and he gave Bianca another hug. "I'll see you next time."

"Bye, Jayden."

She waved as the truck pulled away, then a movement on the side of the house drew her attention. Otis cocked his ears and glanced at her, his black eyes strangely expressive. The dog was a mystery to her, always hanging around like he was tied to the ranch and this family, but never coming close enough to truly belong.

EJ remained convinced he could turn the stray dog into a pet, but Nate repeatedly reminded him the dog would eventually need to be captured and taken to the county shelter. She found it hard to believe Nate could so easily give up the animal that seemed to be devoted to Sugar and had also rescued EJ, but maybe that was wishful thinking.

She felt a little bit like a stray in the world. With Eddie gone, there was no one to claim her. She'd come to the ranch—to Nate—and while she'd never admit to needing rescuing, she definitely wanted a place to belong.

She wanted to belong to Nate.

Yet would he discard her the way he seemed willing to do with the dog?

As Nate and EJ approached, she shook off her ridiculous thoughts. They both knew this arrangement was temporary. It was silly to pretend anything different.

"I miss Sugar." EJ leaned against Nate's leg. Nate immediately bent down and swung the boy up into his arms.

"She'll be back in a couple of weeks, and you have Twix to take care of while she's gone."

"And Otis," EJ said, pointing to where the black-and-tan dog was trotting toward the barn.

"We need to stop feeding him," Nate said, "or call in the humane society to help catch him."

"No," EJ cried. "You can't let them take him away, Mr. Nate. I *need* him."

The ferocity in her son's tone was a shock. "EJ, you know Otis doesn't belong to us. If Nate wants—"

"Never mind," Nate interrupted, as if he couldn't stand to upset the boy. "We'll deal with the dog at another time. I'm in no hurry."

EJ gave a hiccupping sigh. "I need him," he repeated and rested his head on Nate's shoulder.

The sight melted Bianca's heart and she swallowed back the emotion that clogged her throat.

"Aren't we a glum bunch?" Nate asked with a rough laugh. "How about we go into town tonight? We can have dinner at Rosa's then get ice cream at the soda counter in the grocery store."

Bianca smiled. "Convenient that both businesses are in the same building."

"The blessings of small-town life," Nate said with a wink.

EJ lifted his head. "Can I get two scoops?"

"With whipped cream and a cherry," Nate promised then quickly added, "as long as it's okay with your mom."

"It's a two-scoop kind of day." Bianca leaned in and placed a soft kiss on EJ's cheek, trying to ignore how right it felt to be standing here with Nate holding her son. Trying to pretend that this didn't feel like the family she'd always craved.

What made Nate think it would be easier if they went into Paseo for the night? He hadn't anticipated that Bianca was already a part of the community. Yes, she'd made trips into town during her stay to work on her new business venture. But he'd forgotten how welcoming the people who lived here could be, generous in their willingness to wrap their arms around a stranger and make her one of their own.

That's what had saved his mother when she'd come through town, alone and pregnant with triplets. And clearly Bianca had made a place here just as quickly.

Rosa greeted her like an old friend when they moved from the gas station/grocery to the restaurant housed in the back. Just as many people stopped by their table to talk to him as they came to visit with her. She seemed uncomfortable with the attention, but at the same time radiated happiness as she deepened the connections she'd made on her visits to town.

Everyone clearly approved of her, and moreover people

seemed thrilled to see him out with a woman, even though it could hardly be called a date with her son in tow. Well, everyone but Tiffany Garcia, who'd moved back to Paseo last year after a difficult divorce. She spent the evening shooting death glares at him from across the tiny restaurant. Nate and Tiffany had gone on a couple of dates, although nothing had come of it. He hadn't thought he wanted anything more than a casual encounter, at least not until Bianca arrived on his doorstep. Tiffany obviously wasn't happy he'd changed his tune.

Had he changed?

Could he change?

The questions and doubts warring in his mind had plagued him through dinner, although between Bianca and EJ they more than kept the conversation going.

The boy reacted with wide-eyed wonder at the size of the ice-cream sundae Rosa made for him, and Nate managed to quiet some of his uncertainty. If only everything in his life could be fixed with a double-scoop ice-cream sundae.

Bianca talked even more on the way home, sharing stories of her childhood and the exploits she could remember from Eddie's teen years. Nate's anxiety subsided even more, and he matched her anecdotes with tales of his own. Eddie might have been wild, but between the three Fortune brothers, there had been plenty of mischief.

He laughed as he told one particular story of when the boys decided to make an after-school snack of brownies. "None of us was particularly neat, so when chocolate batter got all over the kitchen, we decided to clean it up with dish soap. But Grayson accidentally stepped in it and discovered how slick soap can be on a linoleum floor. Of course we had to make a skating rink and poured the entire bottle onto the floor. It was like Olympic speed skating until Mom walked in."

EJ cracked up from his booster in the back seat of Nate's truck and Bianca had gasped, then shook her head.

"I can't believe it," she whispered in horror. "What did your mom do?"

"As I remember she was about ready to kill all of us just on principle."

"That's funny," EJ shouted.

Bianca choked back a laugh. "I don't think you should share any more stories." She grinned at him then rolled her eyes. "I'm not even sure I should let my son near you."

Nate returned her smile but her words ripped into him like bullets tearing through flesh. She *shouldn't* let EJ near him. Or at least she shouldn't trust him as much as she did. He wanted to be a permanent part of her and EJ's lives so badly he could taste the need like the first bite of a summer strawberry on his tongue. It was sweet and a little tangy, almost unfamiliar even though it felt like he'd been missing the flavor forever.

He listened more than he talked the rest of the way home, then made a stupid excuse about needing to run to a neighbor's place when they stopped in front of the house.

Bianca frowned as she got out of the truck, her mouth pulling down at both corners. Damn, he wanted to kiss the smile back onto her face.

"I'll see you later?" she asked hopefully. "EJ's going to go to bed soon."

"I'm not tired, Mommy," the boy said as he unbuckled his seat belt. "I had too much sugar."

"You're fine," Bianca told him then looked to Nate. "Later?"

He shrugged. "Maybe. But it could take a while. Don't wait up."

She looked like a puppy he'd just scolded. "Okay," she said with a too-bright smile. "Thanks again for dinner."

He cursed himself as ten kinds of a jerk as he watched her walk in the house. Then he drove away, gravel spitting up from his back tires as he plowed his foot into the gas pedal. He drove like he used to when he was a stupid teenager. Too fast. Too reckless.

He peeled out onto the highway, turning away from town and feeling adrenaline spike in his veins. He recognized the sensation, had spent years as a SEAL shaping it, controlling it, learning to use it to his advantage. Now he was going off the rails over nothing more than dinner and an ice cream.

The truck slowed as he took his foot off the accelerator and pulled onto the shoulder. A few deep breaths in and out helped him get things under control again. It was more than their night out. Bianca had made a comment about trusting him with EJ, and while Nate understood she'd meant it as a joke, the truth of her words burned in his gut.

He was no longer a kid who could afford to be reckless. Bianca and EJ needed him. He owed it to Eddie to be there for them. Hell, he wanted the two of them to be able to count on him. He longed to give Bianca the happiness she deserved and to be a father figure to EJ.

But he wouldn't do either of them any good like this. He pulled back out onto the highway and drove at a normal speed this time. For a moment he entertained the thought of heading back to Paseo and texting Tiffany. Maybe if he found an outlet for the need and desire pulsing through him, he could make some sense of everything else in his life. But he dismissed the idea almost as soon as it entered his mind.

He might not have the guts to claim Bianca, but he knew

himself well enough to understand that no other woman would be a substitute for her.

He drove for another hour, counting headlights on the highway and listening to country music on the station out of Wichita Falls. A mix of relief and disappointment filled him as he returned home to a darkened house. It was better that way, he'd told himself, even though the lie was harder to stomach with every day that passed.

Instead of entering the house, he headed to the barn, not surprised to see Otis trotting around the edge of the corral. The dog was already waiting for Sugar's return. Nate whistled low, and the animal's ears twitched. He turned and slowly walked into a pale sliver of moonlight, near enough that Nate knew he was responding but not close enough to touch.

"She'll be back in a couple of weeks," Nate said as the dog looked toward the house and let out a pitiful whine. "You've got it bad, don't you?"

The dog cocked his head and met Nate's gaze, as if to say, "Takes one to know one, buddy."

Nate laughed softly and shook his head. What the hell was going on that he was imagining himself having a conversation with a dog? He was worse off than he thought.

He entered the barn and began stacking bales of hay. He didn't look up as Daisy snickered gently. He stayed focused on the physical labor, waiting for the mindless task to clear his head as it had so many other times.

It was nearly midnight, and the world was quiet other than the faint rustling of the wind and the soft sounds of the animals. Nate had always been a night owl, but growing up on a working ranch had conditioned him for early mornings, and nearly twenty years as a soldier had taught him to take sleep wherever he could find it.

He still appreciated the peace of this late hour, although his brain and body didn't get the message that they were supposed to relax. He felt like his insides were an engine revving with no clear destination. He remained stubbornly stopped, unable to move forward or go back. His feelings for Bianca roared through him without pause, and he had no idea how to regain control of his life.

Or even if he wanted to.

"Can't sleep?" a soft voice asked and he whirled around to find Bianca standing in the middle of the row of stalls.

She was so damn beautiful, wearing an oversize sleep shirt with a faded illustration of the Eiffel Tower on the front. Her dark hair was down around her shoulders and her legs were bare. The shirt grazed her knees, and she was wearing her well-worn cowboy boots. At the most there was about six inches of skin showing between the hem of the shirt and the top of her boots. But she might as well have been in a lacy negligee based on the reaction Nate's body had to her.

He almost laughed at the irony of the hours he'd spent working to clear his mind. Because right now he couldn't form even the suggestion of a coherent thought. His brain had gone totally blank.

"Haven't tried yet," he said, pulling off his leather gloves and tossing them onto one of the hay bales. He wiped his hands across his jeans.

"Did you have fun with the neighbor?"

"Didn't make it to the neighbor's."

Her hands clenched into fists at her sides. "That was never the plan, was it?"

He shook his head.

"You just needed to get away from the ranch?"

"Something like that," he answered, inclining his head.

"Was it that woman in the restaurant?" Her dark eyes flared as she asked the question. "The one who was staring at you the whole time."

"Tiffany?"

"I don't know her name, but she was sending you some 'come hither' looks."

"Come hither," he repeated with a soft laugh.

"It's not funny."

There was a catch in her voice, and he realized with a start she actually thought he'd left the ranch to be with another woman. Maybe it wasn't funny. Hell, he'd entertained the idea for a lightning-fast second. But it would have been an effort in futility because the only woman he wanted was standing right in front of him.

Still, he couldn't quite give himself permission to claim her. She was so damn perfect, and he was terrified of contaminating her with the mess in his head.

"No," he agreed carefully. "And I wasn't with Tiffany. I drove around for a while to clear my head then came back here and started on a few chores to distract myself." He took a step toward her then stopped. He could feel his chest rising and falling like he'd just run a marathon. Like he was using every ounce of strength he had to keep from closing the distance between them. "From you."

She sucked in a breath and bit down on her bottom lip. His knees almost buckled.

"Why?" she whispered.

"Can't you see how broken I am?" he asked, his voice hoarse. "The things I've done, the horrors I've seen." He paused, then added, "The ways I've failed the people I care about."

"We're all broken in some way," she said with a sad

smile. "But we keep going. You've kept going. You're helping your family because you're loyal to them."

"It sounds like you're describing a family pet."

Her smile widened. "You're also hot as hell." She pressed
her hands to her cheeks, as if saying the words out loud
embarrassed her. "You make me want things I can't even
name."

"Try."

The word hung between them for a few long moments,
and he thought she'd walk away rather than give voice to
her desires. But his Bianca was braver.

So much braver than him.

"I want you to kiss me." Her fingers traced her lips then
trailed down the graceful column of her neck. "I want to
kiss you." She swallowed. "Everywhere."

Nate stifled a groan, but she wasn't finished.

"I want you to touch me and I want to explore your body.
I want everything you're willing to give."

He closed his eyes, trying to keep his body from trembling. "You're killing me here, Bianca."

"Look at me, Nate."

Nate had never been one for classic literature, but he
felt a sudden affinity for that poor sop Odysseus trying to
resist the Sirens. He focused his gaze on Bianca, and she
must have read in his eyes the desire he was sick of denying.

Her lips curved into a sultry smile as she grabbed the
hem of her shirt and tugged the fabric up and over her head.
That left her standing in front of him, shivering slightly
from the cold evening air, in a pale pink lace bra, cotton panties with smiley face emojis all over them and her
cowboy boots. It was the most erotic moment of his whole
damn life.

Chapter 10

As she tossed the comfy cotton shirt off to one side, Bianca glanced down at herself and almost died of embarrassment.

How could a man take an attempt at seduction seriously when the woman seducing him wore smiley face emoji panties?

Of course, she hadn't come to the barn expecting to seduce Nate. She'd been resolved he needed to make the next move if their relationship—if it could be called that—was going to progress to the next level.

But he looked so alone in the quiet night—like he was purposely keeping his distance as some sort of self-induced punishment she couldn't understand. Somehow she knew deep inside that he needed the connection between them as much as she did.

More even.

So she'd ignored her doubts and thrown caution—and

her nightgown—to the wind. But as Nate's gaze met hers, his face was unreadable. The only thing that made her think he was affected by her impromptu striptease was the slight tremble of his hand as he lifted it to massage the back of his neck. Another of Nate's tells.

Or was it?

He stared at her for a long time without speaking. Probably only seconds in reality, but the moments felt like hours. Days. Months and years of her being exposed, baring herself for judgment and ultimately rejection.

Oh, God. Bianca couldn't take any more rejection.

"My bad," she whispered with a strangled laugh and bent to retrieve her nightgown from the barn's dirt floor.

"No."

The word was spoken with such intensity, Bianca froze, her arm stretched out like a statue.

He was in front of her a moment later. She could feel the heat radiating off him, seeping under her skin and warming her entire body. She pulled her arms close to her chest, an automatic reaction, and straightened until she was looking up into Nate's brown eyes. In the soft light they looked lighter and were rimmed with gold. Or maybe that was the emotion in his gaze.

"You're beautiful," he whispered.

"Having a baby changes your body forever," she said then mentally kicked herself. Maybe she should grab a tube of lipstick and circle all the flaws on her body in case he hadn't noticed them.

"I wouldn't change a thing about you." He circled her wrists with his long fingers and eased them away from her body. She bit back all the excuses that wanted to tumble off her tongue. For her shabby lace bra with the frayed edges to her silly emoji panties. For wanting to seduce him but not having any idea how to go about it and bungling the whole thing.

The way he was staring at her made her feel like she hadn't spoiled anything. The mix of desire and tenderness in his eyes made her heart sing.

"The next move was supposed to be yours."

"I couldn't make one, even though I wanted to so badly. I'm not good enough for you." He lifted his hands and grazed his fingers over her collarbones. When he got to her bra straps, he gently pushed them to the edges of her shoulders but no farther. A shiver passed through her as the calluses on his fingertips tickled her bare skin.

"You are," she countered.

He shook his head, and his gaze remained focused on the patterns his fingers were tracing. "I'll never be good enough for you. There's too much of the past that's—"

"Stop." She placed her hand against his mouth. "Look at me, Nate."

He pressed his lips together but lifted his gaze to hers.

She cupped both his cheeks in her hands. "I don't want to talk about the past tonight. I don't want to think about the mistakes either of us has made. Trust me, you're not the only one who's done stupid things."

"You have no idea what I've done."

"Are you here with me now in this moment?"

"Yes. I'm here."

"Then this moment is what we have. It's all we need. *You* are all I need, Nathan Fortune."

His nostrils flared and his eyes intensified even more. He bent his head and claimed her mouth in a kiss that lit her body like a brush fire, fast and all consuming. She was nothing but an empty canvas—a blank landscape for Nate to do with what he would.

He twined his arms around her waist and pulled her tight against him. The soft cotton of his shirt brushed her nipples through her lace bra and she moaned deep in her throat.

"So damn beautiful," he said against her mouth. She gasped as she felt the evidence of his desire press against her stomach, and he took the opportunity to sweep his tongue into her mouth. This was everything she'd imagined, and she gave herself over to the sensations bursting through her.

Suddenly one of the horses gave a loud whinny, and then a cacophony of answering snorts and whickers rang out in the barn.

Nate stilled, which made Bianca giggle. "We've got an audience," she said, trying to muffle her laughter.

"I love hearing you laugh," Nate said, grinning down at her, "but right now I could do without the livestock peanut gallery."

He lifted her into his arms like she weighed nothing, looping one arm behind her knees while he supported her back with the other. She giggled again then settled against him, the warmth of his chest chasing away the evening's chill as he hurried across the driveway to the house.

She kissed the underside of his jaw, loving the taste of salt on his skin. He tilted up his chin, stumbling a step, then chuckled low in his throat. "Save that thought until we're in my bedroom, darlin', or I'm liable to face-plant going up the stairs."

"I like having that effect on you," she admitted.

"You have no idea the effect you have on me." His voice was a low rumble, and it made her tingle from head to toe.

Opening the door to his bedroom, he turned to fit through with her in his arms. The door to Nate's room had always been closed, and as intrigued as she was, she'd never allowed herself to sneak a peek into it. Somehow that had felt too intimate, like she needed to wait until he invited her in before she could satisfy her curiosity.

"I haven't changed much in here since I moved back," Nate said, watching her gaze sweep across the room.

There was a double bed with a colorful patterned quilt, a tall dresser and a simple wood chair pushed against one wall. The walls were painted a soft green and several trophies sat on top of the dresser along with a glass bowl filled with loose change.

"It's nice," she said.

"You're nice," he countered, pulling back the covers and laying her gently on the sheets.

She shook her head, sitting up and kicking off her boots. She wiggled her bare toes and tried not to let nerves get the better of her. "Not tonight. Tonight I'm wild and crazy."

"Really?"

Well, wild and crazy to Bianca was ice cream for dinner. But instead of admitting that, she reached behind her back and unclasped her bra. The straps were already almost off her shoulders and she shrugged them all the way down and tossed the small strip of fabric off the bed.

"Uh-huh," she said, wishing she could think of something cute or sexy to say. Right now she was trying hard not to spontaneously combust. Sexy talk was beyond her capabilities.

"You're seriously going to kill me," Nate whispered, his tone reverent, like she was a fine piece of art or a priceless treasure.

It gave her the confidence to pull her shoulders back and drop her hands to her sides. She'd never put herself on display for a man this way, but she wanted to be someone different with Nate—a woman she barely recognized but enjoyed trying on for size.

The truth was, she'd only been with one man in her life—her ex-husband. She'd been grateful for any attention, but their time together had always been more about his pleasure than hers. Suddenly trying to claim her sexuality felt like skydiving without checking whether her parachute worked. It was exhilarating, but was she in for the mother of all crash landings?

She was already hurtling through the air, so she figured she might as well enjoy as much of the view as she could.

"There's one problem," she told him, arching a brow like she knew what the heck she was doing.

"Not from where I'm standing."

"You have too many clothes on."

"Easily remedied," he answered and unbuttoned his shirt. Bianca had gotten a few glimpses of his toned body, but her breath caught in her throat when he pulled the shirt off and tossed it to the side. His chest was all hard planes and angles; a sprinkling of dark hair covering his bronzed skin.

"More," she whispered, pointing a finger at his jeans.

One side of his mouth kicked up. "Wild, crazy and commanding. I like it."

He toed off his boots then undid his jeans, pushing them and his boxers down over his hips. Bianca couldn't even stop the little whimper that escaped her mouth as he moved toward the bed.

She blew out a breath. "Wow."

Nate grinned. "I'll take wow." He climbed on the bed and stretched out next to her. "I'm feeling a little 'wow' myself right now."

Reaching out a hand, she splayed her fingers across his

chest, through the dusting of hair covering his skin. The muscles there twitched at her touch, and her hand looked so small against him. Now that she'd seen him—all of him—she realized he was big everywhere. Big enough that she wondered if he'd actually fit. So much for her minute of confidence in the bedroom. She was back to feeling like she had no idea what to do next. She was back to reality. As usual, reality was not her friend.

"Hey." Nate placed a hand on her hip, squeezing gently. "I lost you there for a minute."

"Sorry. I was just…um…thinking."

He dropped a soft kiss on the tip of her nose. "If you're thinking right now then I'm not doing this right."

"You are," she said quickly. "It's me. I thought I could be someone different tonight but—"

"I don't want you to be anyone but who you are." He kissed her, gently sucking her bottom lip into his mouth.

Bianca moaned once and then again as his fingers moved to graze across her belly, then lower.

"Do you want this?" Nate asked against her skin.

"Yes," she answered without hesitation. "I want everything."

"Then trust me, darlin'. Trust us." His head moved lower, blazing a trail of openmouthed kisses down her throat. Then he was at her breast and she gave a tiny cry when he sucked one sensitive nipple into his mouth.

Her body felt like it was melting into the bed, and she relaxed her legs, opening for him. Letting him in. Trusting. She arched back as his clever fingers found her center, even as he moved his attention to her other breast.

Pressure started to build inside her, and she wanted to chase it, to hunt it down and claim whatever brilliance she could feel shimmering on the other side. But Nate seemed in no hurry. He took his time, wringing every ounce of pleasure from her.

"Now," she whispered when she couldn't bear it any longer. He claimed her mouth, kissing her deeply as his fingers moved against her, inside her. He was everywhere, and she lost herself in the feel of him. Then she was breaking apart and it felt like a million stars raining down over them, bright and hot and more dazzling than she could have ever imagined.

He broke the kiss to reach across her, pulling a condom packet from the nightstand drawer. She was boneless and satisfied, but as he adjusted himself at her entrance, need built low in her body once more.

"I want everything," she repeated, lifting her head off the pillow to kiss him.

He entered her as their mouths melded, his tongue mimicking the rhythm of their bodies. She grazed her fingers over his shoulders and down his back, pressing him closer. They moved together, a tangle of limbs. Nate whispered sweet words against her hair then nipped gently on her earlobe.

It nearly sent her over the edge again, but he cupped her face in his hands and whispered, "Wait for me, Bianca."

She'd wait forever if that's what it took. If she'd known how easily she'd fall for this man, how tender and sweet he could be...well, she would have gotten in her car and hightailed it to Paseo long before now.

She wrapped her legs around his hips, tilting her own so she could take him even deeper. There was nothing she wouldn't do to give him the same release he'd given her. She felt a tremor pass through him as he kissed her again.

"*You* are my everything," he said, lifting his head to gaze down at her. "You are mine."

"Yes," she breathed and broke apart again. Nate groaned as he came and buried his face in the crook of her neck, and it was hard to tell where she stopped and he began.

All Bianca knew was that this moment changed everything. Nothing between them would ever be the same.

Nate wasn't sure how much time passed before his breathing slowed and he trusted himself to lift his head and look into Bianca's dark eyes again.

It could have been minutes. It was probably minutes, but it felt like an eternity to him. Because that's how long it would take until he regained control of his heart.

Which was stupid because he'd had enough great sex in his life to understand that hearts didn't need to be involved for bodies to fit together perfectly.

Being with Bianca didn't change anything, he told himself, even though he knew it was a lie.

"Is it always like that?" she asked, a sleepy grin on her face.

"Not always," he said.

Never, his brain screamed. *Only with you. Only with us.*

But how could he tell her that without admitting everything he felt? Hell, he barely understood his emotions for this woman. They were unfamiliar, and the unknown scared him half to death. It was like walking through an Afghanistan landscape that could be breathtaking in its peaceful beauty, and the next moment a land mine would explode and he'd be blown into next week.

He rolled onto his back, taking Bianca with him as he did. Her body curled into his as if she was made to fit against him.

"You've got some crazy mad skills," she said, draping an arm over his chest. She turned into him, and her long dark hair cascaded over her shoulder and spilled across his body. She was soft in all the places he was hard, and he wanted to explore every inch of her until he knew what she liked, the kind of touch and kiss that would drive her crazy. He had the undeniable urge to claim her as his for as long as she'd allow it.

As satisfied as he was at the moment, desire began to spark inside him again, his body humming to life at the thought of taking her again.

"I could say the same about you."

She laughed and lifted her head. "You're joking, right? I've got no skills and very little experience."

He shifted so their legs were tangled together and he saw her eyes widen slightly when she felt him against her hip.

"You're the sexiest woman I've ever known," he told her, sifting his fingers through her hair. "I can't get enough of you."

She arched a brow. "As in can't get enough right now?"

"You probably need to sleep. It's fine. Ignore me."

But she didn't ignore him. Instead, she reached between them and… Oh, hell. She was going to send him over the edge with her featherlight touch.

"Do you know an unexpected bonus to being with a single mom?" she asked, her tone teasing.

Right now he could barely come up with his own name.

Her mouth quirked as if she understood the power she held over him and reveled in it. "I'm used to functioning on a tiny bit of sleep." Her fingers squeezed and he arched off the bed, then reached for the nightstand drawer again.

"Then I'm going to keep you up all night long," he promised and kissed her again.

Chapter 11

Bianca blinked awake and drew in a breath that caught in her throat as she became aware of Nate's trembling body next to her.

She hadn't planned on falling asleep in his bed, but after he'd made love to her a second time she'd been so relaxed and happy. He'd wrapped an arm around her waist and pulled her into his chest so they were spooning, and she'd quickly drifted off.

Grabbing his T-shirt from the floor next to the bed, she pulled it over her head then checked the clock on the nightstand—not even five in the morning. The sky outside the bedroom window was still black, and she wasn't sure whether she'd woken on her own or if Nate's restless tossing and turning had prodded her from sleep.

He was sprawled on his back, one hand above his head and the other at his side, fingers clutching the bedsheet. She sat up and her heart ached at his pained features. He looked miserable, his jaw working and his eyes tightly closed as if he was in agony.

"Nate," she whispered, wondering if he was truly asleep. She hated to think he was stuck in some kind of nightmare he couldn't escape.

"No," he muttered. His chest rose and fell and she could hear his breath coming in shallow gasps. "No. Eddie, no."

Bianca stilled at the mention of her brother. Nate had been with Eddie the night he died. She had so many unanswered questions. Why Eddie? Did he suffer? Was there anything that could have been done to save him?

She couldn't believe there had been. Surely Nate would have moved heaven and earth to save Eddie if it had been a possibility. She hadn't asked Nate about that night. It felt intrusive and too personal, like poking her finger in a still-raw wound. She knew he missed her brother as much as she did.

Clearly the night of Eddie's death plagued Nate. She'd heard of soldiers coming home with post-traumatic stress disorder. Men and women who'd given so much to their country but couldn't fit back into their regular lives because of the intense trauma they'd encountered while deployed. Nate had been a SEAL for almost twenty years. PTSD could be a reality for him. He didn't even have a regular life.

Except now they were creating one together.

Bianca wanted that more than anything.

Between what he'd faced as a SEAL and coping with the knowledge that his birth father was Gerald Robinson plus having a passel of instant half siblings strewn across Texas, Nate was dealing with some heavy stuff.

It was up to Bianca to bring light into the darkness he seemed to feel was his due.

She reached out a hand and touched his shoulder. His muscles tensed, and he stilled but didn't open his eyes.

"Nate, wake up." She gently shook him.

"No," he repeated, but she could tell by the movement of his eyes behind the closed lids that he remained imprisoned in the nightmare. "Eddie, no." He let out a desperate cry. "I'm sorry. No."

Emotion clogged her throat, and she swiped at her eyes. When they'd first gotten the news of Eddie's death, there had been weeks when Bianca's dreams were filled with images of Eddie walking in front of her, just out of reach. No matter how fast she ran or how loudly she called to him, she could never catch up. To know Nate had possibly gone through something worse and that his memories continued to hold him in a choking grasp…

It made her feel both closer to him and so sad at how alone he was in the world, despite his extended Fortune family.

If she had her way, neither of them would ever be alone again. She cupped his cheek, leaning over him, letting her hair brush his bare skin. "Nate, come on. Wake up. Come back to me."

A moment later, she yelped, her heart pounding a crazy beat as she found herself flipped onto her back, Nate looming over her. The look on his face was terrifying. His eyes were open but unfocused, totally empty of any sort of recognition or emotion. He was like some sort of cowboy cyborg, unrecognizable as the man who'd held her so tenderly hours earlier.

"Nate." She breathed his name through clenched teeth, afraid any sort of movement might set him off. Might put her in real danger.

He blinked once…twice. Sweat beaded along his hairline. With a muttered curse, he threw back the covers and scrambled off the bed, stalking to the edge of the bedroom.

She watched as he bent forward, sucking in air like he'd just run a marathon. Slowly she sat forward, swinging her legs over the side of the bed. He put a hand up, palm facing toward her like he feared she might approach him.

"I'm sorry," he said, his voice hoarse.

"It's not a big deal. You were having a bad dream."

He turned but didn't move toward her. He stood in the shadow, light from the window playing across the muscles corded along his arms and chest and the black boxers he wore to sleep. "I could have hurt you, Bianca."

"No." She made her voice firm, ignoring the way the hairs at the back of her neck stood on end. "You'd never hurt me."

"I don't want to," he whispered, and his eyes were so miserable she could feel his suffering like a physical force between them. Keeping her away at the same time it drew her toward him. "But you saw me." He swore again and ran a hand through his hair, the ends sticking up in wild tufts. "I hate that you saw me like that."

"It had something to do with Eddie. You were dreaming about him."

He gave a slight nod.

"I used to dream about him," she said, forcing her shaking legs to stand. "It's normal."

"Nothing about me is normal anymore. I'm broken, Bianca. I told you I wasn't good for you. You have to believe me. This proves it."

"What does this prove?" He backed up as she approached him, until he was standing against the tall dresser. "You're human. You lost a friend, and you miss him. You saw things—did things—that no man should see or do. You protected our country."

"Don't make me into a hero."

She reached out a hand, pressing her palm over the place where his heart beat a wild rhythm in his chest.

"It's hard not to when you keep acting like one."

"I'm not."

"Fine," she agreed, sliding her other hand up and around the back of his neck.

"You should go before EJ wakes up."

"Not quite yet." She closed her eyes and laid her head on his shoulder, plastering her body to the front of his. He remained rigid, but she paid no attention. She knew what it was like to be alone, unsure if you could overcome all the fears and doubts weighing on your shoulders.

Her fingers splayed over his heart as her other hand gently massaged the back of his neck. She'd seen him do it enough to know it relaxed him. His hands gripped her waist as if he would set her away from him. Instead he held her closer, bending his head until it rested on the top of hers.

Neither of them spoke, but slowly Nate's breathing returned to normal. His hold on her was tentative, as if even now he didn't trust himself with her.

"I'm sorry," he said again.

"Do you want to talk about it?" She tipped up her head to look him in the eyes. "Your dreams?"

"Nightmares," he corrected. Then he shook his head. "Not now." She must not have been able to hide her disappointment because he quickly amended, "Not yet."

"Thank you for last night."

One side of his mouth quirked. "Thank *you*, Bianca. For everything you are."

When a bird chirped outside the window, she pulled away from him. "I do need to go."

He nodded, but his lips pressed into a thin line. He'd

tried to run her off minutes earlier but now it felt like she was hurting him by leaving. "You're protecting EJ."

"I'm protecting all of us. This is too new for him to know about. He'd have expectations. He might not understand that sometimes two people are together and it doesn't mean anything."

She waited for him to argue. It's what she longed for—Nate to tell her what was between them meant something to him. She was quickly falling in love with him. With the tough, hardworking rancher and the scarred, troubled ex-SEAL and the sweetheart of a man who'd borrowed a pony so her son could learn to ride.

"I understand," he said tightly, and she wanted to scream as the invisible wall he kept around him snapped into place again. Every time she broke through his defenses, something would happen to rebuild them just as quickly. One step forward and a million miles back.

"Are you busy today?" she asked as she picked up her boots from the floor. She didn't want him to see the disappointment that must be apparent in her eyes. How was she supposed to hide how she felt? She'd always been an open book with her emotions, and it's what had often gotten her in trouble. At least she was learning that if she couldn't hide them, she needed to keep them to herself as best she could.

"The usual work," he said. "Why?"

"I was wondering if this afternoon would be good for a riding lesson?" She held the pile of underwear and boots in front of her stomach like a shield. What if Nate said no? What if after one night she was out of his system? "I'm going to work with EJ on his numbers and letters this morning, and I'd like to finish organizing the garden storage shelves in the shed. But after lunch—"

"How about I pack a lunch and we eat it on the ride?"

"Do you mean in the barn?" Her voice sounded high-pitched to her ears, like she'd just inhaled a giant shot of helium.

Nate's features relaxed fully as he smiled. Good to know her obvious terror helped him regain his equilibrium. "I mean on the trail. You and EJ haven't been out to the windmills yet. It's the spot where Jayden and Ariana got married last year."

"Shouldn't we stay in the corral? You made EJ stay in the corral on his first ride."

"EJ's four."

"But he's way braver than me."

"You can do it, Busy Bee."

"A trail ride." She swallowed and forced an even breath. "Okay. Can Twix handle a trail ride?"

"EJ can ride double with me. Normally I wouldn't do it, but we'll let you get comfortable in the saddle before I put him on his own horse for a trail ride. Trust me, he'll love it."

"I'm sure he will." She wasn't sure about herself. "No running."

"You mean galloping?"

She nodded. "That, too."

"I promise I'll take care of you."

She wanted him to trust her with his demons and doubts, and turnabout was fair play. "I know you will. We'll meet at the barn at eleven?"

"I can't wait. And, Bianca?"

"Yeah?"

"As far as last night…"

She licked her lips, a strange mix of dread and anticipation sifting through her. "Yes?"

"Once with us is not enough." His eyes darkened. "Nowhere near enough. If this thing is happening between us, I'm all in. You good with that?"

"Very good," she answered and hurried out of the room before she did something embarrassing like rip off his shirt and pounce on him.

Nate got to the barn twenty minutes before Bianca and EJ were meeting him. He'd left the house before the boy woke this morning, not sure he could face the four-year-old with the knowledge of the night he and Bianca had shared burning through him like a wildfire that had spread out of control.

How was he supposed to curb his feelings for her when he wanted so much more? Along with his need came an equal amount of fear. He knew the things he was capable of, and even though Bianca thought she understood Nate's life as a soldier, she didn't.

She couldn't.

She was light to his shadow. Goodness to the darkness that dwelled deep inside him. He craved her glow, but at the same time he was terrified of contaminating her with who he was on the inside.

Or worse…hurting her.

The nightmares that plagued him were vivid and real, at least to his unconscious self. The line between waking and sleeping blurred more nights than not. When he'd first left the navy, he'd spent months sleeping with a knife under his pillow, his hand wrapped around the handle. It was the only way he could force his body to relax enough to get any rest.

What if he'd had that knife when Bianca had woken him? Hell, he didn't need a knife to hurt her. He knew a dozen different ways to kill a person. Bianca was beautiful and delicate. The thought of putting his hands on her in anger made the breakfast he'd eaten hours earlier churn in his stomach.

So what was he doing here cinching the old Western saddle he'd loved riding on as a kid with Earl Thompson? He and his brothers had fought over who would get to accompany the rancher on the trail ride he took every Sunday afternoon after church. It hadn't been long until they'd gotten good enough in the saddle to warrant their own horses. He thought of EJ, who was showing a natural gift for animals of every kind. Even now, Nate glanced up to see Otis sitting calmly in the corner of the barn.

He'd stopped pretending he wasn't going to continue to feed the stray dog and secretly loved EJ's attempts to tame the animal.

Nate loved everything about having Bianca and EJ in his life, which made him the most selfish bastard in the world. They deserved a man who could give them unconditional love and devotion. Not the person who'd failed to save Bianca's brother. Not the man who had so many demons he didn't know where to begin fighting them.

Yet he couldn't let them go. Not yet.

"Mr. Nate, I'm ready," EJ shouted as he ran into the barn. He climbed up onto the bench Nate had set in front of Cinnamon's stall so the boy could watch him groom the big horse. "I wrote my whole name and spelled it right." He held up his hands like he was a preacher calling down the Holy Spirit. "Edward James Shaw. That's me."

"Edward James Shaw," Nate repeated, wondering at how he hadn't realized the connection before. "Like your uncle."

Bianca came to stand next to her son, a shy smile on her face. "He will be a Shaw. I've applied to have EJ's last name legally changed. He was named after Eddie, so I want him to fully be a Shaw."

"I bet your brother loved that he was named after him."

A shadow crossed her face. "Are we ready to go?"

He studied her for a moment but chalked up her sudden change in mood to nerves.

"You're riding Daisy today."

She swallowed. "What about you and EJ?"

"We're on Cinnamon, Mommy. I told you."

"Is that a good idea?" Bianca asked. "That's the horse that almost came down on EJ."

"I've been riding him for years," Nate assured her. "He's spirited but with the right rider, he's an angel."

"He's so tall."

"You trust me, right?" Nate asked.

"Yes," she said without hesitation, and his heart soared.

"Let's go, then."

He led Cinnamon out into the corral and dropped the reins.

"Won't he run off?" Bianca asked as she followed.

"Nope. He's used to being ground-tied so he's not going anywhere. EJ, I want you to help me get your mommy settled on Daisy. Can you do that?"

The boy nodded. "Come on, Mommy. I'll teach you how to hold the reins."

EJ took Bianca's hand and led her toward the stall that held the dappled mare. Nate followed, giving Bianca an encouraging nod when she glanced over her shoulder.

"Are you sure this is a good idea?"

"The best." Nate grabbed the horse's bridle from its peg on the wall and opened the stall. He led Daisy out into the aisle and attached her to cross ties. "The first thing you'd normally do is make sure she's been groomed so there's nothing under the pad and saddle to irritate her. I've taken care of that part so why don't you grab Daisy's pad and put it on her?"

"Always walk up to a horse on the left, Mommy," EJ told her when she took a step forward.

"Thanks, buddy. I'll remember that." She picked up the pad and approached the horse, then frowned as her gaze flicked to Nate. "Why are you smiling?"

"The look on your face makes it seem like you're approaching a fire-breathing dragon."

As if she'd heard him, Daisy gave an indignant snort. Bianca tightened her hold on the saddle pad but kept moving. "Not at all," she said, her voice dramatically gentle. "Daisy is a sweet girl. She's calm and docile and she'd never buck or kick." She lifted the pad onto the horse's back and adjusted it so the sides were even. Daisy turned her head, her eyes focusing on the new person at her side. "We're going to a have an easy day together. Right, girl?"

Nate watched as Daisy shifted position so she could sniff at Bianca. "Take a breath. She can sense your fear."

"Horses as far away as Mexico can sense my fear," Bianca shot back but reached out a hand and stroked the velvety tip of Daisy's nose.

The horse snuffled and rubbed her head against the front of Bianca.

"She's a cuddler," Nate told her, earning a small smile from Bianca.

"Mommy likes to cuddle, too," EJ announced. "When I used to have night terrors, I'd sleep in her bed. She snuggled me too much."

Bianca threw a tender look toward her son. "There's no such thing as too much snuggling."

When her gaze met Nate's, pink rose to her cheeks.

"I agree," he said quietly. "Let's get Daisy's saddle on her then you can lead her out."

"Or we could just call our little visiting session good for the day."

"Mommy," EJ said with the type of exasperation only known to young boys. "I'm starving. I want to ride so we can eat lunch."

Nate pulled the saddle from its rack and hefted it onto the horse. Daisy sniffed but didn't move as he tightened the front and flank cinches around her. "We'll adjust the stirrups after you're on. Ariana was the last one to ride her, so they should be close in length."

He put the bridle over the horse's head and showed Bianca how to fit the bit in her mouth.

Her eyes widened. "I'm never going to do that."

"Never say never," he told her with a laugh then handed her the lead rope. "We might make a horsewoman out of you yet."

They walked together into the afternoon sun. The day was clear and crisp, a gentle breeze blowing from the south. Winter was one of his favorite times in Paseo. After years spent sweltering in deserts across the Middle East, he enjoyed the mild Texas winters, when temperatures could dip below freezing at night but warmed to near perfect during the day. This was one of those perfect days, and he thanked his lucky stars to be able to spend it with Bianca.

He could hear her murmuring to Daisy but couldn't make out what she was saying. The horse's ears twitched, as if she were hanging on to Bianca's every word. Nate could relate to that.

Bianca stopped a few feet from where Cinnamon stood. The big horse gave a foot stomp and Daisy seemed to answer with several twitches of her ears. "They're friends now, right? Cinnamon isn't going to mess with Daisy?"

"Mommy, you can see them talking with their bodies. It's like when Reed Parker pushed me so he could cut in line on the first day of school." EJ held up his hands as if he was a teacher explaining a concept to one of his students. "He was just nervous and didn't know how to use his words. Then he learned and now we're best friends." The boy frowned. "Well, we were when I went to school. Maybe he won't remember when we go back."

"He'll remember," Bianca said gently.

Nate wanted to argue—not that EJ's friend wouldn't want to be his friend but that the two of them weren't going back to San Antonio anytime soon. It had only been a few weeks, but Nate couldn't imagine life on the ranch without Bianca and her son.

"Time to saddle up," he said to Bianca instead. "Do you want a block to stand on?"

She shook her head. "I can handle this part."

Nate came to her side anyway, holding Daisy's bridle with one hand and turning out the stirrup so it was easier for Bianca to manage with the other.

She swallowed, fit her boot into the stirrup then grabbed the horn and lifted herself up and over the saddle like a pro.

"You did it, Mommy," EJ called.

"I sure did," she agreed with a too-bright smile, her voice breathless.

Nate handed her the reins and squeezed her leg. "You're doing great."

"Liar," she breathed, her smile not wavering.

"Keep Daisy a few lengths back from Cinnamon. We'll go slow to start."

"We'll go slow the whole time," she corrected.

"Do you have the food, Mr. Nate?" EJ asked.

"I have a ton of food." He pointed to the saddlebag positioned behind Daisy's saddle. "We've got sandwiches and chips and fruit—"

"And cookies?" EJ asked hopefully.

"You bet. Ready?"

EJ nodded and Nate swung him up on the thick pillow at the front of the saddle. He mounted Cinnamon behind EJ, being sure to give the boy enough room. "Once we get on the trail, I'm going to let you take the reins."

"Mommy," the boy called, "I'm going to drive the horse just like you."

"Uh-huh," came the choked answer from behind them.

Nate kissed the air and pressed a thigh to Cinnamon's flank, giving the horse direction. Cinnamon loved trail riding, so he didn't need much prodding. With a shake of his head and mane that made EJ giggle, the horse turned and started for the field leading to the path that wound its way through the entire property.

"Give her a little nudge," he instructed, glancing over his shoulder to Bianca.

"Don't leave me," she called.

He gave Cinnamon's reins a gentle tug. "Whoa, boy."

"Mommy, come *on*." EJ didn't bother to turn around as he shouted the command.

Nate patted the boy's shoulder. "Be patient with her. Remember, a man's job is to take care of the women he loves. You love your mommy very much." He turned perpendicular with the trail so he could watch Bianca's progress. "You're doing great. Daisy can be kind of lazy when she sets her mind to it. Give her a kick with your heels."

"I'll hurt her."

"She's a thousand pounds. You won't hurt her. Do it gently—just like I showed you back in the ring. You're telling her she can't have her own way."

Bianca popped her heels into the horse's sides then yelped when Daisy trotted forward a few steps. The horse quickly slowed to a walk, and Nate gave Bianca a thumbs-up.

The horses fell into a rhythm, and Nate played the part of tour guide, pointing out landmarks on the ranch and explaining the history of the area to Bianca and EJ.

The boy settled back against his chest, making Nate's heart twist. Even Bianca seemed to relax, becoming somewhat of an expert on tugging Daisy's reins when the horse tried to stop and eat grass.

"How much farther?" EJ asked when his stomach rumbled loudly.

Nate chuckled and pointed to the west of the trail. "The pond and windmill are just over that rise. Only about ten minutes longer until we break for lunch. Maybe we should have had a snack before we started."

"I can wait ten minutes," EJ told him. "Come on, Mommy."

Those words had become the boy's refrain during the ride. He continually turned and looked around Nate's arm to ensure Bianca and Daisy were keeping up with them.

"I'm with you," she called back. Nate saw her press her thighs against Daisy's side when the horse slowed.

"If we teach her to shoot a gun, your mom could be a regular Annie Oakley on that horse," he said to EJ when Cinnamon started down the trail again.

"I don't know Annie Oakley," EJ told him.

Nate chuckled. "I'll introduce you."

"Do you love her?"

"Annie Oakley?" Nate flexed his fingers against the fabric of his jeans. "She's dead now and I only knew her through her reputation, of course. Grayson was a bigger fan when we were younger. She was a famous sharpshooter but an excellent horsewoman, as well. Annie Oakley could—"

"I mean Mommy," EJ interrupted.

Nate sucked in a breath, jerking back on the reins enough to make Cinnamon pin his ears for a moment. He glanced behind him, but Bianca only smiled and waved, looking almost relaxed in the saddle.

Clearly she hadn't heard EJ's question.

"What do you mean, buddy?" he asked, keeping his voice light. Were his feelings for Bianca that obvious?

"You said a man takes care of the women he loves. Since we came to visit, you've been taking care of Mommy." EJ tipped up his head to look at Nate. "Is it because you love her?"

Oh, hell. That question was as loaded as one of Annie Oakley's Wild West Show pistols. Of course he didn't love Bianca. Not like EJ was talking about. Nate didn't even know if he was capable of that kind of love. The situation was...

"It's complicated."

EJ blinked, his gaze remaining focused on Nate's face. "What's comp-ki-lated?"

"Well, your mom and I are friends. I care about her and about you. Your uncle Eddie was my best friend. So we've all got some shared history. We're like family."

"Uncle Eddie was family," EJ countered, "but you're not really."

"True," Nate admitted, wondering how the hell he was going to get himself out of this conversation. "Let's put it this way—the way I was raised, a man looks out for women, especially those he's friends with—"

"And loves," EJ interrupted.

"Or that he considers a friend," Nate clarified, feeling

sweat bead between his shoulder blades. "But all women really… You have to be a gentleman with all women. Does that make sense?"

"Kind of."

That was a start since Nate felt like he was babbling nonsense at the moment.

"So you don't love Mommy, but you'll take care of her because she's a girl?"

"Well, I'm not sure I'd put it that way."

"How *would* you put it?"

Nate shifted in the saddle. Lord save him from boys with a one-track mind. "I guess I'd say—"

Bianca's high-pitched scream cut off his words. He yanked on the reins, turning Cinnamon just in time to see Daisy veer off the well-worn path. The horse galloped across the field like she was being chased by the devil himself, Bianca bouncing precariously in the saddle as she screamed Nate's name.

Cinnamon jerked hard just as EJ yelled, "Snake!"

The boy lurched to one side, and Nate pulled him in tight at the same time he dug his heels into the horse's flank.

Cinnamon came up on his hind legs again as a Western diamondback curled in a defensive coil on the trail in front of them and the telltale rattling sound reverberated through the air. After a quick glance to where Bianca and Daisy hurtled across the field, Nate backed Cinnamon off the trail and out of danger. As soon as they were clear of the snake, Nate readjusted EJ in front of him.

The boy let out a hiccupping breath. "Mommy," he whispered, his tone clearly terrified.

"We're going to get her, buddy. Are you ready?"

"Yes," EJ answered, his voice shaky.

"Then hold on tight."

Chapter 12

Bianca did her best to hold tight to the reins, as Nate had instructed, even though it felt like her teeth were going to rattle right out of her head.

"Whoa, Daisy," she shouted, doubtful the horse could even hear over the pounding of hooves. She wanted to turn around and see how close Nate was. Every moment she expected to see him gaining on her, but it felt like Daisy could outrun even a Triple Crown winner at the pace she was going.

She tried to remember the exact instructions Nate had given her for stopping a horse. She'd dropped one of the reins, which was flapping wildly next to Daisy's head, probably only adding to the horse's panic. The snake had come out of nowhere, or at least that's how it had felt to Bianca.

Daisy lost her footing for a second, and Bianca grabbed hold of the saddle horn, squeezing her eyes tightly shut, expecting to end up thrown or crushed under the animal's massive weight. But the horse righted herself again and kept running.

Pull back on the reins and down, she remembered what Nate had told her. Not up because that will make the horse rear. Bianca yanked on the rein, and Daisy changed direction but didn't seem to slow.

"Whoa," Bianca shouted, trying to make her voice deep and commanding instead of terrified. Terrified wasn't going to help her in this situation. She leaned forward and reached for the loose rein, then yelped as she almost lost her balance and toppled off Daisy's back.

Where was Nate? Why wasn't he coming to rescue her?

Maybe something had happened with EJ. Maybe the snake had spooked Cinnamon, too. The thought gave her a burst of adrenaline that had nothing to do with her own fear and everything to do with worry over her son. She was going to have to rescue herself.

She leaned forward again, wrapping her right hand around Daisy's sweaty neck as she stretched out her left. Her fingers grazed the rein but couldn't quite grab hold, so she reached farther and...

Nate's big hand closed around the rein.

"Hand me the other one," he shouted, and she quickly straightened and passed it over Daisy's neck. Her breath caught in her throat at the sight of EJ tucked against Nate's chest, his big eyes wide and his cheeks wet with tears as he stared at her.

"Whoa," Nate repeated the command over and over as he galloped next to the horse.

Immediately she felt a shift in Daisy, a slowing in the pounding of hooves and the merciless jostling. She held tight to the horn until the two horses had come to a stop in the middle of the grassy field.

"Mommy," EJ cried.

Nate dismounted then pulled EJ off Cinnamon's back and into his arms.

"I'm fine," she said, her voice trembling.

As soon as EJ was safely on the ground, Nate reached for Bianca. She accepted the help because her body was shaking so badly she would have ended up in a puddle on the ground otherwise.

"We didn't talk about snakes," she whispered as his arm tightened around her shoulder and he pulled her close.

EJ launched himself at her, wrapping his arms around her legs. Nate bent and picked him up, and they stood in a group hug without speaking for several minutes. Nate's breathing was ragged, and EJ whimpered softly, but eventually she could feel them each begin to calm. It was as if they silently pulled strength from holding each other.

Bianca's brain felt jumbled in her head, but she knew she had to pull it together for her son's sake. That's what moms did, after all.

"What an adventure," she said softly and kissed the top of EJ's head, using the pads of her thumbs to wipe the tears from his cheeks. "Did you even know Daisy could run so fast?"

The boy gave a soft laugh. "I didn't think Cinnamon was going to catch her."

"I knew you and Nate would manage," she said, then took him from Nate. The boy wrapped his arms tightly around her neck. His skinny legs clamped her waist.

"It's not because he loves you," EJ said against her ear. "He takes care of all of his friends."

Bianca forced her knees not to buckle at the strange and oddly prescient comment. "But you love me," she told him, "and we're in this together. No silly snake is going to hurt me."

"Snakes are scary, Mommy. Not silly."

"You did good staying in the saddle." Nate's voice was hoarse and she saw his Adam's apple bob as he swallowed. "We usually don't see rattlers on the trail this time of year, or you hear them with enough distance to change direction. I'm sorry, Bianca. I was paying attention to EJ and not—"

"I'm fine, Nate." She reached for his arm, ignoring his slight flinch as she touched him.

He took off his hat and wiped a sleeve across his forehead. "I'm not. I was scared out of my mind watching Daisy tear across the field with you on her back."

"So much for our beginner trail ride."

Nate's mouth thinned.

"This wasn't your fault," she told him. "If I had more experience riding, I could have handled Daisy's reaction better."

"I should have seen the snake."

"You did." EJ lifted his head from Bianca's shoulder. "The snake scared Cinnamon, too, Mommy. He went up on his back legs. But Mr. Nate held on to me so I wouldn't fall and then we came after you."

"You two rescued me," she said, pressing her forehead to EJ's.

"It looked like you were doing a decent job taking care of yourself," Nate told her.

She found it easy to smile at him. "Was that before or after the part where I was holding on to a runaway horse for dear life?"

His eyes were guarded and she couldn't understand why he looked so miserable. Yes, Daisy getting spooked had been scary and could have ended badly, but it hadn't. She was fine. EJ was fine.

"I'm still hungry," her son said, rubbing his stomach.

Nate moved forward and pointed over her shoulder. "You took a shortcut."

She turned to see a metal-framed structure situated on a slight rise above the trees about a hundred yards away. The windmill's fan turned in the breeze and the pond in front of it was surrounded by high grass. "We're almost there." She brushed EJ's hair out of his eyes. "Do you want to walk or ride the rest of the way?"

He thought about it for a moment, then said, "Ride. Will you ride, too, Mommy?"

Her chest tightened as panic seeped under her skin, but she nodded. "Of course."

Nate lifted EJ out of her arms and up onto Cinnamon's saddle. "Are you sure?" he asked.

"I have a way better understanding for the term 'get back on that horse,'" she told him.

He tucked a strand of stray hair behind her ear. "So damn brave," he murmured.

Bianca had never felt brave, but maybe she needed to change her definition of bravery. She'd always thought of courage as reserved for people like her brother, who purposely put themselves in harm's way to save others. Not someone like her, who spent far too much time scrambling for purchase on the endless mountain of life. Fear often motivated her. Truly it was her constant companion. Fear that she wouldn't be able to provide for EJ. Fear that she'd turn into the screwup her mom had always made her believe she was. Fear that, in the end, she wasn't lovable. She'd never be chosen.

But every moment with Nate felt like he was making a

choice and it was her. When she'd first arrived at the ranch, she'd thought his attention was a gift, but what if it was actually her due?

Maybe she needed to start believing she deserved to be the one chosen. Maybe she had to start choosing herself.

"You're right," she told him, earning a smile. "But I think I've depleted my stores of bravery for the morning." She held up a trembling hand. "I'll take calm and uneventful for the rest of the day."

He slid his hand into hers and kissed each one of her knuckles. "We can walk the horses over to the windmill."

She shook her head and turned to Daisy. Running a hand along the horse's damp neck, she moved forward until she was directly in front of the animal. "No more freaking out," she said gently, and gave Daisy a scratch between the eyes. The horse snuffled as if her breakneck run across the field was already forgotten.

"Mommy, she's a horse. She can't understand you."

Bianca moved to Daisy's side, placed her boot in the left stirrup and hoisted herself up and into the saddle. "She senses that I mean business." She pointed at EJ and wiggled her eyebrows. "Just like you do when I tell you to take a bath."

The boy giggled, and Nate mounted Cinnamon behind EJ, smiling as he settled EJ against his chest.

"Let's go find our lunch spot," he said, "We all need a break after that."

"He's so happy here," Bianca said as she watched EJ chase a grasshopper from the copse of trees where they'd had lunch all the way to the water's edge.

"It's a good place for a boy to grow up." Nate broke a cookie in half and handed her the larger piece.

"Does terror burn off calories?" She plucked it out of his fingers, moaning softly as she took a bite. "Because I can't get enough to eat right now." She waved at EJ, then flopped onto her back on the wool blanket Nate had packed. "Thanks for bringing everything for lunch. This has been a wonderful afternoon."

Nate shook his head. "How can you say that after your scare with Daisy? I'm really sorry. I told you to trust me and then—"

She placed a hand on his back. "Don't you dare blame yourself, Nate Fortune. You didn't put that snake on the trail."

"But if I'd been paying more attention, I would have seen it first. Just like with—" He placed his elbows on his knees and hung his head between his hands. "I would have protected you. I failed."

She sat upright again, scooting closer so her arm and leg brushed his. "Take off your shirt."

"What?" He darted a glance toward EJ before turning to her. "You want me to undress right now?"

"Not really." She gave him a playful nudge. "I mean, I wouldn't complain, but I was really just trying to figure out if you were wearing your superhero cape underneath that denim shirt."

He snorted. "Not funny, Busy Bee."

"Neither is you making the situation today into something more. Yes, I was scared. Yes, something bad could have happened. But it didn't. I'm fine." She poked his rock-hard bicep. "Do you know why?"

"Because you're amazing," he said softly.

"Hardly," she said with an eye roll. "But when Daisy was out of control, and I thought for sure I was going to be thrown or trampled, I heard your voice in my head. All those instructions you gave me as we started out on the ride."

"You had a few minutes of riding tips. I should have never let you—"

"I'm a grown woman," she interrupted. "I wouldn't have climbed on that horse if I didn't want to."

He blew out a long breath. "I was so damn scared you were going to be hurt." He draped an arm around her shoulder and pulled her close.

"That makes two of us." She turned her face into his shirt and breathed him in, the scent of mint gum and the earth and laundry detergent. "Thank you for taking care of EJ. I was most worried about him."

"I had him," Nate whispered.

"I know." Somehow the knowledge of that soothed her soul in a way she barely understood. She'd come so far from the morning she'd hightailed it out of San Antonio. She was stronger now. Strong enough to ask—

"Did Eddie suffer?"

Nate stiffened next to her, and suddenly it felt like she was snuggling up to a glacier. He was silent for so long, she didn't think he would answer. Finally he said, "No. It was fast."

"Do you think he was scared?" She couldn't imagine her strong, brave brother scared of anything, but she had enough distance and experience now to understand that Eddie hadn't only been the bigger-than-life hero she'd worshipped as a girl. He'd been human.

"We were all scared." He hung his head again. "Hell, Bianca. Fear and adrenaline were our bread and butter over there. Eddie was one of the bravest men I knew. He saved at least a dozen men on that last mission." He paused, then added, "He saved me. But don't think for a minute he wasn't soil-his-pants scared when it was going down."

"I associate being scared with weakness," she admitted. "That's how it always seemed to me. Eddie was strong. You're strong."

"Not like your brother."

She shook her head then covered his hand, which was resting on his thigh, with hers. "Think of all you've been through."

"I can't," he said on a ragged breath. "When I think about it, I feel like I'm going to lose my mind. I don't want to think. I don't want to remember."

"But the nightmares… Talking about it might help."

A shudder passed through him and she squeezed his hand, leaning in closer. "You're not alone," she whispered.

"I've been alone so damn long." He said the words more to himself than her, but they broke her heart just the same.

She was torn between pushing him, wanting to know more about Eddie's death and the demons that made Nate suffer so much, and simply soothing him. Was it fair to force him to relive the traumas or atrocities he'd seen in the line of duty?

"Not anymore," she said finally. "I'm here for you as long as you need me."

He pulled away, got up off the blanket, paced a few steps and then turned back to her. "There are things you don't know about Eddie—about that last mission."

"Do you want to tell me?"

He closed his eyes. "Yes. No. I'm so messed up, Bianca."

She drew her knees to her chest, as if they could protect her heart from whatever pain she was sure to endure in learning the details of her brother's death. "Whatever it is, I can handle it."

"Mommy, I caught a grasshopper."

She sucked in a breath, her focus switching to EJ in a split second. "Bring him here," she called, shielding her eyes from the Texas sun. "Let me see."

As EJ ran forward, Nate backed away. It felt like more than just a physical distance between them. Somehow the connection they'd shared moments earlier had been severed. His mask was in place again, and she wanted to rip it from his face. Until Nate was truly honest with her and himself about how Eddie's death had affected him, could they really have a chance at making this work?

"Look at his big eyes." EJ came to stand at the edge of the blanket, his small, dirt-smudged hands cupped in front of him. "He's green."

"So cool," she whispered.

EJ smiled. "He tickles my hand with his legs. Can I keep him?"

"No, sweetie. His home is out here on the grass. He probably has a grasshopper family waiting for him."

"What if he's alone?" EJ asked.

She could feel Nate's gaze on her and glanced up, but his eyes were unreadable under the wide brim of his Stetson.

"I doubt he is," she answered.

EJ scrunched up his face into a frown but then opened his hands. The grasshopper rested on his palm for several moments, probably stunned by being captured. Then the bug hopped into the grass and disappeared in the high stalks.

"There are a thousand more you can catch," Nate told EJ. "Grayson, Jayden and I used to chase those things all over the place."

He smiled at her boy, and Bianca's heart stuttered. She had to convince him to face his demons because she needed a future with Nate Fortune like she needed her next breath. She'd fallen hopelessly in love with him.

Not the start of something that felt like love. Not a little bit. Full force with everything she had. It was difficult to fathom how that was possible given the brief amount of time she'd truly known him, but it was her reality just the same.

She wasn't going to give him up without a fight.

"We should go." When both Nate and EJ turned to stare, she realized she'd shouted the comment. She was willing to fight but didn't quite know how to start. That made her nervous, and when she was nervous she talked too much… or blurted out random commands.

She'd never had the nerve to fight for anything she wanted. Everything in life had simply happened to her and she'd made the best of it. This was different. She was different in Paseo, and as much as she yearned to embrace it, the thought also made fear pound through her. She took a breath and thought of what Nate had told her about Eddie. Her brother had been scared, but he'd kept going. She could keep going. Or at least try to keep going without making a fool of herself.

"I mean…" She tapped a finger on her watch. "It's probably time to head back to the ranch."

"Sure," Nate said, giving her a questioning glance. "Are you feeling okay?"

She grinned, wondering if her smile looked as fake as it felt. "Fine."

"Then let's pack everything up." Nate placed a hand on EJ's shoulder. "You ready, buddy?"

"Fifteen more minutes, Mommy?" EJ asked, his eyes darting toward the windmill on the hill. "I'm not done exploring."

Bianca sighed. "Fifteen more minutes."

EJ pumped a fist in the air and ran toward the windmill.

"Would you like to see it, too?" Nate approached her slowly, as if not sure how she might respond.

Perfect. He thought she was a crazy person. What a great start to her plan to fight for him.

"I can show you the spot where Jayden and Ariana said their vows." His voice was gentle. "Are you sure everything's okay?"

I'm in love with you.

"Yep," she said quickly, pressing a hand to her stomach.

"I don't think so." Nate slipped his hand into hers. They began walking toward the windmill, where she could see EJ bobbing up and down in the tall grass, clearly still on the hunt for grasshoppers.

"Does this have something to do with what we were talking about?" His voice was hollow. "About me being messed up?"

"No," she answered immediately, hating that her own tumbling emotions had made him think she was judging him.

"Because I wouldn't blame you. You and EJ are important to me. Getting to know you is one of the best things that's happened in my life in forever."

"Me, too."

"But I don't know if I can give you what you want."

"Then give me what you can," she blurted.

"Bianca." He shifted so he was in front of her, blocking the path. "You can't mean that."

"It's not forever," she told him, forcing her gaze to remain on his. A spark flared in his coffee-colored eyes, like her words disappointed him somehow.

Was it possible Nate wanted forever with her?

"What I'm trying to say is I can be patient. You've been through a lot. I get that. We can go slowly. It doesn't have to be a rush. You and I have all the time in the world, but I'm not going to give up because I'm scared and you believe you're messed up." She bit down on her lip, took a breath. "I'm going to fight for us. I believe this is something special, and I refuse to let it go."

He lifted his hands to cup her cheeks and leaned in to brush a kiss across her lips. The touch was featherlight, but she felt it to her toes. There were things he couldn't say yet, secrets he wasn't willing to share. But the kiss was a promise of more. It felt like a pledge, as if he was giving her an answer to a question she hadn't even known to ask. But the "yes" in his kiss meant everything.

"How did you get to be so amazing?" He pressed his forehead to hers, their breaths mingling so that it felt like they were connected even by the air around them.

She tipped back her head and laughed. "I was born that way."

"Mommy, I got another one!" EJ's voice rang out across the meadow.

Nate looped an arm around Bianca's shoulder and they walked toward her son. Suddenly the fear that had become Bianca's constant companion dissolved, hope blooming in its place. Hope for a real future with the man she loved.

Chapter 13

It was a week later that Nate got the call he'd been expecting since Jayden left the ranch. He driven into town to pick up materials to replace a section of fence that had been damaged by a windstorm just after Christmas. His phone rang as he loaded the back of the truck, and he sent the call to voicemail.

Almost immediately, the device buzzed with an incoming text.

Don't you dare screen my call, Nathan.

He finished sliding a piece of timber into the cargo bed and punched a button to return the call.

His mother answered on the first ring.

"It wasn't on purpose," he lied. "I'm in the middle of fixing the south pasture fence. It's not a great time to talk."

The familiar sound of one of Deborah's patented sighs

came through the phone. "Talk to me, anyway," she told him. "I've been trying you for days."

"I've been too busy to get to town."

"You're not answering the house phone, either. Did you get my messages?"

"I meant to call you back earlier."

"Lucky for both of us, you made the right choice today."

He shut the back of the truck and leaned a hip against the tailgate, resigned to get this inevitable conversation out of the way. His mother wasn't going to let him off the hook. The truth was, he'd been secretly waiting for her call. He was a grown damn man, but sometimes he wanted his mom to help smooth the rough edges of his life. Of him. The way she had when he was a boy. Even though Deborah had been busy raising triplets and working, she'd always made time for each of them as individuals.

"Hi, Mom. How are you? How's Grayson? I hear you're heading to Tulsa."

"Fine. Fine. Yes," she said in rapid succession. "Are you going to explain why I have to hear about your new girl-friend from Jayden?"

"She's not my girlfriend," he said, which was both true and not. He'd never taken Bianca out on an official date but he felt closer to her than any other woman in his life. "She's Eddie Shaw's little sister."

"Jayden explained that part. He told me she has a son."

"EJ," Nate explained. "Edward James." Guilt twisted in his chest as he added, "Named after Eddie."

"He also said you're different with her."

"Different how?"

"Happy," Deborah said, her voice a caress across the miles that separated them.

"I was happy before," he argued but couldn't manage to put any conviction in the words.

"No, you weren't. Not for a while, Nathan. I've been worried about you." His mom had a knack for ignoring the nonsense her three sons tried to feed her and cutting through to the truth. "I'd like to meet Bianca and her son."

He took off his hat and swiped an arm across his forehead, sweat beading along his hairline despite the cooler January day. "I don't know how long she's staying. She hit a rough patch and is trying to get her life back on track."

Deborah let out a soft laugh. "I can relate to that."

"You'd like her. She's smart and funny and she loves her son more than anything. She'd do anything for EJ."

"I can relate to that, too," his mom answered. "It's how I feel about all three of you, even though you're grown men now."

"What about you?" he asked. "How are you, Mom?"

"I told you I was fine."

"Fine doesn't mean anything to me. Or to you. We both know that. Did Jayden tell you he had lunch with one of Gerald's kids when he and Ariana stopped in Austin?"

There was a charged silence on the other end of the line. "He mentioned it," Deborah said finally.

"How are you dealing with the fact that our father is still alive now that we've all had some time for it to sink in?"

Another pause. "The same as you, I'd imagine."

He laughed. "Well, that doesn't reassure me you're okay."

"Oh, Nathan."

"We'll make it through."

"We always do," she agreed. "One thing I've been thinking about is what I might have done differently back then. The regrets I have about letting Jerome—or Gerald now, I suppose—walk away."

"Mom, he made that choice."

"I didn't stop him. We had a stupid argument, and I let fear and pride dictate my actions. I didn't fight."

Nate sucked in a breath. Bianca had told him she was willing to fight. Hell, she was so much braver than he imagined. Than she gave herself credit for.

"You couldn't have known," he insisted, "what he would do to break ties with his family."

"You're right, of course. It's the past now, anyway. It doesn't do anyone any good to let regret take over and dictate how you live your life."

Nate didn't answer. What could he say to that?

But his mom knew. Even though he hadn't talked about Eddie's death to her—to anyone except the tiny snippets he'd shared with Bianca—Deborah didn't need words. She had that spooky maternal sixth sense, where she understood what he and his brothers were going through without them uttering a word.

"You know this, right?" she asked, her voice still gentle. "Regret is not a way to live your life, Nathan. You can't change what happened in the past." He heard her draw in a breath. "You can't blame yourself for Eddie's death."

Of course he could. He did.

"I want to talk about Eddie Shaw," he told her, "about as much as you want to discuss Gerald Robinson."

Deborah chuckled. "You're like him, you know."

"Eddie?"

"Your father," she corrected. "You're strong like he was. And so darn stubborn."

"I thought I got that from you," he said, letting humor lace his tone.

"From both of us," she admitted. "Don't let it change the course of your life. If you care about this Bianca, tell her."

"She knows how I feel." But doubt niggled the back of his mind as he said the words. What did Bianca really know? That he'd opened his house but not truly his heart. That he wouldn't share the details of his past. That he was willing to make love to her every night but would sneak away after she fell asleep, afraid of what she might witness when he was in the middle of one of his nightmares.

"Take it from the voice of experience," his mom said, as if reading his thoughts. "A single mom who's built a life around her son needs to know a man is committed to her and her son. The stakes are too high any other way."

"There are things about me she doesn't know," he admitted. "The night Eddie died…" His voice cracked and he swallowed.

"Tell her," his mother urged. "If she's the kind of woman I think she is, the two of you will find a way to get through it, Nathan." She let out a delicate sniff. "You deserve happiness."

"Mom, I don't want to upset you."

"You're not. Sometimes I just wish things had been different for our family. That I'd been able to give you boys more."

"You gave us everything."

"You were always sweet," she said. "A teddy bear heart in a tough navy SEAL body."

He smiled. "Bianca called me a teddy bear the first day she showed up in Paseo."

"I like her already. Remember, no regrets," she said. "I love you, Nathan."

"You, too, Mom. Say hi to Grayson for me."

They disconnected and he got in the truck and headed for home, surveying the land that he'd grown up working on as he drove. The ranch had been a kind of salvation to him when he'd left the navy. A place to escape and hide out, where he could lose himself in the backbreaking labor and honest sweat of a hard day's work. He'd needed a reprieve from life and from the hell his existence had become the moment Eddie died, but he was quickly realizing there was no way to outrun what he'd gone through.

He thought he could escape the bad memories by ignoring them, but in doing that, he'd allowed the past to dictate his future. He didn't want that. He wanted Bianca and EJ.

He wanted to be the man they both deserved.

As he approached the ranch, he noticed a car he didn't recognize parked in front of the house. Not that he knew every vehicle in Paseo, but the cherry red sports car seemed out of place in this part of Texas.

In front of the old farmhouse, the Miata gave the impression of nail polish on a pig. The car wasn't new. It had several small dents in the back bumper and the paint's shine was worn down on the hood. He did a mental eye roll at the car's bumper sticker, which read My Other Ride Is… Your Mama.

Nate didn't know who was visiting the ranch today, but he could guarantee they were no friend of his.

He parked the truck and took the steps two at a time, not sure why his heart was hammering in his chest. As he burst through the door, Bianca, EJ and a man Nate didn't recognize all turned to him.

"Mr. Nate," EJ shouted, his voice shaky. He let go of his mother's leg and ran toward Nate.

Nate scooped him up in his arms, holding a protective arm on the boy's back.

Who the hell was the guy glaring at him from across the room?

"Nate, you're here." Bianca pressed two fingers to her temple.

"Yep," he agreed. "I live here."

The stranger's eyes narrowed and Bianca took a step

forward, as if she was breaking up a potential fight on the playground. "This is Brett Pierson. He just arrived." She swallowed. "My—"

"Husband," the man supplied.

"Ex," she corrected.

Brett raised a brow in Nate's direction. "For now," he muttered.

"Don't do that," Bianca whispered, and Nate hated the panicked look in her warm cocoa-colored eyes. She shook her head. "Not in front of EJ."

Brett gave the barest hint of a nod, as if agreeing only to humor her.

"This is Nate Fortune." She gestured toward Nate. "He was a friend of Eddie's."

Brett curled his lip in what could have been a smile but looked more like a sneer. "Right."

Bianca seemed shocked at Brett's reaction. "Really, Brett. I'm sure I mentioned Nate to you. He and Eddie did BUD/S training together. They were SEALs in the same squadron."

"Yeah. I've heard all about him." Brett focused his gaze on EJ. "Come here, *son*." He held out his arms and motioned for the boy.

EJ buried his face against Nate's shirtfront.

"I mean it, EJ. I drove all this way to see you." His gaze flicked to Bianca. "You and your mama. *My* family."

Nate had never wanted to punch a man so much in his life.

"He doesn't know you, Brett," Bianca said. "He was two when you left. It's been a long time."

"He needs to get to know me, and he isn't going to do that with another man holding him. That ridiculous business about changing his name doesn't help, either."

"My name is Edward James Shaw." EJ took a deep, shuddery breath and burrowed farther into Nate's shirt.

"I've got you, buddy," Nate whispered, ruffling his hair.

"Nate?" Bianca turned to him. "Would you take EJ to the barn for a few minutes?"

Nate shook his head. "I'm not leaving you alone with him."

"Are you joking?" Brett held out his hands, palms up. "I'm her husband."

"Ex," Bianca and Nate said at the same time.

Then she turned back to Nate. "I need a few minutes to talk to Brett. We have some things to work out."

"What kind of things?" Nate asked.

"Things that are none of your business," Brett told him, his jaw set. The same kind of firm line he'd seen on EJ's face when the boy was digging in his heels about convincing his mother to give him five more minutes before bedtime. And as much as EJ looked like Bianca and Eddie, suddenly Nate could see Brett in him.

EJ's father.

The man who'd walked away, leaving Bianca on her own with a toddler. The man who hadn't offered one bit of support in the past two years, emotional or financial. But still the boy's father. Nate knew what it would have meant to him and his brothers if Gerald Robinson had come into their lives when they were kids. How that would have changed everything.

What right did he have to deny EJ the chance he'd secretly dreamed of as a boy? Despite the fact that Brett looked like a tool and drove a ridiculous car for a trip across half of Texas, this couldn't be an easy situation to walk into. Was Nate helping anyone by making it more difficult?

Bianca walked toward him, only stopping when they stood toe-to-toe. She put a hand on Nate's arm. She looked miserable and strangely hopeful at the same time. "Please," she whispered, and of course Nate nodded. How could he say no?

"We'll be in the barn if you need anything."

"Thank you."

EJ swiped a hand across his cheek. "You should come, too, Mommy. I bet Otis is out there. He might let me pet him today, and you'll want to see that."

"I do," she agreed. "But I need to talk to your daddy for a few minutes."

"You can give Daisy a carrot."

"Maybe I'll bring Daddy to the barn when we're finished with the grown-up stuff. He can meet Twix."

"He might not like ponies."

"I like ponies," Brett called, and acid burned in Nate's gut. For all he knew, Brett had finally realized what an amazing woman and son he'd left behind. He could be ready to make Bianca and EJ his future.

Just like Nate was ready.

"See?" Bianca asked, smoothing a hand over EJ's back.

"I guess you can bring him," the boy muttered.

She lifted onto her toes and kissed EJ's cheek. As she did, her fingers curled around Nate's bicep and she squeezed, as if communicating something with him she didn't want Brett to know about.

He sure as hell hoped it meant she wasn't interested in reuniting with her ex-husband. That might send Nate over the edge.

And he'd just gotten comfortable on solid ground.

Bianca shut the door behind Nate and EJ, then turned to face Brett again. He gave her one of his stock smiles, a jaunty half curve of his mouth. It was the smile that had melted her heart when she'd first met him.

The girl she was back then seemed like a stranger to her now. How had she been fool enough to fall for Brett, with his slick moves and pretty lines? At the time, she'd been grateful for his attention.

She'd been so starved for anything that felt remotely like love. She'd been coming off a bad breakup after the guy she'd thought she was in love with had cheated on her. Her mother had gambled away her meager savings—literally— so Bianca left school and drained her own bank accounts to pay Jennifer's debts and bills so she wouldn't lose her apartment lease and have one more thing to add to her list of problems. Eddie was in the field, stationed a half a world away on a mission so covert that Bianca couldn't even reach him.

She'd been alone and reeling. Brett had seemed like a fairy-tale prince to her, and she'd desperately wanted to believe the things he'd told her—she was special and beautiful and he wanted to take care of her.

Now she knew better. She wasn't a princess, and her life wasn't a fairy tale. It was real and sometimes a struggle, but it belonged to her. She was in control. No one else.

A part of her wanted to kick him off the Fortune ranch and out of her life for good. But he was EJ's father, and Bianca understood how hard it could be on a child growing up without a dad. She knew Nate did, as well, which was probably why he'd been willing to let her have this time with Brett.

It was clear he hadn't wanted to, and she appreciated his protective streak toward her, but more importantly toward EJ.

"What do you want, Brett?" she asked, crossing her arms over her chest.

"I told you. I'm here to take you home. That stupid business about you filing to have EJ's name legally changed was a wake-up call. I've missed you, babe."

"Missed me? It's been over two years since you walked out the door. You left our *home*, knowing very well I couldn't afford rent on a house like that on my own. I'm changing EJ's name because he belongs to *me*. He's a Shaw. You don't even know where your son and I have been living because you haven't bothered to check."

"Not true." He shook his head, a lock of hair flopping into his eyes much like EJ's did. It was cute on a four-year-old, but Bianca wanted to tell Brett to get a haircut. "I kept tabs on you. When I received notification of the name change hearing, I went looking for you. But you'd moved out of that crappy apartment, so I talked to your mom. She told me you'd left San Antonio, and something in me snapped. It was one thing when I knew you and EJ were close, but to have you out of my reach…"

"That sounds unbelievable creepy," she muttered, "even from you."

Brett flashed another smile. "I hoped you'd think it was romantic."

She couldn't believe she'd married a guy who was so delusional. It was a bigger blow to realize her mother had helped Brett to find her after all this time. The conversation with her mom hadn't gone well, but she thought Jennifer understood that Bianca wanted a fresh start.

"How is it romantic?" she asked, pointing a finger at him. "Or even the least bit acceptable that you've kept tabs on us but haven't wanted to be a part of your son's life?"

Brett shrugged. "I had some things to work out. You know I hadn't planned to get married and become a dad when I did."

"Me, neither," she countered, "but that doesn't change reality. EJ is an amazing kid. You've missed a lot."

"I want to make it up to you. I've gone back to school,

and I've got a great job in sales at a medical device company. They're even paying for my classes."

Her own broken dreams of a college degree and a great career felt like glass shards in her throat. "Good for you. What does that have to do with EJ and me?"

"I'm doing all of this for you." He moved forward and reached for her, but she shifted away. "For us. For our future."

Bianca had never been the violent type. But the urge to punch her ex-husband in the throat was so overwhelming she could barely ignore it.

"We have no future," she said through clenched teeth. "If you want to see EJ, we can work out an arrangement. You'll also need to start sending child support checks You've been dodging payments for way too long. It's going to stop."

Brett scoffed. "He's my son. I don't have to pay to see him."

"Raising a child means responsibility. You can live up to yours if you want to be a part of his life." Bianca pressed her fingers to her lips, shocked at the words coming out of her mouth...at the conviction burning deep in her soul. She was done letting anyone take advantage of her, accepting scraps for herself or for EJ because she'd been taught to believe she wasn't worth anything more.

"Now that you've latched onto one of the Fortunes, you think you've got it made." Brett's blue eyes narrowed. "Is that it?"

She shook her head. "This has nothing to do with Nate," she said, which was both true and not. The conviction that she and EJ deserved to be valued resonated through her, but being with Nate had helped open her eyes to recognize it as a fact. "You and I are over, Brett. I'm willing to let you into EJ's life. But not if you're going to hurt him. He needs his dad to be a dependable presence in his life. This isn't about the money, but I know you. If you have to invest in something, it means more to you." She flashed a small smile. "Maybe that's why we were never meant to be. Neither of us believed you had to try to make our relationship work."

"You're not being fair," he muttered.

"I don't blame you," she told him without emotion. "Not entirely. I let it happen, but I was different then. I've changed, and I'm not going back to who I was before. That's the woman you married. Not me."

"And you think Nate Fortune is that man?" He practically spit the words. "You don't even know him."

"I know he's been generous and patient with me. He cares about EJ." She chuckled. "He cooks."

Brett threw up his hands. "What the hell does that have to do with anything?"

"You wouldn't understand. He's a good man. Eddie trusted him, and I do—"

"He killed your brother."

She took a step back as if he'd struck her. "Shut your mouth," she said, the words hissing out on a painful breath.

"I'm sorry. I know you don't want to hear this but—"

"You're right." She turned, stalked the few paces to the front door and yanked it open. "You need to leave, Brett. You can say goodbye to EJ in the barn, and I'll call you next week about arrangements to see him."

"It's a shock, Bianca, but at least let me explain. I'm not trying to throw the guy under the bus."

She rolled her eyes, anger coursing through her. "Right."

"Has he told you the details of Eddie's death?"

She wasn't about to admit that he hadn't. "I read the report," she answered instead.

"It's not the same thing. You don't know the whole story."

"And how do *you* know it?" she demanded.

"From talk I've heard in the old neighborhood. Your mom confirmed everything."

"She didn't," Bianca whispered, then pressed her lips together, thinking of the veiled hints her mom had made during their last awkward phone conversation. Jennifer had intimated that Nate wasn't the man he pretended to be, but Bianca assumed she was talking about his ties to the Fortune family. Nate had been Eddie's best friend. He'd loved her brother as much as she had. Missed him just as badly. There was nothing Brett could say to change that.

She swung the door shut gently and crossed her arms over her chest. "Fine. Tell me if it makes you happy. It won't change anything."

He walked forward until he was only an arm's length from her. "It makes me unhappy to see you fooled by a man who doesn't have your best interests at heart. He's lying to you."

"Go ahead with what you think you know about Eddie's death," she told him. "But stop trash-talking Nate. I won't have it, Brett."

He blew out a harsh breath. "I don't need to trash-talk him. The truth is damning enough. He deserted Eddie over in Afghanistan. Saved himself but let your brother take the brunt of enemy fire during their last mission. He left Eddie alone, Bianca. What kind of a soldier saves his own neck that way at the expense of another man's life—let alone when that man is supposed to be his best friend?"

"Stop."

"You can't depend on him. You can't trust him. He's in it for himself, and as soon as you're not useful to him, he'll walk away."

"I don't believe any of that."

"Come on," Brett urged. "I can tell by the look in your

eyes that you know I'm telling the truth. I also know by the way you look at him that you're sleeping together."

She narrowed her eyes. "That's none of your business."

He barked out a laugh. "Knowing you, you're half in love with him already. But he's not the man you believe he is."

"Neither were you," she muttered.

"I made mistakes," he admitted. "I let you down, and I'm sorry for that. But I would have never left your brother for dead. Even I'm not that awful." He leaned in, brushed his thumb across her cheek. She flinched, like his touch was electric. "I've changed, Bianca. I'm trying to be honest with you. Even if you won't give us another chance, cut ties with Nate Fortune. He's going to hurt you way worse than I ever did."

"It's time for you to go," she whispered, unable to argue any longer. There was no way what he was saying about Nate was true. It couldn't be. Nate would have told her if he'd had some direct involvement in Eddie's death. She would have known. Eddie thought of Nate as a brother. He'd practically sent Bianca to Paseo, after all. This had to be a ploy by Brett to ruin her new life just as it started.

But she couldn't stop doubt from easing its way in through the shadows of her mind. Despite what she knew about their friendship, she also recognized there were things about Eddie's death that Nate hadn't shared. Then there were his nightmares and the way he insisted he didn't deserve her. She assumed that was the result of his time as a SEAL, the things he'd seen and done over the past two decades, but what if there was something more?

"Say goodbye to EJ for me," Brett told her. He scrubbed a hand over his face. "I'm not going to take the chance of upsetting him more. I have so many memories of him as a baby, but now I'm a stranger to him. None of this went the way I'd planned it, Bianca."

"Maybe you should have made a better plan," she said, hating how snippy she sounded. She sighed and opened the door more gently this time, feeling exhausted and overwhelmed, the way she had so many times in San Antonio. "If you're serious, Brett, we'll make it work."

He nodded. "I'll call next week and we'll come up with a plan for him to spend time with me."

"Call first, then I'll talk to him about spending time with you."

He grinned, only this time it was genuine. "You're going to make me work for this, aren't you?"

"I sure am, and I should have done it a long time ago."

He leaned and kissed her cheek. "You're a better woman than I deserve. Thank you for being such a fantastic mother to our son."

My son, she wanted to scream. EJ belonged to her. But she only held open the door with a smile. "He's the best part of me," she whispered. "Always."

With a last wave, Brett walked toward his red Miata. It was the same car he'd driven when they first met. At the time it seemed exciting and fun, but then she'd had EJ and Brett had refused to part with it. It was a two-seater, so they couldn't fit a car seat in it and she should have seen it for what it was—a sign that he wasn't willing to change anything in his life to accommodate EJ. She hoped he'd changed now, but she still didn't trust it.

Up until a few minutes ago, she'd started to believe it hadn't mattered. Nate had stepped into EJ's life and fulfilled all the hopes she'd had for a father figure for her son. Now she couldn't help but wonder if it had all been a lie.

Chapter 14

"You can't avoid me forever. We live in the same house."

"*You* live here." Bianca looked up from where she was clearing weeds in the overgrown vegetable garden situated behind the kitchen windows in the backyard. "I'm only visiting."

The words were spoken casually, but they cut across Nate's chest like a blade. Something had changed between them since her ex-husband's unexpected visit to the ranch yesterday. He knew Bianca wasn't interested in reuniting with Brett. She'd patiently explained to EJ that his daddy wanted to be a part of his life again, but that they weren't going to be a family in the traditional sense of the word.

EJ had peppered her with questions about his father and why he was returning to their lives now. No matter how she felt on the inside, Bianca had done an amazing job of keeping the focus on EJ and how she'd always protect him and make sure he remained her number one priority. It reminded Nate of his own mom.

Deborah had never once spoken an ill word against the triplets' father or how she'd been left as a single mother. Of course, she'd thought Gerald dead for all these years, but even after they'd discovered that his current wife, Charlotte, had kept a dossier on all of Gerald's illegitimate children, Deborah hadn't made any disparaging comments about what they'd all lost.

"What's going on, Bianca?"

"Nothing. I'm working."

He crouched down next to her. "You're going after those weeds like you have a personal vendetta against them."

She paused in the act of digging out a dry tangle of vines. "I want to make sure the garden has a good start when your mom gets back to the ranch this spring."

"She's going to love it." Nate had made an offhanded remark last week about how much Deborah had loved tending her kitchen garden when the boys had been younger. Since she'd started traveling more with Grayson in the past few years, her herbs and vegetables had been left largely ignored. Neither Jayden nor Nate had the inclination to commit to bringing it back to life. His mom lamented her heavily weeded garden whenever she came home but rarely had enough time to clear it out in the way it needed.

Bianca had decided that this was going to be her gift to Deborah—preparing the garden to thrive again. She'd enlisted EJ's help and between other chores, his lessons and work on her business, the two of them spent time each day in the backyard. She attacked it with such vehemence, it seemed she was determined to finish the task today.

At the moment, EJ was on the far side of the yard with Otis, trying to teach the dog to play fetch. Despite Nate's protests, the dog was quickly going from a stray to a family pet. Or at least EJ's pet. Although Otis seemed amenable to chowing down on the kibble Nate put out for him every morning, the dog wouldn't allow anyone but EJ to pet him. Nate liked to argue against believing the dog belonged to them, but it made the boy happy and Bianca didn't seem to mind.

"Bianca." He placed a hand on her arm, hating that she not only stilled but stiffened under his touch. "Talk to me."

She stood and paced to the garden's border, placing her handheld shovel in his mom's gardening bucket. It was strange how much it meant to Nate to see her using the set of tools he'd watched his mom use when he and his brothers were boys. "I think *you* should talk to *me*," she countered. "About the night Eddie died."

He straightened, kicking a ball of dirt with one booted toe. "You know what happened. Your brother died a hero."

She moved toward him slowly, crossing her arms over her chest. Even standing directly in front of him, the scent of her shampoo mingling with the smell of fresh dirt on the morning breeze, he could feel the distance between them. It was more than physical, and Nate had no idea how to close the divide.

"Yes," she agreed quietly, "but is there more?"

More. What an understatement. He tipped his head up to the robin's-egg-blue sky. His heart pounded in his chest and a shiver raced along his spine as panic rushed through him. Memories came swift and severe. So many damn sounds. Rounds coming in…rounds going out. Mortars…grenades. He fisted his hands and forced himself to keep breathing, afraid he might drop to his knees from the weight of guilt and regret.

He licked his lips, swallowed back the bitterness in his throat. "What more do you want to know?"

She studied him as if she was searching for something in his gaze. Some explanation or promise that things were going to be okay. That the chasm that separated them, quickly filling with his poisonous shame, could be navigated. He couldn't give her that. He realized he couldn't give her anything she needed. Now or ever. But he remained still under her scrutiny, hoping that whatever she saw would be enough.

She drew in a shuddery breath. "Brett told me..." She paused, unclasped and clasped her hands in front of her stomach. "He told me you were responsible for Eddie's death," she said on a rush of air. "He said you killed him."

He would have expected her words to hurt, but somehow hearing them spoken out loud was a relief. His shame and guilt had been a silent, secret companion since that last mission. One that stayed with him always but gained strength in the dark of night.

Now the beast yawned and opened its eyes, blinking against the light of day. Instead of being chased away by the spotlight shining on it, the darkness reveled in the notice, as if being acknowledged made it more legitimate. But to Nate, the demons had always been real, and they let out a long breath at someone speaking the truth out loud.

"I know it has to be a lie," she continued when he didn't answer. "He's only trying to tear us apart. He doesn't want me to move on, but Brett and I have no future. You're my future." She pushed her hair out of her face. "I'm babbling again," she said with a shaky laugh. "But it's been weighing on me. I shouldn't have believed him in the first place. He was trying to warn me away from you, which is crazy." Her mouth curved up at one end, her smile wobbly but sincere, like his silence confirmed what she thought she knew about him instead of the opposite.

It had always been the opposite. As much as he wanted to, he could never be the man she wanted because...

"It's true," he said at the same time Bianca whispered, "I love you."

It felt like his heart was shattering into a million pieces as he watched the hope in her eyes cloud to confusion. "What did you say?" she asked.

He shook his head. He couldn't stand to repeat it, not when all he wanted to hear was her telling him she loved him over and over. Somehow he understood that Bianca's love was the only thing that could mend all the splintered pieces of his soul and patch him back together. She was the only thing that could make him whole again.

"Nate." She raised a hand to her throat, clutching at it like she was having trouble gathering air into her lungs. "You can't be serious. There must be an explanation. You wouldn't have—"

"I killed Eddie," he interrupted, surprised at how calm his voice sounded.

"Mommy," EJ shouted, "Otis brought me the ball."

Bianca held Nate's gaze, tears shining in her eyes.

"Mommy!"

"Go to him," Nate said, wanting to reach for her. To somehow convince her he could make everything right. But he knew nothing had been right in his world since that last terrible mission. Now there was a good chance it never would.

She swiped at her eyes but pasted a bright smile on her face. The mom smile—the one that made it clear that no matter what fresh hell was exploding in her life, she would make things okay for her son.

It was one of the things he loved most about her.

"Let me see," she called, turning and walking toward EJ and the dog.

Love.

The word ricocheted through Nate's brain, wreaking havoc on the parts of his heart that were still intact until his insides were nothing but a sad, pulpy mess.

She'd said she loved him at the exact moment he'd ruined her.

Wasn't that just his way?

He let his gaze soak in the sight of EJ laughing as Otis ran to retrieve another ball, the dog moving so fast he skidded as he tried to grab the ball in his mouth. EJ laughed harder, and Bianca's smile relaxed.

It was suddenly too much. Despite the open space around him, Nate had the sensation that his world was closing in on him. His lungs were in a vise and he could hardly breathe. He needed to get away…to move…to clear his head of the tumult of thoughts pounding him.

One foot in front of the other, striding toward the barn. He moved as if on autopilot, grateful that his body knew what to do since his brain was in the middle of a major meltdown.

Cinnamon's ears twitched when Nate approached his stall, as if he could sense Nate's mood. He saddled the horse, focusing on the scent of the barn and the sound of Cinnamon's rhythmic breathing to keep him grounded. Then he climbed on and took off out of the barn, riding like he used to as a kid, hell-bent for leather across the open fields. He used to race his brothers, but now he sped away from his own demons, hoping that the pounding of hooves and the feeling of being one with the huge animal would calm him.

He needed to clear his mind so he could figure out how to clean up the mess he'd just made of all their lives.

What's wrong, honey?"

Bianca shook her head and smiled, her cheeks aching from the movement. "Nothing, Susan. I just need to return these books I borrowed." She placed her stack of paperbacks on the counter.

"You can keep them as long as you need," Susan told her gently.

"EJ and I are leaving Paseo today. I don't think we'll be back so…" She broke off when tears clogged her throat. She glanced behind her to where EJ sat in front of the computer screen. He had on headphones and was already engrossed in a show, so she had a moment to let her happy-mom mask slip. "I know it sounds strange because I haven't been here long, but I'll miss seeing you."

"Honey, no." Susan stood, moving around the makeshift checkout counter to envelop Bianca in a baby-powder-scented hug. "You can't leave. You're too good an addition to our little town." She pulled back enough to look into Bianca's eyes. "You're good for Nathan Fortune."

Bianca sniffed, embarrassed that she could feel her chin trembling. "I can't," she whispered, then broke down completely, crying into Susan's brightly patterned sweater while the older woman hugged her, swaying back and forth the way Bianca used to when EJ was fussy as a baby.

After a few minutes she took a shaky breath and stepped out of Susan's embrace. She darted a glance at EJ, but he was still focused on Elmer the Elephant's latest adventure.

"Let me get you a tissue." Susan reached over the counter then handed Bianca a wad of them.

"I'm so embarrassed," Bianca muttered. "You don't need me blubbering all over you. I'll pull it together."

"Don't be silly." Susan patted her arm. "Sometimes a woman needs a good cry." She arched a heavily lined brow. "Especially when a man is involved. If your mama were here, she'd give you a big ol' hug and tell you the same thing."

"My mom would tell me that I was a fool to come to Paseo in the first place," Bianca said with a small, sad laugh, "and I'm getting just what I deserve."

Susan made a soft tsking sound. "Because I'm sure she's never made a mistake in her life."

"She's made plenty." Bianca dabbed at her eyes. "I have a feeling she might count me as the biggest."

"Don't say that." Susan wrapped an arm around Bianca's shoulder. "You're a good person and an amazing mother. Look at how hard you're working to get your business started. I heard from Rosa that Nathan Fortune couldn't keep his eyes off you when he brought you and EJ into town for dinner the other night. She said he looked positively smitten."

"I thought he was more than smitten," Bianca admitted. "Or at least I hoped."

"Because you feel more for him?"

"Way more. I'm in love with him."

Susan leaned in and gave Bianca's cheek a smacking kiss. "How wonderful. That boy needs some happiness in his life. I've kept up with him over the years, and he always had such a big smile and easy way about him. But he's been different since he came home this last time. Like he can't quite find his footing away from the life of a soldier. It happens to some of them, you know. Makes me sad that the men and women who give up so much to keep us safe have to deal with that. A fresh start with you and your son is just what Nate needs."

She took a step away and frowned. "Wait. Did you say you're leaving and not coming back?"

"That's the plan."

"But what about Nate?"

Bianca shrugged. "One of the few worthwhile pieces of advice my mom gave me was that loving a man doesn't guarantee a happily-ever-after in the end."

"I wouldn't call those words worthwhile," Susan said, her tone disapproving. "No offense, hon, but your mama sounds like a real piece of work."

"Yeah," Bianca agreed. "But she was right in this instance. Nate and my brother, Eddie, were SEALs together—best friends. Eddie died on their last mission, and there were circumstances Nate didn't share with me."

"It's difficult for soldiers to revisit those bad times. Some of them need to leave the past in the past."

Bianca drew in a breath. How much could she share with the sweet librarian? She didn't want anyone to judge Nate. He took care of that quite thoroughly on his own. Heck, she still didn't understand why he blamed himself for Eddie's death. Yet he hadn't denied Brett's claims.

None of it made sense, but if he wasn't willing to talk about it with her, how could they move forward? She understood letting go of the past, but whatever happened on that last mission still had a choke hold on Nate.

She wanted to fight for their relationship, but not if it was a losing battle. She'd dealt with too many of those in her life already.

"It feels like he's throwing away our future because he can't let go of the past."

"And there's nothing you can do?"

"I need some time to figure it out," Bianca said. "I only just realized that I'm someone worth fighting for. If Nate isn't willing to, then I'm not going to beg." She straightened her shoulders. "I spent too long letting people make me feel less than. I won't do it anymore. If nothing else, I owe it to EJ to be strong and believe in myself."

"You owe it to both of you," Susan agreed. "Honey, I'm awfully sorry to see you go, but I guess I understand. Maybe Nate will come to his senses."

The idea of working things out with Nate had hope blooming in Bianca's heart, followed quickly by a wave of sorrow so strong it almost knocked her off balance.

She'd watched him gallop out of the barn like he couldn't get away fast enough. If that wasn't a clear message, she didn't know what would be.

"I'm going to be fine either way," she said, even though she wasn't sure she believed it.

"You never know how things will work out." Susan walked back around the counter. "Look at Deborah Fortune raising the triplets on her own, thinking all this time that the man she'd loved—the father of her boys—had died." She threw up her hands, her shimmery pink manicure sparkling in the light. "Then suddenly he's back from the grave with a new identity, family and kids crawling out from the woodwork. That had to be a huge shock for all of them."

"But they're getting through," Bianca said. "They have each other."

Susan nodded. "Plus Jayden has that pretty new wife of his from Austin. And Nathan has—"

"It's time to go, EJ," Bianca called, forcing one more feigned smile on her face. She couldn't talk any longer about Nate. Not when she was determined to leave Paseo. If she thought too long about everything Nate had been through and what he meant to her, she'd never find the strength to drive away.

But it wasn't just Nate. The ranch had started to feel like home, and she had one thing to finish before she left Paseo for good.

Because as much as she'd come to love this place, she would never again settle for scraps of a life. Not when she deserved so much more.

Chapter 15

Nate arrived back at the ranch four hours later, hungry and tired but with his head clearer than it had been in weeks. He had to explain to Bianca the full circumstances of Eddie's death. Maybe she'd look at him like the whole tragic incident was his fault, but he had to take the chance. The truth was burning a hole right into his soul, and he couldn't move forward without having everything in the open.

But her car wasn't parked in front of the house. In its place sat Jayden's truck. His brother walked out from the front door as Nate dismounted.

"I've got a problem," Jayden called as he moved to the top of the porch steps. "And I'm hoping you can make it right."

"What's up?" Nate led Cinnamon forward, wondering where Bianca was at the moment. The quicker he got through this conversation with Jayden, the quicker he'd be free to find her.

"It's Sugar."

Nate felt his mouth drop open. "What's wrong? Where is she?"

"In the backyard," Jayden said, crossing his arms over his chest and raising a brow. "With her desolate dog boyfriend."

"What the hell are you talking about?" Nate lifted the Stetson off his head, wiped his brow across the sleeve of his canvas jacket then dropped the hat back into place. "Dogs don't have boyfriends."

"Sugar does," Jayden countered. "EJ's stray, Otis. Since we arrived, that dog has been laying in the backyard, head on his paws, whining. Sugar is beside herself. She can't get him to play or follow her. Apparently she likes being the center of Otis's world, and it's currently killing her. When Sugar is upset, I'm upset. You need to fix it."

"Did you examine Otis?" Nate took a step forward, then remembered Cinnamon was still with him. "Let me put Cinnamon away then I'll come take a look. Maybe he's sick or injured."

"Or heartbroken," Jayden suggested quietly.

"That's ridiculous," Nate said, not bothering to hide his snappish tone. There were times when he was totally in sync with his brothers, and others when it felt like they were speaking another language. "You just said Sugar is with him. EJ is going to freak if something's wrong with that dog." He held out the reins. "You take Cinnamon and I'll try—"

"Where is EJ?" Jayden interrupted, his tone a little too innocent for Nate's taste. "And Bianca?"

"I'm guessing they ran into town. Stop messing around, Jayden. This is serious."

"Is that so?" Jayden tapped a finger against his chin,

slowly walking down the steps. "Ran into town or ran away from town? On the drive in, Ariana and I saw a little hatchback with a woman that looked a lot like Bianca on the highway outside Paseo. She was driving like the devil himself was chasing her."

Nate swallowed as his throat went dry. "Take the reins," he commanded.

Jayden kept moving until they were standing boot to boot. "Did you two have a fight?"

"Take the damn reins, Jayden."

His brother closed his fingers around the leather straps, and Nate immediately bounded up the porch steps, through the front door and up the stairs, taking them two at a time. His breath came out in ragged puffs, like he'd just run a marathon by the time he got to the top, more from the panic gripping him than from any kind of physical exertion. He pushed open the door to his mother's bedroom, his heart dropping when he found it empty of Bianca's things.

Grayson's bedroom—the one where EJ was staying— was also back to how it had been before the Shaws had arrived. The perfectly made beds mocked him, as if these past few weeks had been nothing but a dream and he was back to the lonely reality of his regular life.

There was no note from Bianca or clue as to where she'd gone. She'd simply disappeared.

She'd found out the truth about him, and she'd left.

He rubbed at his chest, willing the walls guarding his heart to rebuild themselves. This was an inevitable outcome. Maybe he'd thought they'd have more time, but there was no doubt Nate was supposed to end up alone.

Except he didn't believe that anymore. Bianca had changed everything, and most of all she'd changed him.

He walked back down the stairs only to find Ariana waiting for him at the bottom.

"I'm sorry, Nate," she said gently. "Do you want to—"

"It's fine." He held up a hand. "I'm fine. I've got some work to do in the yard." His voice sounded distant in his own ears. "Good to have you and Jayden back. I'll see you later, okay?"

She nodded. "Okay."

He went out the back of the house, unwilling to have another confrontation with his brother so soon. Nate needed time to readjust his mask into place. To convince himself it didn't matter that she'd left him, so he could go about convincing everyone else.

Otis lifted his head as Nate moved off the back porch, his ears twitching like Nate might help him find EJ.

"He's gone," Nate said as if the dog could understand him. He scratched Sugar behind the ears when she trotted up to him. "You can stay or go, but EJ isn't coming back."

Otis whined softly, then stood and started following Nate as he made his way toward the shed. Sugar barked once but remained in the backyard, trained not to wander far.

"I mean it." Nate glanced over his shoulder at the dog. "You're going to have to deal with the fact that he left you. They left both of us."

He blew out a breath. Hell, he was having a breakup talk with a dog. How pathetic could his life get?

He set his hat on the woodpile near the shed out back and pulled the ax out of a block of wood. A windstorm just before Christmas had felled several large bur oak trees, so he'd quartered them and left the wood by the shed to chop into manageable pieces of firewood. But other jobs had taken priority, and he hadn't made it to the stack of wood yet. Now he welcomed the mindless task.

Physical exertion was the one thing that had kept him sane during his years as a SEAL. When things got to be too much to deal with, he could rely on grueling exercise to work out all the emotions he didn't want to face. So he swung the ax like he had a vendetta against it, welcoming the first twinges of pain in his muscles.

Otis stayed with him, watching his movements from a patch of shade near the front of the shed. By the time he finished chopping, his shirt was drenched and sweat rolled down between his shoulder blades. His arms quivered and he knew by tonight he wouldn't be able to lift his hands above his head. The pain in his body dulled the ache in his heart, although it still remained, an undercurrent of emptiness that seemed to form the base of who he was.

"You know this isn't Alaska?"

Nate drove the ax into a thick piece of oak then turned to his brother. "I'm aware."

Jayden inclined his head toward the shoulder-high pile of wood to Nate's side. "We've got enough firewood there to take us through half a dozen Texas winters."

"Good to be prepared." Nate wiped his brow then began stacking the oak against the side of the shed.

"Are we going to talk about it now?" Jayden asked, pulling a pair of leather work gloves out of his pocket. "Or do you want me to find some tires for you to throw around?"

"No tires," Nate mumbled.

"Fence posts to dig?" Jayden suggested, walking to the other side of the woodpile and grabbing a piece to stack. "You could run to the county line with a hay bale balanced on your shoulders. I don't know if there's anything else that would beat you down enough to make you happy. CrossFit is all the rage in Ariana's old neighborhood in Austin. Want to try some box jumps? That might make you feel better."

"How about I beat the crap out of you?" Nate asked conversationally. "That would definitely help."

"Ariana wouldn't approve. She likes my face just the way it is."

"And here I thought she had better taste than that," Nate said, ignoring the fact that he and Jayden looked exactly the same.

They worked in silence for several minutes, but finally Nate couldn't stand it any longer.

"She left me," he said, pulling off his gloves and slapping them against his thigh. "I told her I was all in and she left me."

Jayden wiped an arm across his brow. "What exactly does 'all in' mean?"

"You know."

"I don't."

"I was committed."

"As in you love her?"

"As in 'all in,'" Nate repeated.

"Somehow you think that scared her away?"

Nate shook his head. "She found out about Eddie. That scared her. Or disgusted her. I don't know."

"Did you tell her your version or the truth?"

"They're the same thing," Nate answered, glaring at his brother. "Besides, I didn't tell her anything. Her ex-husband showed up here yesterday. He wants her back and was more than happy to explain everything to Bianca so she'd see what bad news I am in her life."

"What exactly did he explain?"

He took a breath, licked his lips then said, "That I killed Eddie."

The string of curses that flowed from Jayden's mouth was so explicit and creative, Nate almost blushed. Nearly twenty years as a SEAL and he was actually learning a few new phrases thanks to his brother.

"Whoa, there." He held up his hands, palms out. "I might not like how the guy treated Bianca, but she was going to find out eventually. I should have been the one to tell her in the first place."

"Birth order," Jayden muttered through clenched teeth, stalking away a few paces then turning back to Nate. "That's the only thing that explains it."

"What are you talking about?" Nate scrubbed a hand over his jaw.

"Your stupidity. It must be a result of our birth order." Jayden pointed an angry finger at Nate. "I was first and Grayson next. You came last, so it stands to reason you got cheated on brain cells. As in—" he leaned closer "—you have none."

Nate scoffed. "Who took your physics final senior year? I did. Don't talk to me about which one of us got the brains. There's no question I did."

"Then give me another excuse for acting like such an idiot. You did *not* kill Eddie Shaw. You tried to save him and could have died in the process."

Nate shut his eyes as images from that last mission assaulted him. "If I'd gotten there sooner, he'd still be alive, Jayden. If I'd taken him out first—"

"You saved four men that night, Nate. Eddie chose to be the last one extracted from the ridge."

"I couldn't even recover his body," Nate whispered, shame making his voice crack. "I had to leave him there."

"He would have understood," Jayden said quietly.

Nate met his brother's gaze. It was like looking in a mirror, a reflection of himself, only stronger and more sure. Nate couldn't be sure of anything at the moment. Since he'd returned from Afghanistan he'd been like a boat in the middle of the ocean being buffeted by waves from every side and unable to get his bearings. He'd thought he'd started righting the ship with Bianca and EJ in his life, but now he was lost again.

"How do you know?" he asked, unable to stop hoping for something that might make the world make sense.

"Because he was a soldier. He knew the risks."

"I was supposed to have his back. We took care of each other for almost twenty years. He was ready to get out—to have a real life—and I took that from him."

"The men who fired the guns and launched that final grenade took that from him." Jayden stepped closer. "What if things had been reversed? If you'd been the one injured, would you have wanted Eddie to save you first?"

"Of course not." Nate felt simmering anger rising inside him, hot and sharp. "But I never would have gotten myself into that position." He shook his head. "I told him we needed to wait for backup. He insisted on going in with just our squadron. He was so damn stubborn. Then it all went to hell."

"Which was *not* your fault," Jayden insisted.

"You don't understand. Someone has to take the blame. I should never have agreed to it. I had a gut feeling. And I told Eddie—" He broke off, regret choking him.

"What did you tell him?"

"I said 'you got us into this, you better get us out.' The way he did that was by sacrificing himself."

"He made the choice, Nate. He knew the risks."

"I'm sick of the anger and guilt. It's like Gerald Robinson, you know? All our lives we thought our dad was dead. Only to find out he was in Texas all along and had his own family. It makes me so damn mad, Jayden. It makes me feel guilty that I didn't push Mom for more information on him when we were teenagers and I got curious."

"You remember what happened when we were younger and I wouldn't stop asking her about our dad."

Nate gave a sharp nod. "She cried."

"It was awful. She didn't want to talk about him."

"But what if I'd demanded to know his identity and I'd tracked him down and figured out that Jerome Fortune had faked his own death? That would have changed so much for all of us."

"You had no way of knowing," Jayden said quietly. "Just like you had no way of knowing what was going to happen in Afghanistan. I get your need to take care of people, Nate, and I admire it. I do. But you're not some sort of all-seeing, all-knowing superhero. You're a man who makes mistakes, but you try your best." He paused, then added, "I think you have that in common with Gerald Robinson."

Nate shook his head. "I don't have anything in common with our father."

"You do if you let Bianca walk away. The same way Gerald let Mom go. I think he really loved her. There's a good chance he still might. But a lot of water has passed under that bridge. You've got time on your side." Jayden made a show of checking his watch. "About three hours based on when we saw her."

Nate threw up his hands. "What am I supposed to do?"

"You could start by calling and apologizing for being the biggest ass on the planet."

"She left."

"Or you pushed her away."

"I've got work to do." Nate grabbed another piece of wood. "No more talking."

"You're not meant to be alone. You deserve way more

happiness than you're allowing yourself to have." Jayden shoved his gloves into his back pocket. "It's scary as hell to put yourself out there, but trust me when I tell you it's worth it in the end. Think about it."

Otis perked up his ears and watched Jayden walk away.

"Feel free to go after him," Nate told the dog. "He's heading back to the house. You know Sugar will be waiting. No sense in both of us being miserable."

The dog inclined his head then gave a soft whimper and lowered his body to the ground once more.

Nathan stacked the wood then moved on to shoring up a few loose pieces of siding on the back of the shed. At the rate he was going, he'd be caught up with projects around the ranch by the end of the week. He couldn't allow himself to stop. If he didn't keep moving, the heartache of losing Bianca would overwhelm him.

Ariana brought him a plate of food to the barn when he missed dinner.

He mumbled, "Thank you," but didn't slow his pace.

"It's not too late," she said gently before she left him alone again.

Alone.

He'd been alone for so damn long. It felt right when he'd first come back from Afghanistan. He needed the time by himself to readjust to regular life. But he'd used his guilt over the last mission as an excuse for staying isolated.

Until Bianca had broken through all of his walls.

Around midnight he returned to the darkened house. He knew Jayden and Ariana were worried about him, and while Nate appreciated the concern, he didn't know how to assure them he'd be fine. It felt like he'd never be fine again.

He'd gone into town for supplies and gotten a text from Bianca saying she'd stopped for the night near Stallworth, a small town about four hours from Paseo. She wasn't ready to talk but didn't want him to worry.

As angry as she might be, his Bianca couldn't help her caring nature. It was one of things he lov—

No. He couldn't go there right now.

He showered and put on clean clothes, but instead of making his way to his own room, he sat on the bed where EJ had slept. It was impossible to imagine waking up tomorrow without the boy's enthusiasm and energy setting the tone for the day.

He smoothed his hand over the quilt, stilling when it hit a lump under the covers. He reached under and pulled out Roscoe, EJ's beloved stuffed animal. The boy cuddled the raggedy bear to his chest all night as he slept. How would Bianca ever get him to settle without it?

Nate ran down to the kitchen, grabbing the phone from the wall and punched in her number, the teddy bear finally giving him an excuse to reach out to her. The call went straight to voicemail.

She and EJ were out there someplace, and Nate had to find them.

Chapter 16

Bianca was half asleep on the chair outside her room when the bright lights of a familiar silver truck pulled into the motel's parking lot.

It was almost four in the morning, and the world was quiet around her other than the sound of the diesel engine. She'd come out of her room when she couldn't sleep, afraid her tossing and turning would wake EJ, who'd taken hours to finally settle without his teddy bear. The cool air and the slight breeze scented with impending rain had settled her enough to where she didn't feel like she was going to break down and begin sobbing.

Emotion gripped her again and she clutched at her throat, feeling like a deer in headlights as the truck turned into the empty parking spot next to her small car. The engine died a moment later, and Nate emerged, wearing a white T-shirt and jeans, his hair sticking up around his head like he'd been compulsively running his fingers through it.

Bianca gripped the edges of the chair to keep from launching herself at him. What was the point of trying to become an independent woman if she melted into a puddle the minute a man came after her?

He'd come for her. That had to mean something, right?

But as he walked toward her, his eyes were unreadable in the faint glow from the motel's neon sign.

"Fancy meeting you here," she said, trying for a jaunty tone.

"You forgot this."

Bianca gave a choked sigh when Nate brought his hand from behind his back to reveal EJ's beloved teddy bear. She stood and reached for the bear, her skin tingling when her fingers grazed Nate's.

"Thank you," she whispered. "You wouldn't believe what a challenge bedtime was without Roscoe."

"I found him under the covers of EJ's bed."

She brushed her fingers over the stuffed animal's worn fur. "I can't believe he forgot to pack him or that I didn't check before we got in the car. Eddie gave him to me the first time he deployed. He said the bear would keep me safe when he couldn't. It's been the only stuffed animal EJ ever cared about, and I always believed that meant something. Roscoe was our connection to Eddie and—" She drew in a deep breath as she looked up at him. "It's the middle of the night, Nate."

"Technically, it's very early morning," he replied.

"Okay," she agreed. "But you drove all this way to deliver Roscoe?"

"You left him." He paused, then added, "You left me."

She felt her mouth drop open. "I couldn't stay. Not after our conversation. How did you find me?"

"Stallworth is a metropolis compared to Paseo, but it's

still a small town. You texted that you'd stopped here for the night. As much of an early bird as EJ is, I didn't think you'd get on the road again until daylight, which meant I had a few hours. I checked all the hotels and motels until I saw your car in the parking lot."

"You came all this way to bring EJ his stuffed animal?"

Something flared in Nate's eyes. It was a mix of regret and hope that lanced Bianca's heart. "I came to apologize for how I handled our last conversation and for not telling you the truth about Eddie when you first arrived. You had a right to know."

"I need to know *everything*," she said, unable to stop herself from reaching for him. He flinched when her hand gripped his arm, like her touch was charged, but he didn't pull away. She wouldn't have been able to stand it if he'd pulled away. She inclined her head toward the closed door behind her. "I'd invite you in but EJ's a light sleeper." She gestured to the concrete step that led from the walkway in front of the row of hotel rooms to the parking lot. "Would you like to have a seat on my makeshift porch?"

Nate studied her for a moment then nodded.

She let go of his arm as they sat. Somehow she knew whatever Nate was going to tell her would be easier if they weren't touching.

But the urge was strong to climb into his lap and bury her face in the crook of his neck. She'd only been away from the ranch for half a day, but she missed Nate like they'd been separated for months.

She could feel the tension pouring off him and knew the next few minutes would determine her future and whether she'd be moving forward with or without Nate Fortune.

"Tell me," she whispered.

He closed his eyes as a quiver passed through him.

"Eddie was my brother in every way that matters. I never imagined a world without him, and we'd been through some pretty serious stuff over the years. But there was something that felt off to me on our last mission. Our commanding officer wanted action, but the intel wasn't clear and it felt like we were rushing it." He looked at her, his dark eyes filled with regret. "From the start I knew things were going to go bad."

"But you continued, anyway?"

"We were behind enemy lines but so close to finding one of the terrorist cell leaders. Our unit wanted to send a message. Eddie was adamant we move forward. He was worried we were going to let the bad guy slip through our fingers again. It's hard to understand, but there's so much time on a mission spent waiting. So many close calls when you almost get the enemy but you're too late. Guys get antsy. We were SEALs because we could produce, Bianca. We were good at what we were trained to do. Eddie wanted a last chance at making something happen before he got out for good. Whether it was another feather in his cap or to prove to himself he still had what it took…" He shook his head. "We'll never know, but all hell broke loose when we came over that ridge."

"Oh, Nate."

"It was an ambush. We managed to hold them off for several hours, waiting for a rescue force, but a few of our guys got injured." He shrugged. "There was a lot of gunfire. My shoulder. Eddie's leg. He insisted I move everyone down into a ravine where there was more shelter in the rocks. He was going to cover us."

"That sounds like Eddie," she said with a small smile. "He wanted to have everyone's back."

"He had mine that night," Nate told her without hesitation. "Most of us were okay, but there several who were injured. I got three of them out then went back for the one who lost his right leg from the knee down, Dave. I had to carry him out. I got him up to the extraction point and planned to go back for Eddie. The explosion happened as I got to the bottom of the ridge." He pressed his palms to the sides of his head, like it was pounding and he couldn't make it stop. "The hillside had been blown apart. He was gone. I didn't get to him in time."

"You tried," she whispered, wiping at the tears streaming down her face. She couldn't stand the distance between them any longer and scooted closer, gripping Nate's biceps. Needing to connect herself to him. He immediately lifted his arm and wrapped it around her shoulder, pulling her closer.

"The extraction happened so fast." Bianca could hear the tears in his voice. "There was nothing I could do except leave." He took a shaky breath. "I couldn't even bring him home."

"What happened to the other SEAL?" she asked. "You said his name was Dave, right?"

Nate nodded. "He's back in Michigan with his family. He's got a wife and two young girls. I've talked to him a couple of times. It's been an adjustment, but he was fitted for an artificial leg about a year ago and now he's coaching football at the local high school."

"And his daughters have their dad with them."

"Yeah."

Bianca tipped up her head and kissed the underside of Nate's jaw. "Eddie would have wanted that."

"But I failed," Nate insisted.

"Don't say that." Bianca put a finger over his lips when he would have argued. "Don't say that to me ever again. You were a hero, Nate. If Eddie were here he'd tell you the same thing. I don't blame you for what happened to him, and it's past time you stop blaming yourself."

"Then why did you leave?"

She sighed. "I was scared. Not by what Brett told me or listening to you trying to take responsibility for Eddie's death. I know you, Nathan Fortune." She lowered her hand and placed it over his heart. "I know you in here. But I was afraid you didn't care the same way I did."

"I told you I was all in," he said, as if that explained everything.

She rolled her eyes. "Which sounds like you're playing poker or something. I asked you to talk to me about something difficult and you walked away. You wouldn't let me in. It felt like you weren't willing to fight for us. One thing I've realized in the past few weeks—something being on the ranch and in Paseo helped me realize—is that I'm worth fighting for. I needed a little space to figure out what was going to happen next." She felt one side of her mouth curve up as hope, buoyant and light, bloomed in her chest. "And what happened is you came after me."

"Always," he told her.

Her heart stilled. "Always?"

He shifted so they were facing each other and cupped her cheeks in his hands. "I came back to Paseo because I needed a home to make me whole again. *You* are my home, Bianca Shaw. I felt it the moment I opened the door to find you on the other side. It was like the universe sent you to me so I'd have a reason to deal with all the crap I couldn't stand to face on my own." He pressed his mouth to hers, the touch gentle but firm. "I love you. And I'm all in with you. Forever if you'll have me."

"Mr. Nate?"

Bianca turned to see EJ in the motel doorway, sleepily rubbing his eyes.

"Hey, buddy, look what Mr. Nate brought to you." She held up the ragged teddy bear, and EJ ran forward.

"Roscoe!"

EJ took the bear then wrapped his arms around Nate's neck. Nate pulled him onto his lap so the boy was balanced between the two of them. Bianca thought her heart might burst from the happiness of the moment.

She met Nate's eyes and couldn't wait any longer. "I love you, too," she whispered over EJ's head. "I want—"

"I told Mommy not to leave," EJ interrupted matter-of-factly.

"It's okay," Nate assured him. "Your mommy needed a little time-out, but I'm hoping you both will come back to the ranch real soon."

"Like now?" EJ asked hopefully, his brown eyes wide as he looked at Bianca.

"Now seems like a good time to me," she said with a smile.

EJ jumped up and bounded toward the motel room. "I'll pack," he called over his shoulder, then stopped in his tracks when a dog bark sounded.

"I forgot I had a copilot with me," Nate said, standing then pulling Bianca up with him. He opened the passenger door of the truck, and Otis hopped out, trotting over to give EJ a sloppy lick on the cheek.

"I missed you, boy," EJ whispered then looked from Bianca to Nate. "We can keep him, right?"

Nate chuckled. "I don't think Otis would have it any other way."

EJ grinned before disappearing into the room.

"I told you SEALs are big teddy bears at heart," Bianca said.

"Will you come back to the ranch for good?" Nate asked, lacing his fingers with hers. "I love you and I want to spend the rest of my life showing you how much. I want you and EJ and I to be a family."

She leaned in and brushed her lips across his. "We already are, Nate. We're yours. Forever."

Epilogue

"I still owe you a honeymoon, Mrs. Fortune."

Bianca rested her head on Nate's shoulder as he wrapped an arm around her waist. "I can't imagine any place I'd rather be than right here."

It was almost two weeks since she'd returned to the ranch, and Bianca knew she'd come home for good. They'd gotten married three days after applying for a license in the county courthouse. Bianca and Nate both understood how precious life could be and neither of them wanted to wait to join their lives together. As she'd told him at the motel, they were already a family.

The wedding might have been short and simple, but nothing had made Bianca happier than becoming Nate's wife.

They'd celebrated with Jayden and Ariana, who'd left soon after for a research trip to Fort Worth. Now they sat on the porch swing Nate had crafted for Bianca—with EJ's help—as a wedding present, gently rocking as EJ and Otis played fetch in the backyard.

"I'm glad to hear it, sweetheart." Nate dropped a tender kiss on the top of her head. "I'll be counting my lucky stars for the rest of my life that you found me."

"I think we have Eddie to thank. He always said you'd take care of me if he couldn't."

"Did he also mention that I was going to end up needing you like I need the heart beating in my chest?"

She smiled. "I don't think he understood that part."

"Well, it's more than true." Nate's arm tightened around her waist. "I wish I could promise you things will be perfect, Busy Bee. I'm working on it."

"*We're* working on it," she corrected. "And I don't need perfect. I want you, Nate, and everything that comes along with loving you."

"Everything? Are you sure?"

She held up her left hand. "Sure as this ring on my finger." The diamond sparkled, set in a delicate band of gold with a subtle filigree design on either side. It had been Cynthia Thompson's wedding ring, and Bianca was beyond proud to wear something that had belonged to the woman who'd taken in Deborah Fortune when she'd most needed help.

Deborah had been the one to suggest Nate give Bianca the ring when the two of them had called to tell her about their whirlwind engagement. Nate's mom had been sweet and gracious and Bianca was looking forward to meeting her new mother-in-law when Grayson was on his next break from the rodeo circuit and his sponsorship commitments.

"I need to show you something," Nate said, his tone suddenly serious. He shifted, pulling a folded envelope from his back pocket. "This came today in the mail."

Bianca slipped the one-page letter from the envelope, felt her jaw drop open as she read it. "Do you think it's a scam?"

Nate shook his head. "Jayden already told me about his suspicions that Gerald's father, Julius Fortune, held just as many secrets as his son. Ariana uncovered something while working on the *Becoming a Fortune* series last year. I don't know who this Schuyler woman is, but if she is some kind of a con artist, there are Fortunes with a lot more money and power than me she could have gone after."

"But she contacted you," Bianca said with a nod. "In the letter she said she's looking for an honest opinion."

"Why didn't she just call?"

Bianca laughed at that. "You're not exactly the easiest person to reach out here, Nate Fortune."

"I like it that way," he said and took the letter from her, refolding it and putting it back in the envelope. "All I want is a simple life…"

"But complications just keep showing up on your doorstep." Bianca smiled and tipped up her head to kiss him. "EJ and I were a complication."

"You two are the greatest blessings of my life."

EJ let out a whoop of delight at that moment as Otis caught the tennis ball in midair. "Did you see that, Mommy?"

"He's getting to be a heck of a ball catcher," she called.

"Because you've got a heck of an arm," Nate added. "Hey, EJ, what do you think about looking into a T-ball team come spring? There's a community center in the next town over that runs a rec league for kids."

"Awesome," the boy shouted, and the happiness on his small face made Bianca's heart melt.

"Complicated or not," she told Nate, "we'll get through it together."

"I can handle anything." Nate chuckled. "Even a whole new batch of Fortunes, as long as you're with me."

She closed her eyes as he kissed her again, then rested his forehead against hers. "Forever and always," she whispered.

* * * * *

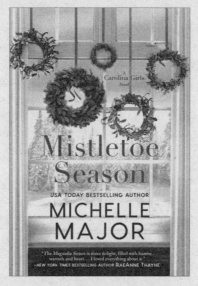

"Who's dating?" Josie, who sat in the front row, leaned forward
in her chair.

"No one," Gabe said through clenched teeth.

"Not even a little." Angi offered a patently fake smile. "I'd be
thrilled to work with Gabe. I'm sure he'll have lots to offer as far
as making this Christmas season in Magnolia the most festive
ever."

The words seemed benign enough on the surface, but Gabe
knew a challenge when he heard one.

"I have loads of time to devote to this town," he said solemnly, placing a hand over his chest. He glanced down at Josie and her cronies and gave his most winsome smile. "I know it will make my grandma happy."

As expected, the women clucked and cooed over his devotion. Angi looked like she wanted to reach around Malcolm and scratch out Gabe's eyes, and it was strangely satisfying to get under her skin.

"Well, then." Mal grabbed each of their hands and held them above his head like some kind of referee calling a heavyweight boxing match. "We have our new Christmas on the Coast power couple."

Don't miss
Mistletoe Season *by Michelle Major,*
available October 2021 wherever HQN books
and ebooks are sold.

HQNBooks.com

PHMMEXP1121MAX

HARLEQUIN

Heartfelt or thrilling, passionate or uplifting—Harlequin is more than just happily-ever-after.

With twelve different series to choose from and new books available every month, you are sure to find stories that will move you, uplift you, inspire and delight you.

SIGN UP FOR THE HARLEQUIN NEWSLETTER

Be the first to hear about great new reads and exciting offers!

Harlequin.com/newsletters

HNEWS2021MAX